D0457781

PAULINE GEDGE

VIKING

VIKING
Published by the Penguin Group
Penguin Books Canada Ltd, 10 Alcorn Avenue,
Toronto, Ontario, Canada M4V 3B2
Penguin Books Ltd, 27 Wrights Lane, London W8 5TZ, England
Viking Penguin, a division of Penguin Books USA Inc.,
375 Hudson Street, New York, New York 10014, USA
Penguin Books Australia Ltd, Ringwood, Victoria, Australia
Penguin Books (NZ) Ltd, 182-190 Wairau Road,
Auckland 10, New Zealand

Penguin Books Ltd, Registered Offices:
Harmondsworth, Middlesex, England

First published 1992

1 3 5 7 9 10 8 6 4 2

Copyright © Pauline Gedge, 1992

All rights reserved. Without limiting the rights under copyright reserved
above, no part of this publication may be reproduced, stored in or
introduced into a retrieval system, or transmitted in any form or by any
means (electronic, mechanical, photocopying, recording or otherwise),
without the prior written permission of both the copyright owner and the
above publisher of this book.

*Publisher's note: This book is a work of fiction. Names, characters, places and
incidents either are the product of the author's imagination or are used
fictitiously, and any resemblance to actual persons living or dead, events or
locales is entirely coincidental.*

Printed and bound in Canada on acid free paper ♾

Canadian Cataloguing in Publication Data

Gedge, Pauline, 1945-
The covenant

ISBN 0-670-84426-8

I. Title.

PS8563.E34C6 1992   C813'.54   C92-093900-7
PR9199.3.G44C6 1992

Also by Pauline Gedge

Child of the Morning
The Eagle and the Raven
Stargate
The Twelfth Transforming
Scroll of Saqqara

The COVENANT

Prologue

*S*he had almost reached the village green when the car pulled up. Her heart sank. She had been planning to go and sit under the welcoming shade of the chestnut tree that dominated the big square of lush, well-tended grass, and read some more before having to make her way home and help her mother prepare the dinner. There wouldn't be much to do anyway, not on a hot summer day like this. They would probably have cold roast beef, perhaps some ham with Father's favourite sweet mustard, cold boiled potatoes and fresh raw vegetables out of the garden. All she would be asked to do was set the table and walk to the village shop for some ice cream for dessert. She still had a good half-hour, she decided, before Mother expected her to start those chores.

But now she had halted on the street and was turning reluctantly to peer in the open window of the vehicle at the woman who was leaning over and smiling at her.

"My dear, I forgot to give you a book my husband's been

saving for you," she explained. "What with one thing and another it went right out of my head today. Do hop in and I'll drive you. He's looking for it now. He put it somewhere safe and then lost it, you know what he's like, but by the time we get there he'll have found it. Be quick! I'll have to drop you home afterwards."

The girl hesitated. The book she had been reading as she wandered along was quite exciting enough and besides, she was a little puzzled at the woman's haste.

"That's very kind of you," she offered, "but couldn't I pick it up tomorrow when Mum goes to work?"

"I'd rather get it out of the way immediately so it doesn't slip my mind again," the woman explained, opening the door. "Hurry up, dear! Get in!"

The girl obeyed without enthusiasm, casting a longing look at the deep shade under the wide arms of the chestnut. Now she would not have time to curl up there and read. Slamming the car door she sat tensely, hands between her overall-clad thighs, as the woman turned the car in the middle of the sun-baked, deserted street and set off. She did not speak again. Her fingers, as she drove, kept gripping and releasing the steering wheel and the girl noticed a bead of sweat along her upper lip. She kept glancing about.

"Is anything wrong?" the girl asked timidly. The woman looked at her, gave her a brief smile, and shook her head.

When they reached the house the woman took her hand and led her inside. The entrance was deliciously cool and dim after the metal furnace of the car. The woman kept hold of her until they were sitting side by side on the sofa in the drawing room, somewhere the girl had not been before. It was not a place for casual moments, she knew. She was a little overawed by the heavy, shrouded furniture, the solemn wallpaper. On the beautiful marble-topped coffee table before her was a jug and a glass. The woman poured.

"I'll go and find the book," she said, "and while I'm looking, do have some lemonade. I'm sure after walking as far as you did you're very thirsty." She got up and went out.

The girl looked at the lemonade. Ice tinkled sweetly in the glass which was already frosting over with condensation. Suddenly she felt an acute thirst but she was becoming anxious. Before long her mother would be glancing out the open door of the cottage to see if she was coming and might even send her sister to find her. That would mean a scolding.

The house was very quiet. She could hear a clock ticking somewhere. The lemonade beckoned mutely. Picking up the glass she sipped it tentatively and it was delicious, not too sour. In large gulps she finished it, wiped her mouth with a corner of her shirt, and sat back, waiting.

The woman did not come, but soon a drowsiness began to steal over the girl. The room seemed to grow bigger, longer, and her eyes wanted to close. I'll have to be rude and leave in a minute if she doesn't hurry, she thought vaguely, but her limbs felt too heavy to move. The book she had been carrying slipped from her lap onto the carpet with a tiny thud.

But then the woman was back, and with her was her husband. They looked strange. Their faces were like huge moons as they hovered in front of her eyes and their voices, when they spoke, seemed to echo.

"Is she under?" the husband asked. The woman nodded. Her nose bobbed up and down very slowly.

"I think so. We can begin. It's such a nuisance that we couldn't get . . ."

"I know," he said impatiently, "but what's the point of fussing about it? Too bad. Nice family. Help me get her to her feet."

The girl felt herself lifted. She could not control her head, which insisted on falling to her chest. Her legs looked awfully long and she giggled. Then she felt embarrassed because they were having to almost drag her out of the room and she didn't like to be a bother to anyone. Crossing the hall she was aware of a touch of the sun's rays on her cheek before the man and the woman turned her from the door and took her deeper into the house. She wanted to protest, to say, This isn't how I can get home, but thank you anyway. But her tongue had grown very fat and filled her whole mouth.

"Easy," the man said. There were stairs going down into darkness, and a moment when she knew she stood swaying while the woman opened another door onto more darkness. A light was switched on. The girl blinked lazily at the sudden glare.

The tiny stab of fear that had gone through her was forgotten when she saw her friend coming towards her, his scarlet shoes with the big gold buckles making tapping sounds on the stone floor. He was smiling. Dazedly she noticed the stiff lace that circled his throat and rested white and delicate over his wrists. His face too seemed very big and his voice came sluggishly, from far away.

"Hello my poppet," he said. "Ready to play a little game with me?"

She was anxious to return his smile, to answer him politely, but she could only stare at him foolishly. Not today thank you, she wanted to say. I'm sorry but I have to go home now. It's getting late. She did not realize that the words remained unspoken.

The man and the woman laid her on something hard and cold. Her friend came and bent over her, stroking her cheek. "How absolutely delectable," he was whispering, still smiling. "How daintily luscious. You are perfect, child. I can hardly wait."

His fingers went on caressing her face, but all at once the man was there too. He had a knife in his hand. She frowned and the fear was back but dull and faint. The man took her hair and tilted her head. Whatever is he doing? she thought dreamily. Whatever is he . . .

Chapter 1

$\mathcal{S}$he had expected to take the airport bus into the centre of London and then inquire about a train that would deposit her as close as possible to the village. But when she emerged from the baggage area, hot and tired, she saw a gaunt, rather sour-looking man in a shabby black suit standing just beyond the barricade, holding a piece of cardboard over his head with her name scrawled on it. Jessica Mortimer. Ruthlessly she pushed through the crowd. "Hello," she said. "I'm Jessica Mortimer."

He responded with a wintry, impersonal smile and lowered the placard. "Good-morning, Mrs Mortimer," he replied. "Lady Eleanor sent me to drive you to the Rill." Firmly but politely he took her two suitcases. "If you will follow me, please, the car is just across the way. My name is Ron." He did not wait for a response but set off towards the exit. Jessica followed, shivering under her thick felt coat as the doors slid open and a gush of bracing, city-tainted air enveloped her.

The plane had been a cocoon of steady warmth for the last eight hours. She was about to step off the kerb when he glanced back. "If you will wait here I will bring the car around," he said and she halted, watching his black, thin back disappear into the gloom of the above-ground parking lot. Pulling her coat more tightly against her body she squinted into the wind.

It was the beginning of June, a month when the English weather was usually stable. Many of the men brushing past her wore light jackets and the women were clad in the ubiquitous English cardigan over their dresses. The sky was a pale, watery blue smeared with ribbons of grey cloud and the pavement gleamed with moisture. At home in Canada, Jessica reflected, a very different summer was beginning.

It won't be easy to become acclimatized again after twenty years, her thoughts ran on. Twenty years. I remember vividly the day we left London, Father, Mother and I. January and a deluge of freezing rain, and Father so white and silent. Even at nine years old I could feel his despair and it filled me with dread so that I clung to Mother's hand as we boarded the plane for Canada and did not let it go until we had been aloft for a long time. I have forgotten much, the memories buried under a need for self-preservation that throws the switches in the subconscious and brings the healing darkness, but that day has stuck in my mind. Here comes cadaverous Ron and his hearse.

The vehicle now pulling smoothly to the kerb was very large and very black. She could tell by its distinctive shape that it was a Daimler, with its solemnly curved rear end and elegantly swooping fenders, and though she did not know much about cars she knew enough to be aware that the cars nowadays called Daimlers were in fact Daimler-Jags. This sleek monster must be at least thirty years old. Ron got out, came around, and held the rear door open for her.

"Your luggage is in the boot," he said. "The trip will take several hours, Mrs Mortimer, but my wife has made up a lunch for you and there are alcoholic beverages provided to alleviate your boredom." Jessica smiled swiftly into his face and was about to laugh until she saw that no hint of humour lit his dour features.

"Thank you," she responded, clambering into the back seat. "But I seem to have eaten my way across the Atlantic. They do stuff you on planes, don't they?" His answer was a polite grunt and he closed the door with a thud.

Jessica shrugged off her coat and sat back. The interior smelt of leather polish and was spotless. In the rear of the seat in front of her was a compartment, walnut and brass, but she left it alone. She was not hungry and she did not want to arrive at Rensby Hall with liquor on her breath. With eyes closed she felt the car purr away from the kerb, away from Heathrow Airport, away from a life that had become insupportable. The seat was long enough for her to lie down on if she bent her knees a little. Still with eyes closed she pushed her coat into a corner and her head sank onto it.

"There is a blanket under the seat in front of you if you require it, Mrs Mortimer," Ron said, and Jessica murmured, "Thank you," and slipped into an exhausted sleep.

Two hours later she woke and sat up, yawning and momentarily disoriented. The car still purred. Ron sat unmoving. We must have passed through a rain shower, Jessica thought, noting the beads of water clinging to the windows. Even inside the vehicle she could smell the damp. I must get used to it again, she said to herself. It's a familiar aura yet foreign, like an old dream half-remembered.

"I trust you were able to rest, Mrs Mortimer?" Ron spoke without turning and Jessica saw him glance at her in the rear-view mirror.

"Yes, thank you," she replied, suddenly aware of her dishevelled hair and sleep-swollen face. "Could you tell me what time it is so that I can set my watch? I'm still on Canadian time." He looked at the dashboard.

"It is three in the afternoon," he said. "We have another

hour's driving and should arrive at the Hall in time for tea. If you would like a mirror there is one folded into the rear of my seat." Jessica thanked him, and pulling open the compartment she found a mirror that slid into an upright position. In her handbag were her comb, powder and lipstick. She made what repairs she could, aware as she did so that he was watching her from time to time, and when she had closed her bag and was gazing out the window at the fleeing countryside he said, "I believe that you are no stranger to our little village, Mrs Mortimer." Jessica wished suddenly that he would call her by her first name. Now that the edge was off her fatigue she was beginning to feel the strangeness of her surroundings and would have appreciated the informality. But she did not want to tread on any establishment toes by suggesting it, nor did she relish being put in her place by this distant man.

"That's so," she replied unwillingly. "I spent my childhood at Rensby's Rill, at least until I was nine. Then my family emigrated to Canada."

"Do you remember the village at all?" he inquired. "I doubt if you will find it much changed. Things do not change quickly in this part of the world."

"I remember small things," she answered. "We had a cottage fronting the green. The walk to school every morning seemed to go on forever."

"I daresay," he interjected. "The cottages are still there, and the only difference I think you will find is on the other side of the main road, beyond the shops. A large housing estate has been erected."

"Between the shops and the creek? Where the big field used to be? My sister and I used to play there and we would wade in the rill to catch frog spawn in the spring. We weren't supposed to cross the main road by ourselves but we were often disobedient. The lure of all that long grass and the clear water was just too much . . ." Her voice trailed away and she fell silent. She and Jane, hand in hand, pelting across the road with tripping hearts, skirting the pub and the village hall and the post office to plunge at last into the sweet-smelling anonymity of the lush early foliage.

"Many of the village children felt the same," he answered, and as he did so a sudden squall of rain splattered against the windshield. "There was quite a vociferous protest on the part of the parents when the decision was taken to allow the estate to be built, but to no avail of course. At least the houses are out of sight of the village proper."

The village proper. Jessica wanted to laugh. "How long ago was the estate built?" she asked.

He shrugged. "My wife and I followed your parents into Sir Matthew's employ, and that would have been twenty years ago," he told her. "At that time the field was still vacant. I believe the estate went up about three years later."

So he knew that her father and mother had worked at the Hall. "You seem to be well informed about my background," she said with an unintentional tartness. "And do you live out, in the village?"

He turned and gave her a quick, unexpectedly disarming smile that briefly transformed his features, and Jessica wondered if it had been prompted by the spark of annoyance she had betrayed. "No," he replied. "Tillie and I have a small suite in the Hall. We have no children, you see. Besides, Mrs Mortimer, we were not originally village people. We came to Rensby's Rill from London. Both of us prefer the quiet of the country."

"Oh," Jessica said. "I see."

Nothing more was said for a while. Jessica went back to watching the impossibly green, highly cultivated Buckinghamshire landscape unroll. The sky cleared, and presently the sun burst out from behind the thinning clouds. At once her spirits rose. Traffic on the increasingly narrow road had become intermittent. The Daimler slowed at a sharp intersection almost buried in the shade of a group of newly leafed beeches and Ron swung the wheel, saying at the same time, "I hope you do not mind, but I am taking a slightly more circuitous route than normal. I thought you might like to drive through the village instead of approaching the Hall from the north, by the church."

"Why thank you," Jessica said in surprise, "I should like that very much." But will I? she asked herself, and leaned forward. Suddenly the air in the car seemed stuffy and she took a deep breath.

"One more bend . . ." Ron remarked. "Ah! There is the school, on your right."

The car slowed. Jessica looked. Sure enough, the old brick and timber building was still there, the bars from which she used to hang until she was giddy still firmly embedded in the paved playground, the crazy pattern of the waist-high fieldstone wall that surrounded it immediately giving her the same rush of satisfaction at its jigsaw perfection that she had often felt as a child. The car glided cautiously through a deserted minor intersection and continued on its majestic way. I remember the road as being so wide, Jessica thought, so intimidating, so fraught with danger, yet now I come to consider it, Jane and I seldom had to stand and wait for traffic to clear. The air of silent desertion it has today is the same, but how it has shrunk! I feel like Rip Van Winkle. Her gaze was still on the right-hand side, the safe side, where the pleasant pub garden adjoined the slightly crooked lines of the Monk's Fast itself and then the cobbled alley and the blank end wall of the library. The pub's gently swaying sign had been cleaned. Jessica remembered it as dully indistinct but now the crude but bold painting of the solemn, brown-clad brother clutching his shrunken stomach made her smile. She forced herself to turn her head.

The thick grass in the village green had been freshly cut and its aroma was filtering into the car. In the centre the great chestnut tree still stood like a benign sentinel, its boughs embracing almost the whole common ground, its glistening foliage already fully open. At the back of the green the truly ancient cottages straggled. Jessica caught glimpses of them as the Daimler moved along, their thatched roofs in good repair, their seasoned gardens boasting splashes of bright summer colour.

The end one, the largest and oldest by a hundred years, was obviously occupied. Its façade and the layout of its tiny front garden had not changed. The door stood open. Jessica knew how the morning sunlight would stream through that doorway and lie warm and golden on the cool flagstones of the cramped hallway. On Saturdays she and Jane would take their dolls and spread themselves just inside the open door, playing happily until the slanting rays moved out of the house, crept up the wall, and disappeared into the woodland behind the cottage. Mentally shaking herself she looked back at the green, now giving way to the crowded beech woods that marched to the northern edge of the village and on into a little girl's concept of infinity.

The right-hand side was open, a wide stretch of farmers' fields across which Jessica craned to see the straggle of willows that clung to the rill all along its meandering banks, and then came the fork in the road and the little, stagnant pond choked with water weeds. On the left the grey stone church was barely visible through the forbidding stiffness of the dark and spindled yew trees. They took the right-hand turn between tangled hedgerows that would lead to their destination. In a few moments they would arrive.

Jessica had always liked the abbey ruins that lay on her left. The walk from her home at the other end of the village to the quiet, warm stones was a long one for a small child and she had not made it often, but sometimes if her mother had been called in to work at the Hall on a weekend she would take the girl in their battered old Austin, and Jessica had spent many peaceful hours sitting cross-legged in the grass under one of the massive, roofless arches making daisy chains, or lying on hot summer afternoons gazing up at the irregular configurations the crumbling walls made against the sky.

Once in a while the place she regarded as her private

domain was invaded by sightseers who used the half-buried paving stones on which to open their packets of sandwiches and left empty bottles of orange squash perched precariously on what had once been the holy water stoup, but the ruins were too historically insignificant and too far from the main artery roads to attract more than a sporadic trickle of the curious. As a national monument, however, albeit a minor one, its preservation and upkeep were a governmental responsibility, and one of the villagers was paid a modest sum to cut the grass and watch the ruins themselves for signs of weathering and further decay. Now, as the car edged carefully past the iron gate on her left, she craned to take a good look.

Ron brought the car to a halt before the tall double gates guarding the Rensbys' estate and got out to push them open. Jessica began to gather up her belongings and passed a quick hand through her hair as the vehicle once more began to move, taking the gravel driveway to the right as it looped around a large section of dense lawn dominated by the gnarled oak tree she remembered so well and coming to rest outside the front entrance. Briskly Ron came round and opened her door. A little stiffly Jessica clambered out, forcing herself to give the man a word of thanks for the detour he had taken through the village though it had unsettled her. She would have preferred to rediscover the place gradually, in her own time. He acknowledged her words with a nod. He was now at the rear of the car, setting her bags down on the gravel, and Jessica had only the briefest opportunity to glance out over the wide, tree-dotted parkland that sloped gently away from the east side of the house before the door opened and a woman came out and stood smiling under the shelter of the grey stone porch.

"Jessica, my dear," she said, holding out a hand. "How lovely to see you again after all these years! I had no trouble recognizing you, you know. You have your mother's dark eyes and your father's stubborn chin. Do come in." She had imprisoned Jessica's cold fingers in her own warm ones and was drawing her into the house. "You can put the car away now, Ron," she spoke to him equably, "but bring Mrs Mortimer's suitcases in first. We were about to start tea," she went on to Jessica as they entered the hall. "I expect you could do with a cup? Tillie! Where are you? Bring the trolley into the sitting room now please!"

Jessica found herself crossing a lofty expanse of wooden floor, past closed double doors to left and right. Ahead and to her left a dark oak staircase soared towards the dimness of the tall ceiling and she just had time to notice the two suits of armour guarding its foot before her hostess pushed through more doors at the rear beside the stairs, took six more steps, and ushered her between yet another set of doors into a cozy room.

A girl unfolded from one of the deep, obviously well-used armchairs beside the window directly opposite and came sauntering over. She was tall and dark-haired, with a pale complexion and a face dominated by a firm but rather sulky mouth. Bright, intelligent eyes swept over Jessica and then the girl thrust out a hand. Jessica shook it.

"You wouldn't remember me because I wasn't born when you left the Rill," the young woman remarked. "I'm Caroline, nineteen years old, art student in London but home for the summer at the moment. Welcome to the Hall." She recrossed the room and flung herself back into the chair, tossing one jodhpured leg over the arm and reaching for the cigarette box on the occasional table beside her. "I must say you're very attractive, Mrs Mortimer. I really didn't know what to expect. My parents described you as the child they remembered and I tried to imagine what a Canadian might be like. Do you ride? They all ride over there, don't they?" She lit her cigarette and blew a plume of smoke into the air. Jessica laughed aloud.

"I don't like horses very much," she replied, settling onto the sofa Caroline's mother had indicated, "and they don't like me. My profession is music. I teach it. And please call me Jessica. You too, Lady Eleanor."

"Thank you my dear," the older woman smiled. "You must forgive my daughter's rudeness. She greets everyone she doesn't know in the same way but she does get nicer upon further acquaintance. I think it is some kind of a test. She calls it frankness. Are you going to change your clothes, Caroline? I detect a faint whiff of the stables."

"After tea," Caroline answered. "What's keeping Tillie?"

At that moment a trolley appeared, pushed by a short, wiry woman with a shock of uncontrolled grey hair. She was wearing a voluminous white apron.

"I made coffee as well as tea today," she announced. "Americans like coffee, don't they?" She raised her eyebrows questioningly at Jessica.

"Mrs Mortimer is Canadian, not American, Tillie," Caroline corrected her gravely, stubbing out her cigarette and looking expectantly towards the food. "We have already established that she does not ride. Perhaps she does not drink coffee either."

"Oh," said Tillie. She lifted the linen cloth from the trolley.

"Jessica, this is our housekeeper and Ron's wife, Tillie," Lady Eleanor interposed. "Tillie — Mrs Mortimer."

The woman came over and shook Jessica's extended hand. "Pleased to meet you," she said cheerfully. "Will you have tea or coffee?"

Jessica wondered if Ron's glum lack of communication was a defence against his wife's joviality. "Coffee please," she answered and watched, bemused, as Tillie poured both coffee and hot milk into a cup before handing it to her and then proffering a handsome silver sugarbowl. The drink was nonetheless strong and comforting and she sipped it gratefully as tea was distributed together with tiny sandwiches, warm savouries and pound cake. Then the housekeeper swept up the coat Jessica had placed beside her and went out. Lady Eleanor stirred her cup of pale, fragrant liquid, crossed her nylon-clad legs, and fixed Jessica with a pale blue, slightly myopic gaze.

"We were all so sorry to hear about the death of your husband," she said delicately, laying her spoon in the saucer. "We just want you to know that we sympathize with you entirely and we hope your stay with us will help you to read-just. To life. You were married for seven years, were you not? Your mother has always kept in touch with us."

Jessica drained her coffee before replying, suddenly very aware of Caroline's attention. She could see the girl on the periphery of her vision, carefully picking crumbs off the plate in her lap. "Actually Michael and I had six and a half won-derful years together," she said slowly. "His death was very sudden, a heart defect no one suspected. I lost him a year ago and I'm still getting over the shock." Lady Eleanor was smil-ing at her encouragingly and tucking wisps of feathery fair hair back into the bun on top of her head. "Sir Matthew's offer of a temporary job was just what I needed. I'm afraid I don't know much about history, though."

"You don't have to know anything," Caroline retorted. "All you have to be able to do is bring order out of impossible chaos. Don't thank my father until you've seen his awful muddle in the library." She got up and put her plate on the trolley. "I'm going to get changed now and give Scott a call," she announced. "See you both at dinner." She flung Jessica an unexpectedly brilliant smile and sauntered out, and Jessica realized all at once that she herself was exhausted.

"You've had a very long journey," Lady Eleanor observed. "Would you like to see your room and rest before dinner? Or have a second cup of coffee? Or a tour of the house? I don't imagine you remember it very well, do you? Matthew won't be home until late and Peter doesn't come down from Oxford for a few days, so the meal will be very informal. I expect Tillie has already unpacked for you." Tendrils of her hair had worked themselves loose again and she was once more vainly trying to discipline them, poking at her head with vague little gestures as she waited for Jessica's reply. In that moment Jessica studied her openly. The woman must be in her fifties, she reflected, but she's as trim and supple as a girl under that rigidly conventional dress. Her skin has a bloom on it that nothing in a bottle can produce, and where are the crow's feet? She might be Caroline's older sister, not her mother. There was something alluring yet unnatural about Lady Eleanor, for her eyes, blue and clear, held the age that her face and body denied. Jessica's gaze moved to those fluttering hands, plump and veinless, the long nails as transparent as those of an adolescent, and remembered the warmth of them imprisoning her own. For some reason, the thought was not pleasant.

"I think I would really appreciate a nap before dinner," Jessica decided, getting up, and immediately Lady Eleanor rose also.

"Good!" she said heartily. "We will find Tillie and she can show you to your room. I'm going to take a turn around the garden and then pop down to the village for a few things, so if you need anything just ask her. There are bells to push in almost every room but they don't always work and Tillie doesn't always answer them." As she chattered on she was shepherding Jessica once more across the hall and towards the stairs, the air in the sombre space now striking chill through the young woman's thin shirt. "Tillie!" she called sharply, and presently the housekeeper appeared from somewhere in the back. "Show Jessica to her room please. If you need me I'll be outside for a while." With a last encouraging smile she left, the heels of her sensible flat-heeled shoes ringing on the parquet floor, her heavy serge skirt, encasing her like a subtle disguise, bumping stiffly against her tightly flexing calves.

"Follow me, Mrs Mortimer," Tillie said portentously and Jessica did so, climbing the stairs woodenly. At the top they turned right, following the landing that seemed to run the whole length of the house. Jessica glanced into two open doors but did not register what she saw. At the end of the landing they turned right again into a small dormer wing and Tillie halted, throwing open a door and pointing across the narrow hall at the same time. "This is the guest wing," she announced. "Your room is here and I'm sorry that the bathroom is opposite, but you won't have to share it with anyone unless the family has house guests sometime this summer. I haven't lit a fire," she went on, sidling after Jessica. "We generally don't have fires after April. But if you need one I'll lay it for you later. I didn't have much time to unpack your things so if I did it wrong you can call me back and I'll do it all again. Dinner is at eight. Shall I call you?"

Jessica looked at her in a daze. "Yes, thank you," she replied at last. "At seven-thirty, if you would. Does the family dress?"

"They change if Sir Matthew is at home but they won't tonight." The woman had untied her apron and was briskly pulling it tight again. "I hope you'll like it here," she ventured, turning away. "Some do. Most don't. If you don't need anything else I'll be getting on." Without waiting for a reply she went out and the door closed softly behind her.

Jessica blew out a long breath and looked about. The room was small but still larger than anything she had ever slept in. To her right a crimson velvet wing chair was drawn up to an empty fireplace, the grate hidden behind a pretty, hinged fireguard that depicted a bouquet of winter flowers. To her left, close to the inner wall, was the bed, and Jessica loved it the moment she saw it. It was huge, deep and solid, a relic from the days when one did more than simply perform the utilitarian practice of sleeping for one's health. Women had received friends and gossiped from such beds, read letters, sipped tisanes, entertained their lovers, and sobbed out their delicate disappointments into the mounded pillows. A lush crimson satin spread enveloped it, and red velvet drapes on brass rings hung down to the carpet from all four corners of the posters. Beside it sat a table containing a bedside lamp, a porcelain ashtray too thinly elegant to use, a water jug of cut glass and a goblet. Jessica hardly glanced at the bureau on the same wall or the vanity table with its oval, gilt-scrolled mirror set in the centre of the big windows.

Ordinarily she would have stepped across to see the view, but now she went to the windows to pull the cord that closed the curtains. They moved soundlessly, their own weight rendering them noiseless, and she ran a hand down the heavy velour before turning back into the now dim room, shedding her clothes as she went. The sheets were cold as she clambered up into the bed and crawled between them but the pillows were endlessly yielding and she breathed, "Oh God how magnificent," as she felt every muscle in her body go limp.

For a while her mind fed her with jumbled images culled from the last two days — her mother's anxious face as Jessica's flight was called, the womb-like atmosphere of the plane in which she floated feeling disembodied, the sight of Ron with her name on the placard above his head, and the unwanted drive through the village that had brought her at last to this cold, foreign house, these strange, foreign people. At the thought of the village a shiver went through her but her body was heating the bedclothes and exhaustion finally overtook her. She slept.

At some point she woke with a start and opened her eyes onto blackness. For a moment she did not know where she was and struggled up half-drugged with sleep, but then the confusion cleared and she was able to fumble for the lamp. As the room sprang to life she peered at her wrist-watch. The time was one-thirty A.M. The jug and goblet on the table had been pushed back and a tray, discreetly covered with a starched cloth, set in their place. Jessica pulled it away to reveal a dinner plate containing slices of chicken, cucumber and tomatoes, bread with two neat curls of pale butter, and a glass of white wine. A small bowl of custard sprinkled with nutmeg completed the meal. Either Tillie had been unable to rouse her for the dinner or Lady Eleanor had decid-

ed to simply leave her alone. Dragging the tray onto her
knees Jessica made short work of the food, washing it down
with the wine before replacing the tray on the table.

Clicking off the light she lay down again. The house was
utterly silent, and so, too, was the night outside. No wind
stirred. The hour ought to have been one of deep peace, but
to Jessica, her mind now less fogged with tiredness, there was
a quality of brooding about it that she liked less and less as
she lay waiting for sleep to claim her again. She had entered
the great stone building, eaten tea, talked to the two women,
tried to take note of her surroundings, in a haze of dislocation
that had now dissipated.

Childish memories of the house jumped into focus.
Herself standing before the two alarming guardians of the
staircase, gazing up in awe at their empty, visored faces.
Herself dwarfed by the stairs themselves that seemed to rear
up and up into a land of mystery.

She had been afraid of the place then. Compared to the
friendly confines of the cottage in which she had lived it was
a vast, formal expanse of dim corners, immovable pieces of
furniture that emitted their own almost-heard warnings of
stern untouchability, and eddies of cold air that blew around
one unexpectedly from elusive, arbitrary sources.

The portraits of dead Rensbys that crowded the walls
had disapproving eyes that followed you until you had scur-
ried out of their sight, and the only way you could escape
their notice was to avert your gaze and creep past them as
quietly as possible. Many times Jessica had grasped her mother's hand and heard the heavy front door close behind them
at the end of a working day with a relief that bordered on
panic.

Children have such odd fancies, she thought now as she
turned over. Such irrational, unfathomable fears. Who would
have thought that one day I should return here to work in a
much more pleasant capacity than my mother every did? She
tried to reassure the child in her that was still starting in

fright at the movement of shadows, but the stillness around her remained unpleasant and the sleep she fell into this time was distinctly uneasy.

Chapter 2

The next time she opened her eyes it was onto a diffused pink daylight. She lay still for a moment, lazily aware of the dim ceiling, the dusky folds of the tight-hanging bed curtains, the end of the bed where her feet did not reach and the slightly distorted outline of the closed door shown in the shrouded reflection of the dressing-table mirror. The house was still silent but Jessica, consulting her wrist-watch, saw that the time was just after seven-thirty in the morning. She wondered when breakfast was, and wished she had asked the night before. The remains of her midnight meal still sat on the bedside table, looking rather sordid. Unwillingly she slid from beneath the warm cocoon of the heavy blankets, and going to the window, pulled the cord that opened the drapes.

The morning was fresh and sunny and she blinked as the light smote her. Rensby Hall's extensive parkland rolled majestically away under her gaze, a regal expanse of smooth green lawn dotted with wide-spreading trees whose lush crowns were on the same level that she was. Beyond it, the row of straggling willows that lined the rill could be glimpsed here and there between the trunks, and closer in to the house itself, before the trees began, a huge grey stone sundial squatted in its own naked area.

Directly below Jessica's window she could see the wide stone steps that led down from the terrace and out onto the grass. On impulse she wrestled with the ancient window and pushed it open. Mild, damp air flooded the room. Either it had rained in the night or the dew had been particularly thick, for the lawn glistened and the terrace steps were slick with moisture. After a moment Jessica regretfully turned away. There would be time enough to rediscover the grounds, but now it was necessary to find the clothes Tillie had unpacked and put away, shower, and face the family.

She crossed the quiet hall to the bathroom, a glaringly white, purely functional room whose chill was barely alleviated by an electric bar heater on the wall which Jessica turned on immediately, but the water was hot and the towels luxuriously thick. After dressing she returned to her room, and sitting before the mirror applied her makeup with hurried expertise. The time was now past eight. With a final pause to gather her wits she picked up the tray and went out, turning right to where her wing joined the landing of the main house and then left along it.

This time the doors were on her right, and they were closed. She strode past them, aware of the loud slapping of her sandals as she approached the elegant sweep of the stairs with its motionless guardians below. At the foot she hesitated, hearing muffled voices coming from an open door at the far end of the hall. Sunlight was streaming towards her through the open main entrance and she skirted it as she came up to what she knew was the dining room on her right. She went in, smiling.

The three of them were grouped casually at the far end

of the baronial oak table amid the remains of their breakfast, more sunlight reaching softly towards them but dying as it washed two ornate silver candelabra. Covered dishes lined the buffet that took up most of the far wall. Jessica had time to briefly notice the rather sombre green and gold flocked wallpaper and the scrolled marble magnificence of the fire-place before the trio fell silent and Jessica herself, tray in hand, came to a stop. There was a split second of silence, a moment during which she wondered if they had been talking about her, but then all three faces broke into answering smiles and the man occupying the tapestried chair at the end of the table rose and came towards her, his hand outstretched. Hastily Jessica slid the tray onto the table.

"Jessica, Jessica!" Sir Matthew exclaimed. "Last time I saw you, you were a shy little bud of nine and here you are a perfect rose! You make me feel positively ancient, my dear. Do you remember me at all?"

He was a big, bluff man with sparkling eyes that nested in a fan of deep wrinkles. He was wearing baggy brown cor-duroy pants and an even baggier houndstooth tweed jacket whose pockets sagged, Jessica soon discovered, from his habit of thrusting his large fists into them with a spasmodic jerk, for as soon as he had shaken hands with her he performed the gesture.

"I do remember you, Sir Matthew," she replied with a half-laugh. "I think I used to be rather afraid of you. You seemed larger and louder than life to me in those days." Yes, oh yes, my God, afraid, she thought with a shock of recogni-tion as he regained his seat. Try terrified, Jessica my girl. The childish emotion of twenty years ago came flooding back with a stupefying speed while she kept the smile pasted on her face. I used to cringe when you touched me, shy away from your bluff, overbearing heartiness. You were always kind and generous to me. Then why the fear?

"There you are, Matthew," Lady Eleanor said with a catch of humour in her voice. "You ought not to loom over children and shout at them as though they were deaf. No wonder the village girls hang back when you try to give them sweets. Come and help yourself to some food, Jessica. I think it is still hot. We didn't want to wake you this morning. We know how wearying jet lag can be. And don't worry about bringing dishes down in the future. Tillie will do that when she makes the beds."

Jessica murmured her thanks and moved to the buffet, removing the lids from the chafing dishes one by one. There were kidneys and bacon, scrambled eggs, kippers, potatoes, toast, coffee and tea. Ladling a small helping of eggs onto her plate, she poured a cup of the strong black coffee. A place had been set for her beside Caroline who was leaning back in her chair, teacup in her firm, tapering fingers. Jessica sat down and attacked the coffee.

"Did you sleep well?" Caroline asked with a measured politeness. Jessica turned to her equally coolly. There was nothing personal in the girl's manner, she decided. Caroline was simply a very self-possessed person who probably had a mild contempt for those who appeared less confident than she.

"Very well," Jessica answered, "although I woke up some-time in the night and was ravenously hungry and very grate-ful for the food someone left beside my bed. I'm sorry I missed dinner."

"You didn't miss very much," Lady Eleanor replied. "Caroline and I ate on our knees in the sitting room and watched a little television." She made it sound as though the two of them had done something rather naughty. "Matthew got back from the city about eleven and then we all went to bed."

"Such an exciting life we lead," Caroline muttered sar-donically. "And what's on our thrilling agenda for today?"

Sir Matthew got up and poured himself another cup of tea. "I suppose you'll do exactly as you please, as usual," he grumbled good-naturedly. "I'm going to take the dogs down to the rill for a swim and then I have a paper to write for the London Archaeological Society. Don't worry, Jessica," he boomed, his eyes almost disappearing as he smiled. "I won't be putting you to work today. Take a rest, wander about, adjust a little. You can begin tomorrow. Or the day after if you like. It doesn't matter."

"It's very kind of you," Jessica protested, "but I've spent a year not doing much of anything and I'd prefer to get to work tomorrow. I certainly don't intend to presume on your hospitality."

Sir Matthew's face became solemn. "I sympathize with your loss," he said. "We're glad to have you. You needed a change and I'm a bit stuck with my research, so you see it has been a happy coincidence."

"A bit stuck? That's an understatement," Caroline murmured. She got up abruptly. "Don't wait lunch for me," she said as she started down the room. "I'm going to take the car out and do some painting while it stays fine."

"I expect you'd like to become reacquainted with things," Lady Eleanor said to Jessica when Caroline had gone. "Do feel free to go wherever you like. I have a meeting this afternoon in the village, the local gardening group you know. You can come with me if you like." She was wearing a loose, short-sleeved silk blouse this morning in a shade of pastel blue that accentuated her eyes and set off her fine blond hair. There were none of the freckles of aging on the smooth white skin of her naked arms, no tell-tale lines or crêpiness about her neck and throat. Jessica thought of her own mother, wide-hipped and coarse-skinned, comfortably and anonymously middle-aged, with scarcely an echo of femininity or sexuality left. This woman gave off an aura of faint yet disturbing perversity in her correct country matron's uniform, her unadorned ears, her sensible shoes, the fluctuation of her manner between the fresh briskness of youth and the measured responses of maturity. She probably spends a fortune on facials, Jessica thought. She probably has a room here fitted

out with all sorts of exercise equipment. English women consider it in poor taste to flaunt their attractiveness but I can
sense Lady Eleanor's sensuality, hidden away under those
ghastly no-nonsense clothes. Deliberately hidden? What do I
remember of her? Very little. Her cheek was always soft and
smooth on the few occasions when she bent to kiss me, and
her perfume was tantalizing. Her closeness did not fill me
with the same discomfort I felt when her husband loomed
over me. Other than that, I have no clear picture of her at all
in my mind. The woman was looking expectantly at Jessica,
who declined the invitation.

"If you don't mind I'd just like to look around the house
and grounds for today," she said firmly.

"Of course we don't mind," Sir Matthew answered.
"Now if you'll both excuse me . . ." He heaved himself out of
his chair, thrust his hands into his pockets, and lumbered out.
Lady Eleanor sighed.

"Tillie is going to scrub down the drawing room," she
said dismally, "and I must give Ron his instructions for this
afternoon. I did have a list of things I wanted him to get in
the village while I'm at my meeting but I seem to have lost
it." She also rose. "I must get busy. Lunch will probably be at
twelve, and if it stays fine we'll have it on the terrace." She
smiled absently and nodded at Jessica. Already an unruly curl
of fair hair was creeping free of the loose bun on top of her
head. "Don't rush your breakfast," she admonished, moving
down the room. "Sit for as long as you like and enjoy this little bit of sunshine." With the still-unconscious smile thrown
in Jessica's general direction she too was gone, and Jessica
poured herself more coffee, letting her chin slip into one
hand as she stared down the impressive length of the table
and out through the glittering window to the swaying tangle
of the flower beds between the house and the path and then
the dazzling whiteness of the driveway. The oak with its twist-
ing branches and the secret, dark thickness of its foliage was
casting a complex morning shadow that scarcely moved

across the lawn, and what sky Jessica could glimpse from her
position of solitary grandeur was unnaturally blue.

For a while she sat in a kind of pleasant torpor, knowing
that she was still suffering a mild effect of her journey and not
caring, until just as she was finishing her coffee the small door
behind her and to her left was flung open and Tillie advanced
upon the buffet. She stopped in surprise when she saw Jessica,
then bade her good-morning. The cheerful racket of a dish-
washer in full spate had followed her and she was towing a
utility trolley. Jessica thanked her for the late supper but the
woman did not seem disposed to talk, and soon Jessica was
able to escape into the relative dimness of the entrance hall.

Here she hesitated, but the inviting morning won out
and she slipped through the main door which still stood
open, feeling the dank coolness of the stone porch slide over
her face before it was replaced by sweet, warm air. She began
to walk east along the façade of the house without having
consciously chosen a direction, her left hand gently trailing
the tightly packed flowers of the weed-free beds. Cowslips,
white daisies, pansies and a few wild snapdragons were in
flower, almost hidden under peony bushes and the rhododen-
drons that stood sentinel at the corner of the house. Jessica
had noted the dearth of wildflowers that used to bloom in
arrogant profusion in the English hedgerows and she was glad
someone here, Lady Eleanor probably, cared enough about
them to ensure their survival in her garden.

Turning the corner, she stopped. The east side of the
house was one great terrace onto which French windows
opened all along its length. Massive stone urns stood empty
at the four corners, waiting for summer shrubbery, but the
climbing rose twining about the protecting stone railing and
balustrade was fully green, revealing tiny buds to Jessica's
closer inspection. Beyond the steps the lawn rolled out on her
right, tree-dotted and now dry, to be lost in the ever-present
blue haze of humidity and the untamed willows and brambles
by the rill. The whole effect was charmingly civilized as only

an English garden can be, and her impression was reinforced as she rounded yet another corner and found the path and beds delineating the beige paving stones of a formal rose garden. Perhaps forty circular bushes stood in the shelter of the large angle made by the north wall of the house and the west wall of the sitting room. Each bush was set in a tidy square of black earth and behind them, right against the house wall, was a stone bench where one might sit and inhale the surely intoxicating summer aromas of the flowers and admire their exquisite hues. Jessica thought that sitting on the bench and watching a revivifying summer rain stir the petals and collect in crystal beads on the spiked leaves would be more to her taste and she moved on.

But she did not go far. Once again she halted, this time with heart quickening, and the roses fled her mind. On her left was the sitting room. Its double, floor-length windows were open and the sound of a vacuum cleaner purred out. The path went by it to a gate that led, as Jessica remembered, into the kitchen garden and the courtyard and the kennels, but her heart and mind were instantaneously drawn to the sea of fragrant white blossoms trembling very faintly though there was no breeze and every now and then detaching petals that wafted daintily to the grass. It was the apple orchard, protected from the park by a tall wrought-iron fence over which the trees, some of them very old, leaned like dignified prelates. The path went between it and the sitting room, took a sharp right-angled turn, and continued on between the waist-high wall of the kitchen garden on the left and the orchard on the right.

Jessica drew a quick breath. Something sprang whole and complete from memory into the present, a childhood vision so undistorted that she was able to effortlessly superimpose the past upon the sun-drenched scene before her. She saw herself approach the sitting-room window and glance in. Her mother, dark head down and arms pumping rhythmically, was pushing the vacuum cleaner over the carpet. Sensing

Jessica's presence the woman straightened abruptly, one hand going to the small of her back.

"Jessica, where have you been?" she asked sharply. "Your dad wanted you an hour ago, to take you home, but no one could find you. Jane's still out looking."

"I'm sorry, Mummy," Jessica had replied, stepping into the shade cast by the house. "I went down to the rill and forgot about the time."

"I know you don't mean to be difficult," her mother had said with a sigh, "but you've got to remember that this isn't our house. It's good of Lady Eleanor to allow you children to come with us to work on Saturdays and if you abuse the privilege and wander anywhere you please she may change her mind. Well anyway." She turned the machine on again and raised her voice. "Go and get Jane. I think she's somewhere in the orchard. Tell her to walk you home now that your dad's finished his work. I'll see you both at suppertime." Without waiting for an answer her head went down again and Jessica wandered away.

The day had been perfect for early June, warm, sunny and still, and the blossom in the orchard had been fully open and almost unbearably beautiful in its scent. The gate leading to the apple trees, halfway down the iron fence opposite the kitchen garden, was ajar. Jessica had paused, and leaning against it, had taken off her sandals before venturing between the trunks. "Jane?" she called. "It's me. Are you in here?" She swung her footwear at a branch above and a shower of petals brushed her face, her hands, and settled in her hair. Picking them off she went on.

"I'm over here!" Jane's voice had reached her, curiously deadened by the regimented thickness of the trees. "Where have you been, Jess? Mum's angry with you, which means that I have to cook the supper tonight." But she did not sound upset about it. Jane was never upset. She took whatever came her way calmly, sometimes with a broad humour. Jessica, catching a glimpse of her sister's bright red shirt and baggy blue cotton overalls and running towards them, knew she would be greeted with the girl's slow smile and she was. Jane jerked her tousled head and Jessica fell into step beside her. Together they strolled back towards the gate.

"I'll peel the potatoes," Jessica had offered, and Jane had agreed with her sagely.

"Yes you will. Did you find anything interesting down by the rill today?"

Jessica made a rueful face. "Not really. There are tadpoles, and the waterweed is much thicker. I think I saw a caddis larva. Jane, I'm tired. I don't want to walk all the way home." They had reached the gate and were strolling back along the path by the house.

"Well you should have thought of that an hour ago when you were ankle deep in the water with your ribbon undone and mud all over your hands. Come on. Maybe Mum will let us stop in the village and have an ice cream." Her fingers had tapped briefly and kindly on Jessica's shoulder and Jessica had glanced up into her face, brown and serious and kind.

The orchard had smelled and looked exactly the same on that day. The shade of blue of the sky had been almost identical. Perhaps a tiny puff of wind caught me as I came round the corner then as it did just now, Jessica thought, and that was what propelled me so vividly into the past for these few moments. She realized that she had drawn level with the sitting room, and the sound of the vacuum cleaner had stopped, to be replaced by a heavy silence in the house and the drowsy hum of bees among the apple trees.

Jessica walked on, but no longer in peace. Sir Matthew called me a bud of nine this morning, she thought, but Jane at thirteen must have been struggling to open out into full flower. I did not realize in those days how difficult life must have been for her, how little of her time was really her own once she had performed her household duties and been responsible for me. Yet she never complained. She was sometimes firm with me but not harsh and I, with the flighty self-ishness of my age, did not appreciate her.

Lost in reverie she would have kept walking, but the sound of a spade hitting the earth caught her attention. Ron, somewhat incongruously clad in a garish red shirt and blue jeans whose cuffs were caked in mud, was digging in the garden. For a moment Jessica watched the rhythmic movement of the tool biting the soil, the man's boot coming up to drive it deep with a jerk of his body, the swing of his arms as he reversed the sod. The shirt was stained dark with sweat along his spine. There's strength under that skinniness, Jessica reflected. He must have sensed her presence for he looked up. She waved and called a good-morning but his response was slow, a grudging twitch of the fingers before he resumed his task, and Jessica's gaze left his bent head and found the wall beyond. It divided the garden from the abbey grounds and ran back to form the whole west wall of the house. Pear trees were trained against its flinty, rough-hewn surface, their branches almost obscured by new foliage. The rest of the garden contained orderly rows of vegetables. Jessica recognized staked tomatoes and the promising hills of potatoes before she moved on, leaving Ron to the work he so obviously preferred to do alone.

She had known it was there, of course it was there, but all the same she was conscious of a dull surprise when it came into view. I'm having quite a walk down memory lane this morning, she told herself caustically. Well I suppose it's inevitable, though I wish I could avoid it. I have done my best to forget about Jane over the last twenty years but now here it is, the arbour, unchanged and as forbidding as ever, waiting to rub my nose in my comfortable amnesia.

It loomed ahead, surrounded by a privet hedge so dense that one could not see through it, its sullen, blackish green height neatly trimmed. A trellis draped with delicate wisteria formed a roof that covered it almost completely and within, Jessica knew, were two stone seats and a small stone table.

The arbour was designed to be a cool refuge from the summer heat, a place for lazing away the endless afternoons or keeping evening assignations, but Jessica had never liked it even when the sunlight was diffused through the yellow wisteria and filled the space with a soft glow.

Jane had loved it, though. Jessica, stepping resolutely through the gap in the hedge where the path ended and the cold paving began, thought how it used to provide her sister with a few hours of precious privacy, a place where she could be free of her responsibilities for a while and lose herself in the schoolgirl novels she liked to read. Neither the noises from the house nor her mother's voice could penetrate here.

Tentatively Jessica walked forward, feeling the fragile wisteria fronds trail across her hair. A few tiny blossoms had drifted down to lie scattered over the seat that faced the entrance, and so thick was the hedge that no breeze was able to sift through and stir them.

Jane had been sitting there the last day Jessica ever saw her. She had been reading, of course, the book held to her nose in both hands, her white blouse under the loose overalls a glimmer in the stuffy dimness. Legs crossed at the ankles and swinging, her dusty toes had poked through the open sandals. Jessica had come up to her, hot and panting.

"Daddy's here with the car and I'm going home with him," she had said. "Are you coming?" The book had not moved but the legs had been stilled.

"No," Jane had replied. "I'll wait for Mum. Tell her I'm still here will you? I'll come up to the house in about an hour. She should be finished cleaning by then."

Later in the afternoon Jane and her mother had begun to walk home and had reached the beech woods by the time Jessica and her father returned for them with the car. Her mother had climbed in but Jane had declined the ride. "I'll walk thank you, Daddy," she had said and he had smiled, knowing she meant that on the way home she would stop to read some more under the giant chestnut tree on the green before cutting across to the cottage. Their father had turned the car and driven away but Jessica, sitting in the back, had turned to watch her sister slowly recede, an amiable, ungainly girl with eyes squinted shut against the bright day and teeth white against a sun-browned face as she smiled.

For months the police had scoured the village and the surrounding countryside, questioning everyone including the tramps and gypsies who in those days enlivened the timeless summers, until eventually the search widened far beyond the county borders, but Jane had vanished as completely as a puff of wind-driven thistledown. After the initial shock, the sleepless nights and anxious, hopeful days, came an exhausted acceptance. Jessica's mother had had fits of almost hysterical weeping but her father had withdrawn into himself, the anger and despair becoming a silent despondency that ate at his mind and at his body too, Jessica firmly believed. A year after Jane's disappearance he had peremptorily moved what remained of his family to a cold western city in Canada and a little later he had contracted cancer. His death had been a lingering and bitter one, and when he had gone Jessica's mother went to work for a maid service, doing the kind of work she knew best. Jessica herself had finished school and had gone on to study music at the university with the aid of government grants and loans. She had continued to live at home, a quiet existence hardly disturbed by her graduation and the students that had begun to call regularly at the little house she and her mother had rented.

I had almost forgotten you, Jessica said to herself, to Jane, bending to run her fingers gently along the edge of the seat. Forgive me. The child protected the child, and then there was the agony of Father and the demands of my studies. Pain and discipline and the not-understanding of the little girl I was; they all conspired to force your memory to the back of my mind. Then Michael came into my life, warm, steady Michael, promising an emotional security I had never known, teaching me how to laugh again, bringing a new kind of order with him. Mother strongly approved of our relationship. Through him, she too began to rediscover something of the humour and optimism that had once been her strength.

Jessica withdrew her hand. The yellow wisteria hung above her, perfumed and motionless. The darkness harboured in the frowning privet hedge even on the brightest days seeped out to discolour the stifling air. It was hell, she thought. It was pure hell, for all of us. How could I have forgotten? This was Jane's special place, the place where she was happiest, with her books and her adolescent fantasies. Then why did I hate to come here? I should be able to sit in this secluded little Eden as she did, in peace, and remember her calmly, yet I sense quite illogically that I am being watched, as though in being here I have attracted the attention of something hostile that is even now rushing invisibly through the orchard to claim me. The dense vines seemed deliberately suffocating. The stone on which she sat began to feed a deadly alchemy into her bones. Yet there was a drug in the cold apprehension she felt. It had a hypnotic quality that kept her waiting, breathless, hands gripping the edge of the seat. All at once she felt herself the object of a mocking regard. Something was with her in the stifling air. Something was watching her in speculation, she knew it.

The faintest of rustles came to Jessica's ears, like the sound of a page being turned, and the spell that had been holding her was shattered. With a low cry she sprang up and fled.

Ron was still sweating in the kitchen garden. The apple trees in the orchard still stood trembling faintly and occasionally snowing the grass beneath them with white blossom. Jessica deliberately slowed to a walk. It's the memories, she said to herself grimly, coming at me thick and fast now that I'm back here, all of them centred on the arbour because I saw her there on that last day and she had such a forlorn air about her, such an aura of fatalism, something I, as a child, sensed but could not articulate, or am I projecting a false precognition back through the years? I jumped at the chance of an English holiday with a simple job thrown in and yes, I am running from the pain and injustice of Michael's death. But perhaps I am speeding towards a long overdue confrontation with the ghosts of the past, mine as well as Jane's. Perhaps there was a thing in me that was ready to come back here and do battle. Or resurrect. Or finally bury. I have always sought safety, whether in my profession or my mother or in my marriage, and sometimes I have disliked myself for it. There will be no safety here, no sheltering wall between myself and the shadowy tableaux of my past. The arbour has just proved it. Act one, scene one, has just been played out.

The late morning sky above the gables and chimneys of the house remained a glorious blue and somewhere off to her left as she rounded the terrace, down in the tangle of untended trees and willows by the rill, rooks were cawing. I must go into the beech woods, she thought, and try and hear a cuckoo. June is the right time. We used to take a picnic there, all of us, Father, Mother, Jane and I, and spend the day waiting for the sound. Why is it that a cuckoo's call always seems to echo?

She was approaching the front door when she heard a furious barking and turned to see Sir Matthew lumbering across the park preceded by two bedraggled, wet dogs heading eagerly in her direction. Stopping, she bent and held out a hand. The golden retriever came up and thrust a cold nose into her palm immediately, snuffling with pleasure, but the Great Dane stood back, hackles raised, and gave a rumbling growl. Sir Matthew approached, beaming.

"They love their morning swim!" he said. "The retriever is Missy, and this huge oaf is Boris. Not very original, hey? Caroline named him years ago." He fell into step beside Jessica and the dogs followed, Boris still expressing his disapproval. "Lovely day. Lovely!" He went on. "Just ignore Boris. He'll get used to you. They don't like coming into the house anyway, my dear, so you shouldn't be bothered too often."

Both animals had halted before the porch. Boris sank onto his haunches, ears suddenly flattened, and Missy had begun to whine.

"But they wouldn't be a bother," she replied truthfully. "I like dogs. My mother has a fat old terrier named Rolly. He's getting on but he can still waddle and puff to the park and back."

Sir Matthew grinned. "Caroline used to literally drag Boris into the house and up to her bedroom when she was younger. I think she would have tied him to the bed if I'd let her. But he wouldn't stay. The moment she let go he'd head straight for the stairs and gallop out the door. Dogs the size of these seem to naturally prefer being outside. Go on then!" he encouraged them. "Go to kennel!" With obvious relief the pair trotted away. "They have warm accommodations in a corner of the back courtyard," Sir Matthew explained as Jessica preceded him inside. "They are still members of the family even though they won't sprawl in front of a winter fire in the sitting room as good English dogs should!" His hands shot into the sagging pockets of the old hunting vest he wore. "And where have you been a-wandering?"

"I've been revisiting the arbour," Jessica said, turning back to him. "I never liked it as a child and I still feel like a cat on hot bricks in there although it's a pretty spot. You'd think by now I would have outgrown such a silly prejudice." He gave her a sharp look.

"Parts of all of us stay locked in childhood," he replied. "But it's a pity you have a distaste for the arbour. I like to go there myself and smoke a quiet pipe or two in the evenings. Perhaps you have an unpleasant memory attached to it?" His gaze intensified and Jessica repressed an urge to wipe a non-existent smear of dirt from her face.

"I saw Jane there on the day she disappeared," she said, and at once he softened and drew back.

"Ah," he breathed. "Of course. Tragic. A terrible thing for you all. Well I must get on. An Assyrian piece to write,

you know. I can get the outline done before lunch, I suppose."
He cast a rather wistful glance back at the brilliant morning,
smiled at Jessica in a way that made her feel as though he had
patted her paternally on the head, and disappeared into the
gloom of the much tinier hall before the sitting room with
what seemed to her like relief. Jessica suddenly remembered
that there were doors to the right and left in that odd
antechamber, the left going to the kitchen and the right to
the study if she remembered correctly, but she decided to
leave a tour of the rest of the house until later.

Passing the two armoured sentinels at the foot of the
stairs she ran up and paced the landing. This time the two
doors on her left were wide open and she risked a quick
glance into the rooms as she went by. The first was obviously
Sir Matthew and Lady Eleanor's, a huge master bedroom
hung in white and turquoise with a heavy Victorian vanity
directly across from the door. Jessica could see little else but
the foot of the high bed with its chest. The room, facing
north as it did, seemed chilly and dank to her and she was
glad she had been assigned sunnier quarters.

The second room was Caroline's, and here Jessica
crossed the threshold for a moment. The girl had an artist's
obsession with light. Her room also faced north, but mirrors
hung in every available wall space to catch and reflect what
light there was. To the left was a fireplace much like Jessica's
own.

Above it hung a large and rather commanding black ink
drawing of the house, done from the park on the east side.
The terrace took its gracious sweep, the eye travelling effortlessly up the steps, between the open stonework balustrade
and across its floor to the impressive range of French windows
behind which, Jessica knew, was the library where she would
be working. The wall and windows of the second storey were
likewise carefully and boldly sketched, but the overall impression the work gave was one of dereliction. Jessica, going closer to inspect it, noted the word "Caro" scrawled in the

bottom right-hand corner. So it was by Caroline's own hand.

Yet the piece had an air of desolation about it. The girl had ignored the flower beds, the fat stone urns for shrubs on the terrace, the outdoor wicker furniture scattered about, and the majestic parade of glass that sheltered the library gave no hint of what was within or any depth to suggest reflections of what was without. It was a sad house, closed in upon itself, breathing an atmosphere of cold foreboding. The sky above it loomed with threatening clouds. Jessica moved back with a mental shrug. Perhaps Caroline is not happy here, was the intriguing thought.

Flanking the undeniably expert sketch were two silver-gilt mirrors. Other mirrors, small and large, were sandwiched wherever they would fit between other examples of the girl's work, all of it technically brilliant, all of it combining to fill the room with an air of discord. Yet as Jessica moved from painting to painting she could find no particular work, apart from the black etching of the house, to account for the mounting psychic disturbance she felt. Like Caroline's personality, her creativity was assertive, self-confident, yet beneath the sureness was something much more difficult to define.

Unaware that she was breathing more shallowly, Jessica swivelled to the bed, a four-poster hung and draped in heavy cream brocade. On the wall at its foot was the largest mirror in the room, a floor-to-ceiling gilded monstrosity that must have had a slight flaw in the glass, for the room it reflected back was strangely distorted. Above the head of the bed another mirror hung, but on the inside wall next to the bathroom door a tapestry took up all the space.

In various shades of brown, from beige to bright gold, it depicted a naked and wistful Eve receiving the apple of the Fall from the serpent. The background was wintry and sere: brittle dead plants, crumbling towers, a lifeless almost desert landscape. The serpent itself was coiled between the woman's parted legs, the apple in its grinning mouth, and with a shock

Jessica realized that its face was human, the skin taut and pale, the eyes beaded black and gleaming with avarice. Such anguished fatalism emanated from the hanging that Jessica turned from it sharply. The thing was obviously very old and probably fantastically valuable, but she did not like it at all.

Entering her own room, a place that seemed the heart of cosiness after Caroline's though the sun had now left it, she found that she was not alone. Tillie was polishing the bureau by the bed and the aroma of beeswax filled the air. She was singing to herself in a high, quavering voice and did not at first notice Jessica, but when she did she gave a shriek and struggled to her feet.

"My Lord you gave me a fright!" she exclaimed, holding out a sturdy hand that to Jessica's surprise was faintly shaking.

Jessica shrugged and smiled. "I'm sorry if I startled you," she offered.

The woman smiled back a little sheepishly. "Oh don't apologize," she said. "Ron says I'd jump at my own shadow, which is probably true. If you want to wait, I'll be done in here in a minute. I've already vacuumed the floor and cleaned your bathroom."

Jessica crossed to the wing chair, sat, and kicked off her sandals. "Please don't let me disturb you," she begged. "I haven't worn these things since last summer and they're pinching me. I'll be gone in a moment."

"They're very pretty," Tillie said approvingly, "but not much good for tramping around the countryside. Or maybe you're not much of a walker?" She attacked the bureau once more.

"I don't know about tramping," Jessica answered her, "but I certainly intend to get reacquainted with the village and the best way to do that will be on foot."

Tillie was rubbing vigorously. "Do you remember much of it?" she asked, and Jessica tensed, knowing what was to come. Oh well, she thought with cynical acceptance. The Rill is a very small community and there's bound to be a renewal of old gossip fuelled, no doubt, by Tillie herself. Best get it over with. "I remember more than I'd thought," she said deliberately. "My family left in very sad circumstances but it's all coming back to me."

Tillie straightened, a gleam in her eye. "Your sister disappeared, didn't she?" she remarked. "A terrible thing, Mrs Mortimer, terrible. But not so unusual for this village. Rensby's Rill has a sort of unhealthy feel to it." She gave a deprecating little laugh. "Oh it's neat and clean and prosperous and I've no complaints about the people. Very friendly most of them seem though Ron and I don't have all that much to do with them, us being outsiders if you know what I mean. But your poor sister wasn't the first to vanish into thin air." She gave the gleaming wood a last proprietary flick of the rag. "Forty-five years ago a little boy left his home to run an errand at the shop for his mother and never got there. And they say you can go back centuries into village history and find the same thing happening every once in a while. This evil old world is full of dark mysteries, isn't it? But somehow I wasn't surprised that such a thing happened here."

"History is necessarily full of coincidences, you know," Jessica objected mildly. Tillie looked disappointed at her apparent lack of interest. She gathered up the pail at her feet, stuffing the cloth into the welter of other rags and bottles it contained. "I suppose you're right," she said grudgingly. "I'm sorry again for yelping at you. I thought you might be the ghost."

"A ghost in broad daylight?" Jessica teased her. She looked solemn.

"They say there is a ghost here," she replied. "It can take on the appearance of anyone in the house, so that you never know whether you're talking to a member of the family or not. Nasty thought, isn't it? I have no idea who it's the ghost of, if you know what I mean. The family just laughs at it but . . ." She shrugged eloquently. "Once I had a long conversation with one of the village girls, down in the cellar. She'd been hired to do some extra laundry for her ladyship after a big party she'd had. We gossiped on about the ghastly winter weather and Ron's flu and whether the potatoes had better be planted in February instead of January. She finished the load and I came back upstairs and got on with the rest of the chores. By the time I got home I was shivering and the next day I came down with the flu myself. That was a beastly year for viruses. Anyway, I missed two weeks of work and when I bumped into her on the village street and happened to refer to our conversation in the cellar, she was surprised. 'That can't be,' she said. 'Milady hired Doris after the party this year. My girlfriend and I were away having a few days in London while it was on.' I was flabbergasted, I can tell you! I think I spent an hour in the cellar with the ghost. Well." She made for the door. "I hope I haven't frightened you. Most people love stories like that. Particularly the tourists."

Jessica glanced at her sharply but there was no malice in her face. "I don't believe in ghosts," she said firmly.

"Well, each to his own," Tillie said cheerfully. "I've nearly done for today but I must get on. It was nice, chatting with you." She paused on her way out and looked back. "Needless to say, Mrs Mortimer, I have disliked doing the laundry here ever since!" was her parting shot.

Jessica listened to her tremulous singing fade down the stairs and quelled a spurt of annoyance. Superstitious woman! Every big house in this country has to have its ghost, Jessica thought in the end, and getting up she opened the closet for another pair of shoes and forgot the matter.

Chapter 3

She ate a light lunch in the warmth of the terrace with a preoccupied Sir Matthew and Lady Eleanor's incessant, somewhat vague chatter that was nevertheless easy on the ear. Her hostess had obviously been raised to believe that gaps in a conversation were a sign of rudeness, and hastened to fill them with anything that came to mind, but she was astute enough to realize that not everyone wanted to participate in her observations and tidbits of local information and so did not mind when a guest fell silent and merely listened. More often than not, Eleanor's ideas died in mid-flow, her sentences fading to be replaced by a fresh flood of words, and in the end Jessica sat with eyes closed, basking in the sun and lulled by the woman's genteel cadences. Missy and Boris lay in the shadow their master cast on the terrace floor, alternately drowsing and watching for scraps. Sir Matthew gave them each a piece of bread smeared with salmon paste. Caroline did not appear.

Shortly afterwards Jessica succumbed to the soporific whisper of the early afternoon breeze in the fully leafed trees of the park, and excusing herself she went inside. Conscious of a deep physical contentment she drifted and soon slept while the mild sun began to sink and the perfect day to fade.

She was horrified to discover, on waking, that she had wasted the better part of the afternoon, but acknowledged the residue of jet lag and refused to feel guilty. When she was a child, going to bed during the day had never been allowed unless one was ill. Her wristwatch told her it was five-thirty. Yawning she slipped out of bed, went across to the bathroom, and washed her face. The upstairs hall was already gathering the evening's murkiness although the sun would not set for some time yet. Refreshed, she looked through the few dresses Tillie had hung in the closet, trying to decide on something suitable for dinner, and with some misgivings chose a soft black jersey Michael had bought her two years ago. "Musicians should always wear black," he had teased her. "Particularly musicians who teach. It makes them look arty and gives them an air of authority." She had flung back some half-serious retort but she loved the dress and it did make her look "arty." She wriggled into it and set pearls in her ears, repaired her makeup, and brushed back her hair.

When she was ready it was still only six o'clock so she sat in the wing chair and read the score of "A Life for the Tsar," an opera of which Michael had been quite fond. She had brought it with her as a sort of talisman, a promise to herself that this painful hiatus in her life would end, the continuing throb of grief over Michael would eventually fade. Then she would be able to teach again, listen to classical music again without the beauty of it tearing her heart to shreds. But the score depressed her and she put it away. She could hear the music too clearly in her head and did not want to encourage the memories that were linked to it.

Getting up, she went to the window. The grass of the park was acquiring a dark hue and the trees cast ominous shadows towards the rill. The window glass, when she laid her palm on it, gave back a breath of cold. Quickly she drew the drapes closed and went downstairs.

Crossing the hall she entered the drawing room. No one was there though a lamp shed a warm circle of light onto an occasional table beside the heavy, long sofa. The room was very large but sparsely furnished with little more than the sofa, a couple of armchairs, a mahogany coffee table topped with a sliver of Venetian marble, and a grand piano whose surface was covered in neatly framed family photographs. The inhabitants' day-to-day living was done in the sitting room at the rear of the house. This room was for formal teas or the entertaining of important guests. Jessica glanced curiously at the photos. Two were studio portraits of Sir Matthew and Lady Eleanor, formal and lacking in any vitality. The rest were of children. Jessica recognized the toddler with the dark hair and beachball clutched to her chest as Caroline. A later picture showed her grinning, a paintbrush clenched like a pirate's knife between her teeth, her whole childish face sparkling with life.

But by far the majority of snapshots revealed a young man in various stages of development. He sat naked, a chubby baby with a startled expression on his face and a blue rattle grasped in his fist. He stood with sturdy brown feet planted firmly in the sand, the ocean behind him and a shrimpnet over his shoulder. Clad in blazer and tie he gazed impassively back at Jessica before the entrance to an imposing, ivy-choked building. This must be Peter, Caroline's older brother. Jessica frowned, trying to bring him to mind. He had been born when she was a small girl. She could vaguely remember him staggering along a path while someone, a nanny probably, held out her arms for fear he should fall. He had made no other impression on her.

Smiling, she was about to turn away when one other photograph caught her eye. This child was sitting primly on an armchair, her doll beside her. A decorous bow perched on top of her head and her expression was solemn. The features were not Caroline's. Of course, Jessica thought, drawing back. There's another daughter. She was about my age, I think, but away from home most of the time so that I can hardly picture her. I would glimpse her occasionally but she seemed so aloof and mysterious that I never asked her to play with me. I suppose she was at the Hall for most of the summers, but Father always took us to Brighton for three weeks then and the Rensbys often went abroad. Her path and mine seldom crossed. What was her name? I can't even remember that. Well I suppose I'll meet her and Peter eventually while I'm here. She left the collection. Almost opposite the door through which she had entered was another door, standing open onto the faintest glow of light. Jessica went across into the library.

It stretched the whole width of the house, a breathtaking, dusky expanse of gleaming parquet floor with a ceiling that seemed to reach up into infinity and an upright field of now dark glass gliding with it on the right. Ten stacks extended into the room from the left-hand wall, each as high as the ceiling itself, and Jessica knew that between the fifth and sixth stack was a vast fireplace that could swallow logs whole. Three reading tables with soft leather chairs were placed at intervals down the room but were lost in the imposing, cavernous space. The room, if one could call it so modest a thing as a room, had thrilled and dwarfed her as a child and she found now, as she passed through the gloom towards that one ray of light falling near the further end, that those childish perceptions of endless space had not changed.

She passed the seventh stack and all at once the source of the light became a door ajar and beyond it Sir Matthew bent over a desk, writing in the circle of a sternly utilitarian angle-poise lamp. But as she approached, something besides the light came to meet her, a draught of frigid air that instantly made her shiver. She gave a low exclamation and the man looked up sharply. For a moment he peered straight at her, his face devoid of all expression, but then his features broke into lines of geniality and he got up.

"Jessica, my dear. Forgive me if I wondered who on earth it was. The library is entirely dark. Come in, do! I am alas still slogging through this wretched paper and wishing I had never heard of the Assyrians." He waved her impatiently forward but she hesitated, suddenly unwilling to enter that room.

"I'm sorry, Sir Matthew," she said. "I had no intention of disturbing you. I was at a bit of a loose end before dinner."

"Dinner?" he echoed her. "Is it that late? Oh do come into the study and have a glass of sherry with me before I have to get changed. I'm incredibly stiff and bored."

She could not refuse the second invitation and stepped forward warily, but once inside her irrational fear evaporated. The room was not cold, in fact it was overwarm, for a fire was burning in the grate behind Sir Matthew's desk, and the impression Jessica received was of a retreat, a place where the man could crumple papers onto the floor, walk about in his socks, and spill pipe ash onto the carpet if he chose. It even smelled different from the rest of the house. Under the aroma of woodsmoke was a faintly acrid, faintly musky odour that made her nose twitch and she wondered briefly if it was something Sir Matthew naturally exuded. The unexpected thought made her smile and he grunted approvingly, ushering her to a chair by the fire and thrusting a glass of sherry into her fingers.

"My goodness how cold you are!" he remarked, taking the other chair and stretching out his legs. "I know how it is. You get used to central heating and even at this time of year you can freeze without it. Be sure and ask Tillie for a fire in your room every night if you need it. We all want you to be blissfully comfortable here." He smiled and dreamily inspected the yellow wine before taking a judicious sip. "Blissfully comfortable, dear Jessica."

Jessica sampled her sherry and tried to smile back but the movement was forced. Something about him was troubling her. "Thank you," she said dutifully, wishing all at once that she had not ventured into the library at all.

It was that look, she thought. The look he gave me before he really came to himself just now. Blank. Indifferent. I would not have imagined that a face so full of affability could be so emotionless in repose. He was talking to her of the time he had spent in Canada during the war, of central heating, of real cold, of the paper he was working on, and she nodded and smiled and watched his eyes. They were nested in laugh lines and that was why, she decided, she had misread him. They did not light up with his mouth though the wrinkles around them deepened.

There is the Sir Matthew who used to stoop to give me candy and rides on his shoulders when I was little, her mind ran on. He would push sugar into my hands — licorice, sherbet puffs, lemon drops — then swing me into the air and toss me up whether I wanted to be there or not. I would scream, I remember, but not with excitement. I hated the feel of his rough jacket against my bare thighs. I shrank from the touch of his red, coarse neck. He would reach up and grab my fingers, forcing them to wrap around his forehead so that I was crushed against the back of his head, and every muscle in my little body would tighten with loathing. I suppose he meant well, and I was sulky and unappreciative to resent him in the way I did, but perhaps the strong, blind instincts of childhood were not so irrational. For there is the Sir Matthew who is the mildly eccentric lord of the manor, gracious to his guests and loved by his family. But there is another man behind those eyes, an intelligent, calculating man, perhaps even a cold man, who moves to a hidden music. She realized that he had finished speaking and came to herself. "I'm sorry? What did you say?"

"I said that you look very fetching in that dress." He heaved himself to his feet. "No no. Stay here by the fire and drink your sherry. I must get changed but Tillie will bang the gong when dinner is served." He left by the door to her back, disappearing into the house.

Jessica forced herself to sit on, trying to enjoy the wine and the warmth of the flames on her legs, but she became increasingly uneasy. The place was too silent, the quality of the air muffling small sounds — the measured ticking of a clock, the fire's occasional crack — and in the end she downed the remains of her drink with indecent haste, set the glass on the hearth, and left the room, her spine crawling.

Half an hour later the gong sounded. Jessica, unwilling to return to her room and too unsettled to venture into the sitting room, had lingered in the vast main hall where a dozen portraits of long-dead Rensbys gazed with a detached arrogance over her head. Each one was identified by a small brass plaque set into the frame and she read them off as she walked from one to the other — Sir Reginald, Sir Crispian, Sir John — thinking that if she was to help her employer chronicle their lives she ought to be able to put faces to the names that would occur in the notes. But in reality she was trying to dismiss the near-panic that had propelled her from the study and by the time Tillie, flushed and with grey hair awry, leaned out into the hall and began to vigorously belabour a large brass gong held under one bare arm, she had succeeded.

A door above immediately slammed and Jessica, looking up, saw Sir Matthew, attired in a dark suit, come briskly along the landing. Simultaneously the double doors between the hall and its smaller equivalent that led to the sitting room opened, spilling the two other Rensbys towards Jessica.

"Food at last," was Caroline's dry comment as she came forward briskly. "I hope you've had a better day than I did, Jessica. I forgot to take a lunch with me and I was sketching halfway to Clapton, perched on the side of the road where I had to clutch my easel and close my eyes every time a car went by." Her half-humorous, half-abrasive way of expressing herself was a relief after the emotional confusion surrounding Jessica's encounter with her father in the study. The girl was a surprise this evening. The lustrous dark hair was piled on top of her head, exposing a very white, long neck against which two large golden discs swung from her ears.

She wore a knee-length blood red dress that clung to her slim hips and left her shoulders bare, and her lips were painted the same flaunting colour. The transformation from the untidy jodhpur-clad half-child of yesterday to this striking woman with an element of sensuous danger about her was bemusing. Smoke trailed from the cigarette in Caroline's negligent fingers.

"I had a thoroughly lazy day," Jessica answered lightly. "And I ended up sleeping the afternoon away."

"Wish I had," was the succinct reply. "Come on. Tillie hates it if we don't start eating as soon as it's ready." She glided away over the gleaming floor, her black stilettos clicking. Lady Eleanor took Jessica's arm.

"I'm glad you slept," she said. "You look better for it. I hope it's given you an appetite, because I believe Tillie has prepared duck tonight. Of course it's not duck hunting season yet, far from it, but Matthew always guts and freezes enough for the year when he goes shooting in the autumn. I wouldn't like duck for a steady diet, would you? But once in a while it's lovely. Tillie does it so well . . ." She prattled on, enveloping Jessica in a pleasant cloud of 4711 cologne as they moved into the dining room. Her hair was down tonight, and fully freed from its inefficient bonds it waved back from her high forehead and settled gently about her shoulders. She was draped in soft folds of grey satin and tiny diamonds sparkled in her lobes. The effect was to bring her clear eyes into prominence. She looked no more than thirty years old and glancing at her Jessica experienced a wave of dislocation.

Sir Matthew ushered them in and closed the doors. Both candelabra had been lit, casting pools of homely yellow light onto the starched white tablecloth and flashing from the heavy silver settings. Jessica was surprised to see Ron standing by the buffet, resplendent in a black suit and white gloves, waiting to serve. What odd people these are, she thought. In the centre of the table stood the most ornate salt cellar Jessica had ever seen, a confection of antique silver turrets and towers that drew her admiring glance. Sir Matthew nodded at it as the others were taking their seats.

"Magnificent, isn't it?" he said. "Been in the family for generations. Costs me a fortune in insurance but what can you do? Don't worry," he smiled as he pulled out the chair to his right. "We won't put you below the salt! Sit next to me. I must say," he went on as Jessica obeyed, "you look very fetching tonight. Very fetching indeed. Black suits you."

Jessica wondered if he was always absent-minded, for he had paid her the same compliment not two hours before. But for all his eccentricity he had given no indication of chronic forgetfulness and she thought perhaps he had repeated his flattery to make her feel more at ease at this moment. She glanced swiftly into his face but saw no hint of collusion.

Then suddenly she remembered Tillie's foolish story. "They say there is a ghost here . . . It can take on the appearance of anyone in the house, so that you never know whether you're talking to a member of the family or not." Her hands went cold and her scalp prickled. Sir Matthew had settled into his chair and at his signal Ron was stepping forward, platter in hand, to serve Lady Eleanor.

"Sir Matthew," Jessica said carefully, "when we talked in the study earlier this evening you mentioned the time you had spent in Montreal. How long were you there?" She was watching him closely and she could have sworn that for a brief second he was taken aback, but his recovery was instantaneous. Ron had now moved to Jessica and was laying thin slices of duck on her plate. His cuffs were spotlessly clean. She could hear his slow breathing and fought the impulse to shrink from his closeness. Her host was answering smoothly, his wife automatically correcting him, he accepting her interjections with evidently habitual good humour, and Ron had returned to the buffet and was bringing vegetables.

The meal was excellent and the wine superior. In answer to the company's questions Jessica spoke a little of her own life as a musician, the foibles of her students, even a word or two about Michael and how they had met at a chamber music concert. At that point Caroline perked up and asked abruptly, "What was he like, your husband? Was he gorgeous? Was he a good lover?"

"Oh Caroline, really!" her mother expostulated. "Must you?" Caroline ignored her. She had turned to Jessica and was waiting for a reply, those black eyes, so like her father's, travelling from Jessica's mouth to her eyes and back again, those red, red lips slightly parted.

"It's all right," Jessica said, though she was annoyed. "I probably won't be able to describe him adequately because I'm pretty biased, and who can be honest about someone they love? I'll simply bore you all briefly with his strengths." They laughed politely, all but Caroline whose expression of almost prurient greed did not change. "He had a raw musical talent that he didn't really care about though he used to play our piano sometimes," Jessica went on. "He had a great sense of fun but a lot of tact to moderate it. He was steady, reliable. Physically he was tall and fit because he used to jog in the early mornings and he liked to ride. He was a good rider. He was dark, like you, Caroline, with warm green eyes. As for his sexual ability, that's private." Put that in your pipe and smoke it, you salacious little witch, she thought with relish, but all at once the girl's hand curled firmly over her own. Caroline smiled slowly.

"He sounds absolutely wonderful," she said. "I'm sorry." The hand was withdrawn and Jessica was left speechless. "Pete comes home the day after tomorrow," Caroline went on. "The son and heir, turning twenty-one this summer. He's already demanded a big party, Jessica, and perhaps it will cheer you up a bit. Personally I want to spend my twenty-first birthday lying on a beach in the south of France with some gorgeous French hunk feeding me sips of champagne."

"Poor Scott," her father said testily. "It's his misfortune to be in love with you." Caroline laid down her fork.

"Oh Scott's all right," she replied, unruffled, "but in his opinion the French are depraved and untrustworthy and only Englishmen know how to be honest and brave. He'd be lost on the French Riviera. To him, heaven is the prospect of inheriting 'Byways' in a couple of years and settling down to be a gentleman farmer like his father, and having scads of children with me. I'll probably do it, too," she added with a disarming ingenuousness. "By then I'll have sold a lot more paintings and I'll be able to get away from domestic bliss as often as I want."

"That is a selfish attitude, Caroline," her mother murmured.

"But realistic!" Caroline shot back, unperturbed.

"Much depends upon this summer," Sir Matthew said quietly, "if you hope to sell any more of your work, Caro. Everything in life must be paid for."

"I know!" Caroline said with a scowl. "Pour me coffee please, Ron."

The meal ended peacefully. Jessica contributed little more to the general conversation. She was wondering whether Sir Matthew's remark meant that Caroline was going to have a show of her work sometime before the autumn, in London perhaps, but she decided not to ask. It might seem like prying, particularly if Caroline was touchy about the subject.

When the coffee was finished Lady Eleanor invited Jessica to join them in the sitting room where she and Caroline would watch television or play cards. Sir Matthew intended to return to the study. But Jessica excused herself as politely as she could and went to her room. Once there she cleared a place on the vanity table and composed a letter to her mother, describing the flight and her first two days in Rensby Hall. "Sometimes they seem like perfectly ordinary people," she wrote, "but sometimes they strike me as very strange indeed. I wonder how you remember them, Mother? The garden is full of a Jane I haven't thought about in years, and in spite of so much coming at me that is new my heart keeps its grip on Michael. I begin work for Sir Matthew tomorrow and I am looking forward to the challenge."

When she had folded and sealed the letter, she prepared for bed, slipped between the cold sheets, and tried to concentrate on a mystery novel she had begun on the plane. But unbidden and certainly unwanted the vision of Sir Matthew in the study kept interposing itself between her and the printed page and in the end she dropped the book onto the rug and lay down to sleep. She left the light burning.

Her dreams were peaceful but towards morning she half-woke, chilled in the heatless room. The thick quilt had slipped to the floor and she leaned over and groped for it, eyes still closed. Pulling it up to her shoulders she went back to sleep immediately but this time her rest was shallow and troubled.

She dreamed she was standing in the doorway to the living room of the apartment she and Michael had shared. He was sitting with his back to her, hunched over the small desk where he used to write the free-lance articles that provided them with extra income, knees loosely apart, dark head down. It was late, and in the dream she wished he would come to bed. He did not seem to be actually working. His body was motionless. She was about to speak to him but all at once the prospect of seeing him move, having his face turn slowly her way, even watching him rise from the chair, became horrifying. She began to retrace her steps, praying that the floorboards would not squeak, afraid to take her eyes off that immobile figure. All at once she knew that he had heard her. He was turning. The chair scraped as he rose. She uttered a low cry and flailed against the blankets but she did not wake, and in the morning she remembered only that she had been cold.

Chapter 4

The same heavy traditional English breakfast confronted Jessica when she entered the dining room and this time she filled her plate and ate willingly. Lady Eleanor outlined her plans for the day, conferring with her husband on certain details that Jessica hardly heard as she deftly sliced her kidneys and buttered her toast with crisp slaps. Caroline ate little and said nothing. She was still in her robe, her hair tousled and uncombed, her hooded eyes swollen. She had obviously not slept well, and as soon as she had finished a third cup of coffee she lit a cigarette and excused herself, brushing behind Jessica and leaving peremptorily. Sir Matthew agreed to meet Jessica in the library as soon as he had taken the dogs for their daily swim and he too got up from the table and went out.

"We are not a jolly lot this morning," his wife remarked. "Matthew got stuck on his paper last night and nothing irritates him more than a job that drags on. You were cold, weren't you?"

Jessica looked up, startled. "Yes I was, a bit. How can you tell?"

Eleanor smiled triumphantly. "By the way you put away your food. I think there's an electric blanket around some-where if you'd like it. I'll tell Tillie to put it on your bed. Just in case." She rose. "Time to get on. Good luck with the work. Take my advice and just ignore Matthew once he's shown you what he wants. He can write twenty pages on the significance of a scratch on an old Assyrian pot, but when it comes to organizing notes and filing information he's a muddle-headed idiot. We all are. Except Peter, of course." She sighed, whether in regret for the family's ineptitude or in admiration for her son, Jessica could not tell. She laid her napkin beside her plate and rose also.

"I'll come with you," she said. "I want a breath of air before I get to work. It promises to be another lovely day." The older woman agreed vehemently and launched into a comparison of this year's June weather with the last as the two of them emerged into the hall. Her parting words floated after Jessica as she walked out the main door into the new sunshine.

Her first impulse was to take the path she had followed yesterday and she had turned left without hesitation before halting abruptly. Something wants me to go back to the arbour, she thought. Something is waiting for me there, some kind of revelation that makes me both afraid and compelled. I don't want to know what it is, not today, not yet. Later per-haps, when I am more at ease here, when I can stop con-sciously trying to wrench my life into a new course and there is the stability that will allow a tentative step into those dark-er avenues of the mind. It is a long way to travel, twenty years, and I'm still not quite ready for such a mysterious jour-ney. Not when all my energy must be spent in grasping the present. How warm the sun is on my skin! And such a clam-our of birdsong!

She turned back and cut across the driveway, passed under the thin shade of the oak tree where the grass was soft and still damp beneath her feet, and rejoined the white gravel that ran to the high wrought-iron gates of the entrance. They were closed. Beyond them the road up which she had been driven in such style two days ago ran between the ruined abbey on her right and the open vista of fields on her left. She was tempted to push open the gates and go into the childish haven of the friendly old stones but she did not want to keep her employer waiting. Reluctantly, taking deep breaths of the faintly flower-scented air, she wandered back to the house. It would be all right, she knew it. Everything was coming together again. The rifts of wounding would be closed, were closing already in this charming but peculiar place, and time would give her back the inner serenity she had lost.

She approached the library from the terrace, mounting the scrubbed stone steps and crossing its pleasing expanse with a light heart. The glittering French windows were all closed. Peering in, she could make out Sir Matthew piling papers on one of the round reading tables and she knocked softly. He came over at once and admitted her.

"A good idea!" he said as she moved past him, and he pushed open more of the floor-to-ceiling glass doors. "Let in some of this glorious air! So you're ready to put yourself in harness, eh? Don't want another day to adjust?"

"No, thank you," she replied, going to the table where he now stood sucking his teeth, hands deep inside his abused pockets. "Please show me what you want me to do, how far you've got. I'm going to find this very interesting."

"Oh Lord I hope so!" he exclaimed as she surveyed the untidy mess that entirely covered one table, drifted over the floor, and had found its way onto several chairs. "Otherwise you'll spend the summer bored to death. There's a typewriter in the study if you need it. You can bring it out here. Set yourself up any way you like and ask me for anything you might need." He waved her into a chair. "The research is all done. I did most of it myself, hired a student in London to do some of the leg work, bullied Eleanor into going over the church records for me. You don't have to worry about that." He patted a mountain of sheets that threatened to topple over at any moment. "The problem is, dear Jessica, that the centuries have become rather muddled. I did my best to keep them apart but I've been at this for years and along the way, well, bits slid under other bits, and pages fell on the floor and got replaced in the wrong section — it needs a stern tidying up. Indexing, writing nice little bridges to join the facts together. Would you like some boxes? You could label them for each century."

"How many centuries are there, Sir Matthew?" Jessica asked slowly. "And yes, I think boxes would be a very good idea."

He nodded vigorously and began to pace. "How many centuries? Well, the Rensbys came over with William the Conqueror—1066, you know. They were plain old squires then. Hadn't been knighted of course. They're mentioned in the Domesday Book. Even then the village was called Rensby's Rill. Forceful and ambitious, the Rensbys were. Still are, I suppose. Had a younger brother in the House of Commons but I didn't like him. Sanctimonious, intolerant prig. He died. Never mind. My ancestors didn't stay squires for long. There was a Rensby on the First Crusade, at Magna Carta, fighting the Spanish for Elizabeth I, at Waterloo, we're part of the warp and woof of this nation." He came to a halt on the other side of the table. "The abbey next door was founded in the late 1200s. It was a small institution. At the time of the dissolution of the monasteries it gave Henry VIII no trouble so he left it alone after carting off all its gold plate, but he had this house built within spitting distance of it, appropriating a large piece of the abbey grounds and using one of the protecting walls, our west wall now, for the work, and part of the abbey's buttery for the cellar. Cunning old fox.

He gave the house to my ancestor Julian Rensby in 1542 and told him to keep an eye on the monks."

His voice had changed. Jessica, bemused by this flood of information, noticed that the fussy amiability had given way to sharp coherence and he was looking at her with bright, intelligent eyes. "What did the monks think of that?" she asked.

He shrugged. "Not much. Relations were decidedly strained and they got worse after Julian caught his wife with a lover and bricked her up alive in the cellar. The monks wouldn't set foot on these grounds after that and the abbot forbade any Rensby to enter the abbey. Not that they wanted to. Ten years later the monks were gone. The church moved them all to new quarters in the north and let the buildings fall apart. I imagine Julian was relieved."

"Bricked her up alive?" Jessica echoed, shocked. "You mean left her to die in the cellar, your cellar, here? Is she still there?"

He laughed. His hands swooped into his jacket and the old Sir Matthew was back. "I'm sorry, my dear," he said. "We're all so used to the story. We grew up with it. But it must sound a bit grisly to you. My grandfather found her bones. He was wiring the cellar, putting in plugs and things down there, and the workmen bashing up the wall found the tiny room, just a niche really, with her in it. The vicar gave her a decent burial and I had her put in the family mausoleum beside her husband."

Jessica shivered involuntarily. The breeze had freshened and was coming in small gusts through the open French doors. The papers before her rustled slightly. "Was there anything else in the room?"

The man straightened briskly. "Nothing but her bones and a rather lovely Tudor chair. I had it restored and it's in the study now, by the fireplace. Anyway, the story is somewhere in my notes and I daresay you'll come across it before long. Boxes. I will get you boxes. Ron will find me some.

Then I simply must finish that bloody Assyrian thing or I'll miss the deadline for the society's journal and I do want old McNaughton to see it in print and write me a nasty letter. Have fun, my dear."

Jessica watched him stroll out across the terrace and vanish into the sparkling morning. Suddenly she wished he would not call her "dear." The word was beginning to have a faintly condescending ring to it that she did not like. She got up and methodically closed the windows, then stood for a moment, contemplating the task ahead in mild dismay. Finally she walked across the room to the large brass button set into the wall by the fireplace and pushed it firmly. By the time Tillie came out of the drawing room and called "Yes?" she was already sifting determinedly through the chaos.

"I'd like a pot of coffee, Tillie, if you don't mind," she called back. "Black, with sugar."

"All right. But I'm baking right now so it might be a minute. I put the electric blanket on your bed." She did not wait for an answer.

Jessica bent to her work but an unpleasant thought gave her pause. That chair, the one found in the cellar. Was I sitting on it in the study last night? She got up and moved so that she would be facing the now closed door to that small, odd-shaped room, but shortly afterwards with a snort of annoyance at her own cowardice she dragged her chair back to where it had been and firmly fixed her mind on the task in hand.

Half an hour later the coffee arrived and with Tillie came Ron, who placed nine envelope boxes on the floor beside Jessica before giving her a noncommittal glance and going away. Nine, Jessica thought. Nine centuries; 1066 to the present. I wonder what other secrets this house holds? She poured a cup of steaming coffee and began to search for a pen.

She worked steadily for the next four hours, becoming increasingly absorbed in Sir Matthew's unordered but lucid notes. Tillie summoned her to lunch but she refused, saying that she had eaten a huge breakfast and was not hungry. She heard movement in the study and knew that her host was engaged in his own task, and she was fleetingly glad that the room was occupied. She tried not to read the words passing under her hands except to determine in which box the pages belonged, but her natural curiosity often won out and a picture of the Rensbys began to emerge.

Forceful and ambitious they certainly were, but unscrupulous also. They had made no secret of advantageous marriages, spurious friendships formed to extract useful information, the petty betrayals and cold, impersonal manipulations that would further their fortunes. Jessica found them fascinating but she did not think that she was going to like them very much. A thread of pure callousness seemed to join one generation with another and she got the impression, after barely scratching the surface of the material she must cover, that the only individuals who had been safe from their acts of self-interest were the reigning monarch and his or her successor.

Yet coupled with their undeniable ruthlessness was a hot-blooded appetite for life that Jessica rather liked. Duels were rashly fought and won, lovers passionately wooed and as passionately discarded, drunken sons whipped for gambling away a year's allowance, and a daughter who eloped and was never heard from again.

All the notes, typed or scribbled, were full of sources credited. Sir Matthew had already completed a monumental task of scholarship and Jessica wondered what was left for her to actually do besides putting it all in a correct order. She had taken the job because she needed a change. Michael's death, coming as it did with no warning, had left her stunned and temporarily unable to function. The shock had gradually diminished but not the nagging ache of grief, nor the ingrained habits of six years of a closely shared routine. At home in the apartment she would wake morning after morning and turn, still drugged with sleep, towards a body that brought her rudely awake by its absence. She still set the table for two when her mind was elsewhere, expected to hear his voice on the phone when she picked it up, ran to open the door when his footsteps sounded in the hallway. Only a small part of her knew rationally that he was gone. The rest quixotically behaved as though nothing had changed and would not accept reality. He had been everything to her, father, protector, friend and companion, a wall of caring between her and the world; an umbilical cord so rudely severed that she simply went on recoiling from the amputation. "You need a total break," her mother had told her. "Not a week on the beach but a few solid months somewhere completely different." She had agreed resignedly. "Would you consider going back to the Rill?" her mother had continued. "You loved it there as a girl. You spent half your time scrambling around in the woods and paddling in the water. I could write to Lady Eleanor at the Hall and ask her if we might rent a cottage cheaply for you in the village." Jessica had considered for a moment. Rensby's Rill. Huge beech trees to shelter a little girl's play. Dimpling water, warm and sparkling in the summer sun, stirred by the eddies of shadowy minnows. The deserted road, puddled by rain, silent and peaceful. Yes, she had loved it. "But perhaps it would bother you," her mother had gone on gently, "about Jane, I mean." Jessica had stirred. Something had moved over and through her, a tremor of anticipation, a subtle washing of both dread and hope. "No, it wouldn't bother me," she had replied slowly. "Jane was the last thing, the bad thing. Before Jane there were so many good things." She had looked her mother full in the face. "But I haven't worked in almost a year. How could we afford the rent?" Her mother had risen briskly. "It won't do any harm to write and ask," she had said. A florid letter had come from Lady Eleanor with what seemed like indecent haste, begging Jessica to consider the Hall her home for the whole of the summer if she wished in return for regular work on Sir Matthew's manuscript. Mother must have exaggerated my need, she thought ruefully, and the Rensbys decided to do her a favour for old times' sake. Poor things! Whatever must they have expected? A weeping, grieving, half-nutty widow? How embarrassing for all of us!

The coffee jug was empty. Jessica drank the cold dregs left in her cup and got up, stretching. Well I, for one, refuse to be embarrassed, she told herself. I'll be positive about all this. I'll maintain the fiction of the job for their sakes, and I'll enjoy a long vacation while I'm at it. And I'll settle with you, Mother darling, when I get home. I do feel more myself already. Michael would be the first one to tell me to haul myself out of the Slough of Despond and simply get on with my life. So be it.

The sound of heels tapping on the parquet made her swing round. Lady Eleanor was approaching, dressed in a very fashionable powder blue suit, a white chiffon scarf around her throat. The jacket was fitted, following the line of her high breasts and her slim waist, and flaring provocatively over her tight hips. The scarf seemed incongruous, an older woman's attempt to modestly cover flesh that, in Eleanor's case, Jessica knew, did not sag. She had a sudden and startling vision of that imprisoned hair falling tantalizingly over smooth, naked shoulders, of the eyes lined in black and somnolently half-closed, and wondered how many men envied Sir Matthew his wife. Perhaps he was the jealous type. Perhaps Eleanor's mode of dress was less the convention of her age and class than a deliberate suppression of her sensuality for the sake of her husband. Certainly Caroline had not inherited her fiery sexuality from her father. Lady Eleanor was carrying a briefcase and her handbag tucked under one arm.

"How are you doing?" she inquired cheerfully. "I don't see any clumps of hair on the floor so I presume you are still sane. Would you like a break? There's a meeting of the school council this afternoon and as I'm president I have to be there. I thought you might drive into the village with me and just enjoy wandering around while I'm busy."

Jessica cast a glance at the still mounded table. Each box had a few pages in it, though. "I'd love to, if it's all right with Sir Matthew," she admitted. "I wrote to my mother last night and this will give me a chance to post the letter."

"Oh I shouldn't worry about that," Lady Eleanor said. "You can just leave any letters on the table in the hall. Ron takes them to the post office every day unless someone else is going to the village. Matthew has finished his paper," she went on, half turning, "and we can post that as well today. He won't mind if you take the afternoon off. He knows you're a conscientious young woman. You can always do more tonight if you want to. Besides, it's a pity to waste this lovely weather." She was walking back towards the drawing room as she spoke and Jessica made up her mind quickly.

"In that case I'd love to come," she agreed. "Just give me a moment to fetch my letter and my purse."

Lady Eleanor drove a beige Austin Mini that reminded Jessica of the old car her father used to own. They bowled slowly to the gates, then on past the ruins. Lady Eleanor signalled carefully and swung left. "What do you think of the Rensby dynasty so far?" she asked as the car picked up speed past the weed-choked pond that lay in the fork between the road that ran from the village and the one that veered north to Clapton. "Have you had a chance to receive any impressions?"

It was an odd choice of words and Jessica smiled inwardly. "From what I can gather so far, they seem to have been a pretty violent lot," she answered. "Sir Matthew told me about Sir Julian's wife, walled up in the cellar."

Lady Eleanor chuckled. "They were a terrible old bunch but strong, you know. Full of vigour. The line has come down unbroken to the present, every generation producing at least one healthy son to inherit the title. Matthew dragooned me into doing some of the simple research for him and I found it quite interesting."

"I think I will too," Jessica said, "but really, Lady

Eleanor, there isn't that much for me to do. Sir Matthew doesn't really need me."

"Oh yes he does," the woman replied, frowning as she scanned the four-way intersection before driving through it and bringing the car to a stop opposite the school. She turned off the motor, and dropping her keys in her handbag extracted a change purse. "You will be doing the part Matthew hates. He could have hired someone from the village, I suppose, but so many of the girls nowadays don't even know how to spell, let alone index and catalogue." She gave Jessica a warm smile. "Besides, you needed us. I think it's a very satisfactory arrangement. Now." She dropped some coins into Jessica's palm and opened the car door. "This should cover the mail. I shall be through in about three hours — I hope! Do you want to ride back with me?"

Jessica struggled out of the tiny vehicle. "No thanks. I think I'll walk." The woman nodded and set off purposefully across the road. Jessica gathered up her letter and her host's bulky envelope and started for the post office.

It was wonderful to be striding out under a benevolent sun. The village seemed deserted, drowsing peacefully, unlike the mood it had projected when she had driven through it with Ron. Then, under an overcast sky, it had been slightly forlorn. She walked past the garden of the Monk's Fast pub, its close-cropped green lawn beyond the sheltering hedge dotted with tables under festive white-and-red umbrellas. They were empty, but a fat robin skittered across the grass to be lost in the shade of a bay tree. The Village Hall, a long, rather ugly red brick building with tiny windows, had not changed, and neither had the post office. Jessica turned up the short path and stepped through the open door.

The large room was still dark and smelled of dust and brown paper. Yellowing, officious-looking posters curled on the walls and the counter was shiny and scored. Jessica, hitting the bell by her elbow, saw that an access had been cut to the grocery store that adjoined the building and through it a large woman was sidling, her feet in bedroom slippers, her hair imprisoned by an old-fashioned net. "Yes?" she said.

Jessica pushed the mail towards her and placed her few English coins on the counter. The woman scrutinized the letter, then her ruddy face broke into seams of pleasure.

"You must be Jessica Carter!" she exclaimed, using Jessica's maiden name. "Staying up at the Hall, aren't you? I remember you well when you were little and your parents too, of course. I was sorry to hear that your father had died. Welcome back to the Rill! Has it changed much, do you think?" She was weighing Sir Matthew's packet and tearing stamps as she spoke. Jessica answered politely, trying to reconcile the gruff giant of her childhood with this homely, friendly villager who was plying her with questions. "Well things aren't what they were, that's certain," the postmistress declared, handing over the change. "Bert and I run the grocery store as well, now. The Archers sold it to us and went to Newbury. Said it was too quiet here. Remember me to your mother, won't you? Yes, Mrs Trent? What can I do for you?"

Someone else had come in. Jessica escaped thankfully into the sweet air and hesitated on the footpath, wondering whether to take a stroll past the cottage where her family had lived or continue on and see the housing estate at the end of the street, but before she had made up her mind she felt a touch on her arm. The woman who had been standing behind her in the post office was stepping back and holding out a hand.

"I heard your name in there," she said as Jessica shook it. "I'm Alix Trent, the vicar's wife. You wouldn't remember us, we've only been in the Rill about five years, but we've heard all about the Carters." She was young, Jessica decided, not much older than she was herself, and quite attractive with her curly hair pulled back into an untidy ponytail, her scrubbed, pale English complexion and long, jean-clad legs. "This is my husband's first country parish," she went on, "and we quite like the life, but we don't often see a new face. Will you pop into the Monk's Fast with me and have a beer?"

It was on the tip of Jessica's tongue to refuse but there was a note of appeal in the simple request. Jessica wondered if she was lonely here, in a place where one could still be classed an outsider after twenty years of residence. "I'd like that," she said. "I was going to wander around the village and get my bearings again but I can do it any time. I'll be here all summer."

"So I hear," Alix said as side by side they retraced their steps and turned the corner. The pub's sign was creaking slightly as it swung in the afternoon breeze. "One can't keep any secrets in a small village. The gossip's harmless though. People know better than to let it influence their relationships. I suppose everyone's been asking you whether the place has changed and do you like being back?"

"Yes they have, but I don't mind. They're just being friendly. I can't see many changes, as a matter of fact, Mrs Trent, and as for liking being back, well, it feels safe and strange both at the same time."

"Oh please call me Alix," came the invitation as they crossed the threshold and threaded their way past the bar on one side and the mullioned bay windows set with tables on the other. The farther door was open, letting a stream of sunlight in to cut through the low-ceilinged, dim interior, and they made towards it. In the garden, Alix settled herself under one of the umbrellas and Jessica sank beside her. The robin was back, watching them from a safe distance on the daisy-sprinkled lawn, its head cocked. A young man came and stood waiting and they gave their order, and as he went away Jessica blurted, "Oh Lord, I'd forgotten. I don't have any bills yet, only traveller's cheques."

Alix waved dismissively. "I invited you and I'll pay," she said, then changed the subject. "Does the weather shock you after Canada?" she asked, "or is it like a familiar old coat that you're able to sort of slip into again? I haven't travelled much but Ben, my husband, has, and he says that the most depressing or exhilarating or inhibiting thing about a place is always the weather."

They talked easily and lightly for some time. Jessica learned that Alix had no children yet, that she liked the parish but was not a joiner and found the various women's groups a chore. After a private education at a boarding school from the age of five she had refused a university education, and had instead become a dance instructor before marrying and now had to be content with running the local aerobics class. Jessica told her of her own career and they discussed music with a mutual delight until Jessica glanced at her watch and said, "Thanks for the beer, Alix, but I must be getting on. I want to make the bank before it closes and then I'll walk back to the Hall."

"I'm going that way myself," Alix said, and they rose together and began to walk towards the pub's door. "Have you started work for Sir Matthew yet?" she asked conversationally. "Is he going to keep you busy? I hope not. I'd like you to come and have tea tomorrow with us at the vicarage. Never having travelled I love hearing about the places other people have been!" She paid at the bar and they escaped together into the balmy afternoon.

Jessica cashed a couple of her traveller's cheques just as the bank was closing, then she and Alix set off along the road, walking slowly and talking easily. By the time they had passed the beech wood and were approaching the gate that gave entrance to both the churchyard and the path that led beyond it to the vicarage, she had decided to accept Alix's invitation. It was not as though Sir Matthew seemed anxious for her to keep strict working hours, she thought. If she spent every day in the library the rather frivolous task would be finished in a matter of a couple of weeks. Besides, she felt comfortable with Alix, and an uncomplicated friend during her stay in the Rill would be pleasant.

"I'll see you tomorrow!" she called back to the other woman as they parted. "I'll expect crumpets and china tea and of course watercress sandwiches!"

Alix laughed and waved. "Of course!" she shouted back. "My pleasure! See you later!"

Jessica trudged up the semi-private road until she came to the ruins. She had intended to go straight up to the Hall but her favourite childhood retreat beckoned, the sage old stones and arches drowsing in a warm silence, so she pushed through the gate and abandoned herself to their allure.

Chapter 5

*A*n hour later the sky began to pale slightly and a rim of clouds had appeared in the west. The weather was changing. A gusty breeze stirred fitfully at Jessica's hair as she left the sheltering lee of the abbey's roofless Lady Chapel and walked across the soft grass to the low iron gate, warm to her touch. Carefully clicking it shut behind her she turned left and in a few steps was through the far more imposing entrance to the Hall.

The wind followed her in under the portico and she was obliged to hold back her unruly hair with one hand as she closed the heavy door to the house and turned into the hall. Then she stopped, nonplussed. The dusky expanse was softened with sprays of purple lilacs, their heavy fragrance rushing to meet her now that the air was still. Several waist-high ceramic vases were set around the walls, obscuring the bases of the dour family portraits, and two pots of blooms reached to smother the two suits of armour. Tillie was vigorously sweeping up the light, stray petals. She glanced at Jessica.

"Thank you," she said tartly as the young woman came slowly forward. "I was about to shut the door myself. The wind's getting up, more's the pity, and there'll be rain tonight. We don't need it."

Jessica nodded. "The flowers are overwhelming," she commented. "Are they from the garden?"

"No," Tillie replied. "Lady Eleanor's friend Vera brought them over. Armfuls of them. She usually provides a few bunches when her trees flower. Milady is very fond of them. Had a nice afternoon?"

Jessica felt dazed. "Yes, very pleasant," she managed, and as Tillie grunted and once more bent to the broom she headed for the library. It seemed to take her a very long time to get there. Lilac twigs grasped for her skirt as she brushed past the vase beside the drawing-room door and she tore it away with a violence that shocked her. The blooms swayed, sending a gush of perfume into her face, and she closed her eyes and hurried on.

Her work was just as she had left it, the chair drawn out from the table, the boxes lying haphazardly on the floor, and she kicked one aside by accident as she sat down. Lilacs. Not a spray, not a modest bouquet, but dozens of the wretched things, sending their stench all through the house.

Michael had given her lilacs when they had become engaged. He had turned up at her door to take her to dinner, resplendent in a suit she had never seen before and never saw again for he preferred jeans and a sports jacket. His arms had been full of the dainty clusters. He had gently pushed them at her and kissed her while they tickled her cheek. "Tonight is special," he had said. "Roses just won't cut it for this occasion," and he had stepped back anxiously, excitedly, to watch her reaction. She had drawn a deep breath, inhaling their sweetness, feeling near to tears, feeling wonderment, for it was January the twentieth and the countryside was locked in the ice of a bitter winter. "Where did you get them?" she had asked breathlessly. "How did you do it, Michael?" He had grinned. "That's my secret," he had replied, and after she had set them lovingly in water and had placed them beside her bed they had gone out and drunk champagne and he had given her a ring. Her whole room had been filled with the aroma of spring, the tender scent of hope, when she had come home. From then on he had always brought her lilacs on January the twentieth and she never did find out where they had come from. California, perhaps? Mexico? One year they had been white and he had apologized profusely because the white ones did not smell.

Jessica looked at her hand where the rings used to be. It was shaking. She had put the jewellery away not two weeks ago in a desperate bid for peace, knowing that she would be coming here, hoping for healing, but now a kind of panic gripped her throat. She knew that her body was rebelling against the scent of the flowers, the powerful memories so suddenly thrust upon her, and she fought the feeling of suffo-cation while the bright day began to dim and the clouds that had been little more than a thin line of warning on the hori-zon an hour ago came drifting to dull the tall library windows.

She had just plunged back into Sir Matthew's paper chaos when there was a knock on the door and Eleanor's head appeared. "Tillie said you were back," she called through the gloom. "My gracious, child, don't you want a light on? It's getting so dark in here."

Jessica looked up. The room was full of new shadows. She got to her feet. "So it is," she said steadily. "I hadn't noticed."

Eleanor stepped briskly forward, throwing switches as she came. Jessica blinked at the brilliance. "I don't think it will thunder," Eleanor was saying, "but we're certainly going to get a shower. I came to tell you that tea is served in the sit-ting room if you would like some." All at once she came to a halt. "Are you all right, Jessica?" she asked. "You look very pale."

"I expect it was the walk," Jessica replied smoothly. "It's farther than I thought, from the village back to the Hall."

"Then you should definitely come and have something to eat," Eleanor insisted. "Did you have a good afternoon?"

Jessica felt herself being shepherded towards the study and did not resist. "It was very pleasant," she answered, following her hostess through the unlit and rather stuffy little space to the tiny hallway and the sitting room beyond. "After I'd posted the mail I met Alix Trent, the priest's wife, and we went for a beer."

Lady Eleanor's spine stiffened slightly. "Oh indeed," she said. "A nice young woman. We are in the gardening club together. But rather too earnest for my liking, Jessica dear, and just a little bit gullible." She waited for Jessica to pass her and then shut the sitting-room door firmly. Sir Matthew looked up from his plate.

"Who's gullible, Ellie?" he inquired. "Hello, Jessica."

Jessica took the armchair where Caroline had been sitting on that first afternoon. She leaned to the tea trolley and poured herself coffee. "I was just telling Lady Eleanor that I had a drink with Alix Trent today," she told him. "I liked her very much. She's invited me for tea tomorrow and I think I'll go."

There was a silence during which Jessica bent over her coffee, but she did not miss the swift glance that passed between Lady Eleanor and her husband as the woman sank onto the sofa beside him. They don't like her, Jessica thought, annoyed. Well that has nothing to do with me. I can do what I want with my spare time. I hope they're not going to become increasingly possessive of me as the summer goes on. Silly old things!

"Good for you," Sir Matthew said, smiling at her. "Alix Trent is an outsider and I expect she can find better things to talk about than crops and weather and all the village gossip. You go, dear Jess."

She did not like to hear her nickname coming out of his

mouth and she answered his smile unwillingly. Both of them were watching her as though they were expecting some comment. The coffee tastes awful, she thought. It's the smell of the lilacs, interfering with my taste buds. She began to talk about the small changes she had observed on her walk back to the Hall but she did not refer to Alix again and they seemed curiously both disappointed and relieved.

Returning to the library she worked for a further two hours, then recrossed the pungent main hall and went upstairs. The landing was softly lit by several sconces on the wall that cast pools of golden light onto the floor and the long, bulky chests that hugged it. A shaft of much brighter light was streaming through Caroline's open doorway and as she came abreast of it Jessica hesitated. The girl had not been at tea. She was about to pass on when Caroline glanced up and must have seen her for she beckoned peremptorily. Jessica went in.

"I hate the hours between tea and dinner," she said without preamble, sweeping several dresses off the armchair so that Jessica could sit down. She was wearing a black silk kimono tied loosely around her small waist and her hair was damp. "There's not enough time to start anything and it's the wrong time of the day for me to try finishing something. Low biorhythms between three and eight P.M. So I bathe and resist the urge to slurp cocktails." She shook a cigarette out of a crumpled packet and pushed it into her mouth. "Got a light?"

"Sorry," Jessica said, taking the proffered chair. "I don't smoke."

Caroline shrugged and began to rummage through the bottles and jars on her vanity table. "Smart of you I expect. It's going to rain. I can smell it. At least I think I can through the scent of the lilacs. A bit overpowering, aren't they?" She raised dark eyebrows at Jessica. She had found a thin gold lighter and struck it but as she held it to the tip of her cigarette her eyes never left Jessica's face.

"A little," Jessica replied diffidently. "Tell me, Caroline, where do you paint? Is there a studio in the grounds some-where?"

"No." The girl perched on the side of her bed and dragged on the cigarette. Her kimono slipped open to reveal one long white leg. "In London I use one of the studios at the school, and as I'm there most of the time it's not worth build-ing something at home. When I'm here I use my room or the guest room next to you and if the house happens to be full I don't work. I simply haul all my stuff down to the cellar for a while." Her unpainted lips widened in a generous smile. "I don't work seriously during the holidays. I just daub to pass the time."

"You're bored at home?"

"More often than not. I know boredom is a bad habit and I do try to fight it, but I usually end up yawning my way through the days." She mashed out her half-smoked cigarette in the little dish by the bed, and gathering up the dresses she had slung haphazardly over the chest at its foot she walked to one of the many mirrors in the room and began to hold them against her body one by one, eyeing herself critically. Jessica was amused.

"Are you planning a show this summer?" she asked, remembering Sir Matthew's remark at dinner the night before. Caroline continued to frown at her reflection.

"What gave you that idea?" she said. "No I'm not. I have to produce enough work by the end of next year to put one on, but I'm not exactly thrilled at the idea. I don't really care whether I graduate from art college or not. Why should I? It's just something to do. Peter will inherit the Hall and marry some debutante who can be trusted to settle down and pro-duce yet another Rensby heir. I'll marry dear old Scott and travel and have affairs, or perhaps I'll simply stay on here with Peter and his wife and grow old and peevish. There's plenty of money, you see. There always has been. Father doesn't flaunt it but there is. There always has been . . ." Her voice trailed away and she stared at Jessica absently for a moment. Then she came to herself. "The green or the pink?"

Jessica blinked. "The green. Somehow pink doesn't suit your personality, Caroline."

Caroline laughed and the pink dress collapsed in a billowing heap on the floor. "You're right. It was a bad buy. All that silly chiffon. I must have succumbed to Mother's nagging some dreary afternoon in Harrods." She strode to the bureau and began to rifle through a cloud of lingerie.

"You don't seem to be the kind of person who would get bored," Jessica said slowly. "You're very alive, Caroline."

Caroline's hands were stilled. "Alive?" she echoed softly. "Yes I suppose I am, although sometimes I wonder. And you, Jessica? Do you think you will be able to live again?"

You are an extraordinary creature, Jessica thought, watching the sure fingers return to the drawer. You have a restless vitality that borders on the neurotic but you are not as unobservant as you seem. I don't know whether I like or dislike you but we may become wary friends after all by the end of the summer. "I don't know," she replied forthrightly, "but I'm here because it's time to try."

All at once Caroline swung from the bureau and came to stand over Jessica. The movement was so sudden that Jessica had to repress an urge to shrink back. "I don't want to like you," she said in a low voice. "I don't want you and I to become involved. It wouldn't be right. It wouldn't be comfortable." A whiff of something faintly acrid rose to Jessica's nostrils from the girl's warm, shadowy cleavage, only loosely covered by the kimono, and her gaze was almost hypnotic. Jessica wanted to push her away. She was shocked and puzzled. But before she could react, Caroline straightened wearily and lifted her hair from the nape of her neck, letting it fall, and walking to the bureau once more. Pulling out a handful of black lingerie she slammed the drawer closed and said without turning, "I'm sorry. I didn't mean anything."

"Yes, you did," Jessica retorted, getting up. "I don't care if you don't like me, Caroline, but wouldn't it be more polite to keep your feelings to yourself?"

"But I do like you," the girl answered swiftly, facing Jessica. "I know you're still grieving and I think you're very brave and I wish I could be like that. I hate emotional pain! I can't take it! Look, Jessica, just forget my rudeness, all right? Do you think you're going to be happy here?"

Jessica wanted to roll her eyes and sigh but she did neither. "I don't understand you, Caroline," she said, "but I suppose I don't have to. I won't be here long enough for it to matter. I'll do my work and eventually get over Michael and go home to my students and my other life. I . . ."

Caroline came close, looking abject but also entirely serious, so that Jessica's next words died on her tongue. The girl's strong fingers closed on her shoulders. "If you find very soon that you can't stick it out here," she interrupted, "If you decide it's not working out and you're homesick or something and want to leave, will you come and tell me first? Not go to Mother or Father but tell me? Please?"

Jessica pulled out of her grip. "You are a very strange person, Caroline Rensby," she managed, half-laughing. "I have no intention of going home, but if I did then yes, I'd tell you first. Are you satisfied?"

"You're making fun of me," Caroline said sulkily. "I mean it, Jess." Then her expression cleared. "Well anyway, I'd better get dressed. Scott's coming for dinner and then we're going to Clapton for a bit of dancing. Want to come? Scott has brothers."

Jessica moved to the door. "No thank you," she said firmly. "I'm not quite ready for a riotous night on the town."

"I am, but I won't get it," Caroline smiled. Jessica stepped onto the landing, but just before she closed the door Caroline called, "Jess?"

"Yes?"

"Do you believe in God?"

Suddenly Jessica longed to be lying chin deep in a hot bath, behind a locked door, in silence. "Yes I do, Caroline, most of the time," she called back, and turned away. But she could still hear the girl's noisy exhalation of breath before she answered, "So do I."

There was no peace for Jessica in her own room. She had no sooner entered it than the smell of the lilacs became insupportable and she saw with dismay that someone had placed a vase full of the blooms on the table beside her bed. Calmly she picked it up, went out onto the landing, and set it on the chest against Caroline's wall. They are good people, she reminded herself as she filled the tub in the gleamingly antiseptic bathroom and slipped beneath the water with enormous relief. They have no idea how haunted I am. I can cope with the things for which I am prepared, but I am still too easily undone by the snatch of Chopin whistled in the street, the sight of a head of dark curly hair set above straight shoulders disappearing in a crowd, the unexpected banks of lilacs in Rensby Hall . . .

She put on black again, slipped into her pumps, and was just finishing her makeup when she heard the gong sound. Caroline, sinuous in the green crêpe wrap dress, her hair pulled to cascade over one shoulder, was just emerging from her room and the two women went down together. The hall was as dim as usual, the one chandelier scarcely illuminating the dusky reaches, but brighter light spilled out from the dining room and there was a murmur of cheerful voices. "Scott's here," Caroline remarked drily. An appetizing aroma of roast lamb almost obscured the smell of the flowers, but not quite. "We need drinks," she said loudly as Jessica followed her. "Scott, this is Jessica. Try not to bore her too much."

Jessica found herself shaking hands with a ruddy, fresh-faced young man whose smile was instant and genuine. His gestures, as he bowed slightly and took her fingers in his beefy ones, were charmingly deliberate. "How do you do," he said, but Jessica sensed that all his attention was fixed on Caroline and as she moved towards the table he rushed to pull out her chair. Amid the small talk and the rattle of cutlery Sir

Matthew poured the wine and Ron, once more in black suit and white gloves, served the soup.

Scott's conversation was amiable and guileless, a litany of farm events and village happenings, family get-togethers and the life of the stable. He and Sir Matthew obviously had much in common, particularly when it came to dogs and hunting, but Jessica, watching Scott with a mixture of warmth and pity, felt sorry for him. Often his hand would close around Caroline's as hers rested briefly on the table-cloth but so far as Jessica could see there was no response. The girl went on smoking or talking to her mother and ignored him. He was obviously no match for her aggressive intelligence — a well-bred, mild-natured, rather simple per-son who could not hide the fact that he was crazy about her. Jessica wondered why on earth Caroline would consider actu-ally marrying him when she spoke of him with disparagement and could not be bothered to acknowledge him at dinner. Perhaps it was one of those odd arranged unions that some-times still took place, though the prospect was unlikely given Caroline's apparent disregard for anyone's desires but her own. One could look at some couples and wonder what they saw in each other, Jessica mused as she waited to be served. One could look at them and be certain that they had no feel-ings for each other at all, but one could never know what went on in the privacy of their own homes. I hope Scott and Caroline are like that. Otherwise the poor boy is going to be dreadfully hurt.

She put some questions to him for the sake of politeness, which he answered readily enough, and she chatted with Lady Eleanor about her afternoon at the school meeting. But mostly she ate quietly and watched Scott try to interact with Caroline and Caroline effortlessly resist. It was a puzzle.

Coffee was served in the drawing room, and here at last Caroline allowed him to sit beside her on the sofa and rest a hand lightly on her shoulder, but not for long. As soon as he had emptied his cup and nibbled on a piece of cheese she rose, pulling him after her. "It's gone nine already," she said, "and by the time we get to Clapton it will be closer to ten. Hurry up, Scott. I want to dance!"

He bade them a hasty good-night and presently they heard the front door boom shut. Jessica sat listening to the sound of Scott's car pulling away down the drive. A sudden squall of water spattered against the window panes, invisible behind thick drapes. "It will probably rain all night," Eleanor observed, hitching forward on the sofa to pour herself more coffee. "I hope Scott drives carefully."

"You say that every time they go out together," her husband reminded her idly, holding out his cup. "Top mine up too, will you, dear?"

Jessica watched them from her vantage point in the corner, curled into the copious armchair. Their heads were together, Eleanor's untidy fair one and Matthew's salt-and-pepper tangle, their eyes on the flow of steaming coffee into Matthew's proffered cup. They mutely projected the unity of companionship they had doubtless developed over the years but there was also an air of smug exclusivity about them that Jessica had begun to recognize and did not like. Lady Eleanor set the pot back on the table, glanced up, and smiled at Jessica.

"I do wish you would play for us," she said, indicating the grand piano whose softly polished surface reflected the silver-framed photos crowded on it. "No one ever touches it and it's such a waste. I used to pick out 'Chopsticks' with Caroline when she was small, but Peter is the only one who bothers with it now."

"I didn't know he played," Jessica replied, and Sir Matthew gave a grunting laugh.

"He thumps out the odd jazz tune but he's got no real musical sensitivity. Come on, Jess. There's not much to do in the evenings here. Play something, please!"

"I'd love to oblige later in the summer," Jessica said honestly and a little guiltily, "but right now I don't think I could get through the shortest piece without making a fool of myself. I haven't practised in a year."

"We shouldn't have asked," Eleanor apologized. "Pour us all some brandy, Matthew, and put some Chopin on the stereo. Jessica, I've got something for you. I found it when I was updating the photo album." She patted the sofa beside her where her husband had been sitting. He had gone over to the neat stacks of records behind the library door and was running a finger along the jackets. "Come over here," Eleanor invited and Jessica slid unwillingly from her cosy nook, and carrying her coffee, did as she was bid.

There was a large brass magazine rack at the end of the sofa, and as the strains of a Chopin valse began to mingle with the steady drumming of the rain Eleanor pulled out of it a fat and rather dusty book. Unmounted photos immediately began to slide from the pages onto the floor. She ignored them. "Now where is it?" she muttered to herself. "I put it in an envelope . . . Ah! Here!" Passing the envelope to Jessica she enclosed the young woman's hand for a moment with both of hers and looked meaningfully into Jessica's face. "I kept this because sometimes when people are bereaved they go a bit overboard and throw away photographs and mementoes of the beloved and then later they regret being so hasty," she explained. "I don't know if your parents were like that but anyway . . ." She relinquished her grip and sat back. "This really belongs to you."

Jessica opened it warily, fumbling a little as she slid out the photograph. It was Jane of course, an old, curling, black-and-white shot, very slightly out of focus. Jane grinning lazily, eyes screwed half-shut against a hot summer sun, one strand of hair blowing softly under her chin. She was standing in front of the thick privet hedge that surrounded the arbour, dressed in a baggy light coloured T-shirt and even baggier pants. One lace on her sneakers was undone. The inevitable book was held loosely in both hands. The whole atmosphere breathed high summer, from Jane's light-drenched face and bare arms to the dry-looking grass under her feet.

She peered directly at Jessica, smiling the contented, enigmatic smile that Jessica now fully remembered, but it was not the sudden jolt of full recall that caused Jessica to take a deep, secret breath and stiffen for a moment. A memory had flashed across her consciousness and was gone in the time it took to recognize the photograph as her sister. It was something to do with Jane in the arbour or the orchard. Something odd, something too peculiar to be believed. But before Jessica could grasp at it, it had receded. She slipped the picture back into the envelope. "Thanks, Lady Eleanor," she said with a smile that included Sir Matthew who was handing her a brandy snifter. "My mother saved a few of Jane's things and all the photos but I haven't seen this one before. I'll keep it if I may."

"Of course you may!" Eleanor concurred. "I just hope it hasn't upset you, dear. Matthew took it outside the arbour that last summer. June, I think. Poor Jane disappeared in mid-June, did she not?"

It wasn't a pretty valse any more; it was one of Chopin's sonatas, a great swell of passionate, uninhibited sound that brought a lump of both appreciation and dread to Jessica's throat. She took a mouthful of brandy and held it for a second before swallowing. "Yes," she said. "June the twelfth. My birthday was the day after. June the thirteenth. It was the worst birthday I'd ever had. I was furious with Jane for spoiling it!" She laughed shortly. "Children can be so thoughtless, and of course I had no idea that Jane would never come home again. Poor little wretch."

"Yes, poor Jane," Sir Matthew murmured. "A dreadful, awful business. It's the . . . the unfinishedness of it that's the hardest, at least it must be so for you, Jess, because you were the last to see her, weren't you?"

Jessica nodded and sipped her drink. "So everyone told me." She set the glass on the table and rose. "It's a great night for reading in bed," she said to them, "particularly if you've got a good mystery waiting. Good-night, Lady Eleanor, Sir Matthew. It's been a pleasant evening."

Thinking that it had not in fact been pleasant at all, Jessica left the comparative cosiness of the drawing room and crossed the hall, shivering from the sudden drop in temperature. She could see water streaming down the outside of the windows that flanked the now firmly closed front door, and the masses of lilacs, drained of colour to a sombre grey in the cheerless, poor light, now smelled rather rank. Carefully stepping round the flowers clustered at the foot of the suit of armour she went upstairs, the envelope still clutched in her hand. The deserted landing was in darkness. Fumbling for the switches located on the wall opposite, she made her way along it. The doors she passed were firmly shut, almost forbiddingly so, and she was not sorry to slip with a sudden shudder through her own doorway.

The pretty fireguard had been stood against the wall, and a fire glowed in the grate, sending waves of welcome heat to Jessica as she advanced. Teeth chattering, she blessed Tillie and hoped that the chill rain would not last, but in another moment she was exclaiming out loud in annoyance. The lilacs were back beside her bed, and in the warm air their fragrance was as fresh and compelling as if they still hung from their shrub. Angrily Jessica swept them up, and marching onto the landing she set them on the chest where she had placed them before, slamming her door when she returned. Tillie doesn't know, she told herself, coming to stand gazing into the fire while outside a great squall of rain was flung against the glass and the drapes stirred. None of them know. It isn't their fault. Still, you'd think someone would get the hint.

Taking the picture of Jane out of the envelope she studied it for a while, trying to recapture the strange feeling that had instantaneously come and gone when Eleanor had handed it to her, but Jane went on smiling lazily and innocently into the camera and in the end Jessica propped the photo

against the lamp on her night table and got ready for bed.
Then she wrapped herself in her dressing gown and curled up
in the wing chair to read. But she could not concentrate. The
rain drummed fiercely on the hidden glass behind her. The
fire crackled sporadically, sending out a steady, drowsy glow.
After several pages she began to yawn and gave up on the
book. Laying another log carefully on the fire she crawled
gratefully between the sheets and was asleep immediately.

It seemed to her that her head had only just touched the
pillow when she found herself instantly awake and fully conscious. The room was cool. Sitting up shivering and drawing
the coverlet to her chin she turned on the lamp and saw that
the fire had gone out. The storm was still raging. Wind
soughed and whistled, mingling with the rain that continued
to lash at the windows. The drapes quivered in the draughts.
She wondered if a sudden gust had woken her but dismissed
the idea. It had been something else, something not so obvious. She had been dreaming of Michael again, lost and hidden in some dark, convoluted maze, calling to her. His voice
still pleaded in her mind. Oh God, she thought, grimacing
into the peaceful yellow light. I've got to get over this.

All at once a door slammed, the echo rolling along the
empty hallways to shudder against her own door. She jumped,
then began to relax and looked at her watch. The time was
two A.M. Caroline must have just come home.

Jessica lay down but did not turn off the lamp. I'm afraid
to go to sleep again, she told herself. Michael lost, trapped in
a place where I can't reach him, begging for my help . . .

But that is where he is. In his grave, imprisoned in the
earth, the flesh rotting from his bones.

Now stop it! Just stop it. In ten or fifteen minutes the
dream will have faded and there'll be no danger of slipping
back into it. I'll wait.

She turned on her side and lay looking into the steady
shadows, trying to think of innocuous, everyday things, but
her eye caught the picture of Jane and a kind of panic seized

her. Life was ephemeral. The sunny normality of everyday things, the sweet reality of, say, the aroma of coffee on a late Sunday morning or the sound of children playing in a park, was an illusion. It was a thin curtain that could shred at any moment to reveal a stark and terrifying truth. Death is more powerful than life. It snuffs out the strongest heartbeat, chills the hottest blood. It is supreme.

Try as she might, Jessica could not stem the tide of despair that had suddenly engulfed her, and as she struggled to regain an emotional equilibrium she became aware that the atmosphere in the room had changed. The stench of lilacs was suffocating her, pressing against her skin, insinuating itself through her nostrils and into her protesting lungs. She could hardly breathe, did not want to breathe, for the smell had the nauseous quality of a funeral parlour.

Flinging back the covers she slid from the bed and looked about for a cause, a small vase of the flowers she had missed earlier, a potpourri of dried lilacs on the mantel shelf, but there was nothing. The odour was now rising from her nightgown, her hair. Lifting a hand to her face she felt it oozing from her skin. It wafted towards her from the stirring drapes and rose from the carpeted floor. Choking, Jessica wrenched open the bedroom door.

The hallway was dark. Stepping out, she sucked up the cold, tasteless air, aware that she was sweating and panting, then she walked to the long upper landing to see if the flowers she had ejected from her room so firmly before were still sitting on the chest against Caroline's wall. Her feet made no sound on the frigid parquet floor.

The landing was very dim, lit only from below by the light left burning in the main hall downstairs, and either end was lost in dense shadows. Caroline's door was ajar. A thin sliver of moonlight fell through the slit and was quickly dissipated in the gloom at the head of the stairs. The flowers were still there, a dark blur. Their scent came to her faintly, sweetly, unlike the cloying, almost physical cloud that had driven her from her bed.

She hesitated, reluctant to re-enter that pressing miasma, and in the moment when she turned she heard a murmur of voices coming from Caroline's room. It had been going on for some time, she realized, a rise and fall of indistinguishable words, Caroline's clipped sentences blending with a man's deep tones.

Jessica listened, mesmerized. She knew that voice. It rooted her to the spot where she was standing and every muscle in her body went rigid.

Michael.

It was Michael in there with Caroline, Michael's abrupt chuckle, the slow, easy cadence of Michael's conversation. What was he doing with Caroline in the middle of the night? Why wasn't he in his own bed, with her?

Then reality asserted itself and she loosened and began to tremble. Not Michael. Of course not. It must be Scott, though it did not sound like the friendly voice of the young man she had met at dinner. The bloody dream, Jessica whispered to herself, teeth clenched. I'm still in the grip of it. Get out of here before you're caught snooping.

Yet the two voices held her. Even though it was not humanly possible, she still heard Michael's achingly familiar timbre come drifting into the gloom. The man laughed again, a quick burst of humour, and suddenly, soundlessly, Jessica began to cry the tears that had been threatening ever since she woke. Arms enfolding her own body, fingers gripping the thin satin of her nightgown, she backed towards the archway where the guest wing began.

Then the band of weak moonlight widened. The door inched open with a tiny creak. Before Jessica could turn, a man came out of Caroline's room and began to stroll towards the stairs. He was tall and lean, and as he moved into the faint but garish artificial light coming up from below, Jessica saw that he was wearing a pair of old jeans and a loose sport jacket bunched over his hands, which were hidden in the pockets of the pants. His stride was easy and self-confident. Dark hair curled over his collar.

All sensation drained from Jessica's body. Everything in her shrank while her heart palpitated wildly. "Michael?" she whispered, and the man paused. His head came round. He smiled. In that terror-stricken moment Jessica saw his face, stark white, as white as death, his eyes black, his teeth glinting slightly as his lips slowly parted. High cheekbones, untidy eyebrows, dishevelled hair, it was Michael. The smile was sardonic, knowing. Jessica thought she screamed, but she did no more than grunt. She tried to run forward but could not.

The man turned away and began to descend the stairs, making no sound. As though she had been released from some spell, Jessica stumbled after him. He came to the foot, and passing between the suits of armour still half-obscured by sprays of lilac he stepped into the full glare of the hall light and strode towards the main door. Jessica halted, looking down.

It was Scott, robust, fair-haired Scott in dress clothes and trench coat, who was now disappearing into the night. The door closed quietly behind him.

Jessica was shaking violently. Clinging to the landing's waist-high guard rail she had begun the long walk back to her own room when she realized that she was not alone. Caroline was standing in her doorway, and lamplight was pouring its friendly stream over the floor. Jessica paused and the two women studied each other. Caroline's mouth was swollen, her eyes huge above violet smudges. "Are you all right?" she asked finally. "Did Scott disturb you when he left? You look awful."

Jessica summoned up the power of speech. It seemed to take a long time. "I'm fine," she half-whispered. "I didn't mean to pry, Caroline. I wasn't sleeping well and heard somebody on the stairs. I thought . . ."

"It's my fault," Caroline cut in. "I should have warned you that Scott sometimes leaves my room rather late." She continued to stare at Jessica and Jessica, still shocked and unnerved, could only nod. The girl had an odd look on her face, neither apologetic nor concerned in spite of her words. It was almost a knowing gaze. Jessica felt physically ill. Without answering she gathered her courage and walked on.

Distraught though she was, the first thing she noticed when she had closed her own door behind her was the absence of any odour in her room. The lilac scent had vanished. Now shivering with cold and reaction she wrapped herself in blankets dragged from the bed and sat once more in the wing chair, before the ashes in the grate. The fire is dead, she thought incoherently. The house is dead, Michael is dead, this is a forlorn, unhappy place and I am a stupid and thoroughly miserable woman. Go back to bed. Dreams are only dreams. But she sat on while the wind moderated to a few intermittent gusts and the rain ceased. She was afraid to sleep again.

Chapter 6

*S*he did her best the following morning to repair the ravages of her sleepless night but she felt like a painted scarecrow as she entered the dining room, greeted the Rensbys, and served herself a breakfast she did not really want. Caroline was there in jeans and a bulky black sweater, already sending clouds of cigarette smoke over the table. She refused to meet Jessica's eye. It was Lady Eleanor, steaming kidneys balanced delicately on her fork, who exclaimed, "Jessica, my dear! You look positively ill! Whatever is the matter?" Jessica was saved from a reply, however, for Eleanor put down her fork and addressed her daughter. "I heard your door slam last night. It woke me and it obviously woke Jessica too. Really, Caroline, must you entertain Scott in your room so late?"

Caroline lifted one shoulder in an indifferent shrug and deliberately stubbed out her butt. "Well we can't make love on the sitting-room floor," she replied coolly. Sir Matthew was stirring his tea vigorously. He frowned at her.

"You shouldn't talk like that," he said. "Jess will get the idea that there are no morals in this house."

"Well there aren't," Caroline objected. "And I didn't mean to slam the door. The wind caught it. Scott and I do our best to be quiet."

Jessica had finished her first cup of coffee and was pushing an unappealing mound of scrambled eggs about on her plate. The conversation was making her distinctly uncomfortable, not because she was particularly prudish but because it had an oddly surreal quality to it due, she was sure, to her own exhaustion and the emotional stress of the night. The weather did not help either. The morning was heavy and dull, the cloud cover thick.

"I'm perfectly all right," she broke in forcefully. "I heard the door too and I got up to see what was going on. I was half-asleep or I'd have realized it was nothing to worry about. Then I had trouble dropping off again." She made herself swallow some of the egg. "The storm upset me, I think. Please, I appreciate your concern, all of you, but don't fuss over me."

"Quite right, Eleanor," Sir Matthew reproved his wife. "Poor girl doesn't get a moment's peace." As his nose was buried in his teacup, Jessica didn't know whether the poor girl was herself or Caroline. The girl was listening disinterestedly, her red-tipped fingers caressing her coffee spoon. Jessica got up to pour herself another cup and Sir Matthew rose also. "I hope you have some idea where you're going with the work," he said to her, smiling, and she regained her chair and smiled back.

"It is a bit of a mess," she admitted, "but it's a fascinating mess. I'll do as much of it as I can before I go to tea at the Trents'."

"Oh do you think you ought to leave the house today?" Eleanor put in rather plaintively. "It is so very dismal outside. Call Alix Trent and put her off. Have tea with us."

"Thanks but I want to see her," Jessica insisted, and Sir Matthew said quickly, "But of course you do. The work can wait. Might as well fill up this sulky day with something congenial." His tone was jovial but Jessica sensed reproof in the words. She was mildly irritated. First they encourage me to set what working hours I like and now they seem offended that I'm taking them at their word, she thought. I'm perfectly willing to co-operate with them, after all they're giving me what amounts to a free vacation and God knows I'm grateful, but I wish they weren't quite so . . . possessive.

Sir Matthew's hand came out of his pocket and Jessica could have sworn that if he had been closer he would have patted her on the head. Instead, he smoothed the front of his jacket. "Still, sulky or not, the dogs must have their swim," he finished. "See you all at lunch." He went out and Jessica turned to Lady Eleanor.

"I'd like to do some laundry when I get back," she said. "May I use the machines in the basement?"

Eleanor's pale blue eyes looked bewildered. "Laundry?" she repeated. "There's no need for you to wash your own clothes, my dear. Just leave them in the bathroom and Tillie will collect them up and do them for you."

But Jessica's North American liberality rose up. Dressing for dinner was one thing. Having a servant handle one's dirty laundry was quite another. "I would like to do my own," she said firmly. "If it's all right."

Caroline stirred. "Of course it's all right," she drawled. "Democracy and all that. We call it a cellar, not a basement, and it's a proper hole, but I daresay Tillie won't mind being relieved of the necessity of an extra ten minutes' labour." She pushed herself away from the table and stood, and now Jessica looked up at her. Her mouth was still very slightly disfigured under the bright red lipstick but her eyes were clear and unshadowed. Now they met Jessica's with a complicity Jessica found distasteful. "I need a long walk this morning," the girl went on. "Care to join me, Jess?"

Jessica could think of nothing worse than being in Caroline's unpredictable company. "Thanks, but I've got to make up for the time I'll be away this afternoon," she answered. The girl raised her eyebrows and sauntered from the room. Lady Eleanor's hands went to her hair.

"We really do have morals, Jessica," she said anxiously, patting and pushing at the errant pale wisps, and for the first time since Jessica had woken so suddenly last night she felt her mood lighten. She laughed.

"You are wonderful people," she said. "Kind and generous. It really isn't important, Lady Eleanor. Now if you will excuse me, I must get to the library."

Society's conventions make us all into polite liars, she told herself as she settled down in front of the untidy pile of papers, kicking aside a half-full box as she did so. They're not as wonderful as I pretend, and in return there is something cloying and insincere about their attentions to me, something claustrophobic. Except for Caroline, of course. Her attention is merely abrasive. Jessica sighed. Outside the solemnly grand library windows the parkland looked mournful and still. The trees seemed indistinct, shrouded in mist, and the stone of the sundial was discoloured with moisture. Some of the dampness had gathered in the room itself and hung in the ceiling and about the murky corners. Jessica had turned on the lights as she went but they struggled against the oppressive duskiness. Work would be therapeutic today. It would take her mind off the weather, Caroline, Scott, the dream . . .

Determinedly Jessica bent to her task but for some minutes she had to struggle against the memory of her husband's voice in the darkness, his face on the stairs, so white, his teeth so foreign, almost feral, yet undeniably his. But certainly deniable, Jessica thought angrily. Deniable, ridiculous, dangerously foolish. Don't walk that way. Don't weave embryonic madness around a dream.

She worked steadily for perhaps an hour. Each time her mind tried to wander to Michael and the events of the night she wrenched it back with an effort of the will. Sometimes she became suddenly aware of her surroundings: the dark and deserted library, the small, open door to the even darker study; but the same determination pushed that perception away. Gradually the intricate and confusing details of the Rensbys' history absorbed her concentration and the nightmares receded. The boxes began to fill.

At last she found herself staring at a few sheets of yellow foolscap, closely typewritten, with the date 1543 scrawled across the top in Sir Matthew's bold, uneven hand. She had not intended to read it, merely to throw it into the appropriate box for sorting later, but her interest was caught by the first sentence — "Sir Julian had long suspected that his wife the Lady Elizabeth was not only light of mind but flighty of morals as well, for her sheets had grown cold to him, though she spent much time fussing and preening before her mirror as though at the imminent arrival of a lover." It was the story of poor Lady Elizabeth Rensby, walled up alive for her sins. Sir Matthew had obviously transcribed it from some social history of the area, for a reference was scribbled in the margin.

Jessica read on. The story was compelling. Sir Julian's suspicions grew. He confronted his wife, who denied his accusation and had the effrontery to burst into tears of seeming innocence and charge him with a cruel indifference to her charms. Sir Julian appeared mollified, but one evening, returning early from an unsuccessful hunt, he had caught her in bed with a young squire from a neighbouring estate. Julian had taken his riding crop to the man and then to his wife, but his wounded pride, his murdered trust, could not be assuaged. Elizabeth had been dressed in her wedding gown, dragged into the cellar, and screaming and sobbing had been immured forever behind a new wall.

With a shudder Jessica wondered how long her muffled pleas and entreaties had resounded through the house. For hours? Days? What had her children thought? What had Sir

Julian felt when his wrath had cooled? Remembering his portrait hanging in the main hall, Jessica doubted if he had been
even tempted to relent. His face, rising from a starched white
lace ruff, was handsome but icy, the nose pinched, the mouth
sensuous but cruelly so. For a moment Jessica turned and
stared at the entrance to the study where that cursed chair on
which Lady Elizabeth had doubtless died had been placed.
But apparently the story did not end there so she read on.

It seemed that the squire, distraught over the loss of the
woman he adored and unable to contemplate her fate, had
hanged himself a month later in his own cellar. To Jessica, his
end had the inevitable fatalism of a Greek tragedy and rounded out the story nicely, but there was more. Intrigued, she
learned that according to the legend Sir Julian had not been
content with killing his wife. It was he who had plotted the
destruction of her lover as well. It was one thing to do away
with one's property under the law, but it was quite another to
cold-bloodedly murder another man.

Julian had enlisted the aid of evil powers. Together with
the local witch he had celebrated a Black Mass, in the course
of which they had called up a demon, and the demon had
been responsible for hounding Elizabeth's lover to his death.
Sir Julian's own fate was more mundane. He died surrounded
by his second wife, his children, and the fortune he went on
to acquire in the latter years of his life.

Jessica shuffled the papers together and dropped them
into the sixteenth-century box, then she sat back, kneading
her shoulders with both hands. It was quite a tale, horrific,
sad, with a kind of galloping compulsion to it that pulled the
reader as well as the unfortunate participants along. The
world is still barbaric, Jessica thought, glancing at her watch,
but in different ways. Poor Lady Elizabeth! I don't think I
would have liked to be married to those implacable eyes and
that uncompromising mouth either. She bent to her work
again.

The next pile of manuscripts contained an almost

impossible muddle of twelfth, seventeenth and nineteenth centuries and Jessica doggedly read through them all, dividing them appropriately. Underneath was a clear run at the rest of the sixteenth century.

But soon something began to puzzle her and she shuffled through the pages she had already read. There was a sameness to the accounts of the family's adventures, domestic and otherwise, after Sir Julian's story. Fortunes were almost lost but somehow regained. The estate was ruined but appeared to be in full flower for the next generation of Rensbys. Barren wives conveniently died. Diseased heirs were seen later hunting, overseeing tenant farmers, begetting more Rensbys. Each monarch had a Rensby hovering somewhere nearby and many Rensby children spent time at court as ladies-in-waiting or pages. Rensby men took high positions in the army. But not a single Rensby after Julian's time went into the Church, which was surprising. The Church in the past could provide as much luxury and power to an ambitious man as a secular career and had often been the choice of third sons, the first being the heir and the second going into the military. But Rensbys had shunned the Church and the Church, judging by the behaviour of the monks next door to the Hall in the old days, had anathematized the Rensbys. Why? Jessica asked herself, this time getting up and stretching. Rensby history is a series of very predictable ups and downs, surely too regular, too predictable, to be coincidence. And not one religious member. Not one. Curious.

"Jessica, we're going in to lunch," Sir Matthew's voice boomed out from the other end of the library. "Take a break and join us. Tillie's done something hot seeing it's such a beastly morning."

"Thanks," Jessica called back. "I'll be right there."

The weather had indeed worsened. It was closing in again, beginning to rain, not the angry squalls of the night before but a fine, steady drizzle that leaked down the library windows with a lulling relentlessness. Jessica walked past the tall stacks, the vast, empty fireplace, the other tables littered with work she had not yet touched, and out through the chilly drawing room into the main hall. It too was murky though the lights were on, and the Rensby ancestors stared down at her from their shadowy frames.

She was halfway across the floor and Sir Matthew had just disappeared into the dining room when a piece of knowledge suddenly burst into her consciousness and she stopped dead as though she had been struck. The photograph of Jane. The odd memory she had tried to recall and couldn't. It was there, filling her inner vision so that for a moment she was blind to her surroundings. But it was so insane that she was not surprised she had suppressed it all these years.

She had gone to the arbour to look for Jane. It had been high summer, that fateful last summer. Heat again, scent of cut grass and roses, sound of bees in the flower beds. On the way to the arbour, anxious as only a child can be, she had glanced into the orchard. Jane had been there amongst the gnarled, leafy trees, wearing the same baggy pants and light-coloured shirt she had worn in the photo. Instead of a book, she was clutching a handful of wildflowers, and she was not alone. A man was with her, a strange-looking man with lace at his neck and around his wrists. He had long brown hair and white stockings. Their voices, Jane's high and light, his deep and coarse, had reached Jessica quite clearly though unintelligibly through the drowsy air. The man's hand had been on Jane's narrow shoulder, his face bent to hers. Jessica had called out to Jane and gone scrambling through the orchard gate, and by the time she had come up to her sister, the girl had been alone.

"Where's the funny man?" Jessica had panted. Jane had stared at her absently, the flowers falling from her fingers.

"What man?" she had queried.

"The man you were talking to!"

"Jess," Jane had said in a tight voice, "there's been no one but me in the orchard for hours. No one. Understand?"

Her expression was still blank, dazed.

"But I saw him!" Jessica had protested. "All in fancy dress! I heard him talking to you!"

Jane had come to herself with a start. "I told you, there wasn't anyone," she said tartly. "You saw the shadows of the apple trees moving. Stop being silly. Now what does Mummy want?"

What man? Jessica thought now, standing in the frigid hall, her heart pounding. No man. Of course, no man. Then why is that buried memory now so sickeningly clear? Slowly she turned, and Sir Julian regarded her with his fixed, secretive gaze.

I don't like this, Jessica's thoughts ran on as she forced herself to turn her back on that calmly ruthless face and continue towards the dining room. Last night and now. Am I beginning to merge reality with fantasy? And if so, why? Are things being shaken loose in my mind, things long hidden behind my own defences? The past was a neat, comfortable, multicoloured blanket but now it is unravelling to be reformed savagely, without pattern, without coherence. I suspect it was not at all the way I have always remembered it. Where is the truth? She glanced to the top of the wide staircase and hurried into the welcome brilliance of the dining room.

By the time she had eaten Tillie's crab soufflé and listened to the Rensbys' entirely ordinary table banter she felt centred enough to return to the library and put in two more hours of useful and uneventful work. Caroline, wet-haired and with a faint flush of healthy pink to her cheeks, had been quite affable as she described her ramble through the wood that bordered the road to the village, and Sir Matthew and Lady Eleanor had argued mildly about what time Peter might be expected to arrive on the following day. Jessica, her equilibrium restored, had excused herself early, recrossing the hall without a second glance at Julian.

By three-thirty she was tiring. The house was quiet. The

rain still fell. Flicking off the library lights she made her way upstairs to her room, ran a comb through her hair, and freshened her makeup. Her reflection, in the dusky glass of the big vanity mirror, showed her a pale, rather preoccupied face and solemn, over-large eyes. Shrugging she pulled a sturdy coat and a pair of oxfords from the closet, put them on, and left the house.

The rain quickly claimed her, fine but clinging, as she stepped across the drive and onto the grass. After one glance up at the blurred, heavy sky she kept her eyes on the sodden ground under her feet. The cool air was good, easy to breathe, sharpening her mind and raising her spirits as she angled towards the gates and through them, pausing only briefly to take in the grey, shrouded serenity of the ruins before striding to the main village road. It was empty, puddled and bleak in the timeless afternoon. Crossing it she walked north a little way, turned left up the path to the church's lych-gate where for a moment the ancient wooden roof protected her from the steady, gentle fall of water, then hurried past the church and was soon ringing the Trents' front doorbell. Alix opened for her almost immediately. She was in jeans again, this time topped by a vivid yellow sweater, and her hair was down, swinging straight and shining against her neck. A gush of warm air billowed out from the narrow hallway beyond her and at her invitation Jessica followed her inside. She closed the door, holding out her hands for Jessica's sopping coat.

"Take heart!" she laughed as Jessica bent to slip off her shoes. "Today we're back to a miserable wet spring but tomorrow summer could return with full force. I'm so glad you could come. Ben's looking forward to meeting you. But I'm sorry, Jessica, I've been asked to drive some of the local ladies into Clapton later for a meeting. I do have time for a good visit though." She shook the raindrops off Jessica's coat and draped it over the newel of the narrow stairs that almost met the door. Then with a smile she led the way towards the rear. Jessica followed.

She was shown into a surprisingly airy room whose lat-ticed windows, framed in climbing roses, were firmly closed. Beyond them the tall flowers and shrubs of a small hedged garden drooped disconsolately. The room itself had the pleas-ing shabbiness of much use. A battered piano stood against one wall, piled with sheet music and photographs. Magazines littered the worn carpet beside a solid old sofa. A stereo sat on a shelf surrounded by stacks of records and the prints on the walls, though few, were of good quality. The word that came to Jessica's mind as she advanced with hand out to greet the man even now rising from one of the chairs drawn up to a cheerful fire was security. This was a safe place. It's all com-pletely sane, she thought as strong fingers curled about hers. The people, the house. There's contentment here.

Ben Trent was a very tall, rather stooped young man with an open, guileless face dominated by two keen, transpar-ently blue eyes. He drew her forward, indicating the sofa. Jessica sank into its welcoming embrace.

"I'm happy to meet you," Ben said, resuming his own seat and giving her a broad smile. Alix had excused herself and left the room. "We don't often get strangers at the Rill, but then, I suppose you're hardly a stranger, are you? One can be born in one of these tiny, tucked-away places, leave for twenty years, and still be greeted by the locals as though one had only popped up to London for the day when one returns." He bent and flung a piece of wood onto the fire. Sparks shot out onto the tile surround. "Conversely, one can arrive from somewhere outlandish and foreign, Clapton say, settle in, and still be treated with an icy politeness on one's deathbed after forty years of service to the community!" He spoke lightly, with considerable humour, but those shrewd blue eyes were measuring her carefully. No judgement hardened his gaze, however. Jessica chuckled.

"That's very true. I hope it hasn't been your experience, Reverend Trent."

"I'm Ben. No it hasn't, and I don't think it ever will be,

no matter where in this country the church moves me. Priests are privileged in that way. We belong to no social class and therefore are usually accepted by all. It makes cocktails with the squire and beer at the pub so much easier!"

Jessica was warming to him quickly. He was disarmingly without affectation. She wanted to pull her feet off the floor and curl them under her, lean into the corner of the sofa, rest her head against one hand and descend into the intimate familiarity one reserves for friends of long standing. "Where were you before you came to the Rill?" she asked. "Alix told me that this was your first country charge."

"It is. We met and got married in London, and that's where I went to theological college. I served my curacy in one of the inner-city parishes."

"The Rill must be a bit of a shock for you then. Did you choose to come here or did you obey orders?"

He laughed at her ironic tone. "Orders, definitely orders! After the inner city Alix wanted something entirely different and I didn't care where we went as long as we had a roof over our heads. She knew of the vacancy here and suggested that I ask my bishop if I could fill it. I did. There weren't any other takers. We quite like it. The pace of life is slower in the country but just as inexorable in the end as anywhere else." A thought seemed to cloud his features and he stirred and changed the subject. "What of yourself, Jessica? Do you feel at all a part of the Rill any more or is it all odd and strange to you?"

She was about to answer when Alix came in, set a tray on the coffee table in front of the sofa, and removed the cloth covering it with a flourish. "Crumpets!" she announced. "Watercress sandwiches! I went down to the rill and harvested the cress myself in the cold and the rain this morning!"

"Little liar," her husband muttered good-naturedly. "You bought it in Clapton yesterday. Pour the tea."

Alix shot Jessica a look of pure triumph. "China," she crowed.

In spite of the lunch she had eaten such a short while ago. Jessica found herself healthily hungry in a way she had not been since she arrived at the Hall. Without apology she piled her plate with the tiny white sandwiches, spread dripping butter thickly on the hot crumpets, drank cup after cup of the delicately flavoured tea. Conversation flowed happily and without the usual awkwardness of first acquaintance and it was not until Alix clattered her cup back into the saucer and rose that Jessica realized, with a flush of sheer delight and astonishment, that she had utterly forgotten Michael for the last hour.

"I have to go," Alix said regretfully. "Mustn't keep the dear old things waiting." She laid a hand on Jessica's shoulder. "It's been great," she told her. "Please come again soon. Ben will see you out later." Moving to Ben's chair she kissed him softly, smiled and waved at both of them, and went out. Presently Jessica heard the front door slam and then a motor start up.

"What a wonderful person," she remarked. Ben agreed vehemently.

"She certainly is. I'm spoiled rotten, having Alix. How about some more cake, Jess?"

The afternoon waned towards evening, and with it the easy camaraderie the three of them had sustained. Alix's departure seemed to inhibit Ben. Jessica attempted to keep the talk going but his mind was obviously elsewhere. He stared into the fire, smiled hesitantly once or twice as Jessica spoke, lost the thread of what he himself was saying, until Jessica, rather disappointed, stirred and made as if to rise. But Ben came alert and put out a hand.

"No, don't go," he begged. "There's something I want to tell you. I've been debating whether or not to mention it. I haven't discussed this with Alix." He broke off and made an apologetic gesture. "It's not always sound, my judgement, but in this case I have to trust it. I think, I hope, you won't end up hating me."

Jessica shook her head noncommittally, mystified. There was a long silence in which Jessica became aware of a clock ticking a ponderous measure somewhere close by. Then Ben said, "Will it be hard for you, trying to get by without your husband? He died recently, didn't he?"

Here it comes, Jessica thought, disappointed. The priestly commiseration. Aloud she said, "I never lacked for students. It will take me some time to build a good clientele again when I go home but I will be able to make a living by myself."

"You've had several bereavements, haven't you?" Ben pressed. "Your husband, your father, and a long time ago, your sister." He gave Jessica a rueful smile. "Village memories are long, and if there's no current scandal to chew on the locals will resurrect old ones. Is it hard for you, coming back here and confronting such a traumatic past?"

Jessica met his eyes and the retort that had slid to her tongue, the habit of village gossip seems to be catching, died unspoken. Ben's expression was sombre, unmarred by the greed for information Jessica had seen already beneath the smiles of those around her. The firelight glowed on the cleancut lines of his face and his hands were relaxed on the arms of his chair. He was waiting calmly.

"Jane disappeared twenty years ago," Jessica said. "Her loss is less traumatic to me now than Michael's. That's understandable. That's why the Rensbys invited me really, and offered me a simple job for the summer. I had forgotten her, pushed her to the back of my mind as I grew up, but I'm finding that she's coming back in a surprising and touching way now that I'm here. I'm beginning to remember a lot about her. Some of it hurts, so yes, in a way it's hard for me to return."

There was another small silence. Jessica stared at the litter on the table and waited. Then Ben said, "Your parents worked for the Rensbys, didn't they? For a long time?"

"For as long as I can remember," Jessica answered readily,

wondering when the man would get to the point. "They came to the Rill from Oxford originally, but that was when they were first married. Jane and I were both born in Clapton Hospital. My parents liked the Rill and they probably would have spent the rest of their lives here if that terrible thing hadn't happened to Jane."

"So they knew the Rensbys very well."

"As well as any employee knows an employer, I suppose. Perhaps better in their case seeing they were so intimately involved with the routine of the household." Jessica straightened and leaned forward. "Look, Ben, I've had a good time with you both this afternoon but you'll pardon me for thinking that you're becoming very personal. I know it's not polite to be so blunt but I wish you'd tell me why."

Ben sighed. "I'm sorry, Jessica," he said. "I must sound like an inquisitive busybody. It's just . . ." He glanced around the cosy room, obviously hunting for words. "Alix and I have been here for five years, as I said. The vicar before me was old Father Frank Jones. You might remember him. He was already sixty when your family left the Rill." Jessica nodded. Father Frank had been a familiar sight as she came and went from the Hall, for he was often pottering in the churchyard opposite the road that led to the ruins and the house, cutting the grass around the gravestones and tending the flowers. "He was having trouble with his sight even then," Ben went on, "and later he became completely blind. But he hung on here with the help of a young curate and the bishop didn't have the heart to remove him. He died in a home for retired priests two years ago in Cornwall."

So what? Jessica thought, but she said nothing. Ben smiled apologetically.

"I expect I'm boring you but be patient. When Alix and I came here, Father Frank stayed on for a few days to help me ease into the parish, give me some background, that sort of thing. The subject of your sister came up."

"I suppose it did," Jessica said evenly, "if you were getting

acquainted with the history of the village. Jane's disappearance was probably the juiciest bit of gossip the village has
ever seen."

Ben looked uncomfortable. "You're angry," he stated. "I
don't blame you. I sound like the worst gossip-monger myself
but I swear I'm not. I feel I have to tell you this even if you
never speak to either of us again."

Jessica tensed. I don't want this, she thought fiercely.
Jane resurrected, discussed, avidly chewed over, falsely pitied,
and all because I am back in Rensby's Rill. I am disappointed
in you, Ben Trent. Grimly she decided to hear him out and
then leave. "Please go on," she invited coolly. Ben shot her a
worried glance. Jessica could see his embarrassment but also,
by the sudden set of his shoulders, his determination.

"Father Frank told me everything, not because he took
any pleasure in passing the story on but because he had something to add to it. He was a bit obsessed with it, you see. He'd
always refused to discuss the matter idly with the villagers. He
said that such a tragedy was not for entertainment. But he
wanted to pass his information on to me because he was old
and moving away and he still hoped the case might be solved
some day."

"It never was," Jessica said tightly. "It never will be. Too
much time has gone by. And even if some young girl's bones
were found somewhere, how could they be identified as
Jane's? There'd always be doubt. What was this information?"

Ben took a deep breath. "I understand that you were the
last person to see your sister alive," he said quietly. "From the
back of your father's car? She was walking along the road
from the Hall to the village green?"

"Yes."

"Father Frank was certain that he saw her after that,
about half an hour later, sitting beside Lady Eleanor in the
blue Fiat Eleanor had then. Frank was cutting the church
hedge by the lych-gate as they slowed and turned up the road
to the Hall."

The cold anger still sat on Jessica's chest but she forced herself to remain calm. Another false lead, after all this time. Another excited imagination drawn into the sordid drama, wanting to be a part of it. There had been dozens of such sightings. The villagers, full of misplaced zeal and often a boastful self-interest, had seen Jane wandering by the Rill, crossing the schoolyard, talking to a strange man, even sitting in a bus to Clapton. The police had dutifully followed every lead but they had all been proved false, a collection of fantasies. Still, for the sake of good manners, Jessica played out this rather nasty little scene to the end.

"Did he tell the police?" she asked. Ben nodded.

"Of course. He said he was as convincing as he knew how because he was completely certain of what he had seen. The police listened to him with more respect than they gave to a lot of the silly tales going around at the time. Priests don't usually lie, you know, not on purpose, and we tend to be reasonably intelligent. The superintendent had Lady Eleanor's car checked for any traces of hair or threads, but there was nothing. Frank said that the Rensbys were very offended at the search, seeing they had been so close to your family. They denied seeing Jane after she and your mother left the Hall on foot that day."

"I expect they did," Jessica remarked drily. "The idea of Jane kidnapped by dear old Lady Eleanor is preposterous."

"You have contempt for me now and I don't blame you," Ben said, "but I might as well get it all of my chest. The police finally dismissed Father Frank's story because of his eyesight. He was already beginning to go blind, as I've said. They told him he was mistaken. But I don't think he was, and neither did he."

Well of course not, Jessica thought cynically. No one finds it easy to give up their pet theories on anything, to admit they're wrong. Oh Jane! This ghoulish eagerness is so insulting to your memory and I'm sorry. "Why don't you think he was mistaken?" she asked.

"For two reasons," Ben said quickly. "First, his sighting was the only one left after all the others had been disproved. It was the least probable, given the Rensbys' reputation and your family's close relationship with them, but it couldn't be discredited. The Rensbys denied it and that was that. Second, Frank had been a sniper during the Second World War, before he joined the church. He was trained to be observant, to note many things that the rest of us sort of let go by on the periphery of our vision. His sight might have been failing, but someone trained as he was would be very careful about what he did and didn't see."

In spite of herself, Jessica was shaken. "Why are you telling me this?" she demanded, longing all at once for a stiff shot of Scotch. "Why do you care?"

"I don't," Ben replied bluntly. "It's nothing to do with Alix and me although we hear it talked about again now that you're back. That sort of aimless gossip will die away fairly quickly. But I believe Frank's story and you're staying with the Rensbys and I . . . ."

"You wanted to warn me?" Jessica laughed incredulously. "You don't like them, do you? Even if, by some outrageous chance, what you say is true, and Jane rode back to the Hall with Eleanor, it would have been for some purely innocent reason, a forgotten book perhaps, Jane was always reading, and Lady Eleanor would quite naturally not want to become a suspect, a foolish, preposterous notion, and rightly just kept quiet. They are good people, Ben, and the idea of them doing me some harm is absolutely ludicrous!"

"Not warn you exactly," Ben said. "I'm sure you know them far better than I. They never come near the church, you know, which is unusual. Local squires usually attend church at least once a month and get involved with things like tower restoration and managing church finances. Many of them still have a say in what priest is appointed to their parishes. That was certainly the case with the Rensbys. But they've never set foot inside the church. Not in Frank's time either. Four years ago Lady Eleanor came to the vicarage wanting to look through all the old registers. She said she was helping her husband in some family research. The registers are all locked in the vestry, in the church itself. I offered her the key for as long as she needed it but she wouldn't accept it. She asked me to bring them to the Hall for her — something about being violently allergic to the mould that grows on old stone and so she couldn't go inside the church herself. But there was an uneasiness about her. After that Alix and I got invited a couple of times to the Hall for drinks and dinner, but we both felt it was a gesture to sort of keep us quiet, to let us know that they were just ordinary people who weren't partic- ularly religious." He paused and gave Jessica a quick glance. "Alix belongs to the gardening club," he went on, "and so does Lady Eleanor. They chat about seedlings and fertilizer and Alix says she's perfectly civil but you're right. I don't like her. Or perhaps don't trust her would be closer to the truth. I don't trust any of them." He rose and paused, one hand on the arm of his chair. Jessica was suddenly sorry for this man who had shown such moral courage. Ben obviously deeply believed in what he had said, and his disinterested honesty was transparently obvious. Jessica, though considerably shak- en, decided to forgive him. She also struggled to her feet.

"I don't know what to make of what you've told me," she said. "I don't think I believe any of it, but I do believe your motives are blameless. Thank Alix for the tea, but I must be getting back." She felt betrayed, as though Ben had whis- pered to someone else a secret Jessica had entrusted to him alone. Ben let out a long breath.

"I want you to come back," he said frankly. "Alix really likes you and she wants to get to know you better. As I said, I didn't tell her I was going to discuss any of this with you and I won't tell her I've done so now. I'm sorry."

Jessica did not reply, and after a moment Ben led the way out into the now frigid hall. But instead of showing her the door he pulled out of the closet a dark mackintosh. "I'll walk with you as far as the main road," he offered. "I could do with a breath of fresh air."

They walked side by side in silence down the short path from the vicarage to the grounds of the church. The rain still fell, misty and now imbued with the pall of the coming night. Just past the church, where gravestones crowded the path, Ben halted and gestured. A huge stone monument disfigured by patches of moss was set back under a ragged, dismal yew tree and surrounded by sharp iron railings. The masonry was crumbling, and the whole edifice breathed such an air of melancholy that Jessica felt the last of her enjoyment of the afternoon drain away.

"The Rensby mausoleum," Ben said, his voice falling flat and timbreless in the motionless air. "Curious, isn't it, that a family whose members for generations have spurned the church should insist, sometimes almost hysterically, on a Christian burial?"

Through the wavering fog Jessica could make out frozen faces with mouths agape, cherubs with closed eyes, apocalyptic beasts caught in mid-snarl. She shuddered. "Are they in there? Is Sir Julian in there?"

Ben nodded. "All of them, including poor Lady Elizabeth's bones. I believe Father Frank performed the ceremony for her after she was discovered in the cellar. He was a young priest then."

Jessica did not want to hear any more. She turned away. "I really am grateful to you for the tea," she repeated, "and I'm not an unreasonable person, Ben. I'll think about what you said." Ben shook her hand warmly and they parted.

Jessica forced herself to walk rapidly, and as she recrossed the road, still deserted and gleaming with moisture, some of the irritation and anxiety Ben's story had caused began to seep away. She briefly considered mentioning it tactfully to Lady Eleanor but quickly dismissed the idea. Even if Father Frank had seen Jane in Eleanor's car, which Jessica doubted, her reason for being there would of course have been entirely innocent and it would not have been surprising that later the Rensbys wanted to keep quiet about it. Anyone would, particularly when it became obvious, as time went by, that the girl had truly disappeared. Lady Eleanor would not want to be known forever as the last person to see Jane alive. That honour, Jessica thought grimly as she crunched across the gravel of the driveway and cut past the oak, was mine. Best let it lie. What difference could it possibly make now whether Eleanor was passing and Jane had begged a ride back to the Hall to pick up something she'd forgotten? I'd like to see more of Alix this summer, Jessica said to herself, but I won't allow either her or Ben to bring up the subject of Jane again.

Chapter 7

Stepping into the hall and closing the heavy front door behind her, Jessica was immediately in night although outside the evening light of an early June struggled against the oppressive weight of the weather. She peered at her watch, shivering in spite of her walk, and was horrified to see that the time was already seven o'clock. Dinner would be at eight. Pulling off her coat and shoes, noting that her feet were now wet, she tiptoed towards the stairs, taking a quick glance in the direction of the drawing room as she went. It was empty but a tiny slit of light showed under the door beside the stairs leading to the minor hall and the sitting room beyond. The Rensbys were probably having their pre-dinner cocktails. No time for a bath, she thought as she passed between the ever-silent armour sentinels whose vacant shapes still managed to convey a threatening awareness. With her shoes clutched in her hand she felt like a teenager sneaking home long after a curfew. The image made her laugh aloud. The sound travelled the dusky walls, floated to the murky ceiling, and came back to her overlaid with a rather sinister note that caused her to close her mouth grimly and waste no time in reaching her room.

It was as dank and cold as the rest of the house. The fire-place had been cleaned and the makings of a new fire set. Tillie would come up sometime after dinner and put a match to it, Jessica supposed, and wondered rather irritably why Sir Matthew did not convert the house to central heating if, as Caroline had said, there was plenty of money. Old habits die hard, she reminded herself as she stripped, hung up her things, and pulled on a cream wool jersey dress that hugged her body and lapped her in warmth. Gathering together her laundry, she paused. Beyond the sound of her own small movements the house was vastly quiet. No creak and crack of settling wood or shrinking stone, no human footstep or voice rose up to challenge the deadening stillness. Nothing ever will, she thought, her nostrils full of the musty odour of age released by the chill, damp air. Inhabited or abandoned and crumbling, this house will always hold the power of its silence like a cup brimful of stagnant black water, quickly drowning the echoes of laughter and pain alike. The idea was disturbing. Jessica considered the handful of dirty clothes on the bed. Leave it until tomorrow? Better not. My wardrobe is distinctly limited. I still have time to at least load the washer. She scooped up the pile and hurried downstairs.

Tillie was in the kitchen, presiding over clouds of fragrant steam. Jessica had not been there before. The room was done in yellow and white, a warm friendly space of sparkling modern appliances and appetizing smells. To Jessica it was as though the house had grudgingly allowed it to be an area of neutrality.

"I don't mind taking care of it," Tillie remarked, jerking her chin towards the clothes in Jessica's arms. "But I don't mind if you do it either. That's the cellar door, opposite the pantry." She went on tossing the glistening salad. "Dinner

will be ready in about fifteen minutes so you'd better hurry."
Her crisp speech was softened by a quick glance and a preoccupied smile. Jessica thanked her and opened the door she
had indicated.

Old wooden steps ran away from her feet into pitch
blackness. The light switch was on the wall by her left hand
and she turned it on. The light itself was a naked bulb hanging at the bottom of the stairs, but in spite of the burst of
harsh illumination Jessica hesitated. There was something
forbidding about the area that had opened beneath her, something cold and unwelcoming that made her shrink back
instinctively before she was able to descend.

The two machines were set a few feet from the base of
the steps against the right-hand wall. They were lit quite well
from the one source, but the rest of the cellar was cloaked in
its own mysterious shadow.

Jessica put her clothes on the drier, opened the washer,
deciphered the instructions, and began to sort her small load.
But gradually the feeling of a hostile yet curious presence
watching her movements from that chilly dimness grew until
she had to check the impulse to glance over her shoulder and
her actions became quieter and more cautious. She could
hear Tillie moving above in the kitchen, but the sounds were
strangely muffled as though the frigid, dank air down here
had a weight of its own.

Dropping the laundry into the machine she sprinkled it
with powder and pushed the starter. The machine purred to
life, the sound a sudden shock. Hush! she wanted to admon-
ish it urgently. Don't disturb it. It might wake up. The
thought was immediate, instinctive. She had no idea what
"it" might be.

She turned, facing the small play of hard-edged light
that cut a diagonal slash against the long wine rack, almost as
high as the ceiling, that isolated her from the rest of the cellar. The niches were full of cobwebbed bottles, most of them
covered in a layer of grey dust. The vaster darkness that lay

beyond seemed to seep between them, insinuate itself across the floor, creep in the space between the shrouded ceiling and the top of the rack to battle silently and subtly with the innocent whiteness of the light. For a second Jessica imagined the bulb fizzling out and herself defenceless against the triumphant rush of that malicious force, then she mentally scolded herself for being a fool and walked resolutely to the corner of the rack. Everyone's afraid of basements, she thought deliberately. They're always dark and full of old junk and feel like traps. The thing to do is take a look. She peered around the edge.

To her left she could just make out a gaping aperture from which the odour of stored vegetables wafted. That must be the root cellar. To her right the blackness gathered and she could barely make out a wall that rapidly disappeared into its hidden heart. I don't need to see any more, she thought hastily as a surge of uneasiness gripped her. I'll wait in the kitchen for my laundry. Maybe I'll have dinner first.

Then she heard her name. The voice was unclear and seemed to come from a distance. Turning with relief she called back up the stairs, "Yes, Tillie?" There was no answer. The housekeeper's heavy tread could be heard, and the crash of a kettle being returned to the stove. "Tillie?" Jessica shouted, looking to the open cellar door above her, but there was no response.

Puzzled, with a growing sense of dread, she was hurrying to the foot of the steps when she was called again.

"Jessica!"

She stopped dead. There was no mistaking the summons this time. It was louder, the voice more imperious.

Jessica ran up the stairs. Tillie was loading the trolley, a silver sauce-boat in her hand. "Did you call me?" Jessica asked breathlessly.

"No," Tillie answered promptly. "How's the laundry coming? I'm about to load the sideboard now."

"Are you sure you didn't call me?" Jessica pressed.

"Where are the others?"

"In the sitting room with their tongues hanging out, waiting for me to bang the gong," Tillie replied tartly. "But it'll be a few minutes yet. Hurry up or you'll miss out." She pushed the trolley towards the door and Jessica watched her in dismay.

Go into the sitting room and have a drink, she told herself. You can finish the washing anytime. It was a comfortable idea and she almost obeyed the impulse, but the thought of the fear growing the longer she put off going back down into the cellar gave her pause. Don't give in to a completely irrational emotion, she commanded herself sternly. What's the matter with you? If one of the family called you they can wait. Get your chore done.

The bulb still burned relentlessly. The machine was spinning with a throaty rattle. Nothing had changed, and yet Jessica was cold with apprehension as she slowly went down the stairs. Everything around her, the dusty necks of the motionless bottles pointing towards her in their orderly rows, the sharply geometrical patterns formed where the light met the darkness, the stale smell and the gritty floor, had undergone some invisible transmutation that left only their outward forms the same. She stood with one hand on the vibrating washer, her whole body tense, eyes scanning every cranny. Hurry up! she spoke silently to the machine. I've got to get out of here.

"Jessica."

It was a sigh with an edge of satisfaction to it, the voice of a child, and it was coming from somewhere back there in the dark.

"Jessica, is that you?"

Jessica stared into the cavernous space, her throat drying up.

"Who is it?" she whispered. The sound gathered strength from the shadows and went hissing into nothingness. . . . is it . . . is it . . . is it . . .

There was a silence. Jessica sensed the whole cellar become alert and listen. Then —

"How can you ask?" the voice whispered back. "Jessica, Jess, Jessy, you've got to help me! I'm down here and I can't get out! Quickly. Quickly!" The tone had changed, become louder and more strident.

Jessica froze. No one had ever called her Jessy except . . . "Jane?"

As if in acknowledgement the voice grew more shrill and was accompanied by a flurry of thuds. "Help me, oh help me, Jessy! It's dark dark dark! Pleeease, Jessy!"

There were two switches on the wall above the machines. With hands trembling so hard that she fumbled her first attempt, Jessica rammed them on. The remainder of the cellar sprang into life but the wailing did not stop. It increased to a shriek mingled with a booming that reverberated throughout the cellar.

"Jane!" Jessica shouted, and fled around the wine rack.

Harsh light showed her the cement floor, the entrance to the root cellar, and along from it another door. She stumbled into the root cellar. Nothing was there but a few sacks of last year's produce.

The other door was solidly closed and had no knob or handle. A Yale lock gleamed on its surface. Panting raggedly Jessica pounded and pushed on it but it did not so much as creak.

The rest of the wall was completely bare and met the far wall, which was entirely different in character. It was made of chunks of rough-hewn grey stone. "Where are you?" she screamed, flinging herself upon it, Jane's hysterical, pleading voice battering her.

But the moment she placed her hands upon the wall, the sounds stopped.

Stunned, Jessica closed her eyes and put her cheek against the sharp rock. Sweat was trickling down her spine. What happened here? she asked herself dimly, incoherently.

What? Happened? Here?

The cellar was quiet once more. No sound came from the kitchen or the rest of the house. The Rensbys were drinking in the sitting room.

All at once Jessica wanted to laugh. The Rensbys at cocktails. In the sitting room. Recognizing the impulse as an hysterical one, she pulled herself away from the wall and walked unsteadily round the corner of the rack to the machines. The washer, having finished its work, was mute. Automatically Jessica lifted the lid and began to pull out her damp clothes with violently shaking hands but her mind could not sustain the moment of denial. Leaving the lights on and her clothes in a pile she fled. As she ran under the bulb hanging above the foot of the stairs it exploded with a loud pop and the steps went dark.

The four of them fell silent and stared at her as she stumbled into the blessed warmth of the sitting room. Tillie was putting dirty glasses onto a tray. Lady Eleanor, one stockinged leg crossed elegantly over the other, was twirling an olive in the remains of her martini. Caroline sat slumped at one end of the sofa. She was regarding Jessica steadily, seemingly unimpressed, one booted foot swinging.

It was Sir Matthew who reacted first. Heaving himself to his feet he bent over the table, picked up a bottle, and sloshed something into a glass. Jessica managed to collapse into one of the armchairs. Her teeth began to chatter. She felt deathly cold. Sir Matthew thrust the drink at her and she gulped it willingly. The Scotch burned its way into her stomach.

"Didn't you hear it?" she blurted.

"What are you talking about, dear?" Eleanor said.

"The knocking and banging and the voice calling me, wanting help. You must have heard!"

They were looking at her blankly. Then Lady Eleanor deftly slid the olive between her teeth. Sir Matthew plodded back to his seat. There was a moment of embarrassed silence.

Jessica finished the Scotch in one long swallow and

cradled the glass to her chest. The fumes made her eyes instantly water. She laughed shakily. "I'm sorry," she managed. "Obviously you didn't hear anything. I went down there to do my laundry and I swear Jane called my name. It gave me quite a shock."

"It was the ghost," Tillie put in solemnly, and Lady Eleanor snapped crossly, "Oh don't be silly, Tillie! None of us have ever seen anything. There's nothing to see. It's just an absurd story the locals like to tell. You can go now." Tillie pursed her lips, and grabbing up the tray left the room. Eleanor turned to Jessica. "There really isn't anything, my dear," she said briskly. "You probably heard all the pipes down there, gurgling and groaning. They tend to be noisy if there's water running anywhere in the house. Have another drink, for medicinal purposes this time. Sometimes alcohol does wonders to restore one's spirits, don't you think?"

Her crisp common sense was reassuring. Gladly Jessica allowed Matthew to pour for her. This time she tasted the bitter liquid.

"Better?" Sir Matthew asked with satisfaction. "A calming and strengthening invention, Scotch. Feel calmed and strengthened yet, Jess?"

They were obviously concerned, Jessica thought, but their sympathy was curiously superficial, as though her emotions of shock, fear and bewilderment were foreign to them. They could not identify with her at all. "I am feeling better," she admitted. "Now I just feel foolish. I ran away and left my washing down there. All the lights on too. I suppose . . ." She put down her glass with clumsy fingers. "I should go back down and start the drier." She heard and loathed the hesitation in her voice. Caroline got up.

"I'll come down with you," she said. "I want to choose the wine for dinner anyway. Tillie's doing lamb and Father's choice with lamb is always too light." She strode out of the room without a backward look and Jessica scrambled after her. The last thing she wanted to do was plunge into that mysterious pit they called the cellar but neither did she want to be branded a coward by the Rensbys or most of all, by herself.

At the head of the stairs Caroline paused, flicking the switch on and off. "Bulb's blown again," she muttered, turning to rummage in a kitchen drawer. "The men Grandfather hired did a rotten job on the wiring." Jessica kept silent. She watched while the girl pushed past her, extricated the remains of the old bulb from the socket, and put in a new one. Not until Caroline called, "Well come on!" and beckoned her briskly did she respond.

Nothing had changed down there. The lights still burned whitely. Her washing still lay in an unappetizing pile on the washer. The air was motionless and stale. Caroline wandered along the rack, pulling out this bottle and that while Jessica heaved her laundry into the drier and turned it on.

Then Caroline beckoned. "Tour of the cellar," she announced, the chosen wine under her arm. Jessica smiled briefly but followed the girl around the rack. "Root cellar," Caroline said. "Ron's domain. A rather nasty, gritty place where he does strange things in the dark with vegetables that were perfectly happy lazing around in the sunshine." She moved on to the locked door. "Storeroom. Carefully locked because it contains valuable stuff — old paintings, Rensby heirlooms, gold plate, crown jewels, that kind of thing. Personally I see no point in owning any of it if it can't be used and enjoyed. And here," she drew Jessica towards the rear and stopped. Her long fingers described a vague oblong. "This wall belonged to the ancient abbey and not only forms the west side of the house but runs on to become the back wall of the garden. Here the nasty Sir Julian bricked up the faithless Lady Elizabeth. My grandfather hauled her out again and resealed everything. No ghosts. No things that go bump in the evening. End of tour." She looked closely at Jessica. "You're really on the edge, aren't you?"

There was no defence against her brutal frankness. Jessica nodded. "Yes."

"You reckoned without Jane's disappearance coming back to haunt you, didn't you," Caroline stated. "Honestly, Jess, can't you just forget it? Here you are still young, good-looking, intelligent, but you're shying at old shadows and continuing to yearn after a man who was obviously wonderful but who is now dead. Have you any idea how many wonderful men there are in the world? Would Michael want you to put your life on hold like this?"

For a moment Jessica was tempted to confide everything in Caroline — her mistrust of the arbour, the lilacs, mistakenly seeing Michael, and now Jane's memory translated by dimness and the alien aura of old stone into the semblance of a living voice. But an image of Caroline's face last night as she stood outside her room came to Jessica, the faintly mocking, knowing expression to the bruised mouth, and she held her peace. "The odd thing is, I'm not exactly grieving," she responded. "I know, I accept the fact, that he's gone. I'm not angry any more, or bitter. But I can't shake him. The pain doesn't seem to get any better or worse, it just stays the same, as though time has stopped inside me." She grimaced. "I'm not pitying myself. I'm usually a pragmatist. Coming here was a way to make that clock inside start ticking again but instead I feel as if it's whirring backwards. Now I'm hearing things. Maybe I should pack up and go home but I hate running away."

Caroline's face was thoughtful. "He who fights and runs away . . ." she quoted softly. "If you do decide to leave of your own free will, remember that you promised to tell me your decision first. OK?"

"OK." It had seemed an odd promise at the time but Jessica saw no harm in humouring the girl.

"Good. And let Tillie get your things out of the drier. Would you like to come riding with me after dinner? Scott's busy with some farmers' meeting."

Jessica blinked. "Riding in the dark?"

"And the rain," Caroline grinned. "I love it. It's fun. Kind of other-worldly. You don't know where you're going and in the end you don't care. Want to try it?"

The prospect of an idle night alone in her room was less than appealing and Jessica considered the offer, but in the end shook her head. "Thanks but no thanks," she replied. "I've had my dose of bracing English air already today."

"Oh yes," Caroline responded indifferently. "So you have. With sweet little Alix and good old down-to-earth Ben." She was already moving towards the stairs.

"I really liked them, Caroline," Jessica objected, annoyed at her superior tone. "What have you got against them?"

"Nothing I suppose," Caroline answered. "I find them boringly wholesome, that's all. Are you coming?"

Jessica forced herself to take a sweeping glance around the cellar before turning off the lights over the machine. The drier hummed and churned. The long rows of bottles lay motionless in their niches. But at the far end, the shadowed end, something invisible seemed to stir and draw breath in the wake of Caroline's firm retreat, something that knew Jessica was about to be alone. It took all her courage to turn her back and walk away from the small but audible sigh.

Dinner was a warm and cheerful affair, the food excellent, the room redolent with the smell of candles and the women's perfume. During lulls in the conversation the wind could be heard, less fierce and gusty than it had been on the previous night but still rain-laden. No one referred to Jessica's experience in the cellar and by the time they all rose from the cosy litter of the table shortly before nine-thirty it had shrunk in her own mind to less realistic proportions. Caroline disappeared upstairs to change for her ride and Eleanor invited Jessica to join her and her husband in the sitting room for coffee and brandy and a few hands of rummy. Jessica, comfortably torpid with Scotch, wine and dinner, accepted.

The sitting-room fire blazed a welcome. Sir Matthew

grumbled as he set up the card table and chairs. "Fires in June!" he commented. "We should have emigrated to Australia, Ellie, and raised our children on some sheep farm where the temperature never drops below boiling point."

"But I detest sheep, except to eat," Eleanor said, laughing, as they all settled around the table, "and besides, I don't suppose I could grow my prize roses in such a harsh climate, could I? It's one of his little fantasies, Jessica dear," she went on as they cut for deal and Sir Matthew shuffled the cards. "He was on an archaeological dig once with a team from Sydney and got friendly with one of his fellow scholars. I personally find Australian men sexy but impossibly abrasive. Would you agree? Forceful in bed but unfortunately forceful out of it as well."

Sir Matthew was dealing. He chuckled at Jessica's expression. "She's not speaking from experience you know. Heaven forbid!" he exclaimed. "But I rather think she envies my sister Dorothy who married an Australian doctor and found herself transplanted very happily to Bermuda where she grows wonderful roses. Ever been to Bermuda yourself, Jessica?"

Jessica picked up her hand and began to sort it, not knowing how respond. Was he teasing her? There was a subtle sting of superiority in his question, as though it was highly unlikely that someone such as herself might have been to so exotic a place. She looked at him sharply but he was waiting with a smile for her to speak. "No," she answered him belatedly. "No I haven't," and he snorted.

"Well don't bother. Too green, too blue, too pink, that's Bermuda. Unless you like golf, of course. Stupid game, golf."

He was breathing heavily and frowning over his cards. Lady Eleanor had laid hers down on the green baize table and was passing cups of coffee and snifters from the trolley at her elbow that Tillie had replenished. Jessica reached for the brandy. Play began.

An hour or so passed. The coffee pot emptied and the

level in the brandy bottle sank. Jessica had been content with a few small sips but the two Rensbys seemed to have a vast capacity for liquor. They drank and concentrated fiercely on the game. Sir Matthew lit his pipe and sat leaning over the table, legs apart, blowing smoke out of the corner of his mouth. Conversation was desultory. Jessica fell into a state of daydreaming where her mind wandered to her mother and the life she had left behind. Had full summer come back home? Had her letter arrived? Probably not yet. She could imagine her mother sitting by the living-room window of their apartment, the unstinting northern sun pouring through the glass, a cup of coffee at her elbow, smiling as she read. She would answer immediately she received it, a chatty, cheerful page or two full of the small but reassuring details she knew Jessica would enjoy. How the melting snow looked down in the street. Playing cards with Mrs Andrews next door, both sipping sherry and trying to cheat. Bumping into this one or that one while shopping at the mall. All the sane, blessed things that represented continuity and peace. The things, Jessica mused, that were safe for me, that required no risk and were no challenge.

Perhaps that is why I have unwittingly made a shrine out of my marriage, she thought suddenly. I have been living the predictability of middle age, where the present is so fixed that only the past holds interest. The realization shocked her back to her surroundings and she glanced up. They were sitting staring at their cards, motionless, waiting for her to make a play, and Jessica was all at once aware of that terrible weight of soundlessness that seeped into every corner, hung expectantly above every room. It was here now, subduing breath, bending necks, daring the body to make the slightest gesture. Calmly she put down her hand and rose.

"Forgive me but my head's buzzing and I don't think I can play another round," she said. "I'm off to my room. Good-night."

"Good-night, Jessica dear," they chorused, smiling, and

Eleanor added, "sleep well. Let's hope it's a sunny day tomorrow!"

Resolutely Jessica navigated the vast expanse of the main hall, slipped past the armour and mounted the stairs, deliberately not looking at the painted faces that leered at her from the wall. She did not stop to turn on a light. Once gaining the security of her room she flicked on the lamp by the bed, stirred the embers of the fire that now sent a warm glow to greet her, and then sat gazing into its orange depths.

She was physically tired but her mind was feverishly active. The events of the day were thrown against her consciousness in no particular order, flaring and then dying like the quiet flames of the fire, and she moved restlessly as though by doing so she could bring them under control. Ben's crazy story, the mausoleum wreathed in mist. Laundry in the cellar, and a voice. Lady Elizabeth choking and pleading out her life so long ago and yet so pressingly near, just the other side of that rough wall. And Jane. Jane.

It's all been a bit much, Jessica thought, cheek sliding into the palm of her hand, eyes still on the minute, secret vitality of the fire. The last few days I've had one thing thrown at me after another, an emotional and physical onslaught that churned me up and tipped me off balance and had me projecting the confusion onto the atmosphere of the cellar. I'm not used to action, interior or exterior. My life has been a predictable, quiet one, easily upset by changes in routine, I might even say dull. Since Father died I've always chosen the safe path. The womb of music studies, civilized, disciplined. The ease of working at home, the certainty of my mother's efficient care and then Michael's authority. I loved you, darling Michael, there's no doubt. I loved your cheerfulness, your sense of humour, your charm. I loved your physical grace. But I'm beginning to wonder if I loved your reliability more, the certainty of your care, the security of the little cocoon you wove around us. I think you would have had a great deal in common with poor Scott. Is that why the pain doesn't go away? Because I'm missing the security, not the man?

She sat upright, aghast at the speed with which her thoughts had suddenly slowed, swirled, and then arranged themselves in this surprising way. I loved you. You were solid inside yourself, dependable, easy with people, intelligent. Mother adored you. Mother adored . . .

Yet walking on your arm I was often disturbed by a curious restlessness. My eyes would stray, follow this man, assess that man, not because I was consciously unhappy, no. You were as concerned for my happiness in bed as you were out of it. And so I felt guilty and ashamed for my wandering gaze, and called myself disloyal. Yet bed, too, was predictable. Can it be that I longed for something more, something wild, in spite of or yes, yes! because of the blessed sanctuary in which I lived? Was my exaggerated need for safety an unnatural thing, superimposed upon me by myself for some reason buried deep in the blind recesses of my own subconscious?

Her agitation brought her to her feet and she began to pace. Something alien and yet familiar was trembling inside her, struggling to burst into the pitiless light of her consciousness, but she fought it in panic. I loved him! she whispered aloud. He was everything I ever wanted and I didn't deserve him! Maybe he wasn't the greatest lover but he could have been. Maybe it was my fault that he wasn't. Maybe I looked too long at the others, the strutters and swaggerers, oh I remember my guilt, the quick suppression of my disloyal thoughts! Nasty Jessica! Naughty, lustful, ungrateful child! What woman doesn't long for the kind of unconditional love Michael offered?

The alien thing was curling back to sleep, and Jessica breathed a sigh. Too much, that's all. The day has been too much.

She was about to poke the fire when someone knocked softly on the door. Opening it, Jessica saw Caroline standing there.

"I wondered if you were still up," the girl said abruptly. "Come and have a drink with me. I'd like the company."

Several excuses sprang to Jessica's tongue. I've already drunk too much today. I'm tired and it's late. But being alone tonight might mean a return of those threatening thoughts before she was exhausted enough for sleep to obliterate them so she nodded and stepped out into the hall, following Caroline without a word.

"I keep a bottle of the good stuff in my room," Caroline said as she held her own door open for Jessica. "A physic against boredom or night terrors when Scott isn't available." She sighed. "And God, I get bored so easily!"

Night terrors. Jessica gritted her teeth and did not reply.

Once inside, Caroline put a match to the fire and a cigarette almost simultaneously, and disappeared into her bathroom to reappear a moment later with two glasses which she set on the low table before the strengthening flames. Jessica was already in one of the chairs, leaning gratefully towards the blaze. Unobtrusively she watched Caroline, cigarette dangling languidly from her pouting lips, shed her jacket and toss it on the bed before striding to the bureau and extracting a bottle. "Now!" she said, slopping generous amounts of the Scotch into the glasses and pushing one in Jessica's direction. "Drink first to him and then to us, and when we're thoroughly warm inside we'll have nice hot baths and go to sleep. What a life, eh?" She had curled gracefully into the chair opposite Jessica, wreathed in smoke, her dark eyes brilliant. Jessica picked up her glass.

"To him?" she questioned. "Which him?"

Caroline grinned. "To them all," she answered. They clicked and drank. The liquor slid down Jessica's throat with an ease she did not quite like. I could get used to this very quickly, she thought. "Cigarette?" Caroline offered.

They sipped and talked but Jessica, in spite of the welcome loosening of tension the Scotch provided, found she could not relax. The many mirrors on the walls created movement just on the periphery of her vision, reflecting a dozen times over the flickering of the fire and Caroline's animated gestures and repeating the girl's strange, stark art work so that the atmosphere of restlessness and disturbance that emanated from each piece was magnified.

Caroline herself seemed increasingly on edge. Though she talked easily enough, giving Jessica a vivid look at a student's life in London and wittily describing the motley crowd of friends she had made there, it was as though in the end she was entertaining herself. She had begun by asking questions about Jessica's own routine at home but had then pulled back. She doesn't want to know about me, Jessica thought. She is already regretting whatever quixotic urge made her invite me into her room. Either she is totally egocentric or she is afraid to get close to me. Tonight she is going through the motions, being polite, but her head is somewhere else. Her animation is not for me. Perhaps Scott is going to come creeping into the house tonight. Over the rim of her rapidly emptying glass, Jessica observed the girl's gestures becoming slower, more sexually charged, the huge eyes more lidded, the mouth softer. I'm right, she thought, and her heart began to pound. Caroline is expecting her lover.

An odour had been growing in the room also, at first almost imperceptible under the honest scent of horseflesh on Caroline's clothes but now rapidly becoming unbearable as the girl shook out her lustrous black hair and dragged on another cigarette with head flung back in unconscious provocation. Dense and musky, Jessica felt it mingle with the alcohol in her blood, making her suddenly unsettled. The room was too hot, the Scotch too rich, Caroline too close.

"I think I'd better go now," she said abruptly. Getting out of the deep velvet cushions was surprisingly difficult. Her limbs felt heavy and languid.

Caroline did not argue. Rising in one fluid, entirely erotic motion the girl came near, bringing a miasma of that peculiar aroma with her. Overpowered by it, Jessica did not know whether it was completely repellent or entirely sensual. Suddenly she wondered what it would be like to place her mouth over Caroline's, to feel that lithe body moulded to her own. In a moment she knew. Caroline leaned forward and kissed her roughly on the lips.

"That would be best," Caroline said huskily. "You've had a rather nasty day, haven't you, Jess? Poor Jess!" Jessica felt herself pushed towards the door. "Go on, get out," Caroline ordered coarsely. "Tomorrow our precious little Peter comes home. You'll like him a lot better than you do me. Most people do, but I don't care. I wouldn't want to be in his shoes for all the tea in China, as they say. Or all the Scotch in the Highlands." She fell back into the chair and stared moodily at the fire. Jessica managed to open the door and a rush of cold air from the hallway diluted the scent now hanging triumphant in the bedroom.

"Thanks for the drink," she said. "I do like you, Caroline, although you try to convince me I shouldn't. Enjoy your evening."

It was a stupid thing to say, she realized as she flipped on the light in her own room. Her heart was still racing and there was a metallic taste on her tongue. The fire was almost out and a smell of ashes was in the air. Shivering, Jessica undressed clumsily and crept between the cold sheets.

Jane was smiling her unchanging smile, leaning against the bedside lamp. The sight of her made Jessica slightly nauseated. That smell, she thought vaguely as she reached to turn off the light. I know it from somewhere long ago. It was on Jane in the orchard, that's right, when she said she was alone but I could have sworn . . .

Old houses sometimes stink . . . This house stinks . . .

Graves have an odour too, and coffins even though undertakers try to disguise it. Michael darling, I bent to kiss you in your coffin and it was on you, and my tears slid over your waxen skin . . .

She woke with a bursting bladder about an hour later,

and drugged with sleep, staggered into the hallway. It was not fully dark. A shaft of sombre light dusted the angle where her wing turned into the upstairs landing, and almost without volition, with a dim curiosity, she went towards it. It flowed narrowly from Caroline's door, not properly closed, and Jessica, now more awake, would have retraced her steps if it had not been for the noises.

Caroline was moaning, low animal sounds of pleasure and abandon, and someone else was grunting. Jessica felt her scalp prickle as she listened to that guttural, rhythmic thrust of exclamation that did not vary in its deep pitch or strangely inhuman tone. Caroline's lover had arrived, and Jessica did not think it was Scott. She crept closer and put her eye to the crack in the door.

She could not see the bed itself but three mirrors showed her the candles guttering around it, Caroline naked on all fours with hair a dishevelled halo and full breasts swinging, her tongue between her teeth, and the man pushing savagely into her. His dark head was down, his dark arms taut against the tousled linen. Jessica watched his sweat-slick buttocks thrust and withdraw, thrust and withdraw, while those bestial deep cries issued from his throat. It was definitely not Scott, sunny, earnest Scott, who was drowning Caroline in this barbaric passion. Quietly Jessica moved away.

It was not until she had gone to the bathroom and returned to her bed that she realized she had brought more than a secret knowledge back with her from Caroline's door. Her nightgown was impregnated with that now odious stench and for quite some time it prevented her from sleeping.

Chapter 8

$\mathcal{P}$eter came home in the middle of the morning. Jessica, working in the library, heard the blare of a car horn followed by excited voices in the hall. Breakfast in the renewed warm sunshine had been full of suppressed anticipation and she had escaped as soon as possible, feeling that she did not want to intrude. Now she sat listening to the commotion, bags dropped on the floor, Lady Eleanor's exclamations, Caroline's drawl — "Damn it, Peter, is it all books?" — waiting so that the family could hold their reunion in peace.

Today the library was a drowsy haven. Dust motes hung glittering in the light that cascaded through the tall windows. The polished parquet floor gleamed. Outside, Ron was sitting on the mower, cutting the lush grass that had sprung up with the rain, and the sound of the motor was a pleasant purr. Birds shrilled in the shining foliage of the trees dotting the parkland and one robin sat on the terrace, fat and unafraid, peering in at Jessica.

She had done some sorting, but her mind kept returning to the events of the previous few days and her concentration was not improved by the monotonous nature of the work Sir Matthew was requiring. The contemplation of the figure she had mistaken for Michael on the stairs, Jane's voice in the cellar, Caroline's brutish lover last night, was dangerous. She wanted to dissect the experiences, relive them, try to fathom their roots, but she had already decided that they had jumped from the dark recesses of her imagination into an illusory life. Longing for Michael and a child's irrational guilt over Jane's disappearance needed to be dealt with, probably in the company of a professional.

But there was another reason why she did not want to examine Michael. She had been terrified, listening on the landing, it was true. But along with the terror there had been something else, a flash of pure wishful thinking, a yearning for the unfortunate Scott to somehow magically transform into Michael. To touch him again. To smell his maleness, to fit her body around his as she drifted off to sleep in his comforting warmth, to see his slow smile. It could never be. Never. Michael was dead.

But Michael was an old habit fixed in her head, in the very pores of her skin, lying disused but able to be reactivated with the slightest encouragement. Michael had not, could not, come back. Therefore that part of her that obviously refused to accept her loneliness as it should have, and allowed her to heal, was insisting that the habit be brought back to life. Ghastly. Unnatural. But not, she thought with a sigh as she studied the play of sunlight on her hands folded over the papers, unusual. How many people have seen dead relatives out of their own frantic misery? Fight it I must. But perhaps not here. This house is doing weird things to me. An unlucky juxtaposition of perfectly innocuous objects and people that have innocently combined to unbalance me. I may have to leave, but not yet. Stay away from thoughts of Michael and

Jane. Consider, instead, Caroline's lover. I wonder who he is? I don't think I would like him very much though I only caught a glimpse of him last night. Something about him . . .

The hall was now quiet. Jessica presumed that the family had retired to the sitting room to catch up on the news so she was surprised to hear footsteps coming through the drawing room. Then the far library door was flung open and a young man in a loose white shirt and jeans came hurrying towards her. He was short and slightly, even delicately built as so many Englishmen were in her opinion. He had unruly dark hair, one lock of which waved deeply on his forehead before sweeping back behind his ear, and lively brown eyes. His relationship to Caroline was unmistakeable, but the overall impression Jessica received as she rose to greet him was his likeness to his ancestor Sir Julian whose portrait hung in the hall. She smiled and held out her hand but he ignored it, putting his arms around her in an impulsive embrace.

"You're Jessica," he said, stepping back. "How pretty you are! You weren't at the door to say hello. I was crushed. Do you remember me at all?"

"Hi, Peter," Jessica responded, answering his wide grin. "It's wonderful to meet you at last. I do remember you, but as a baby just learning to toddle."

"Well I'm still toddling," he replied cheerfully, "but in different areas. You're inspecting me rather thoroughly. Do I have something on my teeth?" He pushed aside a pile of papers and perched on the table, his hands going into his pockets in a gesture Jessica recognized as his father's.

"No, I'm sorry," she said. "I was rather taken aback by your resemblance to Sir Julian."

He chuckled. "The old reprobate! I am a bit of a throwback. Everyone tells me so. I'm scared stiff of getting married in case I'm mysteriously compelled to brick the old girl up in the cellar, but of course I have to eventually do my duty and provide a Rensby heir so that's that." He made a face. "How are you enjoying your stay in the ancestral hall? Cold and bored I should imagine."

Jessica laughed. He was boyishly magnetic, absolutely sure of himself as only an adored child can be, and as frank as his sister, but he had none of Caroline's cynicism or sarcasm. Jessica felt immediately at ease with him.

"It's different all right," she admitted, "but your family has been welcoming and the work is simple."

"You mean excruciatingly pointless," he said, folding his arms. "Father and his obsession with our history. I heard about your husband. I can't say I'm sorry because I never knew him and I don't really know you yet, but I hope being here will make things better for you."

His honesty was a relief. "Thanks," Jessica replied. "It's just life, I suppose, or fate or whatever, tossing us around. I'll get over it."

He glanced at her keenly. "I think I like you, Jess," he pronounced. "Can I call you Jess? I've got a brand new Ferrari sitting outside. Come for a burn around the countryside with me after lunch. I want to heft a few in the pub anyway. Practise my paternalism and all that. *Noblesse oblige.*"

"I can't," Jessica said regretfully. "I must put in some proper hours of work. But thanks."

He shrugged and slid off the table. "Oh well. Never mind. I don't suppose you allow strange men to kiss you, do you? I thought not. See you at lunch, Jess."

He sauntered away and Jessica resumed her seat, feeling as though she had been picked up and then gently deposited by an amiable whirlwind. Her spirits had risen. He was not to be taken seriously of course, but his very presence seemed to lift everything in this dour old house. She resumed her work with a will.

Lunch was taken on the terrace. True to form, the English weather had made a complete change and the diners sat in a warmth mitigated by a slight and delightful breeze. Tillie had prepared a cold fruit soup and prawn salad which she served in a simpering fluster. Peter was obviously her favourite, indeed it was clear to Jessica that the young man was the pet and idol of them all and took their adulation as his due. Even the dogs, Missy and Boris, fawned on him, leaning against his legs and gazing up into his face with the slavish devotion of, as Caroline put it, "saints gaining the Beatific Vision."

The girl's reaction to her brother puzzled Jessica. She was pleased to see him, that was clear. She joked and argued with him in the easy way of those who are entirely comfortable in each other's company, taking his teasing with equanimity, but there was an added sharpness to her and occasionally Jessica caught her gazing at her brother with a brooding, speculative expression.

It would not be beneath Caroline to be slightly jealous of him, Jessica thought. His personality is as strong as hers. She can't dominate him as she tries to dominate everyone else, and she can't claim the attention he gets. But then, she said last night that she would not want to be in his shoes for anything, so perhaps there is something going on I know nothing about, some private family matter or perhaps simply the fact of his being the Rensby heir, that makes the spotlight he gets justifiable.

She listened to him talk carelessly of his studies in what he blithely called "dead languages and absolutely useless to anyone but fascinating," while he fed the dogs snippets from the table and calmed his mother who had been thrown into what appeared to be a panic over his twenty-first birthday party a few days away. He has a kind of control over them all, Jessica thought, and yet the source of it is not apparent to me. He's a very nice young person. The nice young person suddenly yawned then rose abruptly. "Come on Jess," he said. "We're going for a ride in my car."

Startled, Jessica protested. "Peter, I have to work. But I'd love to later."

"Not later," he said firmly. "Now."

Lady Eleanor had also risen and was clinging tightly to

her table napkin. "Peter, that is not a good idea," she said with a cold precision Jessica had never heard from her before. "After all, Jessica will not be with us for long."

"I agree," Sir Matthew nodded. "Not a good idea at all. Take Caroline."

What's going on here? Jessica wondered. Is Peter some terrible kind of lecher who tries to seduce every woman he meets and they're trying to protect me? Or am I supposed to be kept away from him in case I might sully the son and heir?

"But I want to get to know her," Peter objected. "I want to know everything about her."

"There isn't time," Sir Matthew insisted. "What's the point?"

"Yes dear," his mother put in. "It won't do you any good."

"Look," Jessica broke in impatiently, "I don't think I'm quite understanding this conversation, but Peter already asked me to go for a ride and I refused because I must put in a day's work."

An astonished silence fell and they stared at her as one. Jessica had the distinct impression that until she spoke they had temporarily forgotten she was there. She felt awkward, excluded and embarrassed. Caroline sighed ostentatiously.

"Good for you, Jess," she said. "Don't go. Peter's a lousy driver and he'll kill you." Yet there was nothing humorous in the way she spoke and the silence merely deepened. She was squinting up at Jessica, eyebrows raised.

"I want her to come," Peter warned. Jessica suddenly excused herself and turned towards the library.

"I have to get back to it," she said shortly, gesturing at the laden table visible through the French windows. "Thanks anyway." She pushed the window open and left them, seating herself and bending over her work. Presently she heard the murmur of conversation start up again, but not before Caroline had said sharply to her brother, "You're a bloody fool!" and stalked away over the lawn. Jessica was unable to hear anything more. Nor did she want to.

Shortly afterwards she heard a powerful car roar down the drive and presumed that Peter had either found another companion or was going to amuse himself. Tillie cleared the terrace and Ron put the garden furniture away with a doleful preoccupation. Jessica worked on.

Some time later she fancied she heard shuffling in the study followed by a cough and a sigh. Heart in mouth, all her fears returning, she got up and crept to the study door to be greeted by a cloud of pipe smoke and an absent wave from Sir Matthew. "Another erudite essay to be tried," he said to her vaguely, his gaze still fixed on the desk before him, and Jessica went back to her space by the window and laughed at herself.

She was interrupted twice more that afternoon. Once Lady Eleanor peered round the drawing-room door, a sheaf of yellow papers in her hand and her hair awry, and called, "Oh, Jessica dear, have you seen Matthew? This is my guest list for Peter's party and there's a problem. Matthew wants some of his archaeology cronies, you know, and it's upsetting the dinner seating."

"Try the study," Jessica called back but Eleanor shook her head.

"Not there. I looked. Oh bother the man," and slammed her way out.

Peter seems to have put them all on edge, Jessica thought as she dropped a third of the sixteenth century into the appropriate box. I suppose for people like these, a twenty-first birthday is an important event. I'll be thirty myself in a couple of days. Thirty! Unbelievable! Mother won't forget. I hope she hasn't written and told Eleanor. The poor woman has enough to worry about at the moment.

The second interruption took the form of Tillie who came marching into the library armed with bucket and cloths.

"I'm supposed to do the stacks today," she said. "It's a man's job in my opinion, all that teetering on the ladder, but

Ron digs his heels in about something and there you are. Women are so much more amenable, aren't they? We get things done. Will I be disturbing you?"

"Not in the least," Jessica told her, rather glad of the company, and while the woman prattled away, her voice sometimes echoing from the other end of the long room, the sun began to go down.

At last Jessica decided to call it a day. Rising and stretching she was just about to cross to the drawing room when Peter burst in.

"Come on!" he said breathlessly. "I've shown the beast off to everyone else. Now it's your turn. Work's no excuse. Look. The sun's over the yard arm. Let's go to the pub." He gave her no time to protest. Jessica found herself propelled through the hall and out the open door to where a glistening, scarlet, low-slung sports car purred on the gravel. "Mother says I'm juvenile," he went on as he handed her in and ran around to the driver's side. "It's tasteless to have toys when you're an adult and even more tasteless to flaunt them." He shifted into gear and they started off with a jerk that almost dislocated Jessica's neck. "But I'm not officially an adult yet, and then I'll do the proper wailing and mourning. What do you think? Am I being juvenile?" They were speeding by the abbey ruins and turning out onto the village street before Jessica could answer.

"It's a great machine," she shouted over the sound of the wind. "My husband always wanted one of these. He'd envy me now!"

"Would he?" Peter shot back. They were through the village and careering along a country road with the sun in their eyes. "Discriminating man, your husband. Tell me about him." He slowed down until they did not need to bellow at each other, and Jessica began to talk about Michael, about herself, about life as it was now.

Peter seemed genuinely interested. Brown eyes alert, he prompted her when she faltered, thinking that she must be boring him. By the time they had drawn up outside the Monk's Fast he had encouraged her to confide more in him than she had in her mother. Before he jumped out of the car he reached over and squeezed her hand. "Maybe I'll love like that one day," he said seriously, "but I doubt it. I'm too shallow. Fickle, you know. I like my life fast and thin on top and I'm not looking forward to the day when dear old Dad kicks off and leaves me Rensby Hall plus appurtenances. Ready for a drink?"

The public bar was crowded. It was about half past five and the local people were enjoying their pints before going home to supper. With an arm around her shoulder to shield her from the crush, Peter shepherded her to a corner, answering cries of recognition as he did so. He was obviously as popular in the village as he was at home. "Back in a sec with gin. OK?" he said to her, and was gone.

Jessica felt a hand on her arm and turned. It was Alix. Her hair was loose and she was wearing an attractive white short dress.

"Hello, Jessica!" she exclaimed. "Everything all right up at the Hall?"

Jessica was pleased to see her, too. "Hi, Alix. Everything's fine. Is Ben with you?"

"Yes, over there. We often pop in for a quick one on a warm evening." Then she laughed. "What on earth am I explaining to you for, as if you care whether the vicar tipples or not! Ben. Ben!" Jessica followed her with difficulty to a table where Ben was rising in answer to her call. He greeted her with genuine pleasure and the three of them talked a little under the general hubbub, then Alix said, "How about dinner? Will tomorrow night be all right? At seven for a cocktail first?"

"What, you want to see me again?" Jessica said in mock horror. "So soon? No, no," she protested. "Don't answer that! I'd love to. I'll walk over to your place about seven. If it isn't raining again, that is!" They laughed, and at that moment

Peter pushed his way beside Jessica. He was carrying two glasses. Jessica made room for him. "Have you met?" she asked him. "Peter, this is Alix and Ben Trent."

"I know," Peter said shortly. "We've met."

Ben indicated their table. "Will you join us?" he asked. Peter handed a glass to Jessica and abruptly grabbed her elbow.

"No," he almost snapped. "Jessica and I are busy getting to know one another and if you'll excuse us we'll get on with it." He pulled Jessica away. Annoyed, she shook off his hand.

"You were a bit rude, weren't you?" she said. "They're completely inoffensive people, Peter. I'm having dinner with them tomorrow."

"Well be prepared to be bored to death," Peter sneered. "She's just too squeaky clean for words, and he tried to make out that my mother had something to do with your sister's disappearance, did you know that?"

"Yes I did," Jessica answered tartly. "It wasn't that way, Peter. It's a silly story but he's a priest, for heaven's sake, not a gossip. He's not vicious."

"Jealous sod," Peter muttered. He took a long swig of his drink. Jessica sipped hers judiciously as the noise and congestion around them grew. She was prepared to be impatient with this good-looking, possessive, rather impulsive young man who drove as though he had nine lives, but in a minute he was grinning at her once more and teasing her gently and she could not help but respond.

Even his pettishness seemed short-lived. On their way out they passed Ben and Alix and this time he gave them a friendly wave. "Well why not?" he said in answer to her look. "You think they're harmless. Maybe they are."

This evening she joined the family for drinks on the terrace, limiting herself to soda water while Sir Matthew dipped into the sherry, holding it up appreciatively in his blunt, age-freckled hand against the cloudless pink light of a perfect sunset. Peter attacked the jug of frosty martinis with relish.

Caroline, looking vague and paint-smudged, sat on one of the stone steps, a tumbler of Scotch beside her, and Lady Eleanor, flushed but indomitable, shared the sherry with her husband.

"I was talking to Miss Brown today," she said. "You know, the rather wispy little woman who plays the church organ. Actually she was talking to me. She accosted me outside the post office. Almost ran her bicycle over my toes. They're trying to put together a village concert to raise money for repairs to the organ. She asked me if we would care to help by letting them use the library or our main entrance hall."

"What's wrong with the village hall?" Caroline flung back over her shoulder. Lady Eleanor shrugged elegantly and buried her nose in her glass. The sinking sun caught her valiantly disordered hair as she moved and turned it briefly fiery.

"Well nothing really," she blinked. "That's what I asked her. She sort of bobbed and flittered and then told me the village hall didn't have enough tone. They want it to be quite a fancy affair. I refused, of course."

"I should think so!" her husband barked gruffly. "Give them money. That will shut them up."

"Miss Brown's a brave little woman," Caroline put in. "She's always trying to involve us in church activities."

"She's a leech," Sir Matthew said bluntly. "Was there any mail, Eleanor?"

"Oh yes." Eleanor reached down to her bulging handbag and began to pore through it. "I forgot. The postman would have brought it but Mrs Evans gave it to me. He hadn't started his rounds." She extricated several letters, one of which she passed to Jessica. "Mrs Evans says that the summer will be long and too hot. She's warning all the farmers. She's giving them a spell for the grasshoppers."

Jessica recognized her mother's handwriting on the envelope but she did not open it at once. "A spell?" she repeated incredulously. "Are you serious, Lady Eleanor?"

Peter got up and drained the martini jug into his glass. He licked his fingers. "Oh perfectly," he assured her. "Mrs Evans, dear old fat person, is our local witch. She believes herself to be descended from the witch Sir Julian consulted when he wanted to do away with Elizabeth's erstwhile lover. Unlucky man that he was." He resumed his seat and laughed across at Jessica. "Can you imagine our garrulous but esteemed postmistress in her rollers, hairnet and grubby slippers, calling up a demon? She probably waddles around the fields in the dead of night whacking grasshoppers to make sure her spell works."

"She deserves some respect!" Sir Matthew rebuked him sharply. "Don't joke about it, Peter."

"Her clairvoyance comes from steaming open the mail," Caroline said, her words slurring faintly. "Shut up, Peter. You'll give Jessica the heebie-jeebies."

"No, I think it's fascinating," Jessica returned. "And people in the village actually take her seriously?"

"Of course!" Lady Eleanor said firmly. "Mrs Evans has the gift. It is inherited. I myself occasionally give successful seances for a few choice friends. Please do open your letter, Jessica dear. We shan't mind. I would like to know how your mother is."

Jessica did not want to comply. She wanted to hug her mother's words to herself in private. Reluctantly she slit the envelope and read silently.

"Your opinion of the Rensbys is interesting," her mother had written. "I agree — I always thought there was something a bit off kilter about them though they are the soul of kindness and generosity and I'm sure they are taking good care of you. They are definitely English eccentrics. Is Peter home by now? And are you getting along with Caroline? Give them all my fondest regards. Have you seen anything of the older sister? Her name was Susan or Sandra or something like that. Eleanor never mentions her in her letters and she was so seldom home as a child that she's not even a face in my memory.

I wonder if she caused some family scandal? Anyway, this part of the world is cold and mushy again but the sun strengthens every day. Yesterday I opened a window for the first time this year and the air smelled very good . . ." The letter chatted on as Jessica knew it would, contentedly and sanely, and ended with a wish that Jessica be happy and find a little peace. "My mother is doing very well," she said at last, folding the letter away. "She sends you all her affection."

"Well send it back," Lady Eleanor beamed. "A wonderful woman, truly wonderful. Caroline, I wonder if you would run inside and ring for Tillie? It is already a little past dinner time. And wash and dress, darling. Dinner is always formal when your father is present and it is Peter's first night home."

Caroline rose with an exaggerated sigh. "Peter sweetie, do you care if I dress for dinner or not?"

He met her gaze coolly. "Yes, as a matter of fact I do, Caro lambkin," he replied smoothly. "Family dignity and tradition and all that. What have you been painting today?"

"Your birthday present." Caroline came up the steps and headed for the open library windows. "Something permanent to remind you always of what it means for the Rensby heir to turn twenty-one."

Peter muttered something as she brushed by him. Jessica could have sworn he said, "Bitch." Sir Matthew's head was flung back. He was staring at the rapid approach of twilight. Lady Eleanor reached across and squeezed Jessica's hand.

"You look lovely," she said. "I like that black dress more every time I see it."

Jessica searched the carefully rouged face for sarcasm and found none. All the same, she was distinctly uneasy. Increasingly she was feeling that the Rensbys were marching to the tune of a different drummer and she was stumbling along beside them, trying to get in step but not quite able to do so. Conversations and actions, reactions and gestures, though outwardly straightforward, seemed to belong to some family agenda of which she was unaware. Not that they were rude to her, indeed, they were the soul of hospitality. But sometimes it was as though she did not exist as herself, Jessica Mortimer, to them, and they in their turn sometimes forgot that she was there. It was all so nebulous, so imperceptible, as to be ridiculous.

Caroline was yelling for Tillie somewhere in the house. Lady Eleanor was rolling her myopic blue eyes and tutting in exasperation at her daughter. But the two men were absolutely still, Sir Matthew lying back, Peter's eyes fixed on the gathering dusk of the lawns. Jessica sensed a complicity between them, something cold and perhaps unhappy. Her fingers found her mother's letter and she folded it into her fist. I want to go home, she thought with a sudden desperation. I really don't like it here.

Caroline came to dinner in a stiff gown of such rich scarlet satin that Jessica's eyes ached if she stared at it for too long. Diamonds encircled her neck and wrists. A diamond tiara sat in the cascade of her hair. Her behaviour was demure and Jessica wondered if she was mocking them all. Peter's arrival had pleased her, that Jessica knew, but it had somehow upset her deeply as well.

Tillie had set the table impeccably. The starched white linen rustled and dazzled. The silver shone. Ron, immaculate in black, served the food with more than his usual quiet unobtrusiveness. The civilized yellow glow of the candles gave a soft beauty to all their faces. Eleanor tried to talk about the coming birthday party but Peter cut her off.

"The party itself's not that important, Mother," he told her. "I know you. Don't get bogged down in domestic details and drive yourself to a frazzle. Hire a band, hire caterers from Clapton, buy flowers or steal them from Vera, drag up the champagne and then enjoy yourself. It's the day I get the keys to the world that means the most to me."

"Your friends should mean something to you as well," his mother retorted, nettled, and Peter shot back, "What friends? I didn't go the local school and all my boarding-school buddies have scattered. There's my crowd in Oxford and I want a few of them here of course, but on the whole I think this is your and Father's celebration. Mine takes place on my birthday proper, this Friday."

He then changed the subject and the meal became quite lively. Jessica earned a moment of disapproving silence when she told them that she was going to dine with the Trents the following evening but Peter rescued her by saying, "Oh come on, you lot! You're behaving like sulky autocrats with a wilful servant. Be ashamed of yourselves. Jess deserves the kind of fun she wants and there'll be no harm in it." He looked at his father. "No harm in it at all."

"I am suspicious of all religion and the perpetrators of it," Sir Matthew said portentously. "My dislike of Ben Trent is not personal." He smiled loftily at Jessica but Caroline interjected.

"The hell it isn't!" she said vehemently. "The feud you have with him may be polite but it's been intensely personal since the time he asked you as the local village patriarch to chair one of the church committees and you refused. What was it he said to you then?" She closed her eyes and raised one finger as though trying to remember. The diamonds in her ears flashed wickedly. "Oh yes," she went on, opening her eyes and grinning at him. "He said, 'I am disappointed, Sir Matthew, that a man of your influence should choose to deny his social and religious responsibility.' He'd accosted you outside the library. I was there. I applauded his guts. The incident was the high spot of my week."

"Caroline!" her father thundered. "Be silent! Where is your respect?"

"Father," Caroline shot back, "respect has to be earned." She picked up her wine glass and drank, unperturbed.

Jessica expected the dinner conversation to falter after this disturbing interchange but she was learning that these people had a remarkable facility for simply ignoring what might have upset anyone else for hours. Before long they were laughing and sharing jokes again, pouring *bonhomie* on her, telling stories.

She remembered how as a child she would look high into Sir Matthew's seamed face, how huge and awesome he had seemed to her then, how his hand would slide innocently down her body and cause her to shrink. Body? She frowned. No, of course, a mental slip, I meant head. She signalled Ron for another helping of rum trifle.

That night she slept deeply and dreamlessly and woke late to find that she had missed breakfast. The house was quiet. It seemed that everyone was out, for as she passed along the upstairs landing the bedroom doors were standing wide. It was a glorious day. Sunlight poured in through the front doors to lie warmly on the hall floor. She saw Ron walk by outside pushing a wheelbarrow, the sound of his feet crunching on the gravel.

Jessica turned sharply at the foot of the main staircase and went through the tiny back hall to the sitting room. It was empty but the aroma of pipe smoke hung in the air and a crumpled newspaper lay on the couch. Retracing her steps she pushed wide the swing doors leading to the kitchen from the small hallway. Peter was there. He swung round as she entered.

"Oh it's you!" he exclaimed. "Another slothful slugabed. My how edible you look when you first get up. All moist and dewy. Hungry for me or for food, Jess?"

She rolled her eyes at him and laughed, pulling out a chair and laying her arms on the well scrubbed surface of the heavy table. "You're impossible!" she told him. "Is there any coffee?"

"Coffee, coffee, that's all you Americans can think about in the morning. Civilized human beings start the day with sex, but Americans tamed the wilderness and built an empire on coffee. No wonder they've always been so concerned with decent sanitation." He was opening cupboards and laying a plate and a mug before her. "Of course there's coffee." He took it from the counter and poured it, steaming and black, into the mug. "Cream?"

"I was wrong," she retorted, drawing the mug towards her. "You're not impossible, you're disgusting. Don't serve me, Peter. I can get my own breakfast."

"No need," he responded lightly, opening the fridge. "I know where everything is and you don't. Let's see. Toast. Cold sausages. Canadian bacon? I was only teasing you about being American. I can do you bacon and eggs if you're still into fat." He ran an appraising and unsettlingly expert eye over her. "I shouldn't think you'd have to worry, not for another twenty years at least. How old are you, anyway?"

Jessica took a mouthful of the coffee. It was delicious. She ignored his question. "Toast and marmalade will be fine. I don't suppose lunch is too far off. Did you make this coffee yourself?"

He was deftly slicing bread and setting butter and the pot of marmalade by her plate. "I did. My one and only culinary skill. America's not the only place that runs on coffee. Oxford does too. That, and beer. But beer for breakfast's a bit much, don't you think? I almost always sleep in when I'm home." He grinned engagingly at her. "I'm allowed. I'd even get breakfast in bed if I wanted. God I love being the spoiled only son!"

The toast popped and he swiftly slid it onto her plate, pulling up his own chair and watching her as she buttered it and began to eat. She was acutely aware of his nearness; his knee almost touching hers, the faint aroma of his aftershave, his almost over-delicate, gesticulating fingers as he chattered on. Once or twice she met his eyes, brilliant and full of vitality under the wave of dark hair he was always pushing back, and she felt herself succumb to his magnetism. I could ask him about that one photograph, she thought suddenly. He's so easygoing and informal in his manner. I'm sure he wouldn't be offended. She put down her toast.

"Will your other sister be home for your twenty-first?"

she enquired cautiously. "She's older than you, isn't she? I don't remember her well at all, I suppose because she didn't spend much time at the Hall when I was little. She doesn't come up in conversation between your parents and I wondered if there was some reason why. I don't want to commit any glaring faux pas, you see, or embarrass them in any way."

For a moment he looked taken aback. He blinked rapidly and his fingers dove through his unruly hair in a startled gesture. "Actually there is a reason," he said after a moment. "I might as well tell you. She never much liked the Hall or the local people. She didn't get along with Mother either, I don't know why. She disgraced us by eventually marrying a long way beneath her, and that was the end of her relationship with the family. Caro phones her sometimes, and I occasionally have a drink with her in London. That's where she lives." He lifted his shoulders and made a face and Jessica saw that he was uncomfortable with the subject. "She seems happy enough although her husband doesn't earn much. I don't know her very well any more." He brightened and waved at her plate. "Come on, eat up!" he ordered, and Jessica understood that the conversation was over. She resumed her breakfast in silence.

"You look adorable with marmalade stuck to your chin," he remarked when she had finished. "I want to lick it off." Getting up he opened a drawer and handed her a napkin. Meekly she took it and rubbed at her face. He remained standing. "Come on," he ordered. "Take a ramble in the grounds with me. And choke that righteous rebuff about getting to work. Women who are conscientious bore me." His smile took the sting out of his words. Rising she began automatically to clear the table, but he pulled the utensils from her hands and towed her out of the room.

The weather was glorious and the park of Rensby Hall looked like a little Eden. Together Peter and Jessica left the shade of the portico and strolled out across the newly cut grass towards the trees and the rill beyond. Sunlight bathed them, hot but not oppressively so. Scented breezes played gently, erratically around them and then moved on to stir the leaves of the majestic trees that dotted the lawn. A jet passed overhead but high, far away, its drone almost eclipsed by the cacophony of the birds. Jessica breathed deeply.

"The Hall is a fantasy today," she said, "a dream of perfection. How lucky you are to come home to such beauty!"

"Hmm." He took her arm and pulled it through his own, and it seemed the most natural thing in the world for Jessica to curl her fingers about his shirtsleeve. "Where every prospect pleases and only man is vile, eh Jess? Do you regard every man as vile after your husband, or do you think you'll get married again one day?"

She was becoming used to comments from him that were intensely personal but because of his manner did not offend. "I don't know," she replied honestly. "My head says yes. I'm young and life is long. My heart says not until Michael is no more than a memory. The grieving process seems to be a bit prolonged with me. In a year or two I may feel very differently."

He glanced at her, eyes half-closed against the deluge of sunlight. "Why do you still live with your mother?" was his next question. "Isn't that a bit, well, old-fashioned?"

She did not resent his words. He was regarding her soberly, without a trace of ridicule. He had shown that for some reason known only to himself he was truly inquisitive about her. "My mother is a great cook," she answered, "and having cleaned other people's houses all her life she can't stand dirt or untidiness. She takes care of those things. I'm the one who supports us and I really don't have much time for domestic details. It's a good arrangement."

"That's not what I asked," he said gently, and she gave a defensive half-laugh.

"When Michael was alive she lived alone," she pointed out rather too strongly. "She was happy enough but I hated being by myself once my husband had died. So I sold off my furniture and moved in with her. She and I get along very well."

They had come to the middle of the park and instead of continuing on to the rill Peter steered her to the left, behind the orchard. Most of the blossoms had fallen and were already half-rotted and the few clusters that were left looked blowsy and tired.

"Why did you choose music as a career?" was Peter's next foray. Jessica made a face.

"I'm not sure. I drifted into it, I think. I loved my piano lessons as a child and got good at it and it just seemed natural to continue with it at the university. I don't practise as much as I should any more. After a day of teaching I seldom want to hear another note!"

He laughed, then he said, "Do you miss your father? He died of cancer, didn't he? What was he like?"

This time Jessica felt immediately threatened by the question, why she did not know. To talk about Michael and her mother was one thing, but to reach back into the distant past brought a wave of discomfort. "I miss him of course," she forced herself to say, "but by the time he died he was a broken man. Jane's disappearance . . . He never got over it. If he'd lived I don't think he'd have learned again how to be happy." She went on talking, aware that he was watching her almost unblinking, with complete concentration. His attention was flattering but slightly unreal.

"And what about you?" he put in. His elbow had tightened on her arm.

"Me? I shall go home revitalized at the end of the summer. I shall call up my neglected students, see a few friends who've probably forgotten I'm alive, just go on living . . ."

"No," he interrupted. "I mean what about you inside? Do you know how to be happy? Have you been happy, truly blissfully happy, at any time in your life, Jess? If you died this week would you have any regrets?"

She looked at him in astonishment. "Everyone has

regrets," she said. "I regret not having had more time with Michael, not being a better wife perhaps." She shrugged. "Those are the things one thinks of when someone dies. As far as personal regrets go, aren't they a bit vain? What's the point of looking back at something you've already said or done and wishing it could have been different? It never can be different!" Her voice had risen and she realized that she had been speaking with more vehemence than was polite. Glancing away she saw that they had come, by a circuitous route, behind the arbour and Peter had brought her to a halt in front of it. She began to tremble.

"Come and sit down with me for a while," he urged. "Let's get out of the sun."

"I never liked this place," she blurted. Within the tightly woven dimness created by the privet hedge and the twisted arms of the wisteria, the stone seat beckoned mutely.

"You surprise me," he commented, his arm now sliding around her shoulder and exerting a pressure that was just short of bad manners. "It's a perfect spot for loners like you."

"Am I a loner?" she asked, startled, and he propelled her inside.

"Very definitely," he said, "but then so are most people at one time or another. Even me! My father comes here sometimes, I think to get away from my mother's well-meaning nagging."

He lowered himself beside her on the cool stone. Even birdsong can't penetrate here, Jessica thought. No sunlight, no sound, in a way it's like a cell of the house broken off and set down in this remote corner of the estate. I didn't like the house when I was little. It's not surprising, then, that I didn't like the arbour either. But Jane had no such reservations.

"I had a premonition the day my sister disappeared," she said slowly. "I watched her from the car as we drove home and I felt this . . . this tremor. But I was nine years old. You don't reflect much on your feelings when you're nine. You don't think — why am I feeling this way?" And why am I talking this way? she asked herself. The atmosphere in here works on me like an abrasive.

"Your eyes glitter and look huge when they're tearful," he observed. "It's rather sexy," and she smiled in spite of herself.

"You've a smooth tongue, Peter Rensby," she said.

They sat for a while in an intense silence, and Jessica was not at all perturbed when Peter took her hand. "Tell me, Jess," he said very softly, "Do you believe in God?"

His question did not break the spell of intimacy but the air around Jessica seemed all at once to become charged with a dark force, as though an unseen presence crowded close to hear her answer.

"You Rensbys are obsessed with religion although you scoff at it," she offered. "Caroline asked me the same question."

"Did she now?" he rejoined, still in the same almost inaudible tone. "And what was your answer?"

"I told her yes, I do. What about you, Peter?"

He withdrew his hand and sat back, his gaze travelling her face reflectively. "I'm not sure, but at my age why worry? I've got a whole lifetime ahead of me before I need to be concerned with spiritual things."

"But what if you die young? People do sometimes."

"No chance of that," he said flatly. "No chance at all. I'm going to be healthy and happy and die in my bed at ninety-three." He peered at her. "I say. You still have marmalade on your chin."

"No I don't, I . . ."

Before she could finish her sentence his mouth was beside hers, open and moving against her cheek. The shock of it kept her immobile for a second. His hand was on the back of her neck, holding her firmly so that she could not move. His lips, warm and questing, travelled to hers and found them open. With a grunt he kissed her hard, his tongue insinuating itself between her teeth. "Want a little summer romance, Jessica?" he murmured drawing away slightly, his eyes half-closed. "You do, don't you? I can tell." He kissed her again, and this time his other hand slipped inside her shirt. "Naughty, naughty girl," he breathed. "Your blouse is undone."

The voice was not his. A wave of panic engulfed her and she began to struggle. He released her at once. "I'm not I'm not!" she cried out. He looked bewildered.

"All right," he said, "You're not. Though what you're not, I can't imagine. Pardon me for giving it the old college try."

Something was coming, Jessica could feel it. Her skin prickled. Every nerve in her body screamed. Oh don't come, she begged it silently, don't come! Not now, not ever! With a great effort she placed a hand on Peter's knee.

"I'm sorry," she whispered. "You took me by surprise, that's all, and you didn't misread me either. I find you very attractive."

His good humour was restored. Planting an airy kiss on her forehead he stood up. "Course you do! But I think the mood has temporarily fled, my lovely. Perhaps we can continue this interesting interlude later."

She wanted to shout at him — for the love of God don't leave me alone! — but he was gone, sauntering out of the arbour, whistling. The sound faded on the thick summer air. She tried to rise, to rush after him, but her muscles had turned to water. The arbour was waiting. The arbour knew. Naughty girl. Naughty, naughty girl, your blouse . . .

No! Don't come! It's because of Jane, this fear, this despair, Jane sitting here on that last day, of course it's Jane, but it can't be Jane, I hated the place long before that day, you naughty girl your blouse . . .

Your blouse . . .

"Naughty, naughty girl, your blouse is undone," Sir Matthew said roguishly. He was breathing heavily, one arm lifting Jessica onto his knee, the other hand slipping into her blouse. "You shouldn't go about dressed like that, you know. Some nasty man might want to do things to you." Her crayons rolled off the stone seat and scattered over the arbour's paving. Beyond the entrance a stiff wind was blowing apple petals across the path. Sir Matthew smelled of pipe smoke and sweat. "You do like me, don't you, Jessica?" he wheezed. "You do want to make me happy, don't you?"

Jessica cried out, and the arbour gloated. Now you know, it whispered. Now we can be friends, can't we? With eyes jammed shut she beat her fists against the stone, whimpering no, no, no, while Sir Matthew's hands moved over her, inside her, took her own little fingers and placed them where they should never have been, not just here in the arbour but in the study, the drawing room, the secluded courtyard where the dogs were kennelled, one memory following another with the speed and horrible precision of an automatic camera. She was powerless, now, to stop them coming. Images linked to her other senses, hearing and smell, sensation oh sensation, doubt, fear, awe, the innocent bewilderment of a child, and then the guilt, the shame, sourceless emotions that had dogged her all her life.

Wrapping her arms about herself she began to rock, moaning quietly. The constructions of the past, built by a mind determined to protect itself, shivered, crumbled, and then re-formed. The same events, the same people, places, objects, but now standing like concrete instead of cardboard and her perception of them, so new and strange yet feeling right, right for the first time in her life, made her cry out again. This is what I came back for, she thought under the deluge of pain. This is why I'm here. Something in me was ready to know the truth and it brought me here. No wonder I pursued security! She opened her eyes onto a world that had subtly changed. And what of Jane? she wondered. Did he bring her to the arbour too? Is that why I heard her in the cellar, trapped as I was inside myself? Was it Sir Matthew I saw with her in the orchard, doing something terrible to her, and

I couldn't face it and turned him into someone else? Perhaps. Oh God, my whole life, my whole life coloured grey by this thing, the time wasted, the sourceless anxiety endured, and I didn't know why! Running from safe house to safe house, choosing each prison and letting everyone else lock the door, and I didn't know . . . She pushed herself off the seat and stood shakily. Mother didn't know. Neither did Father, or they would have done something, saved me . . . I want to talk to Mother. I can't tell her over the phone, I must be with her in person, but I need to hear her voice! I can't cry yet. They'll ask me at the house what's wrong. But I can go home now. It's over. Unsteadily she made her way out of the arbour.

There was no phone in her bedroom and the one in the main hall was too public. In the sitting room she might be interrupted. She had not seen one in either the library or the formal drawing room presumably because people using the library would not want to be disturbed and it was simply crass to bother one's guests in the drawing room. That left the study or one of the family bedrooms.

Everything in Jessica cringed from entering the study but she did so, still moving on brittle feet in the aftermath of what had just happened to her. She barely noticed that the room had windows, long French ones from which the drapes had been drawn back. She had not seen them before.

The telephone was on Sir Matthew's desk. She had just picked up the receiver when she sensed that she was being watched. Heart in mouth, still half the child she used to be, she glanced up.

Lady Eleanor's face was pressed against the glass of the window. One gloved hand was on the latch, the other held gardening shears. Behind her the rose bushes twitched in the morning breeze. Before Jessica could relinquish the receiver the woman had pushed open the window and was standing in the room.

"What are you doing, Jessica?" she snapped.

Jessica held onto a semblance of normality with every

ounce of control she possessed. She was sure that the marks of her revelation must be emblazoned on her face for the world to see, but apparently not, for Eleanor's expression was suspicious, almost hostile. "I was about to call my mother," she said. "I suppose I should have asked for permission to use the phone."

Eleanor's expression did not change. "Well no," she conceded. "Of course you don't need permission. But I'd rather you waited until after six in the evening. Our telephone rates are truly outrageous, you see, but they go down a lot later on. Look after the pennies, my father always said, and the pounds will take care of themselves." Her face had relaxed a little but she still regarded Jessica warily. "Is everything all right, dear?" she asked.

"Yes," Jessica said. "I just wanted to hear her voice. I can make it a collect call if you want."

"Of course it's up to you, dear," Eleanor bridled, "but I'd wait. International calls are expensive for everybody, aren't they? What time is it in Canada now?"

Jessica put down the receiver with a feeling of utter defeat and a peculiar kind of foreboding. In that moment she realized that she actively disliked her hostess. Eleanor knows about him, she thought hotly. They all know. I hate them all! "I'll wait," she said shortly. "Excuse me, Lady Eleanor. I should get to work now."

"Why don't you take the morning off?" Eleanor suggested. "It's criminal to waste this gorgeous weather. Take a walk to the village or go along the creek. I believe Caroline is painting down there right now."

She doesn't want me near the phone, Jessica suddenly knew with certainty, looking into those steady, bright eyes from which all trace of vagueness had fled. She doesn't want me to talk to my mother. Why? It can have nothing to do with what I've just remembered, even if she's known about it all along. That would be too much of a coincidence. Then why? What else is going on in this cursed house? All at once she was desperate to be outside again. "That's not a bad idea," she agreed. "No one seems to care much whether I work or not."

Eleanor smiled indulgently but Jessica was sure she detected a sigh of relief cleverly suppressed. "Sensible girl," she said approvingly. "I must get back to my roses. Do talk to your mother tonight."

As though she's bestowing some mighty favour on me, Jessica thought as she went through the library and out into the warm, fresh morning. I'll call from Alix's place tonight.

She strode furiously across the lawn, dappled in light and shade from the great trees under whose arms she passed, relieved to be consumed by an anger that was swiftly replacing the agonized sense of betrayal and loss. The need to tell someone was overwhelming, to tell, to shout, to accuse, and it mingled with the first truly powerful emotion she had ever permitted herself to feel. Hatred coursed through her like a drug and it was clean, it was good.

But by the time she had come to the creek and was standing on its willow-choked bank, watching the stones of its bed dimple as the cold, clear water flowed over them, she was calmer. I'm not going to yell at anybody, she decided. What would be the point in stirring up a wasps' nest of old miseries and sins and perhaps guilt as well? His guilt. Does he feel guilty, I wonder? Does he spare a thought for the destruction he caused? Somehow I doubt it. Before I leave I'm going to speak to him, speak and not lose my temper and scream. And right now I'm going to find Caroline because I have to get it off my chest and I'm vengeful enough, yes, to want her to know just what her darling daddy's really like. I could go to Alix or Ben. Listening to such tragedies is part of his job, isn't it? But I don't want to be told to forgive or turn the other cheek, not that I imagine Ben would actually try to preach at me. He's too honest. Is that why Caroline won't let herself get close to me? But of course not, she's too young to have had anything to do with it. I think she knows, though. Oh I want to hear my mother's voice! Her almost incoherent thoughts propelled her body forward and she began to walk along the creek towards the village.

Chapter 9

$\mathcal{S}$he had not gone far when she caught a flash of colour between the branches and paused. It was Caroline, vivid and gaudy in blue jeans and a loose shirt splashed with as many colours as the palette on the collapsible table beside her. She was bending towards an easel, intent on a canvas that surprised Jessica as she approached, for the scene was bright with a spring-like promise and entirely different from the moody sketches adorning the girl's bedroom. Caroline glanced her way and the brush was stilled.

"What do you want?" she said indifferently.

"I need to talk to you," Jessica answered, no longer put off by her brusque tone. I've changed, she thought curiously. Already I'm different inside and it's good. "Your mother said you'd be down here." She came closer. "But I don't want to interrupt you."

"You're not interrupting," Caroline said shortly. "I'm not the kind of artist who minds if people watch them work.

What did you want to talk to me about?"

Jessica did not reply immediately. The satisfying fantasy of her tearing apart the Rensbys' smug little world seemed daunting and unreal in the light of a Caroline who was decidedly present, standing frowning over her work in the middle of a beautiful morning. She glanced at the painting. The creek was there, and the tangle of willows, sky and a few puffy clouds, all represented in hectic, almost iridescent hues that made her feel, after a moment, that she had eaten too many cream cakes. The technique was masterful but it was as though Caroline had purposely loaded her brush with cloying sentiment.

"Is this Peter's birthday present?" she asked. Caroline laughed harshly.

"God no! Petey would gag on this. I gag on it. Do you?" She was watching Jessica carefully. Jessica grimaced.

"Yes I do. You're very talented, Caroline, but your work is cynical and rather perverse."

Caroline raised her eyebrows. She had braided her hair today and her eyes took luminous prominence over the rest of her face. "My teachers would never put forward such a criticism," she replied. "Don't you know that there are no such limiting judgements allowed in the world of art? Everything is interpretation. But you're right. Cynical and perverse. That's me." She tilted her head, surveyed her work, then fell to dabbing at it furiously. "Do you like Peter?" she asked unexpectedly.

"Yes I do." Jessica found a patch of dry grass and sank onto it. The ground was warm and the sunlit water speeding by made a pleasant gurgle of sound. "He sort of drags you along in the wake of his optimism."

"Well make sure you keep your toes on the gravel," Caroline said tartly. "Petey is a shallow creature who's nice to everyone because it makes life so much simpler. He knows he can get his own way faster with honey than with vinegar."

Jessica remembered the sympathetic touch of his hand in

the car yesterday, the understanding in his eyes. "You don't seem to like him very much," she offered.

Caroline snorted. "I don't like him at all! But I love him very deeply."

A silence fell between them. Caroline continued to daub and examine the canvas. Jessica did not know whether she should keep her new knowledge to herself and walk on, or selfishly share it as she longed to do. After all, she thought, what do I owe Caroline anyway? What do I owe any of them? Finally she said, "Caroline, did you know that your father is a pedophile?"

Caroline's brush did not falter. "Of course," she answered. "Almost everybody around here knows. He's been that way as long as I can remember." She frowned over a leaf of sickening lime green and dabbed it with white. "He had a go at me when I was six. I was on the floor in the nursery, playing with my doll's house. I stabbed him in the hand with a tiny metal-legged chair I was holding and he left me alone after that." She glanced up. "Were you one of his toys?" Jessica nodded, shaken. "I thought so. Why on earth you ever came back here beats me."

"I didn't know," Jessica said in a low voice. "I didn't remember."

"Oh." She put down her brush, wiped her red-tipped fingers on an already filthy cloth, and swivelled to face Jessica. "And now you do. I suppose you'll be leaving as soon as possible. Just as well." She turned back to her work with a sigh. "My vision of summer," she said. "Fat, fertile, and overblown. Good job, Caro."

"Is that all you have to say?" Jessica broke out. "Did you tell your mother? Oh but that's right. She knew. It was old news to her." She could not keep the sarcasm out of her voice. "If everybody around here knows, Caroline, why hasn't anyone done something about him?"

Caroline shrugged. "He leaves the village girls alone now. He doesn't need them any more. As for my mother, she doesn't really care. She's got her own interests."

Jessica sprang up, fists clenched. "Interests! Interests? My God, Caroline . . ."

"Look, Jessica," Caroline said patiently, still surveying her painting, "this is a very old part of the world. Things go on here that might be considered bad, even evil perhaps, elsewhere, but they're customs, attitudes, village traditions that go back centuries and no one gives them a second thought. So my old man liked fumbling village children. So what? That's life. He never hurt them. Their parents knew that. No matter what, the Rensby males have always done their duty by the village, cared for the indigent, fed the people in rough times, found them work whenever possible. Times have changed and their needs differ now, but they still look to the Hall for a foundation to their existence."

"It's sick!" Jessica said hotly. "It's feudal!"

Caroline smiled without humour. "It's an ancient arrangement. That's all."

"And you approve?"

"What a prim little word, approve." Caroline's lip curled. "I don't approve or disapprove. That's simply the way it is."

"But what of the church? Surely . . ."

Caroline picked up her brush. It was a gesture of dismissal. "The church is powerless here," she said.

Jessica swung away. She was violently angry, but she had the uneasy feeling that she had missed something important in Caroline's hard-headed words. "I'll move on," she said harshly. Caroline did not reply, but as Jessica started off along the creek once more something prompted her to look back. Caroline was sitting staring after her, an unlit cigarette between her lips, her expression unreadable. Jessica was glad when she had gone so far that those eyes could not bore into her spine.

The day was perfect. The countryside resembled one of the calendar pictures her mother pored over in the depths of the Canadian winter when she was homesick, but Jessica found no peace in it. Returning to the house just before lunch she chose to eat alone in the library. The tray containing the cold coffee and congealed toast Tillie had provided for her breakfast sat on one of the tables, reproaching her.

Though she was not hungry she forced herself to finish the meal and begin wearily to sort through the snow of untidy notes once more. The act was beginning to acquire the unreflective comfort of a habit under which her mind was free to range. Why do I feel that Caroline tried to tell me something this morning? she wondered. Am I being obtuse, or just suffering the results of emotional shock? If I had spoken to Peter would I have met with the same outrageous callousness? Oh I would like to think not! Yet other people's miseries are usually embarrassing. Perhaps Caroline's reaction was no indication of how she really felt, given her character. Her security lies in scrupulously defending her true thoughts. Jessica smiled grimly. Like me, she told herself. That's the way I used to be. And how is it that in this day and age a whole village can simply accept as normal something so disgusting?

Sir Matthew went by at the foot of the terrace, Peter beside him, both deep in conversation with the two dogs at their heels. Jessica watched them pass with cold eyes. A little later Lady Eleanor's voice could be heard calling for Tillie in the hall. "My mother's got her own interests," Caroline had said. What interests? I'll bet they've got nothing to do with gardening and the school board, Jessica thought cynically, not those strong shoulders, that startling youthful face. She had a sudden sense of claustrophobia, as though all of them were stronger and more ruthless than she, as though their way of life, their daily philosophies, so alien to everything she knew, were enfolding and crushing her because she could not make sense of them. It was like listening to a piece of music when for the first few seconds one was unable to get the beat. There was that dislocation, that anxiety. With great effort she bent to her work and was indecently relieved when her watch showed her that it was time to wash and dress for dinner at the Trents'.

She walked into the sitting room at ten minutes to seven, wearing a tight grey skirt and lilac silk shirt, to let them know she was leaving. They were all there but Caroline. Peter got up and kissed her cheek.

"You look delicious," he said admiringly. "Come and knock on my bedroom door when you get home and we'll have a nightcap."

"You certainly do look nice," Lady Eleanor put in. "Have a lovely time, dear, and be as late as you like."

"Don't walk through the churchyard after midnight," Sir Matthew advised. "Go out the north gate and come back by the road. You never know what might be lurking among the tombs, Jess." He was not smiling. His face was solemn.

He's serious, Jessica thought. Dear God, he means every word. Lady Eleanor was nodding in agreement. Peter winked at her.

"If you do meet something vile, scream and I'll come and rescue you," he promised. "Though I'm sure all you'll need to be rescued from is bad food and boring talk." He resumed his seat and picked up the paperback he had obviously been reading. As she left, Jessica heard Sir Matthew say, "Well, we'd better get dressed for dinner ourselves, Ellie. Poached salmon tonight, I think. Did Tillie find my studs?"

"Absent-minded old coot," his wife retorted, the sound of her fading as Jessica crossed the hall. "I'll be glad when all this is over and you'll start remembering again where you put things."

The early evening was lushly warm and the sky just beginning to flush pink as Jessica stepped briskly down the driveway. She wished she had worn flat shoes but it was too late to go back and change now. She hoped the gravel would not ruin her pumps. But once out the gates the pebbles became paved road and walking was easier. The abbey ruins lay as always, exuding their own atmosphere of untroubled tranquillity, and she cast them a wistful look as she went by.

She would have liked to spend a little time among them. The road curved around them to the right and then straightened again as it joined the village's main street. She had only to go a short way north along the street, away from the village, before coming to the lych-gate that led into the churchyard where both church and vicarage had been built.

Glancing left to make sure there was no traffic, Jessica was about to cross to the gate when her attention was caught by a small figure wandering towards the village on the grass verge. It was a girl, her head down over something she held in both hands. Her loose jeans were dusty, her shirt sleeves rolled up unevenly over bony elbows. The sun, westering on her right beyond the clustering beech forest, was casting long shadows over her and the road.

Jessica's scalp prickled. Tearing off her shoes and flinging them down she ran after the figure. It was moving slowly, absorbed in whatever it was holding, a book Jessica felt sure. She was gaining, panting, heedless of the occasional sharp stone in the roadbed that stabbed her feet, her progress almost silent in the quiet evening. The girl kept walking leisurely. Only when Jessica could have reached out and touched the thin shoulder did she shout, "Jane!"

The figure stopped and turned. For a moment, for a fleeting second, Jane's thoughtful brown eyes smiled into hers, then the face became a stranger's.

"I beg your pardon?" the girl said timidly. She was Jane's height, Jane's build, she even had the texture and colour of Jane's hair. She looked slightly alarmed. Jessica tried to still her breathing but she could not keep the panic out of her voice.

"I'm sorry," she panted. "I thought you were someone else."

The girl smiled timidly and began to walk on. Jessica watched her go, the book in her hand. Oh let this be the last of it, she thought in despair. How often Jane ambled along this road, heading for the cottage with her nose in a book!

It was not until she was bending to put on her shoes that Jessica realized something odd. The book the girl was reading, its title only half-consciously recognized, was *Still She Wished for Company*, a tale of haunting that had been one of Jane's favourites. With a cry Jessica spun round. The shadows on the road lay empty in the soft red sunset.

Though she had paused by the church to calm down she was still bemused when she rang the Trents' doorbell a few minutes later. Alix opened the door.

"Come in, Jessica," she said smiling, closing the door and leading the way along the narrow hallway. "You're right on time. Ben's about to mix the drinks and I've just put my casserole in the oven. You mustn't expect too much," she went on apologetically, ushering Jessica into the airy room whose latticed windows now stood open onto the crowded garden. "Cooking isn't my greatest strength. Come to think of it, I don't know what is. Drink a lot before you eat, that's my advice." Ben had risen from his chair and was advancing with hand extended, laughing. "That's why I've become a skinny drunkard," he said. "How are you, Jessica?"

She took the seat offered, asked for sherry, and began to relax. Everything was all right here, surely this was the way the world really operated. She felt strongly the link between the wholesome sanity of daily life back home and this shabby haven, these uncomplicated people. The Hall and the village were part of a smaller, less important undercurrent, dark eddies in the mainstream of a society filled with people whose motives were good and unselfish, who were eager to do the right thing by their neighbours.

A good smell began to overpower the scent of flowers blowing in on the evening breeze and Alix set down her glass and rose. "I'd better check on dinner," she said, then paused. "Jess, your feet! Whatever have you been doing?"

Jessica looked down hastily. There was a smear of blood on the top of one foot and her stockings had several runs in both legs. Sheepishly she pulled off her shoes. "I was in these

foolish things when I saw a girl on the street I thought I recognized," she told them. "I left them in the grass so I could
run after her, but I was mistaken. I startled her, and gave
myself a bit of a fright as well. I thought it was Jane," she
explained at Ben's puzzled look. "She's been on my mind a lot
lately. You see . . ." She paused and stared into her drink,
then the words came out in a steady stream. She had not
intended to tell them anything, but the healing process she
felt going on inside seemed to be operating on rules of its
own. She finished with Caroline's brutally offhand conversation of the morning.

When she had finished she held out her glass and Ben
obediently refilled it. Alix got up. "I have to turn off the
oven," she said. When she came back she touched her husband on the shoulder. They exchanged glances and Ben
seemed ill at ease. Jessica wondered why. "What a terrible
revelation!" Alix said. "How truly awful for you. I'm so sorry,
Jessica. I know that it has nothing to do with us, but every
decent person must be both sympathetic and outraged at such
a story." She shook her head. "It's appalling."

"Yes it is," Jessica agreed unsteadily. "I can't believe that
Sir Matthew was allowed to accost the village girls for years
and no one did anything about it. Don't these people have
televisions? Don't they know which century they're living
in?"

"You know as well as I do that television's mainly entertainment," Ben said. "It doesn't affect the majority of people
personally. It doesn't make them wonder why they can't
change their own lives. Outside the box, that's reality. What's
inside it is pure fantasy."

"Can't the church do anything about it?" Jessica
demanded. Ben shook his head.

"We've tried. Frank tried. But the root of the problem's
up at the Hall and it sort of seeps down here to the village.
Oh we have a few parishioners who don't want anything to
do with the Rensbys, but on the whole the people regard

their relationship with them as perfectly normal and don't want a word spoken against them. They seem to have a kind of superstitious belief that the Rensbys will protect them from the vicissitudes of life if they remain loyal."

Jessica stared at him. "You're joking!"

"No I'm not. Medieval, isn't it? How can you fight such a deep-rooted myth? When you have a family as powerful locally, generation after generation, and as blithely unconcerned with any kind of morality century after century, you end up with this illusion."

"I see what you mean," Jessica said slowly. "The work I've been doing for Sir Matthew. Unnecessary really. Anyone could do it. But I've been reading the notes as I go and I've been puzzled by the . . ." she hunted for the right word ". . . the sameness of Rensby history. The chronicles are full of adventure, the ebb and flow of family fortunes, disasters and triumphs, but nothing truly tragic." She glanced at their faces. "Nothing catastrophic, in all those hundreds of years, those dozens of generations. A Rensby marries a woman who turns out to be barren but she conveniently dies and the second wife produces the obligatory heir. An only son is dying of a terminal disease and then I read that he's gone off to serve the king in some strenuous capacity. And though they were dreadful gamblers and wastrels they never seemed to permanently lose their fortune. They'd be almost destitute but then they'd be buying racehorses or something." She put her empty glass on the table. "It's not surprising that the villagers would come to think of them as under some kind of protection."

Ben took a breath, hesitated, then said, "Actually, Jessica, according to local lore, pure unofficial village gossip, mind you, the demon Sir Julian and the witch conjured up is still in the Hall and still serving succeeding generations of Rensbys. That's where their protection comes from."

"That's ridiculous!" Jessica responded hotly. "But the rumour's not surprising given the Rensbys' predilection for completely amoral behaviour and the villagers' incredibly antiquated acceptance of the family's supposed right to sei-gniory. It all makes me sick!" There was a small silence. Jessica became aware that the room was gradually filling with darkness and the garden outside was dusky. The sun had gone.

With a convulsive movement Alix got up and turned on a light, then she went to stand close to Ben. He put an arm around her waist. "My dinner will be a bit dry but still edible if anyone wants it," she said, and Ben cut in, "Look Jess, I don't know why the Rensbys invited you but I have a feeling it wasn't out of kindness. You don't have to go back there if you don't want to. We have a guest bedroom. Stay the night and fly home tomorrow." Alix gave him a sharp look, but Jessica heard the offer with a profound feeling of relief. It did not take her long to make up her mind. "Thank you very much," she said. "I'll pack up my things in the morning and come in the afternoon."

"Call Tillie and have her do it for you," Ben suggested. "Don't go back at all."

Jessica considered. "That would be rude," she said slowly after a moment. "I may have a huge bone to pick with Sir Matthew but I'm not a child, Ben. I'll be perfectly OK for one more night."

Ben rose. "Well we're here if you need us," he said. "Let's eat. That wine will have breathed itself into exhaustion by now."

"There's one more thing," Jessica said. "Could I use your phone to call my mother? I'll make it collect. Lady Eleanor didn't seem too keen on me using one at the Hall."

Ben pointed to the table beside his chair. "Certainly. When you've finished, cut across the hallway. The dining room's opposite."

They left. Jessica went to the phone and put through her call. Presently she heard it ring. So far away, she thought. Oh Mother, be home! I need to hear your voice!

"Hello?"

Jessica closed her eyes. "Mother? It's Jess!"

"Jess darling, how lovely! How are you? Did you get my letter?" Oh the sturdy common sense in those aging tones, Jessica thought. Small talk and day-to-day events, specials at the supermarket, hemming a dress, taking the car for repairs, coffee and a doughnut together between students. "I got it yesterday, thanks," she answered. "Are you doing OK?"

"Me? I'm fine. Dolly and I are going to a concert tonight. Brahms. But you're not fine, Jess. I can hear it in your voice. What's going on?"

"I've decided to come home as soon as possible," Jessica told her. "The job isn't much and I'm restless. I might as well be sleeping in my own bed."

There was a pause. Jessica listened to the connection hum. "That doesn't sound like you," her mother said finally. "There's more, isn't there?"

Jessica sighed. "Yes, there's more," she admitted, "but I'll tell you all about it when I get there. I haven't called the airline yet so I can't give you a day or a time but don't worry. I'll phone from the airport when I get in."

"You've still got your open ticket?"

"Of course. And don't fret. I miss you."

"I miss you too. Wish Peter a happy birthday from me. I suppose I'll have to clean this place. I've been a pig while you've been gone."

Jessica had to smile. No one was neater than her mother. "I'll talk to you soon," she said. "Love you. Bye." She rang off, dug in her purse, and brought out the ticket. Quickly dialling the airline, she was dismayed to discover that the first available flight was on Sunday. She argued, but the agent was adamant. With bad grace she confirmed a seat and then was limp with a sense of reprieve. I've done what I came for, she thought. A strange, painful, wonderful thing. My journey to self-knowledge is over. I am going to be free.

Alix's casserole was full of interestingly unnameable things but the wine was good and the company easy. By unspoken agreement there was no talk of the Rensbys. Jessica realized, after being with the Trents for several hours, just how tense she was in the Rensbys' company. Ben and Alix were friendly and unpretentious. Their conversation followed the predictable paths of social convention and Jessica found that inexpressibly comforting. They sat on over Alix's execrable coffee, talking about music, then retired to the sitting room to take brandy. Time went by. Jessica, warm and content, knew she was putting off the moment when she would have to leave this womb. Reluctantly she looked at her watch. It was just past midnight. She stood.

"It's been great," she said regretfully, "but I've outstayed my welcome. Thanks for being so understanding. I'll see you both tomorrow."

Ben picked up his jacket from the back of his chair. "I'll walk you to the road. Leave the dishes, Alix. I won't be long."

The night was calm and the sky clear. Though the stars were bright, thick shadows lay over the churchyard and the ancient yew tree sheltering the graves was drowned in darkness. Jessica was very glad of Ben's masculine presence as they followed the path between the tombstones.

Just before they came to the lych-gate she glanced aside to where the Rensby mausoleum loomed, a brooding, derelict presence. Almost as though something was looking after them, she thought. How stupidly ignorant. How could anyone believe such rubbish? Yet she moved closer to Ben with a shiver.

When they had passed under the wooden arch of the lych-gate and were standing on the grass verge, Ben said good-night and turned back. Jessica crossed the road, now a ribbon of grey running off into nothingness. Steadily she covered the ground past the abbey, its ruins lying enfolded in an aura of lingering sanctity that posed no threat.

Ahead was the gate to the Hall, its two tall halves standing partially open. The closer she came to it the more she shrank. Her pace slowed. The last thing she wanted to do was pass between those formidable though decorative barriers and her heart jumped into her throat when she saw something move just beyond them. Then with a gush of relief she recognized Peter and ran towards him.

"I was getting a breath of air before bed when I saw light in the churchyard," he explained as she came up. "I decided it must be you. Naughty girl, to go that way when Daddy warned you not to!"

"Ben escorted me," Jessica retorted. "I was quite safe."

"I should have given you the keys to the Ferrari tonight," he went on, drawing her arm through his as they moved onto the gravel of the driveway. "You could have arrived and left in style. You could even have offered the poor things a ride they'd never forget."

"You're pretty intolerant," Jessica said. "I'll bet you hate the idea that I might have had a good time and thoroughly enjoyed myself!" But for some reason her apprehension came back in a rush. She was suddenly aware of his body so close to hers and stole a glance at his face, drained of life in the colourless starlight. His fingers, when they brushed her own, were icy. She wanted to free herself but did not know how to do it politely.

With a slight pressure he guided her off the drive and onto the soft grass around the massive oak. Immediately they were in inky shadow. By the tree he stopped and faced her, taking her by the shoulders. "I simply must kiss you again," he smiled. "I've wanted to ever since you rebuffed me in the arbour. You're irresistibly attractive, Jessica." His features loomed above her, all hollows and planes. His eyes seemed sunk in darkness.

He did not wait for permission but bent his head. His mouth opened. Jessica caught a whiff of the odour that had both sickened and fascinated her in Caroline's room, and overcome with a sourceless panic she began to resist. It was useless. She felt his lips meet hers, cold lips. His tongue touched hers, and in spite of her mindless need to get away, she felt a jolt of lust. He withdrew, still smiling. His hand went to his mouth and he laughed.

"Oh Jessy," he said. "Still struggling like a virgin. But it was very nice. Forgive me please."

She could no longer bear the sight of him, why she did not know. All he had done was steal a kiss. Where was the harm in that? Yet she felt entirely alone out here with the lightless house behind her and the night deepening. He tilted his chin, and starlight glinted on his teeth. Sickened, she turned and almost ran towards the main door. He was beside her. "Now don't be angry," he was pleading half-humorously. "It's not my fault that you're so delectable. Let me give you a nightcap in the sitting room."

"No thanks, Peter. I'm tired and I want to go straight to bed," she replied, hardly able to get out the words, fumbling with the door. She was sure that if she looked at him she would scream. "Don't worry about it. I'm not a girl any more. Believe me, I'm flattered. Good-night." She was inside now, and hurrying for the stairs. The hall was frigid. She could not hear him behind her. She did not want him to be behind her.

Flinging herself along the landing she sped around the corner into her own wing, and reaching the door, slammed it behind her. She would have locked it if she could. There was a lock but it seemed to operate only on the outside. Not until she had turned on the lamp on the night table and the room had sprung into reassuring life did she halt to stand trembling by the bed. There was no sound anywhere in the house. She tore off her clothes and got between the bedcovers. One should never sleep with makeup on, she thought, but wild horses couldn't drag me across to the bathroom tonight.

She was groping for the lamp when it occurred to her to wonder how Peter could have seen Ben's flashlight gleam. His window looked out across the parkland towards the creek. If he had been at the front of the house, even by the gates, the trees around the churchyard and certainly the bend in the road would have made such a thing impossible. Jessica withdrew her hand. Had he been waiting for her, hovering by the gate, for half the night? She decided not to turn off the lamp.

He was ebulliently cheerful at breakfast the following morning, pushing back with one hand the sweep of dark hair that dipped over his eye while ladling sausages onto his plate with the other. "So you had a riotous time among the dead and the half-dead last night?" he queried, unfolding his napkin with a flourish, "and came staggering home drugged with the miasma of incense? I hear our vicar is very High Church. Mass with all the trimmings. Oh sorry. I forgot." He graced Jessica with a dazzling grin. "I said that seeing you liked them I'd try to be a bit more tolerant. Still, I missed our nightcap."

"Considering you sat around all evening and drank the drinks trolley dry I'm surprised you even thought of a nightcap," Caroline said sourly. As usual she was picking at her food, a lighted cigarette in an ashtray beside her plate. "By the time I got home from Scott's you were barely able to recognize me."

"Now Caroline," her mother reprimanded her. "Peter deserves a little indulgence at a time like this. He is under some stress, you know."

"Yes I know," Caroline said crossly. "But really all he has to do is turn twenty-one and then everything will be candlelight and roses."

"I gather you had a less pleasant time than Jess," Peter teased her. "Scott must have been nagging you again about the happy times you and your brood of children are going to have if only you'll set a date." Caroline did not reply.

"Only five more days left!" Eleanor said brightly. "I'm getting very excited. Well, four days to the ceremony and five to the party. Oh I do hope Tillie remembered to call the caterers back with the amended menu."

"What ceremony?" Jessica asked curiously. Sir Matthew stirred in his chair.

"It's part of the Rensby tradition," he explained. "A secret rite Peter must go through before he can take his proper place as heir. It has to be performed the day before his twenty-first birthday. I did it. Rensbys have been doing it for generations."

Jessica's appetite disappeared. She had been trying to find the right place in the conversation to tell them she would not be staying on but now her discussion with the Trents came back to her in full force. She put down her knife and fork. "How interesting!" she said carefully. "What exactly do they do?" A secret rite . . . Rensbys have been doing it for generations . . .

What would you give to a demon in exchange for its protection down through the years? she suddenly asked herself.

No, no, impossible.

A secret rite . . .

Her whole body had gone cold.

"We're not allowed to tell," Caroline replied. "It's all very hush-hush. But it better go well, Petey old boy, because I want the rest of my summer to be one long lazy sybaritic fantasy."

Jessica stood up. "There's something I have to tell you," she said through stiff lips. Her tongue felt dead and icy in her mouth. As one they stopped what they were doing and turned to her. Caroline stubbed out her cigarette. Peter stopped smiling. Lady Eleanor's hand went to her disordered hair and Sir Matthew leaned forward. "I'm going home on Sunday," she went on with difficulty, "and until then I'm going to be staying with the Trents. My flight's already booked. I've talked to my mother and called the airline."

"Talked to your mother?" Lady Eleanor repeated sharply. "When? I thought . . ."

"I called her from the vicarage last night," Jessica said. "I didn't want to inconvenience you regarding the phone, Lady Eleanor." She swung to Peter, aware that Caroline, who had remained silent, was rising and coming round the table. "My mother sends you every good wish for your twenty-first," she told him.

"But you'll at least come up to the Hall for my party before you go, won't you?" he pressed eagerly, "and join us for our little private celebration when I do the Rensby traditional thing? I would hate to spend a lifetime saying miserably to myself, Jessica Mortimer refused to come to my party."

Jessica did not answer him. Her gaze was fixed on his father who had not moved. His eyes, meeting hers, were like stones.

"Why?" he barked.

She pushed back her chair and stepped away from the table. "I think you know," she said. "It seems that my faulty memory has all at once been fixed. I don't want to be under the same roof with you any longer than I can help."

At that moment Caroline passed behind her in a cloud of smoke and perfume and whispered, "You promised to tell me first, you silly fool. Now the shit's really hit the fan." Aloud she said, "Enjoy this little scene, my dears. I'm going to do some more on Pete's picture," and sauntered off.

"You've changed, Jessica," Matthew said roughly. "You've become absurdly confident."

"Yes," she returned calmly. "I guess the truth has made me free."

They smiled. Incredulously, Jessica saw the sly mirth on their faces. For some reason her words had amused them. Walking deliberately to the door she paused and looked back. "I want you to know," she said clearly, "that what you did to me was unforgivable. I hate you and I always will."

His expression did not alter. Jessica wondered how she could ever have thought him kindly and genial. "And I want *you* to know," he said maliciously, "that Jane always was my favourite little girl."

Jessica strode upstairs to her room and pulled her suitcase from the closet. Fakes, she was thinking furiously as she opened drawers and flung her clothes on the bed. Everything here is a lie. Last night I spent a few hours in the real world, with genuine people, and I've discovered that I'm genuine too. She swept up the photograph of Jane intending to fling it into the bottom of the suitcase but she paused, staring at it. You poor thing, she spoke to her sister in her mind. You and I, both victims. It must have been Matthew I saw you with in the orchard, that pathetic excuse for a human being. I can let you go, now. I'll never know what happened to you on that hot summer afternoon but it doesn't matter any more. I'm free.

Tossing the photo into the suitcase she caught sight of the opera score already there. She gave it a bitter smile. And I can begin to say a proper goodbye to you too, Michael my love, she thought. I was holding onto your memory for all the wrong reasons. You were sweet and good and I adored you, but you're gone and I'm still here. I have to learn to live all over again.

Yet all at once her knees felt weak and she slumped into the chair by the empty grate.

". . . You promised to tell me first, you silly fool, silly fool, silly, fool . . ."

But Caroline, why am I a silly fool?

Knowing the Rensbys now for what they are, why were they so eager to invite me here?

A secret rite.

Rensbys have been doing it for generations.

She forced herself back to the business of packing, stowing her belongings methodically, but her sense of uneasiness grew until at last she closed and locked the suitcase and went out, making her way along to Caroline's room.

The door to the master bedroom stood wide but Caroline's was closed. Jessica marched up to it and knocked. There was no reply. She knocked again, then tried the knob. "Caroline?" she called softly, looking into the room. It was empty, but Caroline's easel with a canvas resting on it stood turned towards the window, and her palette and brushes were on the collapsible table. Jessica went in, closing the door again behind her. Peter's birthday picture? Her heart began to race. It was dishonest, she knew, but recklessly she crossed the room and faced the painting.

The light was falling fully on it, and Jessica could not repress a low exclamation of shock. Like most of Caroline's work, this was done in an unrelieved black. It showed the front of the house on a gloomy day. Dark clouds hung over the chimneys and gables. The long flower beds flanking an exaggeratedly large entrance porch adorned with many intricate locks contained a tangle of brittle sticks. But where the windows and other details should have been Caroline had painted heavy bars.

Pressed against them, filling the whole aspect, was Peter's face. His mouth was open in a soundless howl. His eyes were wide, his features contorted. Behind him, as though the house stretched back into a limitless eternity, were more faces, all male, all in agony, screaming at Jessica. The intensity of the painting was so great that she took a step back. The power in Caroline's gift was overwhelming, but so was the furious despair with which she wielded it.

Jessica did not even hear the rush of water from the adjoining bathroom or the door being opened. It seemed that Caroline was suddenly there. The girl halted and they stared at each other.

"Don't you know how to knock?" Caroline snapped.

"I did. Twice," Jessica replied, still stunned by what she had seen. "There was no answer."

"Then you should have gone away. But I suppose you feel now that you're leaving you needn't be on your best behaviour." She moved around the bed to the bureau, withdrew a cigarette from the pack lying there, and lit it with deliberate insolence. "What do you want?"

She's genuinely angry with me, Jessica thought. Because I saw the painting? She gestured to the easel. "Is this Peter's birthday present?"

"Yes." Caroline sauntered over and stood next to Jessica, blowing out a stream of smoke as she did so. "Now that you've seen it you might as well give me your admittedly uninformed but perhaps novel opinion."

Jessica ignored the jibe. "It's horrible. It . . . it's cruel. Is it something he'll like?"

Caroline chuckled without humour and Jessica felt that anger still simmering in the tautness of her body. "Like? No, he won't like it at all. But he'll understand it."

"I want to understand it too. Tell me what it means."

"Why should I?" Caroline retorted rudely. "It wasn't done for you."

"Tell me. Please?"

Caroline shrugged and swung away, grinding her cigarette in one of the numerous ashtrays scattered about, then folding her arms and looking, not at Jessica, but out the window. Her vibrant, sullen reflection was multiplied a dozen times in the mirror-crowded room, the blood red lips, the black-rimmed, smouldering eyes, the wealth of untidy, lustrous hair.

She belongs to a different age, Jessica thought, feeling herself pale and passionless by comparison. Her emotions are strong and simple, no sooner felt than acted upon. She is a misfit in this world of moderation and dulling respectability. Scott is not man enough for her.

"Well all right," Caroline said impatiently. "It's all the Rensby heirs. They turn twenty-one and they're chained to this place. Imprisoned. Lords of the manor, condemned to take care of the house, the estate, the village tenants, for the next generation. None of them can run off and be beach-combers in Greece or go to seed in the South Seas. It's a sentence of death for the rest of their lives. Petey doesn't mind — yet. But he will."

Jessica's eyes returned to the painting. Peter howling, the others in anguish, back and back into nothingness, into hell . . . "Your father made a career as an archaeologist," she pointed out. "He's had a full life."

"He poked around ruins in his spare time," Caroline

retorted. "He was never able to devote as much energy as he would have liked to his work. It had to become a hobby. Rensby Hall is a trap!" Her voice had risen vehemently.

Jessica left the easel. "I don't believe you," she said steadily. "There's too much terror in that picture. Your interpretation is too glib."

Caroline rounded on her. "I don't give a damn what you believe!" she ground out. "You're naïve and stupid and deserve what's coming to you!"

"What's coming to me, Caroline?" Jessica pressed in the same tone. "What did you mean this morning at breakfast? Why am I a silly fool? Why was it so important to tell you first if I was planning to leave here? Why are you angry with me, Caroline?"

Caroline pulled open a drawer of the bureau with a jerk and brought out a half-full bottle of Scotch. She banged it on the night table. "Drink?" she said loudly. She shoved another cigarette into her mouth and stood there pouting, a hand on one hip. It was a brute challenge. Jessica strode forward and wrenched the cigarette away.

"I want some answers!" she shouted. "I'm sick of your evasions! Talk to me, Caroline! Or are you just a sick game-player like your parents?"

Caroline had gone white. Without speaking she went into the bathroom and came back holding one glass. Setting it down with mocking care she unscrewed the top from the bottle and poured, deliberately concentrating. Then she drank, closing her eyes and shuddering. "I can't tell you," she said, and Jessica saw that the anger had gone. "I'd like to, but I can't. All I can say is that I'm glad you're running away. For the life of me I don't know why. Perhaps I see something in you that I envy, something I've never had. Do it right now. If you're packed then take your purse and walk out of here, and don't stop until you get home. Peter will just have to manage his birthday without you."

"Peter will what?" The voice from the door shocked

them both. He had poked his head in and was smiling. "Tut tut, Caro baby," he went on, advancing into the room. "Drinking already and it's not even lunch time? Daddy wouldn't be pleased. Neither would Scott. Am I interrupting some juicy girl-talk?"

"You sod," Caroline said mildly, going to fling a piece of sheet over the painting. She seemed calm enough but Jessica saw her fingers tremble. "We were just saying what a decent, clever, charming fellow you are. What do you want, Petey?"

He flourished a fistful of mail. "I have to go down to the village so Mother asked me to take these," he said. "I wondered if Jessica would come with me. I'd like to apologize to her on behalf of the whole family and assure her that I, for one, will miss her a lot." He turned a serious face to Jessica. "My father may be an ogre," he said, "but I'm not. Please, Jess?"

Jessica looked at Caroline. Her head was down and she was holding the glass tightly in both hands. "No thank you, Peter," she replied evenly. "I've packed and I intend to go straight to the Trents'."

"Then let me drop you there," he pleaded. "How were you going to lug your suitcase across the road anyway? I won't be long in the post office. I'll treat you to a picnic lunch on the village green. How does that sound? A loaf of bread, a jug of wine, and me beneath ye old spreading chestnut? It will give me an opportunity to make what amends I can. Please don't hold me responsible for the depravations of my father!"

"God, that's rich," Caroline murmured. She met Jessica's glance. Jessica hesitated. It was true that he was not to blame for what had happened to her in the past. He had treated her with consistent good humour, and it seemed churlish to refuse his offer. What harm could there be in a picnic in the middle of the village on such a lovely morning? Her suitcase would be in the back of the car and she had no intention of ever setting foot in Rensby Hall again once the door closed behind her. Yet Caroline had just shaken her head imperceptibly before lifting the glass to drink once more.

Jessica's gaze went to Peter. His open, agreeable face wore an expression of almost comical pleading.

"All right," she said. "The suitcase is on my bed. If you'll carry it downstairs for me I'll get my purse."

"Gladly!" He took her arm and pulled her to the door. Caroline took a long swallow and the rest of the Scotch disappeared.

"Peter!" she called after them. "Think!"

"I'm on holiday now," he shot back lightly. "I'm not required to think." Shutting the door quietly behind them he ushered Jessica along the landing and down the stairs.

Chapter 10

illie was crossing the hall at a half-run as Peter and Jessica descended the stairs. "I hear you're miserable and you're leaving us!" she called over her shoulder before she disappeared into the back hallway. "I'm sorry!" Not so long ago Jessica would have hurried after her and tried to explain, but now she merely shouted, "Bye, Tillie, and thanks for everything!" as she followed Peter out the front door. He tossed her suitcase into the rear of the car and she barely had time to gather her wits before they were squealing down the driveway. Jessica did not look back. A chapter in her life had closed and she had no desire to carry a last imprint of Rensby Hall with her as she moved on. *I wonder how I shall remember them all in the years to come?* she asked herself. *With a little gratitude and a lot of humour? Or will the thought of them always bring a sour taste into my mouth?*

They came to a halt in front of the post office. Peter jumped out.

"Shan't be a moment," he said. "Do you want to come in?"

"Yes I will," Jessica replied, and before she could work the door handle he was beside her, handing her onto the pavement. "I've known Mrs Evans as the postmistress," she went on, "but I simply must see her now as a witch!"

"Old duffer," Peter remarked as they walked single file between the neat squares of lawn to the post office's open door. "Still, she's well respected around here for her advice. She and my mother get on famously."

Wryly Jessica wondered why. It was hard for her to imagine Lady Eleanor having anything in common with the obese, slightly grubby woman who shuffled to greet them, her moon face wreathed in smiles when she saw Peter.

"Master Peter!" she wheezed. "Good to see you home again. Hello, Jessica."

"I won't be Master Peter for much longer, Mrs Evans," Peter pointed out happily, passing her the sheaf of letters. "I'll be twenty-one on Friday."

"So you will." She opened a drawer and began pulling out stamps. "Having a big party, I hear. I'm looking forward to it. I was a small girl when your father turned twenty-one but I can still remember the excitement up at the Hall. My mother said it was the best time she ever had."

Peter put a scattering of change on the counter. "I think that's enough for the mail. Got any predictions for me?"

She chuckled. "You'll get them at the proper time as long as you're a good boy and do your duty like a true Rensby. We don't want to go jumping the gun now, do we?"

"Yes we do," Peter smiled, "but we can wait. I'm having a picnic down the road with Jessica. Isn't that a nice idea?" They both beamed on Jessica.

"The best," Mrs Evans agreed. "The very best. You cheer her up, Master Peter. I hear she's not happy with us and she's going home soon."

Jessica spoke up, annoyed that they were talking about

her as though she was not present and appalled at the efficiency of the village grapevine. "How did you know?" she asked sharply. "I only told the family this morning."

Mrs Evans laid one fat finger against her equally plump nose. "Word travels fast in a place this small," she said. "But don't worry, Jessica. I'm not the village gossip. I could be, in this position, but it would be beneath the dignity of one who handles Her Majesty's mail. There'd be hell to pay."

"Speaking of hell," Jessica began, "I've been putting Sir Matthew's notes in order, the ones he's made for his family history, and I've been fascinated by the famous story of Sir Julian and the demon. I know about your reputation as a witch hereabouts and I have a question. Was it an ancestor of yours who called up the demon for Sir Julian?"

"It certainly was," Mrs Evans said with pride. "Whether the story's true or not, it's nice to think my humble family's mentioned in the Rensby chronicles."

"I'm very ignorant about these things," Jessica went on. "Once Sir Julian had used the demon, why didn't it turn on him? Demons are supposed to be pretty ruthless things, aren't they? They hate human beings and work for their destruction. How did he protect himself against it?"

There was a startled silence. Peter leaned against the counter and said nothing. Mrs Evans looked nonplussed. At length she said, "Well, if you want to control it you have to draw your pentagram very, very carefully, so that there's not even the tiniest break in the lines. Then you summon it and no matter how much it wants to do you harm, it has to respect the constraining power of the pentagram. Of course if you inadvertently attract one, as ignorant people do sometimes, there's no question of human superiority. It does what it likes and what it likes is always evil. You're doomed." She had been explaining with sure authority, betraying an intelligence Jessica would not have suspected, but now she smiled. "I suppose Sir Julian and my ancestor drew their pentagram very carefully before they spoke the incantation, so that the demon when it came was bound to their will." She busied herself with putting the sheet of stamps away and counting the coins into the till.

"And how could you inadvertently attract one?" Jessica pressed. Mrs Evans did not look up.

"By using the black arts for an amusement," she answered shortly, "or even by being deluded into some seemingly innocent act as quickly forgotten as performed. Young people often pick them up that way and have no idea why their lives never go quite right from then on." Peter straightened.

"Well aren't you full of surprises, Jess," he drawled. "Thank you, Mrs Evans. Come on, queen of my heart. Noon draweth nigh and I'm hungry."

"She believes all that rubbish," Jessica said to him as they returned to the car, and he grimaced. "Yes she does. Hilarious, isn't it?"

They drove the short distance to the village green, parking outside the pub and walking across the road to the warm grass and the welcome shade of the old chestnut. With a sheepish grin, Peter had swung a basket out of the back seat of the car. Jessica did not know whether to be flattered or insulted, for it contained bread, cheese, fruit and cold cuts as well as a bottle of wine.

"You had Tillie make this up before you even asked me to come with you today!" she accused him. "What an underhanded Rensby you are!"

"Guilty," he admitted artlessly as he spread a blanket on the ground and they sank onto it, the basket between them. "I knew you couldn't refuse me. Women never do."

"How boring for you," Jessica responded tartly. "Obviously the feminist movement hasn't made much of an impact on this part of the world."

"It's my winning charm," he retorted. "That's all. They can't help it, poor things. Pass me the bottle opener, will you, Jess?"

They ate and drank in the drowsy heat of noon. No motorists passed. A few children wandered by and looked at them curiously, but on the whole the village lay dreaming in the bright silence.

In spite of her determination to be wary of Peter, Jessica could not help warming to him again. He was so pert, so attuned to her every need. He spread a napkin on her lap, kept an eye on the level of wine in her glass, fed her with affectionate attention, and all the while he joked and laughed, drawing her out and making her feel that she was the most important woman in his world.

No wonder they can't resist him, she thought lazily, leaning back on one elbow and watching him as he lay with both hands behind his head, gazing up into the deep stillness of the chestnut tree. He's the kind of man most likely to be fickle, to break your heart as airily as he won it, and yet women will discard the sober, reliable male to dash themselves to death against this brand of charm. He was squinting a little and humming some tuneless song. She watched his peaceful features, content to be with him beside the sun-baked, quiet, deserted normality of the pretty village street. Then he stopped humming and sat up facing her. He took her hand, his own fingers moving gently over hers. "I can guess why you've decided to cut your visit with us short," he began with a hesitancy she had never seen in him before. "We all know about father's little peccadilloes."

"Little!" she broke in hotly. "I hardly . . ."

"Hush!" he ordered peremptorily and she closed her mouth. His touch went on gliding softly over her skin. "I can't change the past for you," he went on. "I wish I could. I'd give anything to take the pain away. If the words of a sincere apology would do it then I'd say I'm sorry for the rest of my life, but that can't make any difference." His head had been down but now he looked full in her face, and what she saw there made her heart turn over. "I'm asking you not to go," he said in a low voice. "I couldn't bear it, Jessica. I'm falling in love with you."

She sat stunned by his declaration, the drowsy heat of the afternoon, the frightening immediacy of her own response. Something in her rose up, expanded, sang with delight. He was falling in love with her. Peter loved her. But the moment of elation passed and she withdrew her hand. Caroline's caustic judgement came back to her: "Petey is a shallow creature who's nice to everyone because it makes life so much simpler." "That's not possible," she said with difficulty. "You've only known me for a few days. At best it's a mild physical attraction. I have to go home."

His gaze fell to his hands now lying tensely curled in his lap. To Jessica's amazement, all his aplomb seemed to have deserted him. "I know I'm a shallow man," he said, uncannily echoing Jessica's thoughts, "and I've flitted about from girl to girl pretty consistently, but you're different. The feelings I have for you are unique to me, new, strong, rather terrifying actually." He gave her a faint smile. "I suppose you do well to be suspicious of me. I have an atrocious reputation when it comes to women. But you must believe me when I say that I love you and I think I'm right in assuming that you have some rather definite emotions regarding me. Do you?"

Oh yes, she thought, surveying the pale, well-boned face, the troubled eyes, the somehow vulnerable shoulders hunched under the rumpled white shirt. You can move me and lure me in a way that no one, not even Michael, has done before. You're exciting and dangerous and winsome as a child, and the idea that you might do more than just lust after me on an idle afternoon is intoxicating. I am ready for a change from the safe, the predictable, but not for a casual affair. Not yet. She said as much aloud.

"You're right," she admitted with a tremor in her voice. "You're like a magnet to me. You're vital and charming and warm. Who could resist such charisma? But I don't want a summer romance, Peter. I don't want to be another scalp on your belt."

"Oh God what a ghastly comparison!" he burst out. "That's not what I want either! That's not at all what I had in mind! Please come back to the Hall, Jessica. Stay longer. Don't go rushing off in anger and kill any chance we have to be happy! The love is there between us, I know it is, but it's so fragile, so young. Stay here so we can test it, get to know one another better." He leaned forward and put his hands on either side of her neck. The heat of him was both a torment and a delight. She could smell his maleness, and his breath was sweetly flavoured with wine and apples. His mouth was inches from hers. One swift movement and they would connect. "I know your husband's only been dead for a year," he went on urgently. "I can wait. I'd be good to you, Jessica, I promise. You'd never regret your decision to come back with me."

She did not move. Every nerve was almost painfully alert at his nearness yet she studied him expressionlessly, her mind in confusion. I have become a maze of different levels, she thought feverishly. In one is sheer bewilderment at all that has happened to me. In another is relief to be going home to a place where everything is familiar. In a third, a growing, demanding thrust for change that includes my undeniable feelings for this man. A fourth holds memories of Jane, of myself, of Michael, of the beautiful, temperate country of my youth that could very quickly pull me into itself if I wanted. What if I stayed and the bond between us grew and he asked me to become Lady Rensby? It's not impossible. I'd be acceptable here, I'm a local girl after all. The Hall would be mine. But there is a fifth level, she admitted to herself while a fitful breeze stirred the loose, dark wave on Peter's forehead and the need to kiss him became almost insupportable. It's shadowed and full of indistinct shapes that glide away from my conscious mind yet send out a pulse of warning. Something hides in that level, something that makes me uneasy. She sighed and drew back.

"I can't return to the Hall," she said. "I refuse to be

under the same roof as your father. I think I love you too, Peter, but I won't set foot in that place again. Could you perhaps fly over and join me as soon as possible, and we'll take it from there?" She felt the tips of his fingers caress her cheek, the hollow of her throat. Then he too withdrew and was silent for a moment, his arms locked about his knees. He was scanning the sleepy road and the motionless sign of the Monk's Fast beyond it.

"Yes I could," he said slowly, and the happiness burgeoned once more inside her. "I'd like nothing better. But will you do me a favour first, Jess?" His gaze swivelled to her. "Will you stay until after my birthday? It's a very important occasion for me but it won't mean much without your presence."

"Oh, Peter, I can't!" she answered in dismay. "I have too much self-respect to accept your father's odious hospitality ever again. No."

"Well what if I get you a cottage here?" he queried eagerly. "I'll pay the rent myself. It won't be much. You won't have to see any of them if you don't want to. Or a room at the Monk's Fast if you'd rather. Just till after my birthday. Please?"

The confident, teasing Peter Rensby had gone, replaced by a solemnly urgent young man with the fear of rejection in his eyes. I suppose I can still go home on the Sunday flight, she thought. What harm can it do? I want to be with him. I want to make him happy, and if he can find me an empty cottage for a few days I'll be free of everything but the pleasure of his company. The Monk's Fast is too public. Peter all to myself in the privacy of the night. The curtains drawn, the wine uncorked . . . A shiver of anticipation went through her. "All right," she said. "Find me a cottage, Mister Wizard. The Rensbys own the village, don't they? But, Peter," she concluded, sobering. "It's got to be more than a chance to make another conquest. You understand? If you hurt me I'll never forgive you."

For answer he pulled her against him and kissed her, and this time she gave herself up to his mouth, his embrace, opening herself completely. "Hurt you?" he murmured. "Never. Never! From this moment on you are my whole life."

He left her waiting contentedly in the grass. She watched him cross the road and go into the pub, pulling a handful of change out of his pocket as he did so. Every movement he makes is graceful, fraught with sensual appeal, she thought lazily. I don't think he's had a moment of self-doubt since the day he was born, except perhaps a short while ago when he begged me to stay. The memory gave her a pleasant surge of power. I wonder if he's phoning the Hall, telling them what's happened. I wonder what his father will say. She did not care. Lying back she studied the play of light and shade in the thick greenery above. The blanket was soft under her. The air smelled faintly of flowers growing in some garden on the edge of the green. She had almost fallen into a doze when he returned.

"Utterly delectable," he remarked, squatting as she sat up. "Good enough to be fallen upon and devoured. I've found a cottage for you over there," he pointed behind him. "One of the old ones. Some friends of ours are away in France for the summer but I got their permission to open it up. Mrs Evans has the key."

"You called France?" she said, astonished.

He laughed. "Of course. Why not? Charged it to the old man. These people spend most of their time in London anyway. It's a nice little hovel. You'll like it. I had a thing for their daughter when I was eleven and I was crushed when she preferred to be bribed by the librarian's son. Ah well." He began to pack up the picnic things and she hurried to help. He carried the basket back to the car. "Why don't you walk across the green and wait for me?" he suggested. "I'll drive along to the post office, get the key, and meet you there. It's the house right on the end. I'll be five minutes." Without waiting for a response he roared away, and Jessica, after a moment, made her way into the Monk's Fast.

The cramped hallway was dark after the blinding light

outside. She made her way to the public phone hanging on the wall opposite the entrance to the bar, picked up the slim local phone book, and found the Trents' number. She did not want to make this call. For some reason she felt obscurely ashamed to be turning down their offer of a bed. Taking the appropriate coin out of her purse she dropped it into the slot and dialled. Alix answered almost at once.

"Hi, Alix, it's me," Jessica said. Behind her there was a subdued mutter of voices and the clink of glassware. The not unpleasant odour of beer and smoke came to her nostrils. A radio was playing quietly in the background.

"Jessica! I was beginning to wonder if you were coming. Ben's out at the moment but he'll be back in time for tea. Are you on your way?"

"No I'm not." Jessica wondered why it was so hard to get out those words. "Oh I've left the Hall all right. I said my piece to Sir Matthew and packed. But Peter . . ." She paused, hunting for the right thing to say, angry with herself for the necessity. "Peter begged me to stay around until after his birthday and I hadn't the heart to refuse. He's found me a place for a few days. I still intend to leave on Sunday."

There was a pregnant silence on the other end of the phone. Then Alix said, "I hope you're doing the right thing, Jess. Ben and I both felt strongly that you should be here with us. We don't want to tell you your business of course. You know what's best for yourself. Still . . ."

Jessica waited. How dare you judge me, she was thinking. People always say that when they're about to jump on their high horse and give you advice anyway.

"For your own sake, keep in touch with me," Alix went on rather hurriedly. Jessica sensed her embarrassment. "Forgive my presumption, but you're such a nice person and I'd hate to see you made unhappy. And remember, we're here if you need us."

As though I can't look after myself, Jessica said silently. "I'll remember," she said aloud. "I'm really sorry for putting you out like this, Alix, but Peter isn't his father and you've no need to worry about me. I'll certainly see you between now and Sunday."

"I should hope so!" Alix replied warmly. "I'll be available any time but Friday afternoon. I've got to run a few errands in London and I'm getting my hair done at Snippets, but I should be back late in the evening if you feel like a nightcap. Thanks for phoning, Jess. And good luck."

Jessica hung up feeling absurdly guilty and vaguely dissatisfied. Alix's farewell had been definite, as though she did not expect them to meet again. If I've offended her it's just too bad, she thought with irritation as she made her way back out into the sunshine. I'm not her responsibility. She needn't be so possessive.

Peter was already parked outside the tall hedge that surrounded the cottage and its miniature garden as she ran across the green. He dangled a key-ring at her as she came up to him, panting. "I had to call Alix and tell her I wouldn't be there this afternoon," she explained in answer to his raised eyebrows. He took her arm and guided her through the low gate and up the short path to the front door.

"I'll bet she was disappointed," he remarked sharply. "No more excitement for our worthy vicar and his upstanding little wife." Inserting a key in the lock he pushed the door wide and bowed. "Your palace, princess."

There were two steps down, straight into a charming and surprisingly spacious room that obviously filled the downstairs area. The sun would pour into it in the morning, Jessica realized, through the set of modern embrasured windows along one wall, and lie like gold on the thick carpeting. The furniture was casual and inviting. Above the fireplace hung a portrait of a rather intense looking woman with bare shoulders draped in pink chiffon. Several small glass sculptures were grouped on the coffee table. A crowded bookcase stood against the far wall. "He's a doctor, she's a nitwit," Peter said off-handedly. "The daughter grew up to have a big nose and a passion for horses. The kitchen and downstairs bathroom are at the other end, through the passage by the bookcase, and the stairs going to the bedroom are there too. Take a look around while I bring in your suitcase."

Jessica did so. The kitchen was small but adequate. Upstairs there was one bedroom done in restful shades of green, whose window looked out over the great chestnut and the centre of the village, and a bathroom. Everything was unobtrusively tasteful. "They modernized the place for the odd weekend when they feel sentimental about their village roots," Peter commented, setting the suitcase down on the floor and coming to put his arms around her as she stood looking at the view from the bedroom. "They always come to dinner at the Hall when they're here, which is about twice a year. Rather inviting, isn't it?" She nodded. "The bed I mean," he teased her. She did not respond. She rested against him. "I wonder if you remember them," he went on. "Your family lived next door, didn't they?"

Jessica glanced down to the neighbouring front garden, divided from this one by a high wooden fence smothered in climbing roses. "Yes we did," she said quietly. "But I don't think we ever met these people. Perhaps even in those days they were never here."

"Perhaps." With one accord they made their way back down the narrow stairs. At the door Peter turned. "Don't worry about food," he said. "I'll bring you a bag of groceries later this evening and we can picnic every night. It's not for long after all."

He looked so woebegone at the thought that she hugged him impulsively. "You are spoiling me terribly," she protested, and he agreed fervently.

"I am, I am!" he said. "Are you going to make it worth-while? Just a joke," he hastened to assure her as he saw her face. "I'll be back later. Get settled." Then he was gone. She could hear him whistling as he got into the car. The engine started up, then roared away, fading into the distance. Jessica went and sat on the sofa. What are you doing? she asked herself breathlessly. Oh whatever are you doing? I am embarked on a great adventure, she answered herself, and I have never been so scared and excited in all my life.

True to his word he came back in the early evening with milk, cereal, coffee, bread, the minor essentials she would need. He stored them away and laid a starched white cloth on the kitchen table with a flourish, then set out several casserole dishes and a candle in a silver holder. Jessica watched him, entranced. This was a side of him she had never seen, efficient, unsmiling, intent on bringing order. He proceeded to light the candle with an endearing concentration. Jessica lifted the casserole lids.

"What's this?"

"Peasant food. A simple stew, boiled potatoes, salad. Tillie made it up for me."

She firmly replaced the lids and folded her arms. "I didn't move in here to be nursemaided by your family. After what happened it's insulting. They're condescending to me."

He looked pained. "I can't cook," he protested. "I asked Tillie to give me some food for us and I didn't need my mother's permission to do that. The rest of them don't know. All they know is that I'm here with you. Aren't you being a bit touchy, Jessica?"

"Perhaps I am." She loosened and sat, pulling up a chair to the table. He was busy wrestling the cork from a bottle of wine. "I suppose that's from the Rensby cellar?"

He grinned. "You bet it is! Vintage claret. Father would have a fit if he knew I'd stolen it."

"Is that what you feel?" she asked, stung. "That you're enjoying a moment of rebellion from your family and I'm part of it? Was there an argument when you told them I was staying on here because we're falling in love?"

He put down the bottle and came to kneel by her chair, resting a hand on her thigh. "I'll be the master of Rensby Hall on Saturday," he said. "That's the way it's always been. The heir turns twenty-one and all authority passes to him. In my case, I'll go back to Oxford and finish my degree before settling down in the Rill. My parents can remain in the house if they want and I expect they will for a while although they've bought themselves a small villa in Portugal for their retirement. Caroline is free to go or stay. That's unimportant." He reached up to stroke her hair. "When I told them about us my father said nothing at all. My mother fussed and flapped. Caroline told me that given my personality I was just infatuated and being totally selfish and to stop screwing up your life. None of it matters, can't you see? It will all come right because I love you."

She contemplated the earnest face. Why do I feel I'm doing something underhanded, something childish and reprehensible, she wondered? I should be happy, but I feel tainted in some way. "I don't want to eat Tillie's food," she insisted. "I don't want any favours from the Hall. I don't want to be patronized."

He blew out a gust of air and rose, walking calmly back to his place and pouring the wine. "You can't cook here," he pointed out coolly. "There are no supplies in the cupboards. Swallow your pride, for God's sake, Jessica. We could eat out every night but I thought you'd prefer being here alone, with me."

He sounded hurt, offended. With an inward sigh she capitulated. "OK," she said, taking the glass he was offering. "I'll choke down Tillie's stew. But you do the dishes!"

He did not smile. "Very big of you," he said tersely.

But by the time the bottle of wine was empty and they had scoured their plates he was his usual lively self, making her laugh with the jokes and stories he had a knack for telling. He could turn the smallest incident into something hilarious, rattling on with the bottle in one hand and his utensil in the other, leaning over the table at Jessica and pulling faces while she giggled helplessly. They did the dishes together while the sweet summer evening faded into night, then they took the candle into the living room and sat on the sofa, wrapped in each other's arms, watching the yellow flame sway and gutter in the warm draught from the open windows.

He began to kiss her, plunging his hands into her hair, moaning with delight, and she met his passion with a violence of her own, not minding when he unbuttoned her blouse and lifted her breasts to his mouth. "Let's go upstairs," she murmured, and he raised a swollen, lust-glazed glance to hers and nodded.

They did not bother to close the drapes. Moonlight was now flooding the room, lying across the bed where they fell, panting and entangled, draining the colour from their naked skin and turning their eyes to ashes.

"Oh God this is great," Peter was muttering. "You're a gorgeous piece of ass, Jess my love. Open your legs for Petey, there's a good girl."

With a cry of hunger she complied, and felt herself entered. The man lying above her began to move, grunting half-smothered obscenities into her hair. Not like Michael, she thought hotly, incoherently. Not hesitant, not gentle. Wild and passionate and out of control. An animal, like me. The real me. Oh how I have missed this, and not known what it was I was missing! She heard a voice, ragged and coarse, grunting yes, yes, ah yes! and realized it was her own. Sweat made her skin suddenly slippery as she came to orgasm in an explosion of sensation.

With a cry the man climaxed and sank onto her, inert and breathing heavily. For many minutes they lay as one, motionless, then Peter grasped her by the hair and turned her head, kissing her hard. He slid away, rising and standing by the bed. In the washing of the moonlight he looked unreal, a grey figment of her imagination.

"Well aren't you full of surprises," he said. "I've always maintained that the ones who are coldest on the outside turn out to be the wildest in bed." He began pulling on his clothes.

But I'm not like that any more, Jessica thought. I used to

be. Cautious and cool and hard to approach, holding something back all the time although I wasn't aware that I did so.
How things have changed in a scant few days! "Kiss me
again," she ordered.

Laughing he bent and pecked at her cheek. "Greedy little piggy," he said. "Now I have to go. I'll see you tomorrow,
my honey."

She sat up. "Why can't you spend the night here?" she
asked. "What difference would it make?"

He was running both hands through his unruly locks.
"None, of course," he answered lightly. "But let's not rush
things, Jess. I have to get up early tomorrow and drive into
Clapton with my father. We're seeing a lawyer. It's about the
passing of the estate into my hands." He leaned on the bed
with one arm on either side of her. His face was in shadow,
and all she could see was the gleam of his eyes. "I love you
and I'll be back with you as soon as I can. Don't be lonely.
Sleep well." He did not kiss her again. He ran down the stairs
and she heard the front door slam. He did not gun the car. It
slid away with a barely heard throbbing purr and the silence
of the house closed in behind him.

She pulled the covers over herself and lay for a long
time, physically spent, but her mind would not match the
exhaustion of her body. She was aware of an obscure sense of
betrayal and a faint though deep pulse of warning. What is it?
she asked of herself. The fifth level, the place I can't quite
plumb, the place where forms glide and curl across my inner
vision but won't coalesce into anything recognizable. They
say you have to deliberately give your unconscious mind permission to reveal the things it keeps hidden. What's still hiding away down there, trying to get out? No answer came, and
finally she turned onto her side and closed her eyes. It's him,
Sir Matthew, she decided, and Eleanor and that crazy house
and the way I'm defying them, yes defying, by staying on and
taking Peter away from them. What I'm feeling is the vestige
of a juvenile awe they inspired in me and it's got to go. She

tumbled into sleep.

And dreamed. She was in the same small cottage bedroom, its contours barely familiar. The drapes still stood open. Tired moonlight still frayed the edges of the shadows, and out of their blackness Caroline stepped towards her naked, her body alternately a moving darkness and a column of paleness. Her face, with its full lips and marble eyes, was empty of expression. Immediately Jessica was urgent with desire. She held out her arms. The figure bent. Jessica's hands closed over the cold shoulders, slid shuddering down the smooth, unresisting arms, and pulled Caroline onto the bed beside her. Caroline lay waiting, breathing softly. Jessica's nostrils were full of the strong, musky odour the girl had exuded on the night when they had sat and drunk together. In her dream she remembered the kiss the girl had impulsively given her. She lowered her head. This time her mouth met Caroline's slowly, her tongue probing, her fingers trailing over the full globes of the heavy breasts. Caroline's nipples hardened. Jessica felt her own nipples roughen as a cold hand brushed them and flicked over her belly to bury itself between her thighs. She pulled away, straddling the firm hips then inching down until she could thrust her face into Caroline's sex. Caroline's body responded, writhing and quivering. Now that exotic scent had a taste as well, sharp and bitter and inexpressibly exciting. She knew that Caroline had climaxed, and looked up.

Michael was standing by the bed. He was grinning, a malevolent rictus. His exposed teeth were like white pebbles, glinting in the moonlight. His parchment face was disfigured, and he stank of musk and death. Jessica screamed. She scrabbled away from him gasping, clambering over Caroline's inert calves, then all at once found herself kneeling on the disordered covers, wide awake.

The room was empty and the moon was setting. Its light no longer illuminated the dusky shapes around her. Trembling, still breathing in shallow sobs, Jessica pulled herself to the edge of the bed. She could still smell them, the inhabitants of her dream. The odour lingered, and so did the frenzied sexual madness that had gripped her. It's perfectly plain, she thought, shrugging into her robe. Michael presides over my sexual renaissance. He accuses because he is dead and cannot share in it. He is jealous because I am full of sensual possibilities that were impossible before. Caroline . . . She got up and wandered to the window. The village green lay drowned in a soporific darkness. Wind passed through the dense foliage of the huge chestnut, making the leaves quiver, and the shadows beneath its spreading arms flowed, frozen, over the black grass at its foot. I'm still tingling with it, Jessica thought, putting a damp hand to the pane. My nightgown is wet, my heart's thumping. I suppose I'm like the water that crashes through a dam that's just been breached. There'll be chaos, tumult, confusion, until the flood slows and becomes an orderly river.

She was about to turn back into the room when her attention was caught by a movement under the tree. Someone was standing in the dimness, a tall shape that had just tilted its head and was looking up at her. Her hand dropped to her side. A white face, pits for eyes, it was Michael down there with his hostile gaze fixed resentfully on her, Michael, who would not stay dead, who wanted to drag her back to become the woman she had been. Her sweat became instantly chill and she shrank into her robe.

But no. It must be Peter keeping vigil. Just the sort of crazy, romantic thing he would do. She undid the latch on the window and pushed it wide, leaning out and calling quietly, "Peter, you idiot! Come inside!" But the figure had gone. The thick shadows under the chestnut stirred briefly and then were still.

Chapter 11

Brilliant early sunshine flooded the room when she woke, and groping for her watch on the bedside table she saw that the time was a little past six. I should have closed the drapes last night, she thought, and lay for a while listening to the morning song of the birds outside the still-open window and the occasional thrum of a car going by on the opposite side of the green. A gate clanged. Someone called "Good-morning!" in a cheerful voice and was answered from further along the row of cottages. There is life here, Jessica mused as she watched the play of strong light on the ceiling. I was isolated from it in the Hall. It was like a stage set, with only the Trents and Mrs Evans playing their part. If Peter's not going to be back until this afternoon I'll go and spend some time with Alix, maybe invite her to lunch at the pub. I owe her that much.

Rummaging in her suitcase for her toilet things, Jessica went along the landing to the bathroom. For a long time she stood gazing at herself in the mirror above the sink. The reflection gazed back at her solemnly. I've changed, she thought. Not just inside, but physically as well. My features seem sharper to me, more focused. There's a clarity about my eyes now. I don't think I ever really examined my face before. I didn't want to study myself. I hid, because there was always the chasm between the person I should have become and the warped, unnatural one that grew because of Sir Matthew and his filthy fingers. You can grow up without fear now, little girl, she said silently, and the reflection's green eyes and generous mouth smiled in return.

She showered, put on her makeup, dressed, in a mood of energetic well-being. Peter loves me, she sang as she brushed her hair, and I'm going home, and he'll come to get me, and everything will be all right. Downstairs she opened all the windows and the door to the back garden, taking a few steps along the short path that ran between beds of vivid pink and purple flowers she could not name, past a single apple tree, to a rustic shed from whose half-closed door the handle of a lawn mower jutted. The whole space was enclosed by an ivy-choked wooden fence so that even if she had wanted she could not have peered over it into the neighbouring lot. She had no desire to do so. The past was dead at last — hers, Jane's, her father's. The cottage next door could not inspire either nostalgia or anxiety. The day was close. No air stirred and there was a breathlessness about the atmosphere that compressed her lungs and gave her the illusion that she was wading through invisible water. She wondered if a storm was coming. The apple tree was utterly motionless and not a blade of grass trembled.

She fetched herself a bowl of cereal and a glass of orange juice and ate and drank sitting on the back step, waving away an inquisitive bee and watching a hedgehog trundle amiably across the path to disappear under the cool tangle of the border plots. Then she went inside, locked the rear door, rinsed her dishes, and picked up her purse where she had left it on the coffee table the afternoon before. She hoped that Alix would be home, but if not, a stroll through the village and perhaps under the beech trees lining the main road to the church would be pleasant. Stepping up to the front door she opened it. Lady Eleanor was standing there.

"Good-morning, Jessica dear!" she beamed. "May I come in?" She was wearing loose white cotton trousers and a pale blue blouse. Her bare feet were thrust into canvas espadrilles. Her hair was up, revealing the powerful column of her neck. She looked about twenty.

Jessica's happy mood fled. She continued to block the woman's way, her hand on the door. "Actually I was just on my way to the Trents'," she said coolly. "It's such a lovely morning that I thought I'd take a walk."

Eleanor advanced, stepping adroitly around Jessica and into the living room. "I haven't been in this cottage since the Frasers were home last, months ago!" she remarked. "It really is so homey, isn't it? Are you enjoying it, Jessica?" She placed a basket on the table. "We didn't know what you were doing about food, so Tillie sent along some muffins for your breakfast. Can we have a cup of tea?"

Jessica left the door open. She went down the two steps but no further. "I don't think so, Lady Eleanor," she said. "It's good of Tillie to send the muffins but she needn't have bothered. I'm quite capable of looking after myself. Now if you don't mind I'd like to get going."

Eleanor sank onto the sofa and crossed her legs, one hand smoothing her hair in a slow, thoughtful gesture that reminded Jessica vividly of Peter. "We feel so bad," Eleanor said quietly. "We invited you to the Hall and then treated you abominably. And now that Peter is showing more interest in you than he has in any other young woman so far, we feel even worse. We want you to think of yourself as a member of the family, Jess dear, not an outcast. Come back for your last two days, and let us make amends."

"I don't feel like an outcast," Jessica replied steadily. "It has nothing to do with the way you've treated me, Lady Eleanor. I didn't leave in a childish sulk. I left because your husband molested me when I was young. I can no longer treat him with any respect, nor even carry on a normal conversation with him. You didn't drive me away and I'm not squatting here pouting and waiting for you to grovel to me. Please take the muffins back to the Hall."

Eleanor wriggled with distress. "Oh dear!" she exclaimed. "I can't answer for Matthew, that wouldn't be right, but I do like you, Jessica, and Peter is so serious about you that I want us to try to be friends. Have I personally done anything to earn your scorn? Can you forgive me if I have? Please don't equate me in sin with my husband. That would be very prideful of you." She looked up at Jessica appealingly. "Besides, it's your birthday today, isn't it? Tillie is baking you a cake. Will you at least let Peter bring you to the Hall for a small celebration?"

Jessica reached back and closed the door, then came down into the sun-splashed room. "I don't hold you responsible for what Sir Matthew has done to me," she said. "But I'm sorry, I won't spend my birthday at the Hall. How did you know about it?"

"I keep a record of all the birthdays of the people I like," Eleanor said triumphantly. "Besides, your mother phoned earlier to wish you well."

"I'd better call her back, then." Jessica moved towards the kitchen. "I'll make us some tea, Lady Eleanor. What did you tell her?"

Eleanor looked sheepish. "I said that you were out visiting a friend but that you'd be back soon." Seeing Jessica's expression she put out a hand. "Oh my dear, don't be angry all over again! I couldn't bear her to think that we had mistreated you!"

Jessica capitulated. With an inward shrug she busied herself in the kitchen, plugging in the kettle and finding cups and saucers. Peter had brought milk and some tea but there was no sugar. When it was ready Jessica carried the tray into the living room. The sun had slipped from the fireplace wall and the carpet to heat the back of the sofa and linger just inside the windows. Perching on the edge of one of the arm-chairs Jessica poured, handing the brew to Eleanor who took it almost absently and sipped in silence. Her volubility had vanished. When she had finished the tea she set her cup back in the saucer with exaggerated care and relaxed against the cushions. Jessica, annoyed and impatient to be outside and on her way to Alix's, saw that the woman was settling in. She was scanning Jessica with speculation, her face immobile but her eyes suddenly full of intelligence. She's sizing me up, Jessica thought. As a future daughter-in-law perhaps? I dislike her and believe that her fluttering vagueness is nothing but a front, but I suppose I had better try to get along with her. Oh why can't they all just fade away and leave Peter and me to our own devices?

"It's very hot today, isn't it?" she ventured, and as though her words had thrown a switch in the older woman's head, Eleanor came to life.

"Oh hot, yes!" she agreed vehemently. "I've seen weath-er like this before and it almost always means that a big storm is on its way. I'm not looking forward to it. The wind will tear my roses to shreds, even though the rose garden's in a rela-tively sheltered corner of the house. Your mother used to love my roses. Did you know that I gave her a cutting and she planted it in the garden next door? I believe it's still there and doing well. Is Canada good for roses? I don't suppose so. Your winter's too severe, isn't it?" She prattled on. Jessica smiled and nodded or shook her head as the occasion warranted, eventually falling into a trance of boredom while the sun dis-appeared entirely and the air in the room cooled a little. She looked for a break in the monologue so that she could jump up and clatter the tea things, but it did not come. She stifled a yawn. I simply must call Mother before dinner, she thought. Oh Eleanor, shut up and go home!

She had almost summoned the energy to get out of the chair and be mildly rude when she heard the familiar throb of the Ferrari's engine outside. Eleanor rose at once. "Goodness!" she said. "I've been running on for ages and now Peter is here! I'm sorry, Jessica. I've prevented you from your visit. I didn't intend to stay so long."

Oh yes you did, Jessica thought as she went to open the door, Eleanor behind her. You may have come to patch things up, but when I told you I was on my way to the Trents' you very deliberately decided to keep me here. How petty you are with your silly village feuds! I resent being made a part of them.

Peter was running up the path, arms outstretched, a smile on his sun-drenched face, and Jessica fell into his embrace. "I missed you," he declared, kissing her. "Hello, Mother. Been boring Jess to death?"

"She won't come to her birthday celebration at the Hall," Eleanor said in an injured tone. "You try to persuade her, Peter. I must get on. I have to pick up a package from Vera."

They watched her climb into her battered little car and she waved as she pulled away. Peter withdrew into the cottage, closed the door, then kissed Jessica again, more thoroughly this time. "Happy Birthday, love," he said, tugging a box out of his pocket. "I stayed in Clapton long enough to get you this."

Eagerly Jessica opened it. The cluster of rubies glittered like wet blood on their thin gold chain. She gasped in admiration. "Oh, Peter, I've never seen anything so beautiful!" she exclaimed, and he took it from her gently and fastened it around her neck.

"Did you think I'd forget?" he murmured against her ear. "I'm a romantic devil under this tough exterior. Let's go to bed before lunch."

They made love and then Peter insisted on taking her to Clapton to eat. "We can't sit around the kitchen and feed ourselves out of bags on your birthday," he explained. "Besides, you've seen nothing of the countryside since you arrived. We'll have a lazy afternoon doing exactly what we please." Jessica found herself shepherded firmly into the car but she did not protest. A day alone with him would be heaven.

He did not say much as they drove, and Jessica sat with her happiness folded tight inside her as fields, hedges and cottages flashed by. She knew he was taking a long way around. Clapton was only six miles from Rensby's Rill, a fair distance given England's winding country lanes, but not as far as they had already been. She presumed he was giving her a pleasant outing and was grateful for his thoughtfulness.

But eventually he emerged from the sleepy backwater roads onto a main highway and in five minutes was slowing to negotiate Clapton's traffic. After her days in the Rill Jessica felt as though she was waking from a coma. Other cars tooted and wove. Women stood outside stores holding shopping bags, gesticulating to each other while their children ran up and down the sidewalks. Signs blinked. A group of gum-chewing teenagers with hair spiked to the sky swaggered along and one of them whistled, at her or the car she could not decide which, as Peter pulled away from a green light. The sensory blizzard amazed her.

"This is a mean and ugly town," Peter commented. "It has nothing whatsoever to recommend it except a couple of good restaurants and the flea market that replaced the old farmers' market. Want to go pick over the garbage? We can have a late lunch." She agreed, still bemused.

They meandered among the stalls, which held everything from antique glass to cracked mass-produced crockery. Jessica thought how good it was to be a part of the life around her, to smell fish and chips frying, to hear the seductive pitch of the men and women leaning over the merchandise with bargains too wonderful to refuse. Peter had a clever, light word for all of them and soon Jessica too was chatting and

laughing. They drank lemonade Peter bought from two enter-
prising boys who had set up their own rickety table.

The heat had become more oppressive as the day wore
on, and Jessica was glad to relax inside the restaurant Peter
had chosen. It was a pretty Tudor building, once obviously a
private home, and the atmosphere was peaceful and intimate.
Only three other tables were occupied. Looking about her,
Jessica was suddenly ravenous.

Peter ordered martinis for them while they studied the
menu. How unlike Michael he is, Jessica mused behind the
shelter of the snowy white, gilt-edged paper. If he was thoroughly egotistical a woman who was strong enough could end
up despising him, but his self-involvement is mixed up with a
genuine empathy and it throws one off. Michael would have
asked me what I wanted to drink. He would even have asked
me if I liked the table. As if he had read her mind, Peter said,
"Have you decided what you want to eat? Shall I order for
you?"

She smiled inwardly. One to you, my darling, she
thought. "It's so hot," she commented. "I'll stick to a huge
salad."

They ate and drank amicably, talking of meaningless,
everyday things in a harmony that secretly delighted her,
dawdling over the littered table when they had finished the
meal, until the moment when Peter got up and held out a
hand. "Let's go to the pictures," he said. Jessica, after wondering for a moment if Clapton had an art gallery, realized that
he meant the movies. Why not? she decided as she slid her
fingers into his and they left the restaurant. Our time is our
own today.

They sat in the cool dimness of the theatre, sharing pop-
corn and watching a very earnest but almost incomprehensi-
ble foreign film on which the dubbing was so bad it made
Jessica giggle. When they stepped out onto the warm pavement it was early evening and the worst of the heat had abat-
ed. In a contented silence they linked arms and walked to the

car. Peter opened the door for her. "Had a good day?" he asked as she slid onto the seat, and impulsively she kissed the hand that had rested briefly on her shoulder. "You needn't ask," she responded.

They drove back to the Rill in a slowly deepening sunset that filled the cloudless sky with magnificent colours. Peter was soon quiet, handling his vehicle with absorption. Jessica turned on the radio. Massive cadenzas by Tchaikovsky poured out, and it was some time before she realized that the music was not filling her with an aching sense of loss and pain as it had done since Michael died. She closed her eyes. So happy, she thought. Happy and free. I don't want to go home any more. I don't want this evening to ever end.

But this time Peter took the direct route back to the village, and the sky was still light as they passed the church on their right and the road to the abbey ruins and the Hall on their left. They were halfway along the village thoroughfare when Jessica became aware of a car behind them. It loomed suddenly, an old battered Austin of an indeterminate colour but dark. "He came up fast," she observed.

Peter grunted, looking in the rear-view mirror. "Quite the beater," he said disparagingly. "Damn. The idiot wants to pass me." Indeed, the Austin was swinging out. Peter slowed. As the other car came abreast of her Jessica glanced at it, then froze.

Her father was behind the wheel. He looked tired. The hand and one bare arm she could see were coarse and brown. He was wearing one of his work shirts Jessica recognized immediately, a heavy khaki streaked with old oil stains. He was staring straight ahead as was Jessica's mother. Younger, thinner, with short waving hair, she was dressed in one of the nondescript cotton frocks she wore to do her cleaning at the Hall. Her lips were moving. She was speaking to Jessica's father and the man was nodding.

Someone was in the rear. Jessica, fingers gripping the edge of the Ferrari's open window, teeth clenched, craned to see. I remember that day, she thought incoherently. That was the day . . . the day . . .

As the Austin gained she was able to see the back window. A wave of terror washed over her. The little girl's face and one flat palm were pressed to the glass. She was not waving. Her expression was solemn, touched with anxiety, and her eyes stared straight into Jessica's own.

Jane was ambling along with the book under her arm, Jessica's mind ran on feverishly. She didn't want a ride with us so Father picked up Mother and drove on. I had a premonition and I turned as the car pulled away. I watched her recede, grow smaller until she vanished into nothingness. That's me. And I . . . She gave a choked cry. I'm Jane. I'm Jane!

"What's that?" Peter asked.

Jessica found her voice. "That car," she said. "Pass it, Peter, please!"

"Why?" he asked amiably. "It's only one of the families from the housing estate. It'll turn off in a minute."

"Please!"

"Oh all right." He gunned the car and in a few seconds they were abreast of it. Jessica caught a glimpse of three outraged villagers before they swept on, then braked suddenly to swing around the green. Peter brought them to a halt. "Have I insulted anyone you know?" he teased her. Jessica slumped in her seat.

"I thought so," she said dully, "but I was mistaken."

Those eyes, her own eyes, had pierced her with their melancholy. It all began then, she told herself, overwhelmed by a sense of fatalism. This too, sitting here beside Peter Rensby twenty years later and hurtling through the countryside. Destiny looped that moment to this but the circle is complete now. It's over.

In the strengthening dusk she almost stumbled over a carton by the front door. Peter picked it up as she unlocked, and they went inside. "I think this is yours," he told her, putting it on the coffee table and then flicking on the lamp. While he closed the drapes she opened it gingerly and with-drew a cake and a bottle of champagne. The candles leaned drunkenly between the pastel sugar flowers. There was a rather florid card with a heavily detailed painting of some anonymous pastoral scene reproduced on it and the note scrawled inside read, "We all wish you a very happy birthday, Jessica, and many more returns. Love from the Rensbys." She dropped the card as though it had burned her and Peter, see-ing her face, shook his finger at her and tutted in mock chas-tisement. "They mean well," he admonished her. "They are trying to make amends." They are trying to make me feel guilty, she thought mutinously, but I won't. "Cakes aren't Tillie's forte," Peter went on, sweeping up the bottle and going towards the kitchen. Jessica heard the refrigerator door slam. "But she's done her best. We can have a private little party and gorge on sugar and alcohol. We can go out again for dinner if you want."

"No thanks," Jessica murmured, automatically straight-ening the candles. "I won't be hungry for the rest of the night."

He came back into the room. "Why don't you go upstairs and change, and then we'll have some cake and I can toast you in champagne. I think music is called for. The selec-tion is limited here, but I know there's Strauss. Will that do?"

"You've brought women here before when the owners have been away, haven't you, Peter?" she said with a stab of jealousy, and he hung his head, pretending coyness, then met her eye, one hand going unconsciously to push back the deep wave of dark hair that had flopped forward.

"Guilty," he answered sadly. "But that's all in the past now. As far as I'm concerned, you are the first. Always, from now on, you are number one. My memories are expunged, Jessy love, I promise!"

"Swine," she shot back at him, but she was smiling.

She took her time upstairs, choosing a dress with a low-cut neckline that showed off the sparkle of the gems he had given her. All her life she had covered her body in full skirts, loose blouses, baggy sweaters in sober colours, believing that she was putting comfort above attractiveness, not under-standing that she was attempting to hide the shame her sexu-ality had brought to her. This dress with its plunging, heart-shaped bodice, its short, hip-hugging skirt, its blatantly touchable texture, had been purchased in a moment of aber-ration that she had immediately regretted. She had hung it in her closet and never worn it until now. Something told me to bring it when I came here, she thought as she went down-stairs. How mysterious and surprising the mind is!

He had set out plates and forks, napkins and a bucket full of ice in which the champagne rested. He raised his eye-brows as she came towards him.

"You look absolutely fabulous!" he exhaled. "Caroline would be green with envy! She's very jealous of you," he remarked as Jessica slid onto the sofa. "We've always been so close. Fought like cats and dogs but she's never let anyone come between us until now. If she could break us up, she would, but of course she can't."

"Is that why she said she didn't want to like me?" Jessica reflected. "Perhaps she sensed that you would. Like me, I mean. She obviously knew exactly what would appeal to you and felt threatened when she saw a lot of it in me. I'm sorry, Peter. I quite like her myself."

"There's a lot to like," he responded shortly. "And a lot to drive anyone out of their head. Why don't you light the candles and I'll go into the kitchen and open the champagne. I don't want to take the chance of the cork ricocheting onto the sculptures. The glasses are in the fridge anyway." As he went he pushed a button on the tape machine and "Tales from the Vienna Woods" began to cascade into the air. Jessica took the matches he had placed beside the cake and did as he had suggested. She heard the cork explode from the bottle. Once more the refrigerator door thudded.

He was all smiles as he placed the bottle in the bucket and a full glass before her. "Go on," he urged. "Blow them out and wish for something terrific." She did so. I wish for this love to go on growing between us, she said silently, fervently. I wish for a life together, always. He leaned over the candle smoke and kissed her soundly. "I don't get a wish," he said against her mouth, "but all the same I'll wish that all your dreams may come true." Drawing away, he lifted his glass. "To you, my Jess," he announced. "Long life and happiness!"

She touched hers to his. "To us," she said. The champagne was dry and deliciously cold. She took another sip.

"Cut your cake," he ordered.

The confection was spongy and sickly sweet and Jessica put down her fork after a token mouthful. "Stick to the booze," Peter advised. "It's probably better for you." He refilled her glass and she drank again. He watched her speculatively for a moment, then he said, "Jess, I know you told me that you'd stay over until after my birthday, but you didn't say that you'd come up to the Hall for the dinner. Will you? Please?"

She was all at once very thirsty and the champagne was light and quenching. She stared into the droplet of pale golden liquid left in the crystal. Strauss's frothy, summery phrases dipped and swirled around her, speaking of a time of elegance and grace that had gone. "All right, Peter," she gave in softly. "I'll come." She looked at him directly. "Just for you."

"Thank you, darling!" He hefted the bottle with obvious lighthearted glee and Jessica watched the bubbles agitate and then settle as he poured. "You won't regret it. The dinner will be a bit of a bore because Father's insisted on entertaining some of his archaeology cronies, but the dancing afterwards in the library will be fun. Mother's invited a host of people, local and otherwise. Wear the dress you've got on." He bent and planted a kiss in her cleavage. "It'll wow everyone."

She was amused and touched by his boyish enthusiasm. It won't be so bad, she told herself firmly. I can keep out of

Sir Matthew's way. I'll be only one of many and I can leave early if I like. The thought of leaving early brought a sense of relief, as though the party had already taken place and she was back in the cottage, safe and sound.

"I'll drive you to the airport myself on Sunday," he offered, and to Jessica it seemed like a reward for her compliance. She quickly snuffed the unworthy idea, nodding without a vocal answer and lifting the champagne to her lips. For a second she could not feel the rim of the glass against them. It's an insidious brew, champagne, she thought, smiling. You can toss it down without effect and then suddenly it jumps out at you and makes you numb and silly.

Peter was setting his glass on the table with studied care. He put his knees together and folded his hands in his lap. "I have another favour to ask," he said tentatively, "one that you'll probably refuse, but I have to put it to you anyway because it's so vitally important to me and I'm praying it will be to you too." The confusion of his words betrayed his anxiety. To Jessica he looked like a school boy begging for a treat and she almost burst out laughing, full of love and a painful tenderness. She wanted to wrap him up and rock him in her arms. "Ask away," she invited.

His fingers tightened around each other. His brown eyes fixed her with a serious gaze. "I desperately want you to come to the ceremony tomorrow night," he said, and to her surprise his voice broke.

"The Rensby heir's coming-of-age thing?" she queried. "No, Peter, no. You don't need me for that. Don't take advantage of the fact that I agreed to come to your birthday celebration." She was mildly angry and disappointed that he would push her in this way. He held up both hands in an apologetic manner and shook his head vigorously.

"You don't understand. Let me explain." But then he hesitated, searching for words. "I can tell you right away that my father won't be there," he finally went on. "He did his duty when he turned twenty-one, umpteen years ago, and now it's my turn. He has nothing to do with it apart from making sure that I know what to do. It's something very ancient and traditional and the details are very private, and since there's a good chance that you might end up as Lady Rensby one day you deserve to be there with me. Sex is involved, you see," he said earnestly. "The heir is supposed to have sex with a woman of his choice to sort of ensure a continuing good relationship between the Rensby fortunes and the cosmic forces of luck." He glanced away as if embarrassed. "All rot, of course, but I've got to do it. I can't break with the convention of hundreds of years."

Jessica was both revolted and intrigued. It was like something out of a primitive fairy tale. "I've never heard of anything so . . . so barbaric," she shot at him. "So completely pagan and abhorrent to even the most unenlightened modern person! How can you stoop to something so perverse? Did you have someone lined up for sex, Peter?"

"Don't be angry with me," he pleaded. "Of course I had someone lined up. This is vitally important to the family. I invited one of my friends from the university. Pamela's a girl who's game for anything, and she thought a ritual with a bit of sex thrown in would be a hoot. But that was before I met you, fell in love with you!" he said fervently. "I don't want sex with anyone else! The thought of trying to get it up for some ninny I don't even care about tomorrow night is completely distasteful. I want you there. You have a right to be there! You must be there!"

She was taken aback by his passion. Her revulsion was fading, the fascination growing. But under the titillation of something bizarre, the chance for a new experience, was a dim throb of warning. "This has something to do with Sir Julian's demon, doesn't it, Peter?" she said evenly. He made a self-conscious grimace.

"I think that's where it started," he admitted. "Of course there never was a demon. Hardly anyone believes in that kind of claptrap. But the idea of placating fate or binding luck to the family or renewing a cosmic covenant gradually became a Rensby hallmark that no one dares to meddle with. The villagers expect us to go through with it. They're an ignorant, superstitious lot and they're certain they'd lose their own luck if we didn't. Only people like Ben Trent believe there's anything dangerous in it." He grasped her hands tightly. "Say you'll do it, Jessica, for my sake," he begged. "Don't make me perform the rite with someone else!"

The sameness of Rensby history, she thought while his nails dug into her palms. Generation after generation, stumbling but never falling. Coincidence? Caroline's voice, "The church is powerless here."

And what do I believe? she asked herself finally. In demons? No. In the imagination of gullible people? Of course. In the power of luck, that invisible force? The ability some people have of drawing it to them and keeping it? Yes, I think so. She pulled her fingers from his grip.

"I'll do it if you promise there'll be no one watching us," she said. His grin lit up his face.

"I promise!" he vowed. "You'll be safe with me and you'll have one hell of a good time in the process! It's quite the ritual." He left the sofa in one graceful movement, holding out his arms. "Come on," he urged. "Dance with me. I want to dance with you on your birthday." His eyes gleamed with excitement and for just a moment she found herself fearing the strength of his elation. Then she rose and slid into his embrace.

For a long time they danced in silence. Full night had fallen, and the strains of music pulsed through the shrouded room. Jessica was fully aware of his hands feeding warmth through her thin dress into her hips, his breath stirring her hair, his cheek moving against her temple. He smelled of some expensive, beguiling aftershave and under that odour, very faint, was the scent of Caroline's cigarettes. Odour, Jessica thought, eyes closed. Odour. Something I ought to remember, something I've missed. She stiffened and he held her more closely.

"I love you," he breathed. "Isn't it odd how the lives of both our families have stayed intertwined? Years pass since you were a child and your parents worked at the Hall, and here you are again, and here I am, and our lives are still woven together, in a very literal, physical way." He chuckled quietly. "It must be fate, don't you think? The Rensbys and the Carters, linked forever." She did not reply but turned her head to kiss his neck. "This is your thirtieth birthday, isn't it, Jess?" he went on after a moment. His voice was low, a hypnotic caress. "They say it takes courage to face thirty. 'Gather ye rosebuds while ye may,'" he quoted. "'Old Time is still a-flying.' I hope you've gathered all the rosebuds you've wanted to, my Jess. Do you think they've been enough?"

Something in his tone disturbed her. "If I hadn't met you I'd have rushed to gather a few more," she replied, "but you needn't worry that I'll want to stray from you, Peter. You're the most exciting man I'm ever likely to meet."

He made no response and they continued to sway, Jessica pleasantly dazed by the champagne and his nearness. For an age, it seemed to her, they remained locked together, until she felt them as one flesh, a gently moving, indivisible creation of harmony and unity, pleasantly lost in timelessness.

Peter broke the mood. Abruptly he let her go and strode to the tape deck. The music ceased. Bewildered and chilled, the alcohol now souring in her veins, Jessica watched him collect the detritus of their small celebration and carry it purposefully into the kitchen. When he came back it was to turn on the light in the stairwell and extinguish the living-room lamp. "Bedtime," he said firmly. "You look exhausted, my girl. I'm going to sleep beside you tonight." He looked her up and down in the semi-darkness, a curiously intense expression on his face. "Playtime's almost over and I'm going to miss you, baby," he said curtly. "Now up you go. I'll be there in a minute."

She did as she was told, suddenly as weary as he had said

she was. Taking off her clothes required great effort. She washed herself perfunctorily, and by the time she re-entered the bedroom he had undressed and was under the covers. She climbed in beside him. He turned out the light and after a while she was able to make out his profile in the vague illumination filtering through the drapes. He was watching her.

"Peter," she whispered. "Did you come back last night and watch over me from below, under the chestnut? I thought I saw you down there."

It was a long time before he answered. "No I didn't," he said. "Good-night."

She was disappointed that he did not want to make love although she was so tired. Turning over, she closed her eyes. It was then she remembered, with a stab of guilt and dismay, that she had not phoned her mother. There was a telephone on the table by the bed and stretching, she picked it up. No dial tone purred reassuringly into her ear. It was dead.

Peter spoke into the darkness. "It's hardly ever connected," he said. His voice was clear and cold.

Chapter 12

The wind woke her the following morning. It was soughing about the cottage, and an occasional gust rattled the bedroom windows. She lay semi-conscious for a while, aware that the air on her face was cooler, then she rolled over and put out a hand. "Peter," she said drowsily. "The weather's changing."

She was alone. There was a dent in the pillow where his head had been and the sheets were rumpled, but he had gone. Jessica came fully awake. Pulling on her robe she got up and drew aside the drapes. The boughs of the chestnut were groaning under the sporadic onslaught of the gale and the sky was heavy with billowing grey clouds. Going to the head of the stairs she called out, "Peter?" but there was no answering shout from below. In the bathroom she found a note tucked into the mirror. "Party problems," it read. "Mother needs me. Back soon." She had not seen his handwriting before. It was untidy but strong, full of swirls and elongated loops. She folded the piece of paper and put it in the pocket of her robe, then showered, trying not to be disappointed that he had not kissed her awake before he left. While dressing in khaki slacks and a loose beige shirt she wondered what garb would be appropriate for the ceremony she had agreed to attend that evening, then mentally shrugged. I'll probably be asked to pull some ghastly old hooded cape thing over my head and wave a candle before I shuck it all in the cause of Rensby prosperity, she thought, and the image of herself standing naked in some secret room in Rensby Hall, Peter coming towards her equally stripped in the dim candlelight, gave her a spasm of pure lust. You're just a tad depraved, after all, Jessica Carter, she accused herself cheerfully as she went downstairs. And it feels so good. The ruby necklet still nestled in the hollow of her throat. She had not wanted to take it off when she went to bed.

The clock on the kitchen wall told her that it was eight-thirty. The cramped space was gloomy, and so was the living room even though she opened the curtains and also the windows a crack, for the air had a stuffy quality. The wind that puffed against her face was stale and she paused, looking out at the trembling hedge and the swaying flower beds, before wandering back into the kitchen. The view had not been pretty this morning. The village was dreary, even a trifle desolate, under the oppressive pall of the low sky.

Turning on the light she began to clear the debris Peter had left on the counter, scraping the stiff remains of the cake into the garbage, emptying the water in the ice bucket, washing the plates and glasses. She felt bored and a little lonely. I'll walk over to the pub and call Mother as soon as I've put the coffee on, she vowed. She won't be worrying but she'll want to wish me a belated happy birthday.

The friendly aroma of coffee had just begun to lift her spirits when she heard a car draw up outside and a moment later someone knocked on the door. Peter, she thought, and ran to open it. But it was Caroline who sauntered over the threshold, carrying a cardboard box. As always, her presence created an immediate aura. The room seemed to spring to alertness. She was wearing tight black pants and an obviously expensive red silk shirt and the high heels of her boots thudded briskly as she crossed the carpet. Her hair was piled loosely on top of her head. Tendrils pulled loose by the wind brushed her pale face.

"I've brought you breakfast," she called from the kitchen. "Croissants and butter and a pot of honey. I'm glad you've brewed fresh coffee. I haven't eaten yet myself so I'll join you. I decided to escape from the Hall for a while. Mother is already flapping like a distressed hen and Father is glowering and muttering to himself. Oh by the way." She appeared in the doorway, a knife in one hand and the honey in the other. "I suppose I should say happy birthday for yesterday. It was happy, wasn't it? Did Petey play the adoring suitor well?" Jessica saw her black eyes slide to the necklet. "Yes," she said wryly. "I can see that he did." She vanished into the kitchen and Jessica sat down rather abruptly on the sofa, tense with annoyance.

"You could have found somewhere else to escape to," she said tartly. "I simply must phone home, Caroline, and I'm expecting Peter back at any moment."

The girl was returning with a tray on which were the croissants and two mugs of steaming coffee. She slid it onto the table and gestured. "Come on, Jessica. It's a great morning for comfort food. I knew there wasn't much of a breakfast selection in this cosy little love nest so I killed two birds with one stone. I get some peace. You get to eat and enjoy my scintillating company." She bit into her pastry with relish and smiled unreservedly at Jessica. "You've caused quite a stir in the old ancestral seat," she went on smoothly, brushing crumbs from her shirt. Jessica watched the quick, graceful flurry of the red-tipped fingers. "They've been alternating between guilt and mutual reassurances that everything will turn out all right. Bully for you!"

Jessica was suddenly hungry. "Good!" she retorted, pulling her plate onto her lap. "They don't have to like me any more than you do, Caroline, but they do have to accept the fact that Peter and I are lovers and likely to stay in love."

Caroline raised one feathered eyebrow. "Hmm," she said. "Petey in love is an awesome phenomenon. How's he in bed, by the way? All gusto and no finesse? Or all finesse and no gusto? Men seem to fall into one or the other category." She took a gulp of coffee. "This is very good," she observed. "Have some."

Jessica finished eating and picked up her mug. "You seem to have a rather prurient interest in my sex life," she remarked, "why, I have no idea. Your own must keep you very busy." The coffee was excellent, with a faintly aromatic aftertaste. She wondered if it was something to do with the Rill's water supply. Although it was still very hot, she drained it. The dream of two nights ago came back to her with instant force, Caroline in her bed, nude and abandoned in passion, and she kept her gaze on the grounds sprinkling the bottom of the cup.

Caroline laughed, pulled a packet of cigarettes from the pocket of her shirt, extracted one, and lit it with a flourish. "Busy enough," she admitted without a trace of either shame or pride. "Although dear old Scott's not much in the bed department. Lots of snuffling and panting and very little action."

"Aren't you being disloyal, talking about him like that?" Jessica commented drily. "Don't you feel you owe him any allegiance at all? I thought you were going to marry him." The girl grimaced then shrugged, taking a long drag on her cigarette.

"I have other allegiances, or at least I had," she answered. "Scott's like a genial dog who follows me around. I like him a lot, make no mistake about that, and of course I'll marry the sweetie. I'll be good to him too. But loyalty's not a very big word in the Rensby vocabulary."

"Don't you want love, Caroline?" Jessica queried. "Don't you want to feel something more than mild affection for some man? You're so full of passion yourself." Her head had begun to hum, not unpleasantly but disconcertingly, and she put a hand to her ear. The gesture seemed of some interest to Caroline. She watched it with intensity.

"Oh I have passion all right," she said slowly. "But not with Scott."

"I know." Jessica swallowed. Her throat had gone dry. She set her mug back on the table but somehow it missed the edge and fell with a muffled thud onto the floor. "I saw you one night. I didn't mean to spy. I was on my way to the bathroom. Your door was open a little and I saw you both." She laughed shortly. "I suppose in this tradition-bound runt of a village you have to marry suitably, into your own class, but you take a lover as compensation. I feel sorry for you." The dream would not go away. It was weaving itself through the humming in her head, the images so vibrant that the reality of the room in which she sat wavered for a moment. Jessica felt her body relax deliciously and she slumped back onto the cushions.

"Do you?" Caroline said softly, coldly. "Do you indeed? Jessica Carter with her boring middle-class values, her starchy, oh-so-conventional morality. You've changed, baby, but not all that much. You're still dreaming of the perfect husband with you the perfect wife, producing perfect children in the hazy pink glow of a perfect future." She sprawled back, one leather-clad ankle across her knee. "You know nothing. Nothing! I've no idea why I've decided to help you. I've tried to disdain you, hold you in contempt, sneer at your wholesomeness, but something about you has kept knocking away at my sympathy. I wonder if under other circumstances we might have developed respect for each other. Perhaps even friendship. I envy you your innocence. I was tainted from the time I was born. I never had a chance to be like you, and I never will. What's it like to be a normal woman? I don't know. But you do."

Her booted foot began to describe slow circles and Jessica was mesmerized by the movement of the shiny black spiked heel. Each revolution took a very long time. Caroline inspected the glowing tip of her cigarette then looked at Jessica. "I'm not good at examining my own motives," she said frankly. "All I can come up with is that in my opinion you've suffered enough at the hands of my family. My father abused you. Peter is using you and observing the results with the objective delight of a boy who pins butterflies to a board. And speaking of Peter," she glanced at her watch. "I'd better get this show on the road. I'm supposed to be keeping an eye on you until early this afternoon. I was told to use my imagination to fill the time, and by God I have."

"You're talking rubbish," Jessica managed to say. Caroline was far away. A gulf had opened between them and the carpet was running away into infinity. "Peter loves me," she went on with difficulty, for her tongue had swollen to fill her mouth. "He told me you were jealous of me."

Caroline stubbed out her cigarette with deliberate care, then did a curious thing. She came and squatted in front of Jessica, then took her face in both hands, placed a thumb under one of her eyes, and drew the flesh downward, peering closely. "I am jealous," she agreed in a whisper, "but not in the way you think. Feeling a bit numb, Jessica? I want you to listen carefully to what I have to say." She regained the chair and lit another cigarette. The smoke curled above her head with a fascinating slowness that captured Jessica's attention. She stared at it. Caroline's voice had acquired an echo. "I've slipped a little something into your coffee," she said conversationally. "The effects will begin to wear off in about three hours and you'll feel sick but perfectly sane again. Mother and her friend Vera Evans mess about with all kinds of herbal stuff and Mother keeps a good supply in her bureau for the times when she's fed up with Father and the Rill and all the rest of it. I've sampled some of it myself. In a moment I'm going to pack up your things and take you to London, and I drugged you because I didn't want a scene here, protests and struggles and all that annoying brouhaha. You're going to come as peacefully as a lamb." She took a deep drag on her cigarette. Her mouth was huge to Jessica, moist and red, but her eyes were larger. They filled Jessica's vision, cool and speculative and completely calm. She felt Caroline's fingers trail along the skin of her cheek. The oddly impersonal caress resonated through her body.

"They're going to kill you tonight," Caroline went on, every word echoing in waves through Jessica's brain, horribly ponderous and yet crystal clear. "They killed Jane all those years ago, before I was born. I know because they told me about it after I was . . . addicted and didn't want anything to change. Father cut her throat. They're about to do the same to you. Peter doesn't love you. He never did. Why should he bother? You're a victim. Something to study and play with and then throw away."

Jessica made a gesture she felt as violent, but only her shoulders moved. "Jealous . . ." she grunted harshly around the tongue that threatened to choke her. "Insane . . . jealous . . ." Her own words took an eternity to seep towards Caroline, blending with the erratic bursts of air from the partially open windows and coming back in shards to buffet her. Caroline butted the cigarette and immediately fished out another. Striking her lighter she held it steadily against the tube, her dark eyes measuring over its flame. "Only a trad . . . tradition." Jessica put all her concentration into forming what she wanted to say. "Only sex thing. Expected."

"Is that what he told you, to get you up to the house tonight?" Caroline shook her head. The wisps of black hair moved softly against her face and one caught on the vivid scarlet of her lip. She brushed it away. "Clever little Petey. But the stories are true, Jessica. There is a demon at Rensby Hall. He looks after us and we . . ." She blew out a stream of smoke but her gaze never left Jessica. "We make him offerings."

Something in Jessica began to squirm and scream in disbelief and outrage. In fear also, for this young woman in her flagrantly aggressive clothes, her inflammatory boots and heavily made-up eyes was obviously mad. But Jessica was unable to do more than croak.

"You were right, Jess." Caroline flicked the cigarette into the empty fireplace and folded her arms. "I do have another lover besides dear old Scott, the best lover I ever had. He will be anyone I ask him. Any man that takes my fancy, on the street, in the movies, a friend of Peter's. I've even had sex with Sir Julian. How's that for variety?" She smiled slowly. "That night at dinner when I asked you what Michael was like — I was intrigued. So my lover became your husband for me. Every habit, every word murmured, every gesture, was Michael in bed. I've run my fingers through his gorgeous thick hair. I've had all those glorious muscles — he had a wonderfully fit body, didn't he? — lying on me. It was quite an experience. I was thirteen years old when my lover first came to me. I was hooked. No mere man can even come close to giving me the pleasure he does. And for my father he's the guaranteed continuation of our fortunes, as well as every little girl he wants to fondle. He gives my mother youth for as long as she wants it, and you can bet she wants it until well after my father kicks off. Of course he's not a man. He's the Rensbys' luck, the Rensbys' protector. Rensbys don't know how to get along in the world, Jess. They haven't since Julian's time. Every generation gives a victim in exchange for the privilege of that protection. You're Peter's sacrifice tonight."

Jessica tried to stand but her muscles remained flaccid, useless. Oh Peter, hurry and come back to me! she shouted silently. Caroline is dangerous and I'm scared.

"Naturally you think I'm insane," Caroline said flatly, getting up. "What's insane is that I've decided to help you get out of this mess. Why I'm not sure. I think partly because I've begun to realize what a genuinely creative artist I might have been if I'd been allowed to grow up uncursed. I'm going to tell them that I took you out for a drive and you seemed very nervous and then you made a dash for it and I lost you. Pretty weak, but they won't be able to prove otherwise. I hope not, anyway, because if I'm found out he'll punish me. What Petey will do when he can't fulfill his obligation tonight I've no idea. Take someone off the street, I suppose. It's been done before. Don't try to get up." She gave Jessica a gentle push. "I'll be back in a moment."

She stepped out of Jessica's line of sight. There's an audience out there somewhere, Jessica thought painfully, idiotically, waiting for the rest of the dialogue, waiting for the curtain to come down so that they can go to supper in noisy, candle-lit restaurants and discuss our performance. They will go home or to hotel rooms or to hidden corners in parks where they will kiss and murmur to each other, and in the delight of their warm flesh they will forget about us entirely. But once the curtain swishes closed and the stage lights are shut off I will still be sitting here in the dark, waiting . . . waiting . . . for an insane woman to come down the stairs. The wind swooped around her. The greyness of the sky had invaded the room and was pressing in upon her. She could hardly breathe.

Caroline materialized in front of her. She was rifling through her purse. "I'm taking most of your traveller's cheques," that tantalizingly slow voice was saying. Caroline's face, as she bent towards Jessica, was elongated, hideous. "I'll send them to you later. I've left a bit for taxi fare when you get off the plane but not enough to get back here with. Your ticket's in your purse. It's safe. My mother stole it when she was here yesterday morning, you know. Now come on."

Jessica felt herself lifted. She did not want to go anywhere. Looking down made her afraid, for the carpet was many miles below her. She watched her feet stumble across the floor. A strong arm was around her, under her shoulders. "Petey's got the cottage keys, in case you didn't notice," the voice went on. Jessica recoiled as a great blast of air struck her. "You really are pathetically trusting, Jessica." Jessica stumbled down the path. There was a moment of utter confusion, then she found herself facing the dashboard of a car. "I have to get your suitcase," Caroline said. "Thank God the weather's turned so foul and no one's about." Jessica fumbled with the door handle but somehow her fingers would not fasten themselves onto the metal. She was still pawing ineffectually at it when Caroline climbed in beside her, started the motor, and pulled away from the kerb. Peter! Jessica screamed soundlessly. Caroline sighed. "So far so good," she muttered. "Sit tight, Jess, and pray you've seen the last of Rensby's Rill."

Jessica remembered little of the long journey. Time seemed to have stopped. She stared at the dashboard, vaguely aware that rain was now being flung against the windshield and the wipers had been turned on. Their regular motion was hypnotic. A flow of chaotic, half-conceived thoughts drifted through her mind under the constant drone in her blood and she made no attempt to understand or halt it. Sometimes she thought she slept. The car purred. Air from the vents stirred her hair, laying it over her throat where it caught in the necklet, but when she wanted to brush it away she realized lazily that it would take all of eternity to raise her hand and did not bother to try. Consciousness washed and receded.

Caroline spoke twice during the endless afternoon. Once she said, "Ron and Tillie are not involved. No one but the family ever is. They left this morning for a long weekend at the coast. Father and Peter would have dug your grave in the arbour, under the paving with the remains of all the others over the centuries. Except Jane."

The words entered Jessica and fled along an echoing tunnel to be lost in confusion.

The second time, she had slowed to pass through a small town. Beyond the blur of the rain-streaked glass Jessica saw the inhabitants of the streets as faceless, hunched creatures without sentience of their own, moved by the power of the storm. "They were truly sorry about Jane," Caroline said. "They told me so. They liked her and never intended to do her any harm. They really wanted Billy, the idiot child always drooling in the village streets. No one would have missed him, least of all his long-suffering mother. But at the last moment they discovered that she'd taken him away for a holiday. Jane was in the wrong place at the wrong time. That's also why her body was walled up in the niche that had held Lady Elizabeth. Father knew there'd be a serious investigation when Jane went missing — a far more thorough one than if Billy had dropped off the face of the earth." Jessica heard the indicator flick on. The ticking was loud and she flinched. Caroline glanced at her. "Coming out of it a bit?" she said. "Good. They wouldn't have needed anyone at all if Father hadn't gotten himself into a financial mess with disastrous investments. We were about to lose everything, our holdings, the estate, everything. We needed help, but for that he demanded more blood. Today it was to be your turn. Your mother's letter to my mother, full of how depressed you were and how your husband's death was affecting you, was like a gift from Hell. The timing couldn't have been more perfect." The car picked up speed again and Jessica's head lolled back. "If you'd disappeared, everyone would have presumed you'd gone off and killed yourself. All neat and tidy." She reached across and turned on the radio. Loud rock music blared suddenly, assaulting Jessica's brain, beating it into life. The hum that had been constantly lulling her began to break up like static. Jessica moaned and struggled. "Time to wake up," Caroline ordered. "We're almost there."

A few minutes later she brought the car to a stop and got out, and presently Jessica's door opened and she felt herself pulled out of the cocoon where she had rested quite comfortably. She protested weakly, groaning as fresh air buffeted her, but found she could stand. Her movements were almost coordinated but her mind remained undisciplined. Caroline hefted her suitcase out of the rear of the car and supported her hesitant steps through doors that opened of their own accord. A blast of noise and activity crashed down on her and she gave a cry, wanting to turn and bury herself in Caroline's arms, but Caroline was propelling her towards a seat and easing her into it. Her suitcase was placed on the ground beside her.

Caroline took her chin, forcing her head up. "It's four in the afternoon and I can just make it back in time for the ceremony," she said carefully, deliberately. "Sit here for as long as you like, but when you're feeling stronger I suggest you lose yourself in the building just in case someone comes after you. Even if Peter manages to find another victim, he may worry that you suspect too much. You're in the terminal you want for the airline on your ticket. Stay here until your flight leaves on Sunday. It won't kill you to starve for a day and sleep sitting up for a couple of nights. God, what a nuisance you've been, Jessica Carter!" Her fingers found the nape of Jessica's neck and she undid the ruby necklet and slipped it into the pocket of her fiery red shirt.

"No!" Jessica mumbled, her heart palpitating, the agitation in her brain so great that she thought it would burst. Caroline ignored her outstretched, shaking hand.

"I'll leave you with the fascinating story of the Rensbys' secret lives," she finished. "I don't care what you do with the information. Nobody'd believe you anyway. Goodbye, Jessica. It's been a slice. Remember that in spite of your rather arrogant contempt for me, I've saved your life."

Jessica tried to reply but was unable to push any words past her now diminishing tongue. She watched Caroline stride to the doors, an upright, confident figure in her tight pants and clicking, high-heeled boots. She did not turn. The last Jessica saw of her was a splash of scarlet silk rapidly lost in the press of people trundling into the terminal.

For a long time Jessica sat motionless, her purse clutched in both hands against her thighs, trying to assimilate the cacophony around her. Colours still merged with sounds,

odours with the feel of the hard chair beneath her. The pub-
lic-address system blared incomprehensibly. People hurried in
and out of her vision. But gradually her surroundings began to
be sorted out in her mind. The crowd shrank, slowed, became
individuals bent on their own business. Sounds achieved sep-
arate coherence. A woman sat down beside her with a tired
sigh, lit a cigarette, and opened a magazine with a rustle.
Jessica's head began to ache. Her feet were chilly, and shivers
attacked her spine. She told her leg to move and it did, clumsily but obediently. There was a slight gap between herself
and everything going on around her, as though she held a
telephone receiver to her ear but could not communicate
because of a satellite delay. Those few seconds put her a tiny
fraction beyond reality and the experience of dislocation was
distressing. She sat on, breathing harshly, until her senses and
her perception ceased to be distorted, then she looked at her
watch. It was not on her wrist. Slowly, feeling as if each
movement was entirely new to her, she dragged her suitcase
to her feet and opened it. Caroline had flung all her belongings in haphazardly but the watch was there, entangled in her
lingerie. She was not able, yet, to perform the precise task of
strapping it to her wrist but she closed the suitcase and then
consulted it. The time was five o'clock.

I've got to get back to the Rill, she thought desperately.
Peter will be expecting me, he won't understand, if I'm not
there for the ceremony he'll end up making love to someone
else and I couldn't bear it! Caroline will tell him that I've run
away. He'll be so hurt, so puzzled and angry. I've got to warn
him that his sister's completely insane, perhaps dangerous as
well, oh what can I do? She's always been an autocrat, a law
unto herself, strong and willful, but now all that force has
become a kind of delusional omnipotence and it's focused on
the demon story. Her lover is probably just some village man.
Poor Caroline. But what if she tries to do someone some real
harm tonight? Act out the fantasy? There's no point in phoning Peter. By the time he gets here to pick me up the ceremo-

ny will be over. But no. Surely if it's only him and me he could postpone it. But would he believe me if I told him Caroline had drugged and kidnapped me? Wouldn't he just think that I'd got cold feet and deserted him? I couldn't convince him over the phone. I must let him see my face, plead the truth to him in person. A phone call will just waste precious time. How can I do that?

She went through her purse. The ticket was there, and some loose change, but all but one of her traveller's cheques were missing. Caroline had not lied about that. With an exclamation of frustration she closed her eyes against the now violent pounding in her head and tried to think logically.

Alix.

Jessica's eyes flew open. Alix Trent. What was it she had said? "I'll be available any time but Friday afternoon. I've got to run a few errands in London and I'm getting my hair done at Snippets, but I should be back late in the evening if you feel like a nightcap."

Snippets. Jessica stood. Her legs felt rubbery but they held her upright. Unsteadily she made her way to the bank of telephones to the left of the main doors. The London Directory was piled under them like the volumes of an encyclopaedia. It took her a long time to find the heading she wanted and she endured bouts of nausea that she did her best to ignore. "Snippets" was in heavy black print, and six salons were listed. Jessica piled her coins on the appropriate page and began to feed the machine.

She found Alix on the fourth try, and at the sound of the woman's voice as she said, "Hullo, Alix here," Jessica went limp with relief.

"Alix, it's Jessica," she breathed. "I need a big favour. I'm at Heathrow and I simply must get back to the Rill as quickly as possible. Could you possibly come and pick me up?"

"What on earth are you doing there?" Alix asked, bewilderment evident in her tone. "I thought you'd decided to stay until Sunday."

"It's a long story and a crazy one," Jessica answered. "I'll tell you all about it later. Can you come?"

"Of course," was the immediate response, and Jessica silently blessed Alix's generosity and her common sense. "What terminal are you at?" Jessica told her. "It'll take me a full hour to get there," Alix said. "Have tea or something, but do be outside so I don't have to park. OK? And don't fret. I've no idea what's going on but I'm dying to find out. See you soon." She rang off and Jessica put her forehead against the receiver and exhaled gustily. Everything was going to be all right.

She had enough change left to buy a cup of tepid coffee and a rather stale bun, and felt better as soon as she had forced down the unappetizing snack. Then she sat rigidly in the chair where Caroline had deposited her, her eyes on the doors, determined not to give in to the urge to look at her watch every few moments. She thought of the things Caroline had told her, horrible, impossible things, the product of a diseased mind. She knew she should feel sorry for the girl, but her only emotion when she considered what Caroline had said to her, what she had done to her, was rage.

At six-fifteen she walked through the doors and stood anxiously looking about. The rain had stopped but what she could see of the sky was still sullen, obscuring any hint of the position of the sun. The city air was thick and moist. She did not know whether she was warm or cold. The drug Caroline had put into her body was leaching out. Her headache had lessened and she felt more alert.

At last she saw Alix's familiar face behind the windshield of a small red car that was pulling in to the kerb. She was peering at the crowds and frowning. Jessica waved and ran towards her, and before the car had come to a halt she was inside, laughing with a sense of total reprieve, slamming the door and turning to Alix as she picked up speed. "Thank you!" she said. Alix smiled, her eyes on the traffic. Her hair had been waved and lifted from her brow to fall in studied elegance over her shoulders.

"I'm a nervous driver," she responded. "Don't talk to me until we're out of this rat race."

"I love your hair," Jessica said happily, and lapsed into silence.

It was another hour before the city was left behind and the parade of cars became a spasmodic trickle. Then Alix wriggled in her seat and relaxed. "Now," she commanded. "Tell me everything."

Jessica did so, beginning with Caroline's visit that morning, privately marvelling, as she spoke, that it had all taken place in the space of less than twelve hours. It seemed as though Caroline had knocked on the cottage door eons ago. Alix listened without interruption, her eyes on the road. She was driving fast and well. She did not react by so much as a twitch of the eyebrow to anything Jessica said, and Jessica was reminded that Alix was a priest's wife, accustomed to hearing the whispered miseries of her husband's parishioners.

When Jessica had finished speaking there was a hiatus during which Alix pulled down the visor against the now westering sun. She seemed to be considering the things she had heard. Finally she said, "It's all a pile of nasty nonsense of course. I always thought Caroline was a bit unstable. But to treat you like that, spin such tales . . ." She shrugged. "You're going to have a hard job convincing the other Rensbys that the girl is nuts."

"I don't even want to try but I suppose I'll have to. Alix," she hesitated and then went on. "Ben seemed to feel that there might be more to the demon story than history recorded . . ." Alix cut her off.

"Ben's business is religion. Everything must have a spiritual foundation as far as he's concerned. You and I both know that the whole thing is the fabrication of a sick mind stimulated by a silly legend. And speaking of Ben, do you mind if I take five minutes to call him? I usually let him know when I've left London and I'm out of danger!" She chuckled. "He worries about my driving."

"I've no idea why," Jessica put in. "You do very well."

Alix pulled off the road onto a grass verge, turned off the motor, and removed the key before walking to the lighted phone booth across the way. Jessica watched her contentedly. They were already in deep country, and nothing could be heard but the ticking of the engine as it began to cool and the secretive rustling of invisible creatures in the hedgerow beside the car. The road ahead was narrow, winding and then abruptly falling away towards the smudge of a distant forest, its silhouette now darkening against the sunset. Alix was pushing her money into the slot now, and soon Jessica could see her mouth moving as she talked to Ben. She did not look pleased. Her face was drawn and she appeared to be angry. She hung up and got back in the car.

"Is everything all right?" Jessica asked. Alix put the key in the ignition and smiled at her.

"Oh yes, everything's fine," she said offhandedly. "Did I look upset? I was a bit late calling in and Ben was in a tizzy. Sometimes I get just a bit annoyed when he's over-anxious. But he does love me, poor lamb." They shot away from the verge and Alix turned on the lights. "You're anxious too, and I'm not surprised," she went on fervently. "You won't rest until all this is sorted out. Tell me about you and Peter. I must say I was a bit bowled over at the idea of you involved romantically with a Rensby. Are you sure it's what you want?"

The evening slipped away as they drove. Jessica spoke of her love for Peter and the strange turn her life was taking. Under Alix's encouragement she also spoke of Sir Matthew, the recently revealed trauma of her childhood, the freedom, now, to put Michael's death behind her and start again. By the time she had finished speaking it had been fully dark for over an hour. Alix was a good listener, sympathetic and sensitive, and had many positive things to say.

They were speeding along an anonymous road, a small capsule of warmth and companionship in a blackly empty landscape, when the motor began to cough. Alix bit her lip. "Damn!" she said. "I told Ben that the old rustbucket needed attention! Now what? I don't suppose you know anything about the insides of engines, do you?" Jessica shook her head. Anxiety and impatience filled her. Alix brought the car to a stop. "I don't know much either," she remarked, "but I might as well take a look. There are a few old magazines on the back seat. Put on the interior light and amuse yourself. I'll try not to be too long." She pulled the hood release and got out, taking the keys with her. Sighing, Jessica put her head back and tried to relax. No effects of Caroline's pernicious drug remained but a feeling of being physically exhausted, and she did not think she could summon up the energy or the tranquillity to read. Alix was bent under the hood somewhere, invisible. Jessica closed her eyes.

The minutes crawled by. Jessica was too mentally agonized to rest. He'll start without me, she thought. He and someone else, Pamela, was that her name? She's probably arrived at the Hall by now, all agog for the big moment. What fun. Jessica did not dare to consult her watch. Oh come on, Alix! she commanded silently. If the car won't go we'll have to walk to the nearest house and call for help. She waited for what seemed like another eternity and was about to get out and see for herself what was going on when Alix opened the driver's door and climbed in. She inserted the key. "Now!" she said. "Let's see if my fiddling has done any good!" Jessica crossed her fingers. The car started without protest and they grinned at each other in relief. Alix eased back onto the road.

But it was very late by the time the car slowed and Jessica saw the familiar lych-gate and the dark bulk of the Rill's church on her right. She was surprised.

"We're coming into the Rill from the north end!" she commented. "Why aren't we driving through the village?"

"I took a short cut," Alix explained as she turned up the road that led past the abbey ruins and slowed even further to glide through the Hall gates. Jessica saw the new moonlight gleam briefly on their black ironwork before the car crunched on the gravel of the drive and came to a halt in front of the porch and the gloomy outline of the door beyond. At that moment Jessica gave a cry.

"Alix, I forgot my suitcase!" she said. "It's still sitting beside that chair at Heathrow!" Alix was getting out of the car.

"I wouldn't worry about it," her voice floated to Jessica as she too scrambled onto the drive. "I imagine that Peter will be only too happy to give you anything you might need."

The great park was hushed and dark, the trees standing mournfully in pools of deep shadow, the ground around them a dim ocean of nothingness. Something was hunched under the oak tree, a form she could not recognize for the drab mist, and she had no time to wonder at it. The house itself, as Jessica approached, seemed blindly hostile, a lightless, brooding hulk of stone that loomed over her so that a sudden apprehension made her falter. "It's all over," she whispered.

Alix urged her forward, a hand to her back. With the other she knocked confidently on the door. Jessica could have sworn that she heard the sound go rolling ponderously through the unseen hall on the other side. An urge to flee gripped her, a foolish, quixotic impulse to turn and run into the beckoning, sheltering night, but even as her muscles tensed the door swung open. Peter stood there. Though the porch was dark, his face showed very pale. His eyes glittered. A drop of some dark liquid was trapped in the corner of his mouth.

"Hello, Alix," he said huskily, and Jessica saw that his teeth were stained with the same ominous sheen. "They tell me you've had an eventful drive back from London. They said you phoned. And hello to you, Jess. Been on quite the wild-goose chase, haven't you?" He seemed dazed, his speech and actions strangely mechanical. Behind him in the dimness of the hall Jessica caught a glimpse of Sir Matthew's florid face and Caroline's red shirt. Peter took her arm. "Caro's been punished," he went on in that frighteningly unfamiliar tone, "and everything's fine. I'm going to look after you." He smiled slowly at Alix. "Thanks, Sis," he said through those grimed teeth. "Better run along to hubby now before he calls out the cavalry."

There was something terribly wrong. With a convulsive wrench Jessica tried to pull herself away from his grip but his fingers tightened remorselessly.

Alix leaned close. Her lips brushed Jessica's ear, and all at once the air was full of a familiar odour, acrid and musky, as she spoke. "I think I forgot to tell you," she whispered, "that my full name is Alissandra, and I'm a Rensby too."

Chapter 13

Caroline drove back to the Rill with her foot to the floor. She handled the car with confidence and loved speed and besides, as she often told herself, it didn't matter if she smashed herself up. Her lover would make sure she sustained no permanent damage. She had driven drunk, driven stoned, and sometimes in moods of savage fatalism had driven with total recklessness in a deliberate attempt to test the validity of the bizarre contract under which she and her family lived.

But today she drove blindly, aware of the need for haste but more concerned with the furious activity of her mind. She still did not know what had prompted her to play God, to lift Jessica Carter Mortimer out of her death cell and drop her once more into the mainstream of ordinary life. "It's your turn to babysit this morning," Peter had told her, his head appearing round her bedroom door before she was even awake. "I've done my bit. I'm going out with Father and the dogs." He had made a face. "This is his last chance to drown me in fatherly advice. Silly old codger! I'll take over from you later this afternoon. Thanks, Caro." He had slammed her door without waiting for a reply and she had struggled to a sitting position and fumbled for her cigarettes, lighting one and staring blankly into the curtained dimness while consciousness slowly returned. Her dreams had been sombre, full of a kind of melancholy she refused to succumb to in real life. They often were after she and her lover had exhausted themselves with sex for the better part of the night. No, not him, she corrected herself, inhaling the smoke deeply while the details of her sanctum swam into focus. He's never exhausted. In all the years he's been coming at my summons he's never been the one to beg off. He likes the sex, I know. He gets off on the triumph, the power that comes from rubbing my nose in the filth of it and seeing me enjoy it. He crows over my insatiability, throwing fuel on the fire that never dies, sometimes making me plead but not able to refuse me in the end because he's bound by the agreement that's been sealed in blood. I see him naked, the sweat pouring off him, those black, black eyes burning with the greed of possession, those teeth, like freshly bleached bones, bared in anticipation. But there is never tenderness. Of course not. There is no love in Hell, no loyalty, only hate and an endless, devouring thirst for acquisition. I am a specimen to him and his great lust is fed by his loathing. But I don't care. I am an addict of orgasms, hooked on sensations that only he can supply. The human men I've slept with have been like fumbling, inept little boys in comparison. In the early days he used to come to me as a shy teenager with a slightly sullied beauty and simple but knowing hands, teaching me, drawing me on, magnifying that small core of pure sensuality I had been born with until it began to fill my days and rule my nights. By the time Father told me who he really was, I was already lost. Father chose his moment well. What would have happened if I had refused his earliest attentions? Turned my back on the invitation? Well it's too late now. Years too late.

She had dragged herself out of bed, washed and dressed, in a sulky silence. The day had matched her temperament. It was heavily overcast and windy. Shoving the pins into her hair she had been furious with prissy Mrs Mortimer, that paragon of widowed virtue who nevertheless gave off a whiff of latent sensuality that had intrigued Caroline. I warned the silly woman, Caroline had thought as she painted her eyes and reddened her mouth. I told her to take her purse and run, but she ignored me. Peter put stars in those big eyes of hers, the stupid, naïve bitch. But under the angry thoughts was the stirring of a fear that had been troubling her for a long time. I have to watch her die, the fear whispered. I have to drink her blood. I have to forget her words over the last few days, her smile, her bravery in facing up to dear, dissolute Daddy, her hopes for a future that does not exist although she doesn't know it. I have to put her humanity out of my mind and begin to see her as fodder, as a faceless means to a vital end. You like what you've got, don't you, Caro darling? she had asked herself as she went downstairs. You like your demon lover, your life of total irresponsibility, your black womb in which you can experience anything you wish without fear of the consequences. Then you must be prepared to pay for it once, just this once. You can do it. All it's going to take is a strong stomach and an attitude of complete mercilessness. Right in character, Caro sweetie. Right up your street.

She had grabbed up the remains of a box of croissants and some butter and honey from the kitchen, already in a mess since Tillie and Ron had left earlier for their weekend at the seaside, but on the way to the front door she had paused. Her mother was on the phone in the sitting room. Caroline could hear her voice, preoccupied and hurried, and guessed she was talking to the caterer or the florist or the owner of the wine shop about tomorrow. Big party, Caroline thought. Petey preening in his tux, Mother looking impossibly sexy for once because I know she'll shed the dowdy old-lady image on her precious son's twenty-first, Father huffing and beaming and playing the gracious host. Flowers everywhere and mounds of glistening caviar and champagne flowing like baby's pee and later the dancing, the heat, the drunken laughter, all because Jessica Carter Mortimer is going to die tonight.

The hall was empty and dim. Caroline turned and ran back up the stairs. Entering her parents' bedroom she went straight to her mother's bedside table, fished the key out from under the ledge in the headboard of the bed where her mother kept it, and unlocked the drawer. Her mother's collection of virulent herbs and no less dangerous modern chemicals was packed into the space. Caroline knew them all. Over the years she had sampled most of them. Choosing the most innocuous soporific she pocketed it, closed and relocked the drawer, replaced the key, then contemplated her mother's purse which lay on the bed. She knew that Eleanor had taken Jessica's plane ticket out of the young woman's purse the day before as a form of insurance in case Jessica decided to do a midnight flit. Having her in the cottage was a distinct nuisance for everyone, and Eleanor had complained bitterly that Jessica should have been drugged and kept under constraint in the Hall until Friday night. But Peter, intoxicated with the games he was playing, resisted. And as usual he got his own way. I'll leave all my options open, Caroline had thought, quickly rifling the purse and withdrawing the ticket. I'll play this entirely by ear. This is my own game, my secret amusement. The hall was still deserted as she crossed it again, and she let herself out into the sullen morning.

She had still not decided what to do when she knocked on the cottage door to be confronted by Jessica's disappointed face. Even when standing in that cramped kitchen setting out the croissants, pouring coffee, watching in amazement while her own hand took out the little bottle and dumped its contents into one of the mugs, she did not know what she would do. But by the time she was biting into the food, taking the measure of that rather impassive oval face opposite her with its glorious but antagonistic eyes, she felt herself set upon a certain path. My game, she thought caustically, and mine alone. Power to let you die or give you life. What a rush! Yet under the deliberately cynical thought was a strange mixture of jealousy and pity and of course the fear, though she scorned herself for allowing it to exist.

It had all been so easy. And in a curious way she was released from the jealousy and the fear as she told the woman who now sat glassy-eyed and motionless the whole truth about her precious Peter and the rest of them. She did not expect to be believed. Jessica Carter was gullible, yes, but only in certain ways. It did not matter. The pity remained. Getting the semi-comatose girl into the car, driving her to the airport, it was all an anticlimax, and she turned and walked away from the delicate little figure in the terminal building without a backward glance.

But now . . . Caroline lit yet another cigarette as she raced on through the gathering duskiness of evening. Now the ball was in Petey's court. What would he do? She sighed and turned on the radio.

It was just after eight o'clock when she parked her car beside the Ferrari and got out, stretching and yawning. The sky was prematurely dark and the park was already gathering its shadows into itself. She was crossing to the front door when it was flung open and Peter came rushing out.

"Where the hell have you been?" he shouted. "Where is she? Where is she?"

Caroline regarded him critically. He was flushed and his eyes were darkly circled. "She's gone," she said flatly. "I did my best, Pete. She was very restless this morning and she got angry when I tried to stop her from calling her mother. Then she accused us of taking turns to watch her, which of course was true. She went upstairs and packed her things and came down with her suitcase and said she'd rather find herself somewhere else to stay. I think she'd been putting two and two together and something clicked with her." She shrugged and folded her arms. "I persuaded her to get in the car. I thought I'd drive her around a bit, let her talk, try and reassure her. But she jumped out in Clapton and disappeared. I've spent the whole day trying to find her." His gaze moved to the interior of the car.

"Where's her stuff?" he barked.

Damn, Caroline thought. Oh damnation. "I got rid of it," she said evenly.

He stared at her. "You stupid bitch, I thought you had brains!" he yelled, then he slapped her hard across the mouth. Her head whipped round with the force of the blow and she swayed, but quick as light her own hand came out and connected with his cheek. "Don't you ever do that again," she snarled, and began to walk away, but he shouted after her, "You'll have to find me somebody else, Caroline, and you don't have much time! It's all got to be over by midnight!" She heard the panic in his voice but kept on walking.

"I need a drink," she said.

He came running into the house behind her, calling for his father, but she did not pause. Once inside her own room she drew the drapes, fetched a bottle and glass, and collapsed into the chair by the bed. The Scotch was good, smooth and bitter and comforting as the touch of an old sweater. She took a gulp, then pulled off her boots and held the glass to her cheek. Why did you do it, Caro baby? she asked herself, her gaze slowly travelling the mirrors and her sketches that adorned the walls. Didn't think it through, did you? What happens now? Am I really supposed to provide another blood-filled lamb to be slaughtered? Peter will be telling Father and Mother my story and before long one of them will come hurrying up the stairs to let me know. None of us are very big on consequences, are we? You don't learn about consequences when something else takes away your responsibility. She sipped the Scotch reflectively and examined her emotions. There weren't any. The only responsibility a

Rensby has is to bring the victim to the knife on time, she thought with a humour she suspected was a little hysterical, and I've buggered up the one lesson in action-and-consequence I might have learned. Or have I? Must I make things right?

From where she sat she could see herself reproduced in the mirrors several times. The light from the bedside lamp fell softly on the loose tendrils of tousled black hair lying against the strong column of her neck. She studied her own ivory complexion, her full, ripe mouth slightly swollen now where Peter had struck her, the set of her broad shoulders under the shimmering red of the silk shirt. "Well who is it for?" she asked aloud, her reflections mimicking her silently. Not for dear, amiable Scott, who loved her but wouldn't even notice if she shaved her head and wore a sack. Not for her fellow students who were consumed with the single-minded desire to make it, whatever "it" was, and who at this time in their lives could not be concerned with the all-encompassing intricacies of a grand passion. And not for him, the master of her body, who could never do more than don the masks she demanded and pretend an involvement no matter how fully he controlled her responses. "I want love," she said to her listening selves, but she did not know what it was she was asking, and she fell silent, slopping more Scotch into her glass and saluting herself before tipping it down her throat.

There was a knock on her door that she did not answer, and presently Peter came in, closing the door carefully behind him and taking the other chair. He crossed his legs and regarded her quietly for a moment, then he ran his hand through his unruly hair.

"I'm sorry I hit you, Caro," he said with a rueful smile, and she shook a cigarette out of the battered pack beside her on the night table and lit it with an impudent gesture before blowing smoke in his direction.

"No you're not," she replied. "Don't try your bullshit charm on me, Petey. I know you too well. I'm not the least bit sorry I slapped you either. Let's call it quits. Want a drink?"

The smile had left his face. He shook his head. "Not really my thing," he said. "Look, Caro, I've been talking to Mother and Father. Things are a bit desperate, you know. Father seems to think that because you lost Jessica it's up to you to find me a replacement."

"Does he indeed?" She cocked an eyebrow. "Then why doesn't he come and tell me himself? He never could face me down, could he? I'm stronger than the lot of you, and he knows it. I'm the only true Rensby left. Even you, Peter darling, even you wilt and panic and rely on your boyish magnetism to hide the fact that you've got nothing behind those appealing eyes of yours but mush." Suddenly she wanted to grind out her cigarette against his pale cheek, pick up her boot and jab its sharp heel into his mouth. The violence of the images shocked her but she recognized the disappointment behind them, the realization of her own loneliness. In the end he would let her down. He always had. He looked pained.

"You can save your vicious tongue for your favourite whipping boy," he protested. "Scott loves it when you attack him. It reminds him that he's alive. Father won't come and speak to you because he says it's my job to sort out the mess. I'm the one that's taking over."

"So take over," she said indifferently. "What is your lordship going to do?"

A hard, sly expression flitted across his face. "I'm going to order you out into the night, Caroline. You're going to find me a replacement for Jessica. If you fail I'm going to cut your throat."

She burst out laughing. "Sweet Petey!" she exclaimed. "You can't even watch the blood run out of your steak without blenching! You're putting me on!"

He did not move. He went on staring at her. "There's too much riding on tonight to even think of backing out," he said coldly. "You treat me lightly, Caro, and I'm tired of it. I

know I have an aversion to the sight of blood. A lot of perfectly estimable people share my distaste. But I will go
through with the ceremony even if I have to drink the cellar
dry or empty Mother's drug stash to do it. I'm deadly serious.
Get me a sacrifice or be one yourself."

"And who's going to make me?" she sneered over the lip
of her glass. "You? Do you think you've got the guts to grab
me and hold me and tie me down and after all that, put a
knife to my throat? Knowing that in spite of everything we've
been close? Will you be able to look into my eyes, Peter?
What will the memory be like for you, I wonder? Remembering will take guts too."

He did not reply. He sat there apparently relaxed, his
hands hanging over the arms of the chair, his legs still comfortably crossed. His expression did not change but behind his
eyes Caroline saw something familiar, a glint of triumph she
had often glimpsed on another face. Her heart contracted.

"Yes we've been close," he said at last, "and I'll miss you,
Sis. But I won't have to exert myself much. Father will grab
you and hold you and tie you down." He leaned forward and
slapped the arms of the chair in a swift, exasperated gesture.
"Oh for God's sake, Caroline, you don't want to give up what
you've got any more than the rest of us! Get out there and
pick up some befuddled old rummy! What does it matter? It'll
be child's play for you! And hurry up. Time's slipping by."

Now she saw the anxiety beneath the forced calm of his
previous words. He'd kill me if he knew I'd let Jessica go on
purpose, she thought, then laughed aloud at the foolish irony
of the words. She dragged her boots towards her and pulled
them on, took another swig, this time straight from the bottle, and stood. He rose with her. "All right," she said. "I'll go.
To hell with you all." He followed her to the door. If you
thank me I'll turn and knock you to the floor, she thought,
but he said nothing, only closing the door softly behind them.

Before she reached her car her hair and face were misted
with the fine drizzle that had begun to fall. She had not both-

ered to turn on the outside light and she stood for a moment fumbling for her keys and wishing she had brought the bottle with her. She had a large tolerance for alcohol but tonight she wanted to be good and drunk. Someone was watching her from the shadow of the porch, Peter probably, but she did not acknowledge his presence. Putting the car in gear she started down the drive. I should have talked to Father, she thought with exasperation. I can face him down if I want to. Peter should be doing his own dirty work. I shouldn't have meddled with their plans. I should have left Jessica to her fate and the whole thing would have been neat and clean and quickly over. You're an idiot, Caroline Rensby. The memory of the killing would have faded in time and anyway, who knows? Her plane might go down. She might get hit by a car next week. Her future is unknown. Mine isn't, nor Peter's. Nothing can touch us as long as he does his duty like all the first-born male Rensbys before him. My duty is to help him do it. Then why that moment of rebellion? Flouting social mores is one thing. I've always been good at that. But I've put the whole family in jeopardy, not to mention Peter's future children, almost without conscious consideration. Whose side am I on?

She had turned the car away from the village, to the narrow back roads that wound between Clapton and the Rill. No one will be out tonight, her thoughts ran on. Summer, but it might as well be autumn. The pubs will be full, though. Maybe I should cruise until closing time and pick up someone from one of the villages along the Clapton country route. Easy. I've had enough one-night stands that way in the old days. She grinned humourlessly to herself and unlatched the glove compartment, feeling for the cigarettes she kept there. The old days. You're so ancient, Caro. Quite the octogenarian! But her mind filled with a vision of Jessica, at least ten years older than she was but a babe in arms when all was said and done. The woman had always made Caroline feel worldweary. The jealousy was back. Caroline flicked her gold lighter and dragged angrily on her cigarette. To hell with you all, she thought. Away with the whole damn world.

As she had predicted, the roads were deserted, shining black in her headlights, the few straggling hedges and crowding woodland humping ghostly and sliding into nothingness behind her as she drove. I wish I could talk to Alissandra, she thought, but she went up to London today. Alix the oldest, the one I know least, shipped off to boarding school, like Peter, at five years of age, whereas I kicked and screamed and refused to go. Alix, whose adult photograph no longer appears on top of the grand piano because she is the Rensby watchdog, with her finger firmly on the pulse of both the village and the church. Alix would straighten it all out for me in that shrewd, quiet way of hers. Father had been almost speechless with rage when she came home from her digs in London and announced that she'd fallen for a priest. Rage, but fear too. He had threatened to command the beast who shared Caroline's bed to get rid of Ben, but Alix had calmly and with the cold rationality that had always been her underlying character, pointed out the advantages to such a union. Command the unspeakable one to make sure that Ben was posted to the Rill. That way she herself, Alix, could keep an eye on parish activities and also on the mood of those villagers who did not particularly care for the Rensby autocracy. Father had given in. Alix had gone through with a church wedding for Ben's sake. Poor gullible Ben, who knew his wife was a Rensby but believed that she was ashamed of her roots. He applauded what he saw as her courageous decision to keep a distance between them and herself, and as she had requested, he mentioned the connection to no one. If he wondered why she had wanted to return with him to the Rill he probably put it down to a desire for expiation through good works in the very place she most disliked.

Caroline believed privately that her sister's double life suited her temperament very well. She was profoundly and secretly committed to preserving the Rensby heritage but she was also addicted to the complexities of the duplicity. It gave her an almost sexual thrill. Alix the game player, Caroline mused, coasting through the wet, forlorn countryside. Alix, who was such an expert player that Ben's parishioners practically worshipped her and the malcontents had almost forgotten that she was a Rensby. Alix would give me a shake and tell me to get on with it, Caroline thought. She would remind me that blood is thicker than water, that I have a responsibility to Rensby history. She would pour tea down my throat while she gave me the sermon about what happened to the very few renegade Rensbys who were brave enough or stupid enough to try and break the covenant with Hell that good old Sir Julian made. Then she would usher me out the back door and run to kiss her husband as he came in the front. She had rather liked Jessica, Caroline knew. But not enough to have saved her life. Ironic, isn't it? Caroline asked herself. I'm not sure that I liked her at all, but I'm in this mess because I have saved her.

Her headlights, as she rounded a bend, picked up a moving shape so quickly that she braked and swerved with a curse. As she slowed to a halt the figure came running and peered in at her window. Through the spattering of raindrops she saw that it was a young man enveloped in a cape that was slick with water. His hair was plastered to his head but he was smiling. Caroline rolled down the window.

"You're mad to be thumbing on a night like this," she said. He passed a hand over his face.

"I know," he replied apologetically. "I'm trying to get to Danebury. A truck picked me up and was going to take me all the way but it broke down so I decided to move on. I don't suppose you're going in that direction?"

Caroline hesitated. I've had my moment of power, she thought clearly. I've done my bit for honesty and virtue and all that stuff. I may be a spoiled brat but I'm not a fool. "Actually I'm not," she said, and his face fell. "But I live quite close by and I've nothing much to do this evening. I like driving in the dark. If you're not in a hurry why don't you come home with me, have something to eat, dry off, and I'll take you wherever you want to go?" She was an old hand at making her eyes, her body, say the things her words did not, and she knew her own allure. He swallowed.

"If you're sure it's not too much trouble," he said eagerly. "I could do with a bite. I haven't eaten since breakfast." She nodded, waiting, and he hurried around the car and got in beside her. "I'm Michael," he smiled, holding out a damp hand, and Caroline repressed a shudder as she shook it.

"Caroline," she responded curtly, reversing the car until it was pointed back towards the Rill. She did not look at him, did not want to look at him. With both hands tight to the wheel she stared ahead. "Where are you from, Michael?"

"London." He was struggling out of his cape and Caroline saw, out of the corner of her eye, that he was dressed in faded jeans and a baggy sweater that had obviously seen better days. "I'm a student at the university there. Term's over, of course, but I have a summer job selling shoes close to my flat. It's very convenient." He produced a pack of cigarettes from the grubby knapsack that had been concealed by the cape and held it up. "May I smoke?"

"Yes, if you'll light me one."

He did so with a charming and clumsy alacrity. Caroline saw, as he passed her the cigarette, that his hands were slender. Now keep quiet, she ordered him silently. Stay a stranger, a ghost, without flesh, without reality. Don't talk to me.

"I have this weekend off," he went on conversationally. "My parents live in Danebury. I haven't seen much of them this year. But it's my mother's birthday tomorrow and I thought I'd surprise her by showing up. She'll be surprised all right! I deliberately didn't phone her to say I was coming."

Shut up, Caroline thought fiercely. Shut up! I don't want to hear about your mother's bloody birthday. I don't want to know what a wonderful son you are! She could feel him watching her, and in spite of herself she glanced at him.

He was not handsome, but there was a healthy openness about his face.

"You live around here?" he asked shyly. "What do you do?"

Her eyes returned to the road. "I'm a student in London, but not at the university. I'm home for the summer at the moment."

"It must be wonderful to be able to live at home for a while," he said without a trace of envy. "Danebury's only a market town and I wasn't able to get summer work there, otherwise I would've. I miss the country."

He was a lot like Scott, transparently honest and probably uncomplicated. Caroline found herself hating him. "The country's not so great," she snapped. "In fact, it's pretty boring."

Quickly he turned away, looking at the window, and she knew she had hurt his feelings. Oh God, she thought in desperation. Why couldn't you have been some groping old nobody who'd give me an excuse to do what I have to do? "I'm sorry," she said, against her better judgement. "I'm not renowned for my tact."

He turned back to her and his ready smile burst out. "Oh that's all right," he assured her. "Most people share your view. I'm afraid I'm hopelessly reactionary in lots of ways."

Caroline was suddenly assailed by such a host of conflicting emotions that her hands trembled violently on the wheel and her foot left the accelerator. She wanted to burst out into hysterical laughter. She wanted to scream and scream. "Are you all right?" he asked. For answer she brought the car to a shuddering halt. Reaching across him she jerked open the glove compartment and brought out her wallet. Lifting his hand she slapped the notes into his palm.

"We just drove through a village," she said harshly. "It's not much, a house or two and a pub, but you can get a room there for the night and the bus to Danebury will pass through tomorrow morning. You can walk back to it in five minutes.

Get out."

Bewilderedly he tried to push the money back at her. "I've offended you somehow," he said wretchedly. "I'm sorry."

To her horror Caroline realized that she was crying. It was something that had not happened to her in years and she loathed the feeling. "You haven't offended me at all," she choked. "Not at all. Believe me. Go on, Michael. Take the money, and when you're settled in the pub, go down to the bar and have a drink on me. Enjoy your mother's birthday."

Still confused, clutching the bundle of paper, he picked up his knapsack and backed out of the car. He began to thank her for the ride, but she pulled his door shut and sped away, wiping the tears from her cheeks with savage gestures. You're making a habit of this Good Samaritan stuff, Caro old girl, she told herself. You're becoming pathetic.

It occurred to her that she could just keep on driving. She had her wallet. She had credit cards. Why not get lost in London, fly to France, take a holiday and come back when it had all been decided one way or another? Because they'd punish me for certain, she told herself as she slowed to pass through the Rill. This way I have at least a small chance to talk myself out of trouble. If I run I've no chance at all. It would be waiting for me when I came back. She wondered, as she drew up in front of the house, when she had begun to think of her family as "they." Crushed by a sweeping sense of dread and loneliness she let herself quietly through the front door.

Only a small light on the wall beside the dining-room door was burning, its fragile halo soon dissipated by the pressing shadows of the hall. As she began to cross the floor one of the shadows moved and Peter emerged into the pallid glow. Before he could speak she took his arm. "I have to talk to you," she hissed, tugging him towards the dining room. He did not resist, but once she had eased the double doors closed behind them and switched on a light he shook himself free.

He was the colour of putty.

"You couldn't go through with it!" he said loudly, accusingly. "You've backed me damnably against the wall, Caroline. It's already ten. I've only got two hours!" He had crossed his arms and was running his hands up and down the sleeves of his shirt, clutching and kneading at the fabric. His teeth were chattering.

"Hush!" she said violently. "I don't want the others to know I'm back yet. Pull yourself together, Peter. It's not the end of the world!" She had gone around the table and was jerking open the buffet doors. Bringing up a decanter full of sherry and two glasses she set them down and poured, pushing one glass towards him and draining hers in one draught. She refilled it then slumped into a chair.

"How dare you patronize me!" he spat. "You're the one that let Jessica get away, not me! She'd have been perfect, the simpering little do-gooder! Only her mother would have missed her!"

"Her students might have missed her too," Caroline said softly. "She was a music teacher, remember, Peter? A quiet, anonymous music teacher, full of simple ideals. A romantic too. Do you know what it might feel like to be those things, Petey? Idealist? Romantic? I don't. I never have. How could we? Our lives have been perverse, corrupted, from the day we were born. Whole chunks of us went missing or were shrivelled up before they could flower. A romantic sees the world as beautiful, mysterious, compelling, even tragic, but never as bestial and cruel. An idealist strives above all for excellence in everything, even though excellence may be completely unattainable. And what about love?" She drew his untouched glass towards her and stared into the quivering golden liquid.

"What about it?" he queried. "I haven't a clue what you're driving at, Caro."

"I've never felt love," she went on. "Do you imagine for one moment that any Rensby since the time of Julian has? I've felt lust, attraction, mild affection that soon disgusted me by its very weakness. That's what I feel for Scott. Mild affection, and disdain. I've believed that I love you but I don't. Not really. The emotion I call love is simply manufactured out of habit, boredom, imitating others who love." She looked across at him where he stood glowering, his fingers still entwined in his shirt. "Oh I have powerful emotions all right. All of us have. But they're entirely selfish ones, aren't they, Petey? Do we love each other in this family? Don't make me laugh!" She pushed the glass away with a vicious thrust and it skidded over the highly polished surface of the table and came to rest, teetering, on the edge. "It came to me tonight," she went on equably, "that the closest I ever come to love is when I'm painting, when I'm taken entirely out of myself. My work is very good. It's warped, of course, but then so am I. So are we all. The beast has done that to us. The beast has taken my creative gift and turned it into shit and kept me in a prison of sexual highs I always thought was of my own choosing, but it wasn't." She got out of the chair and approached him. She felt exhausted and close to mental collapse. "What has it done to you, Petey sweetheart?" she asked acidly. "Think carefully."

He backed away from her. "Pull yourself together, Caro!" he snapped. "You're talking nonsense."

"Am I?" she breathed. "Look at us, Peter! We were prepared to murder another person without a qualm. Father's already a murderer twice over. You know what's lying behind the wall in the cellar! Can you imagine how Jane's body got there? The blood, the mess, stuffing it in the niche? The Rensbys stepped outside the bounds of decent humanity five hundred years ago and we're demons ourselves and don't know it!" His arms came out and he gripped her shoulders. His face was distorted.

"Well, Miss Lily-white Evangelist, what have you been sniffing or sucking on tonight? A few grains of conscience? You can't tell me that you're willing to give up what you get from our family benefactor in exchange for feeling better about yourself, because I know you, Caroline Rensby, and that's a crock! You're as greedy and addicted as the rest of us!"

"I know," she whispered. "I know. But it hit me tonight, Peter, that although we think we control him, we don't. He controls us. He's always controlled us, generation after generation. Rensby freedom has been an illusion." She grasped his wrists and put her forehead against his. "I can see that you're scared, Peter. So am I. I don't pretend to know what's happened to me. All I know is that you have a chance, tonight, to break the covenant and set us all free. You can do it. Don't you want to see your children grow up without this terrible burden? Please, Peter! Set us all free!"

"You don't know what you're asking!" he croaked. "The few Rensbys who've tried have all died young, and endured horrible deaths. One of them was murdered by his own ten-year-old son, remember? You've read the private archives. How can you even think such a thing?"

"Yes," she said, her voice little more than a sigh. "But they were foolish men, Peter. They tried and failed and went on living here. They should have known better. They should have burned the house to the ground and left the Rill forever. First the intent, then the attempt, then the final act. They balked at the final act, but you needn't. I'll help you. Will you try? Please?"

She felt the sweat break out on his skin. He was breathing heavily, in obvious doubt, and in her own anguish she thought there was a slim chance that something of what she had said had been heard. His hands left her shoulders and cupped her face. His lips parted. But in that moment she felt the door open and he immediately released her and stepped back. Eleanor was standing there and Matthew was behind her.

"So here you are, dear!" Eleanor exclaimed. "We thought we heard the car. What on earth are you doing in the dining room?"

"You screwed up, Caroline," her father boomed. "You

PAULINE GEDGE

were very careless. I hope you've brought another little something home for your brother."

Caroline looked at him squarely, at his choleric, grooved face, his loose mouth, his bright eyes set in their deceiving fans of laugh lines. You hate me, she thought. I've never realized that before. I should have. You began to hate me from the day I stuck the legs of my doll's chair into your fumbling hand, didn't you, Daddy darling? You know I've come back alone and you're glad. You want Peter to cut my throat now, don't you? The first scrabblings of panic seized her but she fought them down. Her gaze met her brother's. "I'll help you, Peter," she repeated slowly, deliberately. "We can do it together, I know we can." But try as she might, she could not hold his attention. He blinked, his own eyes dropped, then he turned to his father in mute appeal.

"What is it, Peter?" Sir Matthew said sharply, and the young man shrugged.

"I'm worried, that's all. I don't know what to do." Caroline sprang at him, shaking his arm.

"Yes you do!" she cried. "For God's sake, Peter, be a man for once! Listen to me! Trust me!"

"What are you up to, Caroline?" her father said suspiciously. "Trying to evade your responsibilities as usual?" He settled his shoulders under the shabby tweed jacket, and to Caroline there was something vastly threatening in the unconscious movement. Peter was still watching him beseechingly. "You know what has to be done," Matthew went on, his eyes steadily, coldly on his daughter but his words for his son. "Caroline is your only hope, now, to fulfil the contract. Caroline must take Jessica's place."

"No I can't! I can't kill Caro!" Peter wailed, the muscles of his arm rigid under her grip. "I want to break the agreement! I want us all to be happy!"

Eleanor cleared her throat. The sound was small, polite. "Caroline dear," she said. "Jessica's plane ticket is missing from my purse. I know I haven't touched it since I put it there yesterday. Do you know anything about it?"

Caroline looked her mother full in the face. "No I don't," she said calmly. "You're absent-minded sometimes, Mother. You probably put it somewhere else. Perhaps you even ripped it up. That's what you should have done anyway." She made herself remain still, a slight smile on her lips, but gradually she felt Peter relax and with an inner shrinking, a slow, freezing contraction that she felt in her bones, she knew she had lost. He shook himself free, and putting a hand under her chin, turned her to him. She dreaded what he might read in her eyes. He knew her better than anyone, as she knew him.

"Well, Caro baby," he murmured. "Been doing a bit of petty thieving in your spare time?" She could see no trace of the pain of his previous indecision in his expression. It was now bitter, mocking, but she thought she sensed a hint of disappointment behind it. In the split second before she acted, the alternatives flashed like fire across her mind. I could go on arguing innocence. No. Waste of time. Suggest Father as victim. Tempting but useless. Father, by performing his own initiation into bondage years ago, has guaranteed his own safety. Make up another lie. I took the ticket to use myself because I couldn't face the ceremony. Laughable. They know me too well.

She coiled and thrust, and Peter staggered back against the table. Eleanor gave a bleat and grabbed for her husband just as Caroline pushed him hard and he went down, landing heavily on one hip. Caroline did not pause. She fled across the gloomy hall, fingers flailing for the door. Somewhere in the house the phone began to ring, the shrill sound shocking her, and out of habit she almost swerved to answer it. Behind her she heard her father shout, "Get her, Peter!" and then she was out and the gravel was slippery under her feet.

He was already coming. By the time she reached the car he was out of the house. She could hear him panting, hear the driveway crunch. "Stay cool," she commanded herself under her breath. "Stay cool cool cool." She had not locked the car. Wrenching it open she fell inside. He was reaching for her. His fingertips grazed the glass of the window as she slammed the door. "Caro!" he was shouting, his voice muffled, his figure blurred by the raindrops. "Don't be a little fool! I'd never let him hurt you!" But she knew he was lying. Quickly, grimly, she thumbed the locks on all the doors. He was darting round, trying to get to each one before she did. Keys, she thought. Not in ignition. Pocket? They were in her pants. Gasping she eased them out, noting grimly how her hand shook as she tried to select the right one and insert it in the slot. He was beating on the car now, yelling incomprehensibly. Caroline started the motor, rammed the gear lever into first, and shoved her foot to the floor. The car shrieked. The rear end fishtailed. Teeth clenched she fought for control as the vehicle lurched forward and she headed it straight across the wide circle of grass in which the oak tree stood, ignoring the curve of the driveway.

But suddenly she was no longer alone in the car. The beast, her lover, was there beside her in the passenger seat, and he turned his dark, pale face towards her and said coarsely, "Not a chance, sweet Caroline. Not a chance in Hell."

She screamed, and at the same moment the car hit the tree with a screech of buckling metal. She was thrown forward and then back. In a daze she heard her door pop, and when she peered at it groggily she saw it bent and half-open. She looked beside her. The car was empty.

She sat there limply, trying to collect her wits, trying to overcome the shock and make her legs obey her, but it was too late. Peter's arm appeared, grasped the front of her shirt, and hauled her roughly onto the wet grass. As he did so something slipped from her pocket and became entangled round his thumb. He held it up and gave an abrupt exclamation. "Father was right!" he said. "You deliberately let her go, you selfish little bitch! I refused to believe him. I stood up for you after you'd slapped me and gone running up to your room. 'She's betrayed us,' he said, but I denied that you'd ever do such a thing. I made a fool out of myself on your behalf, Caro." He glanced down at her where she sat, her head on her knees. "You could have covered your tracks perfectly if you'd wanted to. Left the ticket and bought her another one. Left her bits and pieces in the cottage. Hidden the necklet. Why did you put it in your pocket, of all the stupid places?" She stirred and looked up.

"I knew you were going to give it to Pamela tomorrow when you announced your engagement at the party and you'd be angry if Jessica walked off with it. It cost a lot. You meant to get it back after you'd killed her anyway. I intended to hand it to you tomorrow morning. I didn't think, Peter, I really didn't." She smiled faintly. "I acted on impulse."

"You acted like a criminal begging to be caught!" he retorted hotly. "And now you've put me in an impossible situation! How could you?" He was almost whining. "You're a traitor!" She could not bear the self-pity in his tone, the complete self-involvement that always made his feelings of paramount importance, even at a time like this. She struggled to her feet.

"Yes, I'm a traitor," she agreed. "And yes, I think something in me wanted the whole filthy business to end. But it isn't going to end, is it, Petey? You're going to slaughter me and it's going to go on and on into infinity. You could still let me go." She saw his expression and her mouth twisted. "No, I suppose not," she said unsteadily, "and I'm in no condition to fight you. Just promise me that you'll keep the painting I did for you, and look at it sometimes, and think of me."

"Shut up!" he ordered tightly, and grasped the back of her neck. She did not resist. Even if she had wanted to run, her legs would not have carried her far. At least Jessica got away, she thought as she stumbled towards the house. I hope that's enough to save my soul.

Her father was waiting, his silhouette in the doorway bulking misshapen against the timid light from the hall. She went towards him, her head held high.

Chapter 14

There was nothing more to be said. Wordlessly they hustled her through the hall, through the kitchen, and down the steep stairs into the cellar, halting her before the door that had no handle. The deep, waiting silence of the house that had made Jessica so uneasy had intensified until it seemed to Caroline, as she watched her father take a slim key from his key-ring and pass it to Peter, that the whole structure, stones and mortar, wood and glass, hangings and pictures, even the dank air itself, was crowding around her in breathless anticipation. She had felt it before, many times, this sense of pregnant expectation, felt it in a state of tense excitement as it condensed, solidified, became the form of her most private fantasies walking arrogantly into her room. But now she knew that it had become hostile and had turned against her. Grim-lipped, his fingers trembling, Peter unlocked the door.

It swung inwards without a sound and Caroline was ushered through. Neither she nor Peter had been there before. Their father had released the dark power they both had used throughout their lives when he had turned twenty-one and from the time of their birth it had been at their disposal. Or so we thought, Caroline told herself as she saw Peter glance about. Whatever made us think that we were the users?

There were no priceless artifacts down here, as she had known when she lied to Jessica. The walls and ceiling were uniformly grey and completely bare. But the floor was a polished light grey stone and set in its centre, the tips radiating almost to the walls, was a beautiful black five-pointed star, a pentagram. Caroline wondered if it was a kind of marble, and marvelled at how it had been grooved deep into the stone, the inlay so tight and unbroken. Both floor and star glinted very slightly as the harsh overhead light played upon it.

By the far wall was a long, low stone table. It was crudely hacked, obviously very old, and its surface was marred by brownish stains. Under it were placed a plain pewter goblet and a long knife whose blade glinted wickedly at her in the strong light. A spurt of fear pricked in the palms of her hands and trickled down her spine. They're going to tie me down on that, she thought, and Peter's going to slit my throat. The words had no reality. They were flimsy, effervescent feathers brushing by.

Her gaze went to her family. Her mother was fingering the cameo brooch at her own smooth throat and her lips were moving soundlessly. Her eyes seemed glazed. Sir Matthew was just turning into the room having switched on the light. His face was solemn, as though he had entered a church. Peter was surveying his surroundings, his expression inscrutable. This can't be happening, Caroline said fiercely to herself. Most of my life I've know about it, ever since I was thirteen and Father took me into the study and laid it all in front of me, telling me how lucky we were, talking about dreams coming true and unimaginable fantasies realized and how we never had to be like other people, adrift on the unpredictable

ocean of existence, how cared-for we were. Then he drew me
to the desk. I can still remember his eyes. He knew very well
what my fantasies were and how I was already satisfying
them, beginning to plumb the depths of sensuous experience,
drunk with my own discoveries. "I will tell you now what
price the Rensbys have had to pay over the centuries," he had
said, "but first you must swear on oath that waking or sleeping, drunk or sober, you will never repeat what you are about
to hear." He had produced a tiny vial filled with something
liquid and almost black. "This is blood," he had gone on,
thrusting it into her hands and folding his own hot ones
around hers. "Swear, and I will tell you whose." And she had
sworn on the blood of her father's first victim, impressed by
the secrecy and importance of the occasion, intrigued and tit-
illated, for her own young blood was strong and feverish and
she had never seen her mysterious lover in any form but
human. What was a demon anyway? She neither knew nor
cared. And later, when she knew, she still did not care. She
had become his willing captive.

I have given no thought to the nature of reality, her
mind rushed on as she saw her father put a hand on her
brother's shoulder and lead him into the centre of the huge
star that gave off an aura of almost palpable menace. Reality
has always been sunshine, people sitting in their kitchens
reading newspapers and drinking coffee, jets flying, radios
blaring. Reality is the Scotch burning into my stomach after a
hard ride. It's yellow ochre smeared on my thumb and a canvas resting on an easel. It's dancing with Scott, bored to
death but letting the music take me and smiling as I think of
what I will or will not do tomorrow. This is the twentieth
century. What does it have to do with pentagrams and demon
lovers and secret, savage ceremonies belonging to an age of
darkness long gone? I never asked, I just accepted. No, her
thoughts hissed back. You did not just accept. You held out
one greedy little hand towards the ultimate thrill and with
the other you warded off the truth.

You turn the mirror, something whispered inside her. You angle it, just a little, and the jets and newspapers and radios fade and you can see what was not visible before, a world where succeeding cultures are just a crust, where civilization is a thin veneer from generation to generation, and underneath is a darkness as constant and potent today as it was a hundred, a thousand years ago. For me the veneer has cracked and I have fallen into a crevasse. I no longer belong to the world of illusion, the world of everyday little things. I belong to reality. Even out there on the grass by the car I was cocooned in the lie.

All at once an image of Jessica's sister, Jane, blossomed like a hideous black flower in her mind. Jane was close by. Jane was in the wall on the other side of this room, trapped in a prison of her own, nothing left of her but bones and hair. They said that hair and fingernails went on growing after you were dead. For how long? How many curved, yellow inches on the rotting hands? Did the hair grow and grow and tangle around the wounded neck and wind itself across the sunken ribcage? Will they put me in there with her? Caroline wondered, or will they bury me in the arbour with all the others?

"Oh God, help me!" she said aloud in sudden anguish. "I don't want to die!"

Her father had been murmuring in Peter's ear and for just a moment the susurration of his voice ceased but he did not turn around. Presently he began again. Peter's hands were pressed tight against his thighs. He was nodding. Caroline swung to her mother, but Eleanor seemed to be unaware of her presence. Her eyes were closed and her head was flung back. Small shudders gripped her body. Her fair hair hung down her back in a dishevelled stream and Caroline recognized the expression on the woman's face. She had seen it reflected many times in the mirrors of her own bedroom as she waited . . .

She spun on her heel and lunged for the door but there was no handle on the inside either. A key was required to open it once it had clicked shut. Pounding on it, Caroline screamed and shouted in a fit of terror and rage. None of the other inhabitants of the room took any notice of her as she kicked and pummelled.

Then, under the sound of her panic, she heard Peter's voice, loud but unsteady. The words were foreign, harsh, their cadence like a parody of music. They acted on her immediately, cutting through the momentary insanity and filling her with contradictory urges. It was as though a host of sharp-clawed animals were tearing at her mind. Kill. Run. Laugh. Scream again. Tear off your clothes. Dance. Fall to the floor. Her mother moaned. Panting raggedly, Caroline turned.

Her father was leaning against the wall. Peter was beside him, sweating profusely, running his tongue over dry lips. Both were now outside the sharp points and warning lines of the pentagram. But Caroline's glance fled from them to the figure that had appeared and was standing within the confines of the star, one lace-draped hand on its velvet hip, one scarlet, buckled shoe tapping the floor. Its features were very like Peter's. A black satin bow held back its waving hair.

He always did prefer to come to me as Sir Julian, she thought. How beautiful he is in the guise of a sixteenth century nobleman, all that grace and elegance hiding a ruthless, predatory virility. How eagerly I used to strip away those trappings piece by piece until he stood before me naked, his dark skin gleaming taut over those perfectly formed muscles, his image multiplied in my mirrors so that I was surrounded, captured by his overpowering male physicality and crazy with my own desire. In spite of her dread, a spasm of lust shook her. The figure smiled and stepped out of the pentagram. It ignored Matthew, Peter and Eleanor and came striding up to Caroline. The smile widened, and Caroline saw that behind the even, white teeth, the inside of its mouth was darkly red.

"Ah, succulent Caroline!" it breathed. "I know what you are feeling. I have always known your lusts, and answered every subtle grade of wanting with exquisite satiation. What a long and eventful relationship we've enjoyed, haven't we? You were a juicy morsel at thirteen, my lovely, but the taste of you at eighteen!" It closed its eyes and sighed. "What are we doing here, you and I, in this bare, empty cell, when we could be upstairs, on your bed, mouth to mouth, my sex to yours, making time stand still?"

Deliberately Caroline inhaled its acrid odour. Nights of passion came to her with the scent, she and Sir Julian, she and Jessica's Michael, she and Jessica herself—oh that was an unbeatable impersonation!—locked flesh to flesh in the hours that passed like days drugged with delight. "You were better than anything," she whispered. It trailed a long finger-nail down her cheek.

"And you, my raven-haired little animal, I do believe that you have been the best of the lot. All the Rensby women have been passionate creatures, hard to tame. Tall, short, buxom, willowy, hundreds of you through the ages, I've had you all. I've pandered to your secret vices, played out your nasty fantasies, watched the sweet juices of corruption ooze out of you. And sometimes . . ." Its finger grazed a path beneath her chin and came to rest, pressing hard and cold against Caroline's jugular. "Sometimes I've sipped your blood, a bouquet full of a dozen different subtleties. You are challenges, you Rensby females. Prizes worth something. I look forward to sampling the flow from your veins in particular, darling Caroline, tonight. That is unless . . ." Its hand suddenly encircled her throat and it thrust its mouth against her ear. There was nothing erotic in the savage gesture, nothing intimate, only a cold, impersonal strength that shocked her with its force. "Unless you care to fill the cup with someone else's blood," it whispered. "Your mother's, for instance. Look at her, Caroline, the vain, silly hag! What has she ever done for you but nag and pester and bleat? Do you know what is going through her mind right now, with her head thrown back and her body trembling? She is thinking of Peter, Peter her favourite, Peter her angel, Peter who inherits this damp pile of old stones! She doesn't love you. She never has. What do you owe her, my appetizing young accomplice? What do you owe any of them?" It took the lobe of her ear between its teeth, the act both a threat and a promise. "Peter can slit her throat instead," it murmured. "You'd like that, wouldn't you? Revenge, dear Caroline, A proof of your brother's moral cowardice, oh I know how you scorn him, and a chance for Eleanor to make a genuine sacrifice on his behalf. Otherwise . . ." It released her and stood back, shrugging its velvet-clad shoulders. "Otherwise I'm going to miss your big bed and your teasing mirrors and the hunger in that insatiable body."

Oh God, Caroline thought desperately, not this. Not this! A reprieve, a chance to live. My mother's life for mine and he's right, she cares nothing for me. But what does he gain by such an offer? I don't delude myself that it has anything to do with future pleasure, nor can it be a moment of perverse mercy on his part. Hell has no mercy. It was watching her from the perfectly constructed mask of her ancestor's face, and Caroline had the clear impression that it was enjoying the agony of her dilemma. Out of the corner of her eye she saw the others, her mother as he had described her, engulfed in a motionless ecstasy, her father still leaning against the wall with Peter beside him, both also watching her expressionlessly. They had not heard what had been said. Give up, give in, Caroline's mind demanded feverishly. Let her die. She's had more life than you and anyway, she's wasted it hasn't she? You deserve a chance to develop your gift, take your rightful place in the art world, grow up, grow old, go on breathing . . .

But Hell has no mercy. Not for mother, not for me.

What does he want?

And then she knew.

"Hurry up and decide," it said, folding its arms. "I'm getting rather thirsty. I've had nothing worth drinking since little Jane. What an entertaining game that was! Enticing right up to the moment of inevitability! I was her friend, you see.

In the orchard, beside her as she read in the arbour. She thought I was a kindly ghost out of the past she liked to dream about in those books of hers. 'Julian,' she would say. 'Tell me a story of the old days,' and I would grow ravenous as I watched her innocent young face. Your blood will be as tantalizing as hers was—if you make the wrong decision of course." It came close again, its handsome face now full of solemn urgency. "But you won't, will you Caroline?" it pressed. It jerked its head at her family. "Don't throw everything away for them. Compared to you, they're worthless. Let it be you and me, baby, for ever."

Caroline forced herself not to move. He's so real, she thought dully, more real than any of us. We are toys that he plays with, part of some cosmic game that in our arrogance we thought we were controlling. If it wasn't for the pentagram his power would explode into something we can't even begin to imagine. Beside him we are thin shadows without substance. She wanted to fall back, to crawl into a corner and cower, but she straightened and met his compelling gaze.

"No," she said as evenly as she could, though her voice wavered. "My decision is made. Now it's up to Peter to do his part. But I wouldn't be too confident that he'll come through if I were you. Do you think he'll be able to wield that knife when the time comes? I doubt it. He's too weak."

In one swift stride it was on her again, grasping her by the hair and forcing her head back, thrusting its face so close to hers that its red-rimmed eyes filled her vision. All trace of complicity had gone, to be replaced by a barely concealed ferocity that made Caroline faint with dread. "Oh he'll wield it alright," it said hoarsely. "He'll do it because he's all choked up with greed and ambition and fear of my retribution but most of all," it went on with a menacing emphasis, "most of all he'll do it because you've wounded his pride. Yes! Peter will become a murderer because you have let him down." Its grip tightened until Caroline cried out. "Such a deliciously mundane reason," it breathed against her trembling mouth.

"Oh Caroline! What a paltry, meaningless gesture you made! Was the life of that insipid little chit Jessica worth the sacrifice of your own future?"

Caroline searched those foreign eyes, so terrifying in their otherness. She could read no pity there, no human understanding. I've been blind all these years, she thought. Blind and deluded. "I have no future here," she replied with difficulty. "None of us do. This is your house, not ours, and always has been. This is an ante-room to Hell and you know nothing of life, only death. That paltry, meaningless gesture of mine saved my soul, didn't it? If Peter kills me you lose your prize. That's why you gave me a choice."

It recoiled as though she had struck it. The red, slitted eyes blazed with sudden fury and for a second Julian's likeness was gone, wavering into a shape that would have stopped Caroline's heart if it had solidified. But a human face reformed. "How dare you pass judgement on me, you vermin!" it ground out. "Just what do you think you are?" It swung away and walked towards Peter, an ominous purpose in its tread that caused the young man to flinch and shrink back against the wall. "She's made a filthy mess of things hasn't she, the silly little bitch?" it said venomously. "Are you ready to fulfill the terms of the covenant, Peter Rensby, and take up your position as master of this Hall? Or shall I go, and let you all stew in your own juices?"

Caroline sprang to life. "Don't do it, Petey!" she shouted. "Last chance! Get out from under! Take the consequences!"

He swallowed. His gaze flicked from her to the cruel face before him and back to her. Then he clenched his fists and turned away. "Sorry, Caro," he said in a strangled voice. "I'm not going to see my future wrecked because you had a fit of conscience. I've got far more at stake here than you and I'm not prepared to give it up. You're a traitor after all. You betrayed me." He nodded at his father and Sir Matthew stirred into life. He came lumbering across the floor towards her, his face set.

With a scream Caroline flew to Eleanor. "Mother!" she begged, but Eleanor gave no indication that she had heard. Matthew's implacable arms went around her and she was carried, flailing and cursing, to the table. Roughly he forced her down. There were restraints attached to the legs of the table. Caroline had not noticed them before. Now Peter was spread-eagling her, tying her so that she could not move. The stone was chilly along her back. This is crazy! she was thinking hysterically, even as she struggled. This isn't real! Her father loomed over her. Sweat from Peter's brow spattered her neck. Then a mouth was against her ear and her lover's odour enveloped her for the last time.

"Peter doesn't know it yet," he whispered, so softly that only she could hear, "but your parents do. Jessica's on her way back. She called dear Alix from the airport where you so kindly left her, and she's hurrying to her true love's side. Did you really think you could deprive me of my lawful prey? Matthew's weren't the only hands that took her innocence away, although she doesn't know it yet. She's been mine for a long, long time. Goodbye, my Caroline. I'll drink your health in a few short moments."

Caroline opened her mouth to scream again but no sound came out. The last thing she saw was the swift set of determination on her brother's face as he struck.

Caroline's body lay sprawled on the stone table. The top two buttons of her red silk shirt were undone, revealing a jagged and cruelly clumsy gash beneath her ear. Her black hair, matted and wet, stuck to her pallid face and one wisp curled across her staring eyes.

Peter took the ancient goblet from the creature that stood at the foot of the altar. He held it in one unsteady hand, not looking at its contents. The knife was in the other. Chalk-white and swaying slightly he lifted it to his mouth and took one gulp, his throat working convulsively as he fought to swallow. Hastily he passed the cup to his father. Sir

Matthew drank steadily. Then it was Lady Eleanor's turn. She sipped carefully, handed the goblet back to her husband, and wiped a spot of blood from the corner of her mouth with one dainty finger. Turning together to their benefactor the Rensbys bowed deeply. The ceremony was over.

Eleanor put out a hand towards the limp corpse. It was a gesture of resignation and rejection. "The foolish girl," she said. "Her punishment was inevitable but I'm going to miss her very much. Very much indeed. What are we going to say about her disappearance to Scott? To everyone in London, all our friends?" She looked appealingly at her husband. Sir Matthew shrugged.

"She had a chance to take a painting course in Italy," he suggested without interest. "She ran off with some man from London and we don't know where she is. She's hiking round the Continent. What does it matter? Peter has secured our safety and nothing will come of any enquiries the busybodies will want to make. We can look forward to a hell of a party now." He clapped Peter on the back. "Well done!" he boomed. "And don't worry. By tomorrow the shock will have begun to wear off and soon what you've had to do will be nothing more than an unpleasant memory. Concentrate on Pamela and your engagement." Peter gave a sickly half-smile but did not look at him. They all stood in silence for a moment, until Peter stepped away from the table.

"What are we going to do about . . . about her?" he queried in a high, hurried voice, jerking his head towards the table. "She's . . . there's . . . There's blood dripping all over the place."

Matthew exchanged a glance with his wife. "Well I think we'll just leave her for now," he said. "No point in making extra work for ourselves."

Peter glanced at him sharply. A little colour was creeping back into his face. "What do you mean?" he asked. His father pursed his lips.

"You have another small problem, Peter," he answered,

"but I'm sure you'll be able to deal with it adequately, and when you have we can go out to the arbour and lift the paving together." Peter eyed the man suspiciously.

"I don't understand."

Sir Matthew chuckled. "You will, my boy," he said. "You will. At any moment. You see . . ."

The sound of a knock on the front door was faint and muffled but unmistakable. Peter exclaimed in shock but the other two seemed strangely unperturbed.

Suddenly the creature that had been watching this exchange strode forward, snatching the goblet out of Matthew's fingers. It drank deeply. Blood spattered onto the starched white lace ruff around its neck and dribbled down its chin.

"Jessica's back!" it yelled. "Let's have some fun!" Peter stared at it, horror-stricken, for as he watched it shivered, dissolved, and was resolved into a swiftly generating outline he had known for most of his life. He turned to the table. Caroline's body still lay there, flaccid and drained. He forced his gaze to return to the demon.

Caroline was grinning at him wickedly, her red lips parted. The silk shirt shimmered. The spike-heeled boots gleamed. Caroline held out a hand.

"You've got the key, Petey darling," she said. "Unlock the door."